'I really rooted for Robin Wilde in this warm and engaging debut. She's a chatty, winning yet poignant heroine, facing very real and relatable problems.'

Sophie Kinsella

'I'd love Robin Wilde to be my new best friend. In fact, I feel like she's become it through these pages. Wonderfully written and full of humour that had me laughing along from start to finish.

As a mum, as a woman, you can find yourself wondering whether it's only you that feels a certain way or does questionable things, but this book stilled my pondering mind. We're all in this together. Plodding through the murkiness, the judgement, the excruciating emptiness and insecurities of not being good enough. . . only when we know these are universal worries will we learn that all we actually need is a little self-love. Funny, heartfelt, tender and empowering! I can't believe this is Louise's first book. I'm thoroughly excited to read more!'

Giovanna Fletcher

'I'm smitten with this sweet and special story about love, life and motherhood. Reading *Wilde Like Me* feels just like sitting down for a (boozy) hot chocolate with your best friend and I love Robin Wilde.'

Lindsey Kelk

'I adore this book. Louise Pentland writes with so much warmth, heart and honesty – *Wilde Like Me* is a gorgeous, witty, reassuring comfort read. I fell in love with Robin and her family before the end of the first page. If you're having a bad day, I think this book would instantly make it better. Pentland's exploration of mental health issues is refreshingly honest. If you've ever felt like the only person in the world who isn't perfect – and I sometimes do – this is what you need to read. A fabulous mix of escapism and relatability, this is a hug of a book.'

Daisy Buchanan

Wilde Like Me

LOUISE PENTLAND

Wilde Like Me

ZAFFRE

First published in Great Britain in 2017 by

ZAFFRE PUBLISHING
80-81 Wimpole St, London W1G 9RE
www.zaffrebooks.co.uk

A CIP catalogue record for this book is available from the British Library.

HB ISBN: 978-1-785-76293-2
TPB ISBN: 978-1-785-76294-9

also available as an ebook

3 5 7 9 10 8 6 4 2

Typeset by Palimpsest Book Production Limited, Falkirk, Stirlingshire
Printed and bound by Clays Ltd, St Ives Plc

MIX
Paper from
responsible sources
FSC
www.fsc.org
FSC® C018072

Zaffre Publishing is an imprint of Bonnier Zaffre,
a Bonnier Publishing company
www.bonnierzaffre.co.uk
www.bonnierpublishing.co.uk

For Clare, Esther, Victoria and Maddie,
the perfect cure to The Emptiness

PROLOGUE

MY FAIRY TALE ENDING . . .?

'I RESISTED THIS FOR too long,' I think as I step out of my black cab, bubbling with excitement. After a long call and an intense exchange of messages I'd finally agreed to meet him. He invited me to a rather exclusive bar at the top of the OXO Tower, one of London's most iconic buildings on the River Thames with wrap-around views of the city from its terrace and, apparently, cocktails to die for. I was secretly pleased that the job I'd assisted Natalie, my boss, on today – make-up for a shoot in a trendy loft studio in Shoreditch – had finished early. With an entire afternoon to spare, I'd taken the time to pamper myself and really enjoy getting ready for this night.

Stepping onto the pavement and gliding down the pathway to the riverfront, I feel like a peacock parading its feathers.

As I approach the red-brick old factory building, I catch

my reflection in the gleaming windows. For the first time in a bloody long time, I feel beautiful. I've always thought that my 5' 6" frame, conker-brown hair and brown eyes were the dullest of all the potential 'beauty stats'. They're not exactly exotic or outstanding, are they? And they're certainly not hailed as the epitome of perfection in the magazines, but today something feels special. My eyes seem softer and my hair bouncier, as I glimpse myself walking along with my head held high. I don't think, 'slummy mummy' but, instead, 'lovely woman, out on a special date'. Feeling this worthwhile makes me stand a little taller and, oh my God, am I *sashaying* my bum about?

Happily, my make-up looks sultry and glowing. I've gone all out on the contour and highlight, but managed to pull it back before I gave my face actual corners (I still don't regret that luxury make-up binge last month), and I'm in love with my outfit. I'm wearing a knee-skimming black layered lace skirt that I picked up for pennies in a tucked-away vintage shop. In between the light layers of lace and tulle are tiny stars embroidered with gold thread. You can barely see them until the street lights catch them, and then they look like the night sky swirling past. I've tucked a deep V wrap top into the satin waistband and paired it with black-patent heels passed down from my best friend's sister, Piper, before she moved away. If I were deep-down ballsy enough to ask a stranger to take a full-length picture, I'd put it on Instagram with an #OOTD (Outfit Of The Day, for those not as obsessed with social media as I am) and pretend to be a blogger.

Taking a deep breath and reminding myself of everything I am, I pull open the grand glass door, walk confidently to the lift and push the 'up' button.

It's going to be perfect.

It's going to be everything I want it to be.

I say these things over and over in my head. I'm willing the universe to listen and make it so. After four years (and ten months and five days) isn't it about time?

I step into the lift, and take one last look at myself in the mirror, smile serenely at my reflection – without fretting over my make-up caking or my hair looking like a scarecrow.

This is it . . .

The doors open with a shrill *ping*, and it takes me a second to adjust to what I can see.

Instead of being packed full of people, the glamorous blue-lit bar, leading out on to a stylish restaurant area on the patio, is almost empty.

The sight that meets my eyes takes my breath away.

Tiny white tea lights in mottled silver votives run from the doors of the lift, through the indoor bar and out on to the terrace, making a twinkling path for me to walk down. Next to the doors at the end of the candlelit path is a waiter ready to take me to the one occupied table, where *he* stands smiling at me with one arm outstretched in welcome.

Strings of golden fairy lights hang from every railing

creating a warm glow, and there is champagne already chilling in a bucket beside his chair. Our view is of the Thames and all the boats humming along with their coloured lights twinkling up at us, but I barely notice it.

I'm mesmerised by him.

I'm almost breathless at how beautiful all of this is; how beautiful *he* is. I notice the gentle piano melody tinkling in the background and how the breeze is soft on my skin.

I feel like I'm the main character in a perfect-happy-ending movie. If I died right now, in this very moment, I'd be dying happy.

He pulls out my chair.

'Robin Wilde,' he says softly, flashing me the smile my heart skips a beat for . . .

Part One

Badass Single Mum?

9 months earlier . . .

ONE

JANUARY

OPENING MY EYES VERY slowly, I'm greeted by the glare of the mini Christmas tree lights (which I forgot to switch off before I fell asleep) and a hot body pressed up against me, with one arm draped heavily over my chest and the other digging a little painfully into my back.

The first week of January is supposed to feel like a fresh start. This one really doesn't. I've barely slept these last few days, even though I'm exhausted, and when I do close my eyes, I dream of falling into nothing and then wake up with a start.

As my bedroom comes into focus, I roll over and ever so gently stroke her hair. Her lashes are longer than mine but her little nose is the same. I watch her breathe for a few moments and wonder how someone like me managed to have such a perfect daughter. Six years feels like six months. It's true what they say about them growing up too fast. I'm delving into thoughts of how this tiny person makes my life what it is when I'm jolted back firmly to reality. There's a rustling in my kitchen.

I check my phone: it's 7.45 a.m. I stagger downstairs, leaving a half-asleep Lyla where she is, to find my Auntie Kath in the kitchen surrounded by every single thing that lives in a cupboard or drawer. No longer in their assigned place, all my culinary possessions are strewn across every inch of counter surface available. This is a reasonable-sized kitchen and though the counters are scratched and the breakfast bar is a slightly wobbly stub of counter offcut and the dining table cost £4 in a charity shop, I love it. I love my cool mint tiles that Dad helped me put in last year (Granny, who lived here before me, had this waterproof floral wallpaper that even Dad agreed was hideous) and beach-themed art. In the summer, when the light streams in through the glass doors, this kitchen is the brightest, freshest room in the house. In the winter, when there's less light and we string lights over the cabinet tops and make mulled wine ('Mummy's special Christmas Ribena'), it's a great place to sit at the table and wrap presents or make cards. I love this space even more when everything I own isn't stacked up on the worktops or in piles on the off-white lino (OK, my limited funds haven't stretched yet to anything nicer, and, really who wants to spend money on flooring?).

8

Instantly I wish I hadn't given Auntie Kath a set of keys. And I really should have wiped down the surfaces before I collapsed into bed.

'My New Year's Resolution is to declutter!' Auntie Kath says, with way too much gusto for the time of day.

It's six days into the new year and Kath is ready to go. I'd love to be that ready for anything.

I've been alone with Lyla now for four years (and two months and twenty-four days). *Fifty-one* months. It's my fifth new year as a single mum, and my fifth new year with my child being my midnight kiss and cuddle. I'm not *alone* alone, obviously. I have Kath and I have my friends. I do normal things like work and go out; I went to a great party at my best friend Lacey and her husband Karl's for New Year's Eve . . . but I've lost my pep a bit. I smiled politely a lot, and tried to have fun, but I left the party as soon as was socially acceptable (twenty past midnight), claiming I had 'a lot on' the next day. I never have a lot on, though. I'm not sure I could handle a lot right now. I just about manage with 'some', unlike Kath, who is a walking whirlwind of positivity and getting things done.

I stare blankly at her, wondering what planet she's from. A pause. Then she continues: 'You *really* shouldn't keep sweet potatoes in a cupboard, love. They keep better in the fridge.'

There's no explanation as to why she's decided to declutter *my* kitchen. I chalk it up to a 'Kathism' and decide to let her be.

'Right, yeah, thanks, Kath,' I muster as I go to answer the door. Why is the world starting before 8 a.m. on Lyla's first day back at school? Didn't anyone get the memo that it's Teacher Training Morning, and therefore my last lie-in for months? What is this fresh hell?

Paul from over the road is plodding in with his toolkit and a 'youallrighthow'sitgoingwhere'sthebrokenswitchthen?'. I realise he's not fully awake yet either. Kath is, though. She's all over it. You would be, if you were the kind of woman who'd arranged a handyman to call round at 8 a.m. to fix something that nobody needed fixing. The switch is fine; you just have to push it super-hard in the left-hand corner and it works a dream.

'Hello, Paul! I do love to see a man with a well-packed toolkit in the morning!' Chortle, chortle. Someone please make her stop.

Paul heads off to the front room to fix the switch and, assessing that everything is under control, I head back upstairs. I can hear Auntie Kath talking at – not to – Paul.

'How's the missus, Paul? And how are those gorgeous kids? Ooh, I took Mollie to the vet last week. Terrible, she's been. Off her food, off her walks – not like her.' Paul interjects with a series *of yeah*s and *oh really*s? as Kath chatters on. 'Gallstones, they've found! Two! Poor thing, no wonder she's been off her food, I wouldn't want two little balls inside me either . . .'

10

TWO

AUNTIE KATH, MY DAD'S younger sister, lives five minutes' walk away from us and is straight out of a children's storybook: the lovely mumsy woman with a soft voice, wise words and a cuddle that could solve most of the world's problems. Charity shop bargain-hunting is one of Auntie Kath's main skills. Knowing everything about everyone is another. If there is news, a scandal or drama to be had within a four-mile radius of Edgeton Vale, Kath Drummond has it. With her thrifty shopping finds, Kath has a unique sense of style. Floaty, coloured skirts (often with her own added embellishments of sequins, lace, braiding or beads), crocheted cardigans and bejewelled sandals are her go-to staples and somehow, they work. Her face looks much younger than her fifty-two years with full lips and kind, sparkling eyes. She's a good-looking lady who looks after herself with her 'lotions and potions', as she calls them. She spends her time attending her Cupcakes and Crochet Club (basically just an excuse for her and her friends to eat cake while they craft), or the Quilt Making Club. She also runs a village Dog Walking Club – which, technically speaking, isn't a club. She, Moira and Alan from five doors up take the dogs out a few times a week to spy on the neighbours whose houses back on to the field.

Apparently Anthea Lamb's curtains have been closed a suspicious number of times *during the day*, coinciding with a large workman's van being parked outside her house. By the time Gary, her husband, gets home, the van is gone and the curtains are open again. Kath, Moira and Alan would never actually face-to-face ask her what's going on, of course, but they're very happy to speculate.

In Kath's working life, she was a hairstylist in Cambridge city centre, but I think she spent more time gossiping in the salon than cutting any hair . . .

I hear her voice again, calling to me this time.

'Robin,' she tinkles merrily. 'I've made a lasagne, love, and left some out for you and Lyla. I'll freeze the rest, shall I?' She is a good egg. Or at least, she tries to be – as much as, at 8 a.m. on a grey and freezing Wednesday in January, it pains me to admit it.

I start to feel stressed because there are too many people in the house, but then remember how the quiet moments don't always feel so peaceful.

I've named that feeling The Emptiness. When I feel far away and isolated, I have days where I am consumed by anxiety and loneliness, and just feel so flat. Lyla will be at school and I'll be at home all alone and feeling like I have no place in the world, or like I am a speck of nothingness, desperate for my life not to feel so sad.

I should be glad to have Kath and her so-called help. She means well, I know she does.

After scaring Paul off (though at least he's fixed the switch, I suppose), wreaking havoc in my kitchen and ensuring I never find my cheese grater or corkscrew ever again, she finally leaves when she takes Lyla in to school at 10.30. It's a bit of a drive and it's very sweet of her to offer. I think she's guessed how I'm feeling. As she walks out to the car, she's commenting on the fact that there was no such thing as 'Teacher Training Morning' in her day and that they all just 'got on with it'. I don't bother to argue or explain it; I just zip up Lyla's thick purple coat, cuddle her goodbye and let out a deep sigh of relief when I shut the door.

Peace at last.

But as the hours of the day tick by, I realise I'm looking forward to collecting Lyla and having some life in the house and somebody to talk to. I clean out my make-up kit ready for next week's job on the set of an fruit-infused tea commercial. Apparently the creative team want the models' make-up to incorporate a sense of the fruit infusions, so I spend a bit of time trawling the internet for ideas and inspiration. It would seem that 'fruit-infused tea inspired make-up' hasn't gone viral with the YouTube beauty vloggers yet. Can't think why.

Admin done and dusted – and by done and dusted I mean I've ignored the pressing email from the accountant and spent forty-five minutes adding things to my ASOS if-I-ever-win-the-lottery-and-can-afford-to-treat-myself list – it's time to collect Lyla from school.

3.14 P.M., AND I'M AT the school gates a minute early. I enrolled Lyla here at the beginning of the school year. Dad and Auntie Kath released the last of our inheritance from my wonderful Granny so I could pay for this lovely school and I'm still getting used to it all. It's nothing like the down-at-heel and rowdy primary and comp where Lacey and I went to school. Lyla was struggling in her oversubscribed local primary. As always, I blame this on her broken home and emotionally damaged mother. Hesgrove Pre-Prep School is a bit like a giant stately home, with ivy creeping up the exterior and huge stone-framed windows, except everywhere you look there is something wholesome or comforting: a row of low pegs for the juniors to hang PE kits on; artwork on the walls from their trips to the nature area; notices for jamborees or cake sales and that faint smell of new books and poster paints that instantly brings back your own childhood, when you didn't need to worry about broken hearts or council tax bills.

14

I know this is only the first day back after Christmas, but – *deep breath, Robin, and start as you mean to go on* – perhaps from today onward I will *always* be one of those mothers who is here before the bell rings! I look around hopefully, expecting some kind of mutual congratulations from the other smug mothers whose names I've yet to learn. Those who made it here early too. But no one seems to engage. These women are pros, and are unlikely to congratulate themselves (not publicly, at least) on winning first place at the PTA Bake Off, let alone making it to the school gates on time. They stand here waiting in their Hunter flat boots and skinny jeans, which somehow disguise any hint of a mum tum or muffin top. Please God let them have muffin tops! I glance around at their almost identical navy-and-white striped Bretons under padded Joules gilets with grey cashmere scarves, and swear never to succumb to the 'mumiform'. My ripped jeans (*avec* muffin top), loose slogan sweater and leather (OK, pleather) jacket may not scream elegance, but at least, I tell myself, I'm not hiding my pyjamas under my trench coat today. I do wish that, given the January weather, I'd perhaps considered the grey scarf bit, though.

I've noticed a thing about the PSMs (Posh School Mums). They all have their car keys in hand. I mean, they have handbags – very nice soft, slouchy ones with room for a bento box and sensory play pack – but their flashy car keys are always on show. I suspect it's some kind of status symbol

15

or initiation into their secret Mumarati Club. I look down and I'm clenching my own Nissan Micra keys in my pink, cold, unmanicured fingers. To be fair, my nails are usually in pretty good nick – it's important for my job that I make a good impression on that score – but lately things have slipped a bit. Still, keys are in hand, though; a girl's got to try.

I spend most of my life desperately hoping that Lyla is emotionally and mentally nourished. I'm constantly worried that the split from Simon has in some way irrevocably damaged her. What if one day she finds herself in counselling, talking about how unavailable her dating-website-addicted mother was or how much she wished we'd been outdoors more, holding hands and making daisy chains, like characters from an Enid Blyton book? OK, note to self: remove all traces of Enid Blyton from house and replace with more suitable titles like Jacqueline Wilson's *The Illustrated Mum*.

3.15 p.m., and the foyer doors open. There she is, my little brunette beauty! The children don't pour out and run eagerly into our arms like at our old school. There are strict security measures. Each child must be signed out and ticked off a clipboard by Mrs Barnstorm, the Head of Pastoral Care. I could do with some bloody pastoral care.

'Hello, Lyla's Mum!' Mrs Barnstorm is thin and pointy, like a ferret. She greets us with a clenched-teeth, plastic smile. I don't have a name any more. None of us do. We birthed children, so exist only to be 'Tabitha's Mum', 'Natasha's Mum' or 'Ava's Mum'.

'Hi!' I reply to Mrs Barnstorm with an overenthusiastic wave – not because she scares me. Oh shit, she's coming over. OK, fine, she scares me.

'Bit of an issue today, Mum!', she says condescendingly. 'Lyla was short of some of her PE kit and so was forced to go out in her ballet socks instead of her gym socks.'

An expectant pause, and a few heads turn our way.

'Oh. Right. Err . . . I thought they were in there. I did put them in there.' Did I? I don't bloody know. They're both pairs of white socks.

'You didn't.' She returns to her forced smile. 'It's important the children have the correct uniform on for their own safety. Gym socks next week please, Mum!' She ticks Lyla off the clipboard and I'm left with a beetroot-red complexion. Undermined in front of the PSMs. Again. I bet they have drawers full of the correct pairs of socks, all in neat little rows, just waiting to be gently tossed into PE kits and placed lovingly by the door the night before, ready for their easy, breezy school run. I bet *they* don't have to ask eighteen times, 'Have you eaten your cereal? Can you eat up, *please*? Have you finished your breakfast yet, lovely?'

Screw it, I've got this. The day isn't over yet.

A slight setback in motherhood, but hey! It's character-building.

* * *

ONCE WE'RE LOADED INTO the car – you'd be surprised how long it takes to get into a car when you have a six-year-old: there's the argument about which side they're sitting on, do your seat belt up, do it up *now*, do the blimmin' seat belt up! Can she have *Frozen* on? Can I bring myself to sit through another rendition of 'Let It Go'?

I decide that today, I can't face going straight home.

The house is a mess, despite Kath's best efforts, and all day I haven't dared look at the new 'organisation system' in the kitchen. So, to kill time, we head off to visit Lacey for a chat and some reprieve from the humdrum twosome routine of 'fun' games and crafts, fish fingers, bedtime schedule and trash TV. At least Lacey won't know the difference between PE and ballet socks either.

Lacey is my oldest, dearest friend. We met when she joined my lower school in lovely Miss Ledge's class and I was made her Playground Buddy – an esteemed job where you had to take care of someone and make sure they had a friend for the entire break, a role I still haven't let go of, apparently. She's the kind of friend I feel so comfortable with that we're almost sisters. Except that she has an actual sister, who I adore as well.

Piper is six years younger than us and what my mother would somewhat insensitively call 'an oopsie baby'. Piper wasn't a planned addition to the Dovington family, but Tina and Michael always told us they were thrilled with their happy surprise and to give their beautiful doe-eyed daughter a sister.

Lacey is stunning. A petite 5' 5" with once-bum-length but now a sensible medium-length curly blonde hair, blue eyes and a size eight waist, she's like a character from a Californian romcom. She's married to Karl Hunter – handsome (obviously), 6' 2", thick dark hair – who works in the City doing goodness knows what in finance, and last year they had the most beautiful wedding in a barn conversion on the outskirts of Cambridge. Think exposed brick and ash beams; white fairy lights at every turn; candle-filled mason jars; hessian and lace adorning every chair; a sweetie bar with sugary poems about love; the works. They are the most Pinterest-perfect couple I know. They take selfies at sunset with golden light and soft-pink skies; they have a wall painted in chalkboard paint for guests to write messages on in their home, and they regularly nip off for romantic city breaks in Europe without arguing over who should have booked the airport parking. They live in Hopell Village, ten minutes' drive from my house, which suits me perfectly. With Karl working long hours, Lacey has lots of time for tea and chats. Come the evenings, though, she's happiest spending time with her husband, catching up on their favourite programmes or planning their next mini-adventure, and I'm on my own again. I don't blame her; Karl's great, and I'm glad she has found her soulmate and lives so blissfully. She's a good one. One of the best, actually.

Lacey inherited her paternal grandmother's florist's, Dovington's, and runs it with the help of a manager, Terri. Lacey's life skills are organisation and efficiency. There's nothing she can't handle. I sometimes think that if we gave Lacey all of the world's problems she'd have them solved before most of us had made our to-do list. I don't think she really needs Terri, but she's been there since the days of Granny Dovington and loves the place. Lacey is happy to have the help. She calls her life 'fluid'. If she fancies sitting and chatting to me for three hours while happy, easy-going Terri flits about creating displays and serving customers, she can. If she fancies devoting all of her time to arranging and hosting Floral Wreath or Flower Crown workshops, she does. Since Karl is the main breadwinner and the shop pretty much runs itself (thank you, Terri), Lacey is the first to say she has a good life. Ultimately she wants to be fully settled with a household of children, golden Labradors and Joules jersey dresses, but right now – though she's working on it – she and Karl are a family of two.

Sometimes Piper, Lacey's little sister, swings by to 'help out' too. She's recently graduated, is living with Tina and Michael again and, I suspect, bored. She studied in London at Central Saint Martins and came out with a first in Culture, Curation and Criticism and I think she thought she'd walk straight into the job of her dreams. Like so many graduates, she's found it's not that simple, and so right now she's 'looking'. She'll pull something out of the bag; she always does. Probably a very fashionable bag, though. She's easily the most stylish young woman I know, and I don't think I've ever seen her in her 'comfies' or with a slightly grubby canvas tote slung over her shoulder with a load of old receipts, tissues, lip balm and coins at the bottom. She exists on a higher level than that. Like her sister, she's gorgeous, but she has an air of mischief that somehow only adds to her appeal. Piper is a total babe. She's one of those people you want to hate, but as soon as you meet her you're bowled over by her warmth, charm and wit. You can't help but love her, a problem many men have fallen victim to. Piper loves the chase, but she's nowhere near her sister in terms of settling down and having a family. It'll be a lucky man that manages to tame her.

'Guess where we're going, Lylielooblue?' I ask in my falsest, cheeriest voice as we turn onto the main road. Fake it till you make it, eh? I don't want her to detect how unenthusiastic I feel for life right now.

'Wacky Warehouse?' replies her hopeful little voice as I see her dark, almost navy, blue eyes light up and her head bob up at me in the rear-view mirror.

'No . . .' Thank God. There's nowhere I'd like to be less in the world than at an overstimulating, slightly sticky, giant corrugated iron building on an industrial estate with a million screaming children in ball pits inside. My actual worst nightmare.

'Auntie Kath's?'

'Not quite!' I think Kath said something about a meeting with Moira and Alan about The Extension. Gordon four doors down is building *without planning permission*. Moira is absolutely scandalised and Alan is writing a strongly worded letter to the council. Kath just enjoys a good nosy, so she's tagging along on their 'research trip'. The research trip will no doubt be a walk across the estate with Mollie, her golden cavalier, and a good look into Gordon's garden.

'Your special hairstyle salon so I can play on your phone!' Oh my God, why does she remember that? One time, *one time*, I had nobody to look after her and no choice but to take her to the wax salon with me for my appointment. I sat her in the corner and let her play a vibrant ADHD-inducing game just to take her focus away from me having the hair ripped out of my nether regions. I explained it to her as Mummy having a special hairstyle in her grown-up place (not that anyone but me has shown my 'grown-up place' any attention in a long while), and there were no further questions. And here we are, seven months on and she's decided to dig it up and discuss it. I really hope this hasn't been a topic at story time with Mrs Barnstorm.

Not wanting to give her any more opportunities to delve into her memory banks, I decide it's safest to just tell her.

'We're going to Dovington's to see Lacey! Won't that be lovely? I'm sure she'll find something so fun for you to do, and I can have a little chat with her. What do you think to that?'

'Rubbish.'

Oh good.

I'm glad she feels such gratitude for the delightful outings she goes on. Like a top CIA agent, I won't negotiate with

22

her or bend to her will. I will show her I am a strong force to be reckoned with.

'What if I buy you some Smarties on the way there?'

'OK.'

THREE

WE ARRIVE AT DOVINGTON's to find Terri carefully bringing in flowers in tall white vases, ready to start tidying up for closing time. You can tell that, for Terri, this job is a labour of love. If she weren't being paid, I suspect she'd still be here every day, tending to the plants, offering advice for their care and making up the most beautiful bouquets.

'Hiya Terri, are you all right?'

'Hello, lovey! Yes, thanks. Look at these wonderful camellias we've had in! Aren't they divine?' Terri is talking about the blush-pink flowers as if someone has dropped off a box of brand new puppies. 'Lyla, have you seen these? They're so delicate, and can you see how they look a little like roses?'

Lyla pootles over to have a look and a stroke while I have a quick scan round for Lacey. It's hard to detect anything at first, because the space is crammed with botanical paraphernalia – stacks of plant pots; rotating wire racks holding cards to stick in bouquets with special messages lovingly written on; wall-mounted spools of ribbon in all the colours of the rainbow; and, of course, buckets and buckets of beautifully scented flowers – but she's not here. She must be in the workshop out the back. This room is my favourite. Unlike the large, wide, front-of-house space with its practical concrete floor and bright lighting, this room is cosy and calm, with mismatched rugs, an electric heater and pretty little lamps dotted about to give a warm glow – the perfect retreat on this cold January night. Originally just a stockroom in the days of Granny Dovington, Lacey has turned it into a welcoming craft space to host small workshops for customers who want to make something incredible out of the flowers. Typically Lacey hosts sedate hen dos for those who want to know how to make floral crowns for the wedding, or groups of well-to-do teenage girls who want to learn how to put together a fresh prom corsage. From time to time Lacey hosts seasonal sessions for making Christmas wreaths or Easter planters, but for the most part, the craft room is our space. We sit around the sturdy giant oak table with cups of tea and we chat, laugh, cry and everything in between. And the real beauty of this space is that it's a creative heaven for Lyla.

Lacey is like an aunt to Lyla and loves her unconditionally. They're very easy around each other and hold no airs or graces. Lyla comes in, plops herself down by the smeared, could-do-with-a-wash window and asks politely for the biscuit tin. I always feel a pang of pride when I hear her use good manners. At least I'm doing something right! Out come the custard creams, out come the felt tips and left over bouquet wrapping paper and many a masterpiece is born. Here and there Lacey will let Lyla deadhead wilting blooms or make a floral crown, and so quite often our little house is strewn with flowery artefacts from the shop.

Thanks to the wobbly start, my telling off at school and the fact it's such a miserable, sleety winter's day, today feels especially bleak so it's with relief that (after the obligatory rummage around the tin for a good biscuit and a flick of the switch on the kettle) we sit down to business.

'I'm a shit mum, Lacey.' I say as quietly as I can.

'What? No you're not,' she says, gesturing to a completely engrossed-in-colouring Lyla. 'Look at her! She's great!'

'I ballsed up her PE kit today and was completely dressed down in front of all the other mums. They already think I'm a mess. This is going to tip them over the edge.'

'They *don't* think you're a mess! They think you're the same as them, I bet. Everyone has bad days, Robin.'

'Lacey, I love you, but no, you're so wrong. One mum saw me getting out of my car with my coat over my pyjama top just before Christmas and said, "In a bit of a rush this morning?" in the most condescending tone I've ever heard. If snobbery were an Olympic sport, these women would be winning gold medals. What makes it worse is that I wasn't even in a rush, I just couldn't see the point in making myself look nice or putting in the effort because all I was going to do afterwards was go home, clean the worktops and watch a documentary about weird cults in America.'

'Why do you care about what they think? Surely you don't give a shit? They don't know you. They don't know how funny or caring or talented you are. They're not anyone special in your life, so they don't deserve such a high opinion from you!'

'I don't know. I just want to be a good mum. I'm so worried I made the wrong choice moving her there. I don't think she's feeling at all settled yet. I'm not helping her, am I? I thought this would get easier, but it's getting harder,' I take a big breath and look at my perfect child. Her dark brown, silky hair is tumbling down her shoulders and onto her arms while she daintily draws the bricks of a house with Lacey's pens. Her skin, like that of most little girls, is perfect. Not a single spot or blemish. Her lashes are long and dark and create the perfect frame around those eyes that get me every time she looks into mine. She's neither the shortest nor tallest in her class, but she sits slumped just now and looks smaller and more delicate than she is. Every time I take a moment to really consider her, I feel such a mixture of emotions. I love her and want to protect her and nurture her and keep her close and not damage her or ruin her zest for life or give her insecurities by making her do PE in ballet socks, or all of the other things that whirl through my tired brain on a regular basis. The Emptiness feels almost overwhelming right now.

Just as Lacey reaches over to squeeze my hand and I'm letting my mind fill with all the ways I'm failing as a parent (is her slumped posture a confidence issue she's inadvertently picked up from me not being forthright with people and generally shying away?) Piper strides in like someone out of *Vogue*. She's wearing tan skintight jodhpurs (I don't think she's ever been riding in her entire life), knee-high chocolate-brown flat boots, a soft cream cashmere jumper and her golden hair in a high ponytail. She is the walking embodiment of country chic perfection. I look down at my fraying jeans and see a little stain from the yoghurt I spilt earlier. Cool.

'Hey Bister,' Piper says to Lacey, walking towards the biscuit tin and giving Lyla a cuddle on her way past. Lyla takes the cuddle with one hand, so used to the women in her life loving her like this, and carries on drawing with the other.

'Hello Lister,' Lacey replies.

Secretly I wish I had a big sister or little sister to do the 'bister'/'lister' thing with. Although Lacey is my *very* best friend in all the world, I know I can't compete with the bond she and Piper have and will never get my own special greeting like that. But then I think how lucky I am to have these two in my life, blood relations or otherwise.

Piper sits down and starts picking at a stray petal on the table. 'Mum's driving me mad at home; I've just got back from a potentially very exciting appointment in London but she thinks I'm wasting my life by not "getting out there and finding a nice chap like your sister", so I've come here to escape.' She looks up at me with big eyes. 'Robin, you don't have a nice chap and you're OK!'

'Am I?'

'Yes, look at you! Successful job in something you enjoy, beautiful daughter, lovely little house, freedom, independence – you're a badass single mum living the dream, doll! I'm stuck at home with moany Mum, still looking for my dream job, despite my best efforts, and actively *not* looking for a "nice chap" to settle down and be boring with.'

'Hey! I'm not boring,' protests Lacey.

'You know what I mean. Not boring, but not doing what I want to do. You *want* to settle down and play happy families.'

'Give it a few years and you'll yearn for a copy of *Country Living* and some good upholstery too!' Lacey says with a grin.

'Please, no! The only thing I want to do right now on good upholstery shouldn't be talked about in front of little ears!'

Lacey and Piper laugh and I try to stifle a giggle but change the subject in case those little ears pick up on the excitement and start asking questions. It'll be the wax salon situation all over again, and Mrs Barnstorm's blood pressure wouldn't take it.

I'm just thrilled that I'm seen as the coolest one in all

this. This is exactly what I needed to hear today. 'Hear that, Lyla? Piper thinks Mummy's cool! Do you think I'm cool too?'

'Mummy, I think you've got yoghurt on your top.'

Oh.

FOUR

STEPPING THROUGH OUR FRONT door at 7 p.m., I wish I'd had the sense to leave a light on before I went out this afternoon. There's something horribly foreboding about coming home to a dark, silent house. It feels eerie. Despite no evidence of a break-in, while that light is off my brain automatically assumes there is a murderer hiding in the shadows and my heart rate shoots up even higher than the time I was cajoled into a spin class with my boss, Natalie. (Natalie, by the way, goes to the gym every morning at 5.45, so couldn't understand why I was on the brink of cardiac arrest a mere twenty minutes into the session.)

Anyway, with the near skill of an octopus, I manage to unlock the door, turn on the hall lamp, put my keys down, drop Lyla's school bag onto the stairs and dump my phone and keys on the ledge, all while holding a sleeping six-year-old, head on my shoulder, with my right arm. We'd ended up staying at Dovington's long after closing time and Terri's departure. The four of us cosied up in the studio and ordered fish and chips. We ate them out of the paper wrapping with the little wooden forks you get in the chip shop, and it was just what the doctor ordered. I know a good, proper mother would have stuck to our healthy Bath, Bed, Story routine. But the thought of coming home to an empty house, cooking alone then sitting by myself for the evening seriously didn't appeal, so I stayed with them for a bit longer and the company felt good. I would have stayed later if I could have.

My little sidekick had fallen asleep in the car – I try to ignore the twinge of guilt that I'm the crap mum who selfishly kept her out too late on a school night – and, being careful not to wake her, I carried her in with everything else. It's a remarkable skill you are gifted with once you become a parent: the ability to hold more than you'd thought possible in your arms in one go.

It's time to put my Lyla Blue to bed.

I used to love this time of night; that special moment at around seven when you clock off from the drudgery of plastic toys, half-eaten fish fingers, pretending to be interested in Peppa Pig and wiping up all manner of bodily fluids, for twelve solid hours, tuck them up in their warm blankets and take a deep breath. You did it. Another day of keeping your child alive (an achievement in itself), and another evening for you to have just one small glass of wine (you won't have one tomorrow, though; best not make a habit of it). I'd watch trash TV about twenty-somethings having exciting lives like I used to; they go out and snog people and eat worms in jungles. OK, I didn't do that *exactly*, but I do like to watch other people do it. The point is, it was my time again. I got my brain back for a while, and it was bliss.

Lately, though, I haven't been enjoying the magic hours. I often see friends on Facebook making heartfelt status updates about how their kids are their whole world and how they can't think of anything they'd love to devote themselves to more. But some days my whole world feels like a huge, dark, empty room, with me and Lyla stood in the corner looking out into the nothing. Does anyone else out there feel like me? I know it's my job to protect her and love her, and I do, with everything I've got, but lately the glass of wine and trash TV aren't filling up the rest of the dark room as the long nights draw in. I want to offer Lyla so much more than that, and I don't know what I'm supposed to do about it. It plays on my mind.

After four years of being on my own, the novelty of this 'me time' has really dwindled. In the dark January nights, when Lyla was smaller, with fluffy PJs and a fresh new notepad, I'd take a bit of time to write a fantasy list of all the things I want to do in the year ahead. Some of them obtainable, like take Lyla to the seaside for a day, and some a bit more wishful thinking like completely renovate the house or fly off to Vegas. But this January, more than any other, just feels flat. I've finally run out of buzz and get-up-and-go, and writing a list of things to do seems pointless. I didn't even bother buying a new notepad this year. I can't face looking forward any more than I can face looking back.

I miss having someone else in the house, even if they're not sitting or interacting with me; I just miss hearing the sound of another human pottering about. It wasn't great when Simon was here, but it wasn't lonely. When he left I was constantly shattered. I'm sure looking after a toddler alone is akin to running a marathon, and each night I'd flop onto the sofa completely exhausted and glad of an evening of nothing. Now, with Lyla at school all day and able to do so much for herself, I have quite a lot of nothing. Nothing for six hours during the day; four hours of play with her when she comes home and then a whole evening of more nothing. The less my body is tired, the more my mind is.

Amazingly, I manage to heave my sleeping girl up the stairs. When did she get so big? When did my arms get so bloody weak?

I lay her hot little body on her bed after I've pulled back the covers and begin to take off the necessary bits. I unbuckle each navy patent-leather shoe and put them on the baby-pink carpet by her bed; carefully unbutton her tiny grey pleated skirt, gently unstrap the watch she got from my boss Natalie and her husband Martin last Christmas and slowly pull the clips out of her hair. Since she's already asleep, it seems cruel to wake her up for pyjamas, and so I let her drift further off in her little red school T-shirt. She is so perfect. I'm obviously biased, but when I look at her, even when I search for one, I can't find a single fault.

I wonder what goes through her head, and what she understands of the world? Does she pick up on how dysfunctional our lives are, what a crap single mum I'm turning out to be, and how much The Emptiness is consuming me right now? Or am I protecting her enough, shielding her from how hard the world feels to me? Realising that I'm never going to know the answers to these horrible questions, I pull the brushed cotton lilac duvet further up to her neck and give her a kiss on the forehead.

Downstairs feels a lot better with the lamps on and candles lit. Pouring myself a glass of Malbec is probably not the healthiest idea on a Wednesday night, but I don't care. Wine helps. It shouldn't, but it does. Even with Kath, Lacey and Piper in it, today has been grey. Here's hoping tomorrow will have more to it . . .

FIVE

AFTER SNOOZING MY ALARM for the third time, and realising it's now gone 7.30 a.m., I get up, take a big breath and resolve that *this* is going to be a good day. Yesterday was tough. I felt completely trapped in The Emptiness, and even though I saw friends and got things done (or Kath got things done on my behalf), I didn't feel myself. Not today though, oh no! Today is a fresh start, and a chance to make the most of my life and count my blessings. I can't face another day of feeling as bad as I felt yesterday.

Robin Wilde, I say to myself in the mirror: *something needs to change . . .*

I can definitely do this.

Just like Lacey said, I'm as good as everyone else, and today I plan to show the world what I'm made of. Rather than schlepping into school in leggings and an oversized coat, I'm going to release the beauty within and take some pride in myself. (I'm basically just going to pretend I'm Natalie, the most self-assured, successful woman I know. If I follow her lead, I can attain her levels of acing it. Right?)

Lyla is already awake: she's a morning person. She sits buidling her Stickle Bricks and playing teachers with her toys; I can hear her instructing them to 'put the bricks in odd and even piles, please', patiently waiting for me to lay her uniform out. She gets dressed, brushes her teeth and tells me that today she'd like 'ninety-ten' plaits in her hair.

'Ooh, ninety-ten is going to be tricky. I don't think we have ninety-ten hairbands,' I reason.

'Make them,' she demands.

Jeez, I'm being bullied by a child. What does this say about my life? But no. I'm not going there. Today Lyla and I are going to *win*!

'Bluebird, I really love how much faith you have in me but maybe we should do just two plaits? We could put ribbons on the bottom and be like Pippi Longstocking!' I offer, in an overly cheery and high-pitched tone. She surely can't resist this.

'Who?'

Oh, yes; sometimes I forget we don't live in the rose-tinted eighties and read *The Secret Seven* and suchlike any more.

'Never mind – she's a character from a story. She has plaits, two plaits, so let's do that.'

'NINETY-TEN!' is screamed back at me with a complimentary foot stamp at the same time. Oh my God, I'm raising a monster.

'Lyla! Stop! It's seven forty-five and we need to leave soon. Let's do two very beautiful plaits and leave it at that. That'll look so gorgeous.'

'Storie does lots of plaits,' she sulks. Good old Storie. Storie is Simon's new girlfriend. I say 'new'. It's been four and a bit years. Of course *Storie* does lots of plaits. She probably does them while singing to the garden gnomes and fermenting her own urine for face cream.

'Well, I'm Mummy and I'm doing two.'

Sensing I'm not backing down, she gives up the fight and lets me work two neat French braids all the way to the bottom of her beautifully glossy long brown hair, and stomps off downstairs once I'm finished. Well, isn't it lovely to feel so valued and appreciated – motherhood is such a gift.

Once her toast is presented to her in the exact formation she likes (God forbid I'd ever cut it into squares instead of triangles), I nip back upstairs to sort myself out.

Today is not a day for the usual drudgery, so I pull on my good skinny jeans (not the comfy ones with a worn-thin crotch – why is that bit worn? Is my crotch so fat it rubs when I walk? I should look into that). I pair it with my white Ralph Lauren shirt – the one I bought two years ago in a discount shop and, thanks to the fact that I barely ever wear it, looks brand new and isn't a faded grey crumpled mess at the bottom of my wardrobe.

I'm already on to a winner.

My hair is never going to play ball at 7.55 a.m., so I praise Baby Jesus for the joy of dry shampoo and then put it up in what I consider to be a 'sleek pony'. When I see models sporting a sleek ponytail I think they look so chic, so effervescent. When I wear one I wonder if it looks like I'm wearing a brown swimming cap with a small plume at the back. Let's hope for chic and stop overanalysing.

Make-up time. This is one of the few areas in my life I know I'm good at and feel confident with. Time is of the essence, so I don't have hours for a full face, but I do have a few minutes for perfectly applied black liquid liner across my lids, a few good coats of mascara, a base of foundation and perfect red lips. (Make-up is something to be eternally grateful for when you've woken up with a red-wine-the-night-before complexion). Nothing says 'I've got my shit together' better than well-applied red lipstick. It's bold and sexy and as soon as I pout back at my reflection in the mirror, I feel good about myself. It might all be a mask but at least it's an effective one. And it feels good to be doing something for me.

We make it all the way to school without any kind of catastrophe. Lyla didn't trap fingers in doors, zips or seat belt plugs; I remembered her school bag and each and every correct component of her ballet and PE kit, as well as a nourishing lunchbox with proper foods in it like veggie sticks and hummus (not just a sandwich and a ton of things in brightly coloured wrappers). All that, and I look great. Maybe this motherhood deal isn't as hard as I've been making it for myself. Maybe I AM as good as everyone else. To top it all off, we're on time. We saunter through the gates at 8.50 hand in hand, and I feel overdramatically proud. Good for us.

Walking up beside us are Finola Brennan with her two children, Honor and Roo. Roo (short for Rupert) is seven already and in Lyla's class. Three years older than them is Honor. She's tall and strong and obsessed with the horses and ponies the Brennans keep. Finola is a sturdy sort of mother. She takes no nonsense, and believes in fairness and character-building. I like her a lot and secretly really want her to like me too. I'm also slightly terrified of her.

Next comes Gillian with Clara, who's also in Lyla's class and is a sweet little thing who believes fervently in fairies and magic and unicorns. Gillian seems pleasant enough.

Finola and Gillian are friends, and strike me as yummy mummy types who went for morning coffee dates in cafés with their babies and who didn't sit at home, alone, in jogging bottoms and a tangled topknot, resenting the fact that they felt too inferior to go to the mummy groups themselves and make friends.

'Morning!' I chime in a merry tone, as casually as possible flicking my ponytail off my shoulder in a bid to show off that I've brushed AND styled it. Wow, I really do feel great today!

'Morning. Honor! Roo! Go and hang your bags up and then come back for a kiss goodbye,' Finola orders them briskly.

'Hello! Oh, Clara, poppet, I've asked you four times now, can you not pull on my arm like that, you're really hurting me, darling,' Gillian pleads timidly with Clara, clearly not having the best morning.

'You want to raise your voice a bit, Gillian. Children are like dogs and respond best to an authoritative tone,' offers Finola.

Gillian looks a bit shocked, but thankfully her innate politeness kicks in and she just says to her friend, 'Oh, er, yes, thank you, Finola, I'll give that a try next time,' and blinks quite a lot.

Lyla sees all the others running for the cloakroom and follows suit, while we mums walk slowly in and stand by the hall doors waiting to walk them through to their form rooms. We always stand here. It's an unspoken rule that you pick your Foyer Spot on the first day and that's it for life. If someone were to violate this code of etiquette, all hell would break loose. Where would the now displaced mother stand? Who would she talk to? What if her precious child came looking in that spot and they weren't there? It doesn't bear thinking about.

I've learnt the hard way that there are a lot of unspoken rules to be taken very seriously. Joining the school in Year One instead of Reception was tough for both of us. While Lyla was learning the rules of the classroom and playground, I was tackling the etiquette of the foyer and car park.

It's so good to see Lyla running and playing with the others, though I do worry she's still hovering on the outskirts. I'm hoping that each day, as she settles in further, I can maybe be a bit more pally with these women. They all seem to have their cliques and groups, and aside from my when-I-can-face-it cheery hellos and the odd wave here and there, I've no idea how to get in.

'It's such a beautiful day today. So good to see a bit of sun shining,' I offer as a starting point. I'm determined that today I am going to start fitting in. I'm sick of feeling out on the sidelines. My mother always said, 'You can't go far wrong with talk of the weather, how well you slept or what you're cooking for dinner'. Mum clearly has all the bants – in fact, I remember at primary school hanging around at her side at the end of my school day while she talked for England with the other local mums. I'd be dying to go home and hoping she'd stop boasting about her latest Cambridge Front Gardens in Bloom competition win – but in this case, she's not actually wrong. Weather chat *is* a winner.

'It's marvellous. We got all four horses out for a good hack this morning and watched the sun rise.'

Of course Finola did.

'You do so well to do so much!' says Gillian. 'Clara wouldn't like it if I gave so much of my attention to something else. She still likes to have her special mummy time in my bed in the morning after Paul has left for the City.'

'Aww, I wish Lyla still did that; I'd like the company!'

Apparently this was the wrong thing to say. Finola and Gillian look at me, then at each other, then both appear stuck for what to say next. Perhaps we're not supposed to admit we're so lonely, our children are our friends?

'You look really glamorous today, Robin, are you off somewhere special?' Gillian asks nicely, conversation inspiration clearly striking.

'Or husband-hunting in Sainsbury's again!' I hear Val's seething voice from behind me. She's head-to-toe in designer clothing and tottering over on her high-heeled ankle boots smiling to herself (definitely not at me). Valerie Pickering is the worst of the PSMs. Mother to six-year-old Corinthia (who I suspect is a little cow, because they say the apple doesn't fall far from the tree) and married to Roger, who's eleven years her senior, severely balding and absolutely loaded. Val is brutally competitive and, for some reason, hates me. I've never done anything at all to her, but not once has she been able to say something to me that wasn't loaded with sarcasm or an attempt to put me down in front of everyone else. My only form of defence with this woman is to ignore her or, through gritted teeth, play nice and be polite. She makes me feel like shit.

'You *are* looking very *glamorous* today,' she laughs. She's clever; she's saying it like a compliment but I can feel the sting in it.

I'm not going to let her dampen my spirits. After that

miserable solo night on the sofa yesterday, I've made a bloody good effort, and I'm not going to be derailed.

'Yep. Thought I'd treat myself to a bit of me time this morning,' I say as curtly as possible.

'Ahh, yes. Being on your own you must have quite a lot of "me time" to spend dolling yourself up, eh?'

Wow. That was a low blow. I'm taken aback for a few seconds.

To my surprise, I catch Finola puffing her chest out and gearing up to rescue me. 'Valerie, lovely to see you! Edgar tells me Roger has been staying in Huntingdon since Christmas. I expect you're rather enjoying an increase in "me time" too, aren't you?'

Val's eyes widen in shock and Finola continues to give her a steely glare until Gillian meekly chips in, breaking the tension. 'That's a lovely shade of lipstick, Robin,' she says.

I'm so overcome by how perfect Finola and Gillian were just then that I'm blinking back tears. It's been a long time since someone stood up for me like that.

'You'll have to tell me what make it is so I can pick some up myself,' continues Gillian. 'You look really nice.'

Before I can thank them both, the bell rings and the foyer descends into chaos. All the children zip back to us like magnets; mothers are rushing through to classrooms issuing orders to their little cherubs as if they'll never see them again. 'Make sure you wear your gloves!' 'Your judo kit is in the blue bag!' 'Don't you dare fight with Hugo today!' And we're swept away in the commotion before Val has a chance to retaliate to Finola's revealing shutdown. I'm sure that won't be the end of it; it never is with Val, but for now I'm grateful not to have to deal with her. And still a bit in shock that Finola stood up for me . . . Maybe she's not as much of a cold fish as I thought.

Once the children are settled with their oh-so-smiley teachers (how do they manage to be that happy at 9 a.m.?), we make our way out to the car park. Val is nowhere to be seen. She's obviously shot off ahead of us.

'Thanks, Finola, I didn't know what to say to her. I can never think of something in the moment. I really appreciate you stepping in there.'

'Not a problem, Robin. Women like that are like pack dogs; once they know who's boss, they soon settle down.'

In Finola's world, everyone is like a dog or a horse.

'Edgar and I are always available for a good canter if you want to get some air in your lungs of a morning. Does you a world of good.'

'Thanks, Finola. Thank you,' I say, and walk off swiftly in the direction of my car before she sees the tears in my eyes. The thought of me going for a 'good canter' on a horse is ridiculous, but the offer was there and that felt good.

ONCE HOME, I DOUBLE-CHECK that I've got everything ready for next week's job on the set of the fruit-infused tea commercial. Mostly, The Emptiness doesn't touch my job. The occassional jobs I've been doing have, more and more, been like a holiday for my brain. Instead of feeling stuck and sad, I feel like I can run wild with ideas in a way I can't in my mummy life.

After five more hours of 'research' (the lemon tea needs a 'fresh and zesty' model, whereas the berry flavours need the model to look 'warm and inviting'), which has consisted of 30 per cent work-related internet browsing, 20 per cent getting lost down a YouTube wormhole of girls showing what they bought on their latest shopping sprees and 50 per cent clicking on every pointless link or humble-brag post friends have shared on Facebook. I don't know why I even bother going on Facebook, it's so depressing. Everyone I know is planning a wedding with huge lit-up marquees, showing their baby off in its new John Lewis matching outfit or posing for photos on the beach with their tanned boyfriend. Clicking on and scrolling through all this is like self-torture. Fortunately I can't dwell too long, because before I know it it's time to collect Lyla and click back into Mummy Mode.

The pickup goes smoothly; Val is nowhere in sight but instead sends her mother (an older, bonier version of her) for Corinthia. She looks down her nose at me – but I'm not going to let it bother me, at least now I see where Val gets it from. I drive Lyla home for dinner. I don't yet feel completely drained, which is better than most days, so I seize the moment and steam some veggies, grill some chicken, throw a few alphabet-shaped chips in the oven (I was doing so well but fell at the final nutrition hurdle) and sit down with Lyla to eat.

'Mmmm, Mummy, look at this dinner! It's like we're in a restaurant tonight, isn't it? The Mummy and Lyla Restaurant!'

I could cry. She didn't say anything yesterday when it was Smarties before fish and chips, but today, with chicken and veg, she's a happier kiddo. This is full-on validation.

'It is! Let's cheers to that, my Lylielooblue!'

We clink our glasses, spend the evening snuggling on the sofa with books, BunBunBear, an array of Stickle Bricks stuck in my side, CBeebies bedtime hour and a good feeling in my heart. A swish of lipstick really does make all the difference. Note to self: tomorrow it's the boldest, brightest red I own. It's going to be a big day.

SIX

Today, i'm asissting my boss, Natalie Wood, on my first big job and I can't afford to mess it up. After I've dropped Lyla off at Early Risers Club (an hour earlier drop-off for parents who work or who just want to have sixty minutes' more reprieve in their lives, so no PSMs at all today), I have to race home to gather up my kit and make sure my face looks socially acceptable and not like a three-week-old potato. For some reason, I'm having a wobble about going to work today. I haven't been on a job since just before Christmas, and insecurity is creeping in. That just leaves space for The Emptiness to rear its ugly head. Not today, please not today!

Natalie and I need to be at the studio by eleven to help set up. Simon is collecting Lyla from school today, so after a stern word with myself I decide I feel quite excited about get stuck in with some adult time and doing something I'm good at.

Natalie arrives at ten thirty sharp and waits on the drive for me to come out with my kit. I hate to make her wait, so I'm ready at the door with my shoes on as if I'm a cheeky little six-year-old waiting to be taken out for ice cream. Natalie's silver Range Rover is spacious and dust-free, quite the opposite to my messy little Micra. I throw my case in the giant boot, jump in and we drive straight off. Even though we've known each other for four years, it would be weird if she came into my house. Our relationship isn't like that. I've been to her trendy three-storey townhouse a couple of times to drop bits of kit off that have been mixed up in our cases, but never just to socialise. Natalie always says it's important to have boundaries, and she's so right. As she is about everything! We work together and respect each other, and it just works.

Honestly, Natalie astounds me. First, she's absolutely gorgeous. Imagine Michelle Obama but even more gracious and kind. Dark brown skin and shoulder-length jet-black hair that I have seen in so many styles, each one perfectly suiting her; deep brown eyes that exude wisdom and lips so full she can wear any shade and look sensational. She always looks immaculate. Second, she has three perfect teenage sons, Nathan, Daniel and Maxwell, who are all doing amazingly at school and university; a phenomenal husband in Martin, who has happily let his career take a back seat and

49

cared for the boys while she established and grew the agency; and she totally rocks her job. She started straight out of school on the make-up counters at Debenhams, then went freelance as a make-up artist and then, just before her first son, Nathan, was born, set up the agency, MADE IT. She's calm and generous, and ambitious. Natalie is basically a goddess. I've no idea how she does it, but she's the woman who has it all. I want to learn from her. Oh, fuck it, I want to *be* her!

I met her through Lacey. Martin used to work with Karl in the City (before he left to support Natalie and handle the childcare), and after my split with Simon, Lacey put in a good word so I could pick up a few agency jobs here and there. At first they were very sporadic, but that's exactly what I needed. With a two-year-old at my feet almost every day, it was near impossible to work solidly and I could only ask Kath to do so much. The times I did take on jobs, though, were brilliant. I kept my foot in the door, had some time talking with adults and, most importantly, kept that creative outlet open. Three years later, here I am – assisting the agency director on some exciting shoots.

We arrive on set early, and while Natalie confidently walks over to talk to the photographer about his creative vision, I lay out all the kit: apparently the director now wants the models' hair to embody the movement of the tea as it's poured into the cups. I can see the hairstylists, Chloe and Jodi, at their station frantically searching through Instagram for ideas now that the pre-agreed tight, clean bun has been thrown out the window.

We decide that deep berry-coloured eyeliner and a lot of bronzer seems to be the look that says 'fruit tea' on a human face. Initially they wanted to go for a deep (sludgy) brown on the lips, but after an under-the-breath comment about 'shit for lips' from a runner (who won't be invited back for the next shoot), the seed of doubt was sown in the directors' minds and a nude gloss was applied instead.

The eight models (eight flavours of tea to be embodied, after all) glide in and we begin. We work together seamlessly, having danced this dance many a time before. I'm pumped that Natalie liked the ideas I put forward from my research yesterday. Today she askes me to prep each face with moisturiser, serum, primer and foundation, before she takes over to complete with eyeliners, shadows, brows, lashes and lips.

As the models are called on set, we stand back behind the soft box lights and gigantic tripods ready to be called on for any touch-ups. This is a lovely part of any working day. Less intense, time for a bit of conversation while watching photographers make their magic.

Natalie leans over and whispers. 'How did Lyla get on with her horse riding?'

My heart sinks. In a move I now think Finola would approve of, I'd taken Lyla, before Christmas, to the local stables for her first ride only to find Lyla completely detests the sport (before the move to Hesgrove I'd never have considered putting Lyla on a horse, but I was so determined she'd fit in). I don't know exactly what motivated her to shout very loudly as we arrived, 'I bloody hate ponies! I want to go home!' and then start to cry, but I was mortified. One, that we'd offended the stable owners, and two, that she'd sworn. I mumbled something about her hearing it from her dad (they'll never know) and left at speed, red-faced and forty quid – forty quid! – down.

'Oh . . . er . . . Really great, thank you! She loved it!'

'Do you think you'll keep it up?'

'Yes, I think so. Lyla has such a lovely bond with animals,' I lie. I probably won't admit to my boss that my child couldn't give a shit about the natural world and that I worry it's because she's been emotionally stunted by her father leaving me when she was a baby.

'Well, you'll do better than me, then. I used to try and take Nathan before Daniel came along, but no matter what I did, he didn't care for it. He cried and cried. We quickly gave up and I realised I was far better off leaving him to play at his crèche while I got some work done than I was forcing him to develop an unwanted bond with a pony.'

Oh. Could have just told her the truth there. I keep forgetting she's normal and not actually Superwoman – or a PSM.

'How's Nathan getting on at Oxford?' Naturally Natalie's eldest son is in his second year at a top university studying Engineering Science.

'Really well, he still loves it! Daniel's been looking into a rugby scholarship for next year, so it's all go. Four more years and Maxwell will fly the nest, so it'll just be me and Martin left. We're thinking about doing some travelling together,' she replies calmly and smoothly, and without a hint of arrogance or smugness.

'Oh, how nice. That'll be lovely. And well done to Daniel.' God, she's lucky. Three high-achieving boys and a fit husband to go travelling with! I can't wait to grow up and be a Natalie.

Maybe sensing my silent wishes, she straightens up to prepare for the next touch-ups and says, kindly: 'Just you wait till Lyla grows up and heads off. You'll look back on these days of shoots and school runs and miss them. Come on, let's tackle these touch-ups.'

As we pack up I feel good about my day. For the first time in a long while I think I've done well. The Emptiness didn't come and claim me. It's a refreshing change not to feel like I'm blundering through my life, but actually controlling it.

I don't know how I'll do it yet, but as we drive home I resolve I'm going to find a way to make better use of my skills.

SEVEN

FEBRUARY

I HATE FEBRUARY. I thought I'd feel better once January was out of the way, but I don't. If I'm honest, I feel a little scared that I don't. My face is a constant mask of happiness (I chat in jolly tones at work and smile at the girl at the supermarket checkout and sing songs to Lyla in the car), but deep down I feel flat. Very, very flat.

For the last few years I've done everything alone. Shopped alone, spent evenings alone, planned outings for Lyla alone, driven everywhere alone, paid bills alone, slept alone. After a while that takes its toll. I feel like nobody is on my team and nobody has my back. I know there are Lacey and Kath, and Mum and Dad if I really need them, but it's not the same. There's nobody to wake up next to and roll over to give a cuddle to. Nobody of my own to have drinks and Chinese takeaway with when Lyla is with Simon. Nobody to

54

share my happy moments or deepest worries with, and sometimes, when it's very late at night and the house is very still, I wonder if there will ever be anyone at all. Valentine's Day is approaching. Every time I walk into a shop I'm faced with a sea of love-themed paraphernalia reminding me that I won't be waking up to a teddy and a red rose.

Don't get me wrong; I know there are people out there who have a much harder life, but I feel isolated. Everything I do is alone, or as leader of the Robin and Lyla Club, and that gets a bit hard sometimes. I'd love a teammate to just take the edge off. Like how gas and air in childbirth takes you from wanting to rip your midwife's face off to simply wanting to yell obscenities at the walls of your delivery suite. That's what I need – something to just take the sharp edge off the loneliness. What I'd love is a little bit of help and love and companionship. Is that too much to ask for?

I don't want Lyla to ever know how shit I feel.

I want her to feel like I'm her rock, and that whatever happens, however much life throws at us, I'm here and dependable and safe. Right now, secretly I don't feel either dependable or safe, but I sing songs or use a chipper voice to play dollies for the eighteenth time that day. I hide the emptiness that I feel inside to keep her safe. She is a perfect thing that needs to be protected at all costs and so I never want her to carry the burden of knowing *your mum struggles*. She makes me a Valentine's card with a '?' and I play along and exclaim in surprise, 'Oh my goodness, I'm so, so lucky!'

when she tells me it was from her. I don't let on that I'm crying inside at how sweet she is and how much I'd love it to be real.

WEEKENDS AS A custody-sharing single parent can be really hard. To everyone else it looks like the perfect life: time to relax, entire evenings to go out and drink cocktails, read magazines or go shopping, but in reality it's not like that. I crave that family unit and the sound of other people in the house. Right now Lyla is at Simon's for the weekend. I can feel the clouds of The Emptiness gathering again.

Determined not to let it take me over this time, I give Lacey a call and see if she fancies popping round for a glass of wine and a makeover. Lacey can always be guaranteed to come over if a mini-facial and a good smoky eye is on offer. It's been that way since we were naive teenagers in poster-clad bedrooms. Lacey has all the best advice, and I have all the best make-up. I'd pour my angsty fourteen-year-old heart out to her about the boys at school or the girls I hated or was jealous of, and she'd flick through the pages of *Bliss* or *Sugar* and pick out a make-up style for me to try on her.

Things are pretty similar now, except we've replaced teen magazines with *Grazia* and drinks and olives, and I barely hate anyone. Except maybe Val. How sophisticated we are.

'What's the matter, then?' she says, laying the box of Maltesers she's brought over on the sofa and plopping herself down. I love that wherever Lacey is, sweet treats are never far away. She drags my big metal make-up case across the floor towards her and opens it as if it were a treasure chest.

'How do you know something's the matter?'

'Your house is spotless, your nails are done and you've been responding to my messages in under four nanoseconds. Clearly something's going on or your life would be a whole lot messier,' she says with a laugh on the last bit.

'Oh. Hmmm. All good points,' I say, admiring the lilac gloss on my nails. 'I don't know . . . I just feel flat. Every time I think I've got my spark back, something small happens and I feel rubbish again. Today it wasn't even a big thing, but it got to me. I had some spare time – story of my bloody life – and fell into a scroll-through-Facebook-photos wormhole. I went all the way back pre-Lyla and saw our nights out, your hen do, that trip to Edinburgh we had, and I just missed having a bit of fun, I think.' And then I say it. 'I'm bored, Lacey. I'm lonely.'

'Oh, Robin,' Lyla says with a maternal tilt to her head. 'You've got Lyla, though.'

'I know, but she's at school every day and Simon has her two nights a week too. When she was super-little she had every bit of my attention. Now she doesn't need it. Nobody really needs me.' I can feel tears pricking at the back of my eyes.

'*I* need you! I knew you were a bit down at Dovington's last month, but I didn't know things were this bad. You should have called me. I want to help you.'

'There's something missing in my life.'

57

'A man,' Lacey says bluntly, snapping out of her soft, maternal tone.

'Not everything is about men.'

Lacey studies my face for a moment. 'This is, though.' Still being blunt, then.

'I thought you were a feminist, Lacey Hunter?'

'I am. Being a feminist means you want everybody to be equal; to have the same chances, opportunities and treatment as everyone else. It doesn't mean I don't enjoy feeling Karl's arms around me at night, or being taken out for dinner and good conversation, or having someone who takes the bins out when it's their turn.'

'I can't remember the last time that even happened to me. Kath comes over and does such a lot to help, but it's not the same as having your dashing man clean out your dishwasher filter or mow the grass, is it? The last person I had dinner with was Peppa-bloody-Pig!' I laugh sadly.

'So, Robin. I've been thinking about this for a while. I think you need to put yourself out there, meet someone. You deserve to have a bit of fun.'

'I'm never going to meet someone, though, unless a hot single dad magically appears at the school gates on one of the rare days I don't look like an egg, or one of the perilously young male models at work goes blind and suddenly fancies me!'

Lacey throws a cushion at my head and exclaims, 'Robin! First, don't say that! You have a lot to offer any man. And second, you don't have to meet anyone at the school or work. Everyone does it online these days.'

'No, I'm not doing that,' I say as I buff foundation in a tad too firmly. How does Lacey have such lovely skin? After this endless winter, mine is dull and lifeless. 'It's desperate and cheesy. It's full of creepy old men who masturbate over the underwear section of a Littlewoods catalogue!'

'No, it's not!' she exclaims, trying, and failing, to keep her face still. 'It's all changed! You should 100 per cent give it a go. Look at Meredith from school. She was single for nearly ten years, and then she met Peter on an app. Look at her now.'

'Yeah, she's stuck at home crying with the twins while she puts over-filtered photos of them smiling on Facebook and hashtagging #WouldntHaveItAnyOtherWay, when really we all know she *would* have it another way. She'd be wearing clothes without sick on and *not* googling "has my vagina changed since childbirth". That's not where I want to be! I want to be romanced! I want to be seduced!'

'Well, yes, but how do you think he got the twins in her in the first place?'

'This is getting really gross. I don't want to imagine Dating-App Peter getting *anything* in Meredith.' It's surprisingly hard to apply sharp, even, cat-eye flicks in black liquid liner when you're imagining your old school friend being shagged enthusiastically by a man called Peter that she met on 'the apps'.

'You're missing the point, you dingbat. Just give the apps

a try. Let's download MatchMe or something right now. It'll be fun!'

'Oh God, do I have to?' I say, finishing the eyeliner and blending a trio of deep red, mocha brown and gold onto her right eye.

'Yes, absolutely, or I'm leaving right now and you'll be alone all night with nobody to moan to.'

'You're not going anywhere – I've only done one eye and you'll look deranged.'

In the end, she twists my arm and after another glass of wine (OK, three more glasses), it turns out the dating apps are quite fun. Sort of like shopping for men but without having to worry about them seeing you staring or saying something stupid. It doesn't take long before I'm matched with Gareth 34 Engineer, Dylan 32 Freelance Consultant and Phil 37 IT. We scream with glee when the first 'Hi, how are you' pops up.

Why had I never considered doing this before? Man-shopping from your sofa!

Two bottles of rosé later, a wobbly and very giggly Lacey leaves in a taxi and I feel quite excited about all of these dashing potential suitors vying for my attention.

Huzzah!

Playing it cool (on Lacey's orders), I go to bed merrily full of vino and high hopes for my future love life.

EIGHT

I T STARTS TO RAIN as we're driving to Kath's for some respite. I wasn't planning on leaning on Kath today. I never actually plan to lean on people. If I could I would just do everything myself, happily and in indigo-wash skinny jeans that make my arse look incredible and don't bunch round my ankles, but we can't have it all, can we?

I'd planned just on having a lovely Saturday in IKEA to buy some storage for Lyla's ever-growing collection of plastic toys. I read an article on Facebook about how children need to live in feng shui'd environments for their emotional well-being, and so now I'm concerned that Lyla's expanding Shopkin collection is causing deep psychological damage, and that the answer to this is cheap (I don't think the energy of the room will know the difference between IKEA or Harrods, and money's tight living off a part-time salary and inconsistent child support from Simon) stacked tubs in assorted colours.

As with everything in my life, though, things didn't run smoothly. Ikea was rammed. The world and his overwhelmed wife were out in force, ready to stand in aisles bickering over Billy bookcase wood finishes or whether that TV stand would or would not fit in the alcove.

By the time we'd reached the children's department, I was sweating and had already thrown an assortment of junk I definitely didn't need in my trolley. We chose our tubs (very much hoping they sufficiently provide Lyla with the best chance of future emotional fulfilment), and then were forced, as you are in these maze-like places, to go round the market-place. This was my downfall.

I decided to 'treat myself'. I'd been feeling so down and lonely, I reckoned that if I wanted a set of three heart-shaped chopping boards, then I could have them; nobody else was going to be buying me anything heart-shaped, after-bloody-all. And since it's only me who walks on my bedroom carpet, if I wanted that black and yellow six-foot-by-six-foot rug, I should be allowed it. A gallery wall is always something I've wanted, so I liberally picked frames in the art section too. Thank God for my overdraft.

For a moment I felt a bit better. My full trolley had filled my empty heart and I was exhilarated from spending all that money on a whim. I knew I'd regret it at the end of the month, but in that moment, at the lifts to go down to the car, I felt great. Perhaps I'd discovered the solution to The Emptiness.

Minutes later, I realised I absolutely had not.

As soon as I opened the boot, I knew I'd fucked up. Unless there was a massive plot twist and my tiny car was actually a TARDIS, there was no way I was going to get four toy tubs (with lids), eight picture frames, two lamps, three chopping boards, six pairs of scissors (I don't know why) and a six-foot rug in there.

I knew the best course of action was to move Lyla to the front and put the back seats down, but even thinking about everything involved with that tired me. I'd have to read the car manual to turn off the front airbags so she could have her booster in the front, consult the manual again to wrench down the seats, load everything in and return the trolley, and even then I wasn't sure it would all fit.

I looked around despairingly, just in case there was a magic solution, and there they were – the family I was meant to be. A smart dad in jeans with a weekend shirt tucked in was pushing a trolley full of homeware, with a boy not much younger than Lyla hanging onto the front, enjoying the ride. Behind him, his lovely wife, in a soft pink wrap dress clinging to a perfectly round pregnancy bump and holding the little boy's backpack (probably containing low-sugar snacks and wooden puzzles that he excels at). Perfect Mum takes Perfect Boy by the hand and sits him in his booster seat. Perfect Dad packs their things neatly into the boot. The winter sun is definitely shining more brightly over where they are . . .

I'm jolted back to reality by Lyla. 'Mummy, I'm bursting

for a wee-wee! Mummy! Mummy! Muuuuummmyy!' Literally the last thing I want to do is take her back to the shop with my trolley and start this all over again.

'OK, just wait a minute and we'll sort it.' This usually buys me a solid ten to twenty minutes. She's never actually bursting.

I look back at my own parking space and try to focus. After ten minutes of huffing and puffing and a very real sweat patch appearing on my back, I've got one back seat down – the other one is refusing to budge. So many people have passed by and seen me struggling, heaving and grunting, all while Lyla's been sat in the trolley, telling me loudly that she needs a wee (everyone can hear and will be thinking I'm crap for not dealing with that first) and waiting for me to sort her seat out. Just to show her she's not going to be sat in the trolley forever, I lift (more like heave – she's far too big for trolleys now) her out and have her stand safely by the front of the car while I deal with the boot.

Nobody has offered to help.

Why would they? They don't need to. They're in their family units, blissfully unaware of how desperately shit it feels to not have a unit. How crap it is to try to work out how to turn an airbag off while your daughter jumps about on the spot needing the loo. How physically demanding it actually is to feed a six-foot rug through your boot and into the back seat.

I want a Perfect Dad man to do this with me. I want to be wearing a soft wrap dress. I want to not have to look at how desolate my morning has been.

I've crammed everything in and sweated through my top to create oh-so-sexy damp underarm patches, when some guy walks past muttering 'I think your kid needs the loo.' Oh for fuck's sake *I know*! I turn my attention to Lyla who's hopping up and down on the spot like she's trying not to cry.

'Mummy I'm going to wee!'

She says this with a new kind of urgency and that ten to twenty minutes grace window is suddenly more like ten to twenty seconds. Great, so now strangers are more in tune with my daughter's needs. Oh God. I look wildly around at my surroundings, scoping out the nearest facilities and deep down I know they're back in the store. *Shit shit shit.*

'MUMMY IT'S COMING!'

I scoop her up and run through the carpark. My boot and passenger door are still open and fuck, I've left my handbag there too but instinct took over and I couldn't bear for her to have to wet herself. I run like an athlete (a very cumbersome, unbalanced, wildebeest-esque athlete) to IKEA's lobby and practically throw myself and my attached offspring into a loo. Without even stopping to shut the stall door I pull down leggings and pants and sit her on a toilet. Instant relief. We made it. I cannot believe I came that close to making my six-year-old daughter have an accident.

'Ew, Mummy there's a man in here!'.

In my panic and hurry I've taken my little girl to the less than hygienic men's loos. I put my hand over her eyes.

Will I *ever* get this right?

NINE

EVEN AFTER THE MORNING we've had it is almost impossible not to feel your spirits lift at Auntie Kath's tiny Victorian cottage. It is a perfect reflection of her and a living scrapbook of her life. Every nook and cranny is decorated with photographs, tickets, letters and mementos from her past. Every piece of treasure has a tale behind it. The hardwood floors are covered with patterned rugs and swirly carpets; the walls are painted in jewel tones and the curtains are velvet flock. Every piece of furniture is mismatched, and usually with a floral pattern or lurid cushion adorning it. Frames are hung all over every wall, with pictures of Kath's life peeping out from behind the glass, many with Derek's cheery face in too. Derek Drummond, Kath's late husband, was a good man. We all miss him, but of course Kath misses him the most. They were a beautiful couple. They travelled the world and they were the perfect team. Derek was strong and calm and found Kath's scatty eccentricities endearing. When he got ill, Kath cared for him night and day, and when he finally died it really shook her. I think she sometimes feels The Emptiness too. I'll talk to her properly about this one day, but right now I feel so consumed by my own emptiness and self-loathing for being the shit mother that barely even meets her child's most basic needs, that I don't think I can bring myself to do it. I don't think I could be much help.

Looking around, you'd think the whole place would clash and jar but somehow it works. Everything has her touch to it: the shell lamp that probably once didn't have seashells glued all over it – come to think of it hers is the only VCR I've ever seen with shells on; the coffee-table cloth with a pom-pom trim (who has a tablecloth for a coffee-table, please?); the framed map of Wales (we're not Welsh and don't know anyone from there), where she's marked certain towns with stick-on diamantés – everything has been 'Kathed'.

As soon as Kath answers the door, I feel a little lighter.

'Hello, my lovies! I've missed you!' she trills, beaming, even though we only saw her four days ago. Mollie is even more thrilled to have house guests. I really want to love her but she's so jumpy and yappy, and should you leave any piece of skin exposed it's going to be licked.

'No kisses, please, Mollie!' Kath laughs as Lyla nearly drowns in Mollie's slobbery greeting. Kath ignores my barely concealed distaste and waves Lyla through to the kitchen, bustling Mollie into the back garden at the same time. She did notice the lick attack, then.

I can smell something baking in the oven (please be scones, oh please, please be scones!) and all the lamps are lit, creating the perfect warm glow this grey February day needs.

'Auntie Kathy! We've got petals for you!' Lyla chimes before she's even managed to take her shoes and coat off.

Yesterday we stopped by Dovington's for a chat and a cup of tea – hot chocolate for Lyla – and Terri let Lyla deadhead the wilting flowers that couldn't be sold. Lyla revelled in the honour of doing something so grown-up that she'd never be allowed to do at home – not that I see many bouquets of flowers these days. I'd collected them all into a paper bag and messaged Kath because I knew she'd have a genius idea for customising something with them. And now I'm hopeful that idea will take up a whole afternoon and I won't have to leave, or use my brain, or listen to my own thoughts.

I pick up the coat and shoes Lyla's strewn all over the entryway and follow them through to the kitchen. Lyla has already climbed up onto the solid wood worktops, tipped the petals out of the bag and Kath is going through them all with her. 'Oh, Lyla, look at this one, it has little yellow flecks in it, can you see? Mmm . . . smell this one, sweetheart. Doesn't that smell sweet?' I can see from the doorway that Lyla is taking this sorting process very seriously, and dutifully smells and strokes and inspects each petal as Kath remarks on it.

As I walk in, Kath looks up at me and our eyes meet. Over the last few years we've been here more than once. Me in The Emptiness and Kath picking us up. The Emptiness comes in waves. Some months are bad and some are OK, but lately those waves seem to be crashing a whole lot harder than before and after a morning like this morning I'm struggling to carry on standing up in them. A flicker of recognition dances across Kath's kindly face and I know she understands how I feel. As mad as she is, Kath is astute. I love that I don't have to sit and articulate all the horrible feelings in my head and can, in one look, say, 'help'.

Walking over to the stove, Kath reaches out her hand and gives my shoulder a squeeze, which is probably all I can handle without bursting into tears. Kath's got no idea how shit our IKEA morning was, and I don't think I can bear to talk about it all. Sensing my reluctance, she whips into motion and busies about making hot chocolate the old-fashioned way – no instant powder and boiling kettle water for her, oh no! She's bringing milk to the simmer on the Aga and melting a slab of chocolate, and then she pulls some scones (YESSS!), out of the oven. From the fridge, she gets the clotted cream and jam and in no time she's sat back down with Lyla, who is still fiddling with the petals and singing a little song to herself about fairies and magic and all the sweet things that fill little girls' heads. I hope her head stays filled like that forever. I wish mine had.

'Oh, Bluebird, that's a good song you're singing. I think I saw some fairies in my garden the other day, and I thought how much you'd have liked them!' Kath whispers in Lyla's ear.

'Did you?' Lyla asks with wide eyes.

'I did! Next time I see them, I'm going to tell them all about you and your beautiful song.'

Lyla beams up at Kath. I'm so glad there is someone to add this magic to her life; someone she can connect with like this. I wish it was always me every minute of every day, but right now it feels so hard.

I take the bar stool next to Lyla and sip at my freshly poured hot chocolate. It's like little drops of heaven. The scone is still warm and it tastes all the better knowing Kath lovingly made it. When I feel like this I don't want to interact with anyone, but I don't want to be on my own, either. Kath knows and so she carries on around me, letting me be.

'Right then, Missus Blue, what are we going to do with these petals?' she asks Lyla in a mockingly authoritative tone.

'Ummm . . . play with them?' Lyla replies hopefully, twirling her hair around her fingers and smiling in antici-pation. She knows Kath has a plan.

'Well, we can either press them and preserve them or crush them into perfume. What shall we do?'

'Both!' That's my girl.

'All right. We'll do both.'

'Yay! Let's make perfume for Mummy!'

And so they set to work with Kath's marble pestle and mortar, crushing up half the petals to a floral mush and sprinkling them into four different ornate glass bottles that have been collected over the years from markets and car boot sales. They add water, and every so often encourage me to scent-test their creations. Obviously they all smell the same – a bit mulchy, to be honest – but Lyla is carefully telling us which secret power each perfume has.

'This one's for you, Mummy. When you spray it, it will make your heart happy.' My unhappy heart almost breaks. On some level maybe she understands how flat I've been feeling these last few months. She loves me with no agenda or expectation.

Trying not to cry, I say, 'Lyla, this is the most perfect-smelling perfume I have ever been given. I'm going to wear it every single day and have the happiest of all the hearts in all the world because you gave it to me.'

Her face glows with a smile.

We have a little snuggle while Kath fetches the flower press. As she leaves the kitchen I can see a wry smile on her face. She knows what she's doing.

Twenty minutes later, and we're all in full swing with the flower pressing. The Emptiness is fading.

We spend the afternoon carefully selecting the best petals. We go by Lyla's measure. Using tweezers, we lay them on tissue paper, lay another soft sheet over the top, put them in the press and eventually – when every layer of wood, tissue and petals is full – twist down the nuts and bolts. It's gentle and methodic and exactly what I need to lose myself in. I suspect Kath has planned this activity for exactly that reason, even though she insists she just had a hankering for it.

Kath takes Lyla upstairs by the hand to place the flower press ceremoniously in the airing cupboard, where it will stay for a good few weeks to ensure we achieve the finest dried flowers in Cambridge, and I take a moment to gaze out of the window into Kath's garden.

Like her house, her garden has been fully Kathed, too. On wrought iron 'stems' Kath has screwed stacked plates and coloured glasses to make decorative flowers. Wind chimes and tiny mirrors hang from bare tree branches, and if you look very closely, the odd porcelain fairy pokes out from beneath brambles and bushes. I can remember being Lyla's age and being utterly enchanted by them. Kath has such a magical aura about her. She drives me to absolute distraction (I still can't find my corkscrew after her New Year clear-out, and since then she's been in and 'upgraded' my kitchen chairs with gaudy paisley seat cushions I didn't ask for and obviously can't throw out), but on days like this, where would I be without her?

Lyla clatters back into the kitchen with Kath following steadily behind her.

'Feeling a bit better, love?'

'Yeah. Things just felt a bit much, you know?'

'I know. It gets to us all. You've got to put your best foot forward and carry on. Carry on all the way to Auntie Kath's house for a bit of TLC and scones, that's what.'

She comes over and gives me a huge cuddle. Normally I'd feel uncomfortable with such a show of emotion but today, I'll take it. Never one to miss out on affection, Lyla bounds over and clings onto the other side until I'm in a Kath/Lyla sandwich. And it's actually quite lovely.

'Ooh Mummy, you're so squishy with love.'

She's right. I am. My heart is very full, thanks to these two, slightly crazy, very wonderful women.

On the drive home, Lyla is quietly listing the names of all the fairies in Kath's garden, and I am thinking. Having some time at Kath's has given my brain a chance to escape from my mummy-guilt and general lethargy for a few hours.

I realise I've felt most alive recently when I'm designing or making something, and when I'm with other people. Not socialising specifically – gosh, no – but just being around other grown-ups.

I play with the idea of asking Natalie if I can take on a few more jobs and get back into the swing of things. I'm currently working one or two events every couple of weeks, but with Lyla settled in school, Simon's new-found flexibility (Storie has taught him to be 'fluid like the energy of the earth') and Kath's help, I could definitely go up to three or four – or more – and maybe lift myself out of this fog I'm in.

A few weeks ago I would have been stressed to the point of tears just thinking about taking on anything more, so letting myself go there – considering working more and taking a bit of ownership for my life – feels like a big step.

I'm going to do it.

Lyla stops listing names. 'Mummy! You're smiling! You look happy like a rainbow after it's rained.'

I hadn't even noticed, but she's right.

Maybe the rain has stopped.

Part Two

'Fortune favours
the brave'

TEN

MARCH

SPRING IS AROUND THE corner at last and today I have the day to myself. Lyla is dropped to school by Simon and Storie (I expect they're listening to her playlist of hideous wind chime music in their electric car – Lyla told me it sounds like someone gently banging knives and forks on glasses). I have had too many days to myself recently. I start with such grand plans. This will be the day I go through the cupboard under the stairs and list Lyla's old high chair on eBay for some extra cash. This will be the day I cut my wardrobe down by half and donate everything to charity. This will be the day I go to Tesco to buy miscellaneous birthday cards to have in stock at home so that I never again have to flap round the house searching for one. This will be the day I batch-cook a load of nutritious meals to freeze and eat at a later date.

Except it never is the day. None of those days have ever happened in my life. I dream of those days, those never-happening days.

Instead I feel anxious and isolated, watch a lot of daytime TV or get lost in a wormhole of daily vloggers on YouTube who are leading seemingly more glamorous lives than me and being amazing parents. If I'm feeling very low, I'll treat myself to a giant Costa latte and slice of chocolate tiffin, before I do the food shopping (the freezer won't stack itself with oven pizzas and fish fingers) and go to collect Lyla from school. All of this will be done in leggings, slightly bagging around the knees, and an oversized shirt that I try to convince myself looks 'effortlessly stylish' like celebs at festivals but actually just looks effortless.

Still, though, this *will* be the day. I keep thinking about Lacey's pep talk and my idea at Auntie Kath's and it has given me quite a boost. This actually bloody *will* be the day I make the most of the me time and tick things off my list.

Here we go:

Shower and style self. This feels like a given, but after Val's remarks I realise just how downtrodden I've been looking lately and think I might give it a bit more effort. Twice in two months will be some kind of record!

List understairs junk on eBay. My cubbyhole is a TARDIS-like vortex for years gone by. If there were ever a prize for real-life Tetris with baby/child equipment, I'd win it hands down. I've got half of Mothercare stashed away in my house. The distinct lack of romance in my life suggests there are no more little Lylas coming my way, so it's time to let it all go. Like the mini-trampoline I bought last year, thinking I'd go on it every night and be more toned than Julia Roberts in the *Pretty Woman* piano scene in mere months. In reality, I had five or six big bounces and was quickly reminded what a difficult birth Lyla was. Thanks to my bladder, my trampolining days are well and truly over.

Clean out make-up kit and – be brave – message Natalie about more independent jobs. I secretly love sorting through my kit. There's something very cathartic about cleaning brushes and wiping down all the products. Tiny little pots of colour and shimmer. Tubes of concealer and foundation promising the holy grail of perfect skin. Huge flat palettes that open with a satisfying click and are filled with circular slots of every shade you can imagine: some neutral, some iridescent, some you can't imagine how you'd actually incorporate into a make-up look (acid green, I'm looking at you). This is definitely achievable today. You've got to make your list manageable.

Work out. I've had my gym membership for two years now but barely used it. Mum bought me it after a visit up from their place in Cornwall, and I'm not sure if I was more insulted than grateful. Still, it's there, so I'm going to be bold and give it a go.

Right: list written (on unopened phone bill), I should probably add 'open impending doom envelopes' to the list, but I'm not going to be totally unrealistic.

Time to seize the day!

After a long shower (including leg shave and exfoliation – oh, how I'm treating myself), I take a bit of time to assess my wardrobe and pick something out that isn't stretchy or jersey cotton.

This is actually more challenging that I first anticipated it to be. Aside from the odd special occasion dress (I cycle through the same five for weddings, christenings and birthday meals out) and my nice white shirt which now has a red wine stain, dammit, I seem to just live in jeans, T-shirts, smocks or leggings. This is ridiculous.

I quickly give up (story of my life) and throw on some sweats and a tee because nobody in their right mind would tackle an understairs cubbyhole in something without stretch. How ludicrous.

Surprising even myself, I plod downstairs, set my Spotify to 'Motivation' and begin tearing things out of the cupboard with more gusto than I thought I had in me at 9.45 a.m. This is my day! I'm doing it! First I pull out all the things I actually use, like the hoover, mop, a ladder and put them in the kitchen. Once I've scratched the first layer I'm on to the 'sorting through' items. With a bit of effort, I retrieve the high chair, car seat, pram chassis, pram top, pushchair top, separate umbrella pushchair (this kid had a lot of transport options, apparently), a Bumbo seat, the rock-and-vibrate bouncer (that I remember Simon and I having a massive row over in Mothercare, him saying it was too expensive and me arguing that I needed it if only so I could have a moment of quiet and maintain my sanity), a clear plastic tub of smaller toys, a broken plastic watering can, a squashed lampshade, a plethora of half-used tins of paint from when Granny lived here and a dusty bin bag of coloured card from the découpage crafting phase I went through three years ago. With everything scattered haphazardly around my hall and lounge, I can clearly see just how much junk I've been hoarding and feel suddenly quite overwhelmed.

Turning back to the cubbyhole to see if I've missed anything, I'm surprised to find my old shell box. I hold it in my hands, running my fingers over each varnished shell. Kath brought back this beautiful, deep, A4 sized box covered in shells from one of her holidays in the Mediterranean with Derek when I was about thirteen, and I've used it as a memory box ever since. I've thrown in photos and ticket stubs, lucky charms like a miniature troll with red hair and the plastic hospital bracelets Lyla had on her wrists and ankles when she was born. It's so lovely to find it again. I feel all my memories flooding back as I rifle through, and then, at the bottom, I find all the notes and bits of paper I've written on over the years, scrawling out lists and memories and thoughts on the world around me. I'd forgotten I used to do that. I take them out and start to read through them – the thoughts I wrote down the overwhelming day I found out I was pregnant; a couple of pictures of Lyla when we first brought her home – I should put these in the albums with the rest, smiley snaps from when Simon and I first moved in together; a gorgeous photo of Lacey and me in bikinis in her back garden – we must have been about fourteen – I can remember how hot it was, and how we felt like we could take over the world . . . Then I discover a page torn from a notebook, soft from being folded and unfolded so many times. I know exactly what it is. Lacey has so often said, when I've wobbled since Simon left, that having Lyla was an amazing thing. I carried and gave birth to that beautiful baby girl. *I* did it. And if I can do that, she always says, I can do anything. I unfold the pages and read:

Ten days since Lyla burst into our lives. Feels like a decade already. All the days merge into one when you don't sleep through the nights. No one told me breastfeeding would be so hard. I know they say it's all about bonding with baby and 'breast is best', but fuck me, it had better be worth it. Right now it feels like I constantly have 7lbs of flesh attached to me. When she sucks it's like a thousand tiny threads of cotton are being pulled from the back of my chest, through my boob and out of my nipples. Every time she latches on I flinch and make a face. This isn't like the adverts with that mum in soft grey clothes in the perfect airy nursery. I feel so duped. This is horrific.

We were watching Grand Designs when it happened. Kevin McCloud was talking about a building 'blending seamlessly into the surrounding countryside' or something and then all of a sudden, my waters broke. There were no contractions, no warnings, just a massive gush and the sofa upholstery was ruined!

Called the maternity unit, and they told us to wait until the contractions began and then come in. As soon as we'd put the phone down, they began. They were so mild at first that I thought all those women on One Born Every Minute were wimps, but after two hours things heated up. I rolled on my ball while Simon watched the News At Ten, and then I couldn't take it any longer so I manoeuvred my massive bump into the front seat of the car and we drove in.

As usual – even in between contractions – we had a row about the parking. He'd assumed I'd put change for the meter in my hospital bag because I'd said I had 'everything'. Idiot. I obviously meant everything for me and the baby.

Once we were in, things really started to happen, and not in that breathing-calmly-and-thinking-of-your-precious-baby way. There were internal examinations *(basically being fingered multiple times by women I don't even know), soft belts stretched round my giant tummy to monitor her heart rate, gas and air (to 'take the edge off' – ha!) and a lot of vomit. A few people feel sick on gas and air and, lucky for me, I fell into that bracket.*

It was a mess. I was a mess. I really wanted to be one of those women who does it so well. Who 'bears down' and births a beautiful pink baby and then looks up at her husband glowing with contentment, as they hold the bundle.

After four more hours of contractions so painful I wanted to smash my fists into the walls, it was time to push. By this point I'd had so many drugs I felt completely spaced out and alone. It was like I was really far away from everyone and couldn't communicate it.

After an hour of pushing, my incredibly young-looking midwife suggested I needed 'a little help'. Forceps. Huge metal salad tongs to be shoved up my vagina to 'help' me get baby out. I vaguely remember not caring. You'd think you would care about that kind of thing, but I've never felt desperation like this before so I garbled something about 'do whatever the fuck you want sorry for swearing ow ow fuck get her ouuutttt', and in they went.

The next few minutes were a blur. There was pain and people and not a shred of dignity, but then all of a sudden, Lyla was in the world.

Her slimy little body was put on my chest and I realised I was holding my daughter. A brand new life that I had made and delivered, just lying there on my chest.

For a moment she was the youngest thing in the whole wide world. I felt like we were a team. She'd been in there all that time, and now I was holding her on the outside, protecting her from the cool air with my hands and bit of hospital gown . . . my precious baby.

Everyone says you forget. But I don't want to forget, which is why I'm writing this now. It's 3.07 a.m. The house is silent. Simon is sleeping – lucky him – and my tiny baby girl is snuffling in her cot next to me. I look at her. I could gaze at her for hours.

They say you feel an instant rush of love, but that's not how I'd describe it. Love to me is soft and kind and warm. I felt a rush of ferocity. If anyone, at any point, were to try and hurt this perfect child of mine, I'd kill them. I felt instantly protective, and like it doesn't matter what happens to me; I'll take care of her.

I look up from the pages. I *did* do it.

And I can do this.

I quickly gather everything to put it all back in the box. I'll look through them properly later when I'm not seizing the day. Just before I pack it away, right at the very bottom I spot an old card with a heart on the front from Simon saying *Happy Six Months Ro-Ro, Love you forever, Simon xxx.* Wow. That stings.

I don't remember meeting Simon Dessens – he has been in my life forever. Our mums were friends from the community centre where they worked, so we'd played together since we were Lyla's age. Our mums jointly managed bookings for the events or clubs, handled the petty cash, stocked the kitchen with coffee, teabags, sugar and milk and looked after the keys and alarms. They both took great pride in organising the summer fete, and despite their smiles and their florals, they were deeply competitive. The way they talked about it when we were little you'd think they were running the United Nations. Simon and I (increasingly grudgingly as we got older) helped serve refreshments to the old age pensioners at their social clubs and tidied away the chairs from the Weight Watchers' meetings.

By the time we were sixteen, we were in love. Both quite shy kids who lived under the rule of our overbearing mothers, we were kind of each other's security blanket, and felt a connection. Obviously at sixteen you rarely understand yourself, let alone the complexities of deep, proper relationships, and so we felt it imperative to go to the same university as each other. We stayed relatively local and graduated from Warwick, he with a 2.2 in Geography and me with a 2.1 in Communications and Media. Clearly you don't know what on earth you want to do with your life at eighteen, when you pick your degree! I went to an evening course in make-up artistry on the side, and enjoyed it so much more than the education I spent my studen loan on. At the request of our empty-nest-suffering parents we moved back to Cambridge, and by twenty-two I was pregnant with Lyla. I was working as a freelance make-up artist doing weddings or am-dram shows and Simon's dad secured him a steady desk job at a local factory that made drill bits, so we had an income and we could pay the rent on our tiny two-up, two-down terrace.

In our young, blissful ignorance we decided we could manage a baby, and so we were happy. Despite our ages and lack of life experience, our mums were thrilled too; everyone loves the idea of a baby. Though I think my mum was more excited to show her Rotary Club ladies the two-piece baby sets she'd bought in John Lewis than anything else. We had our whole lives mapped out for us, and I was OK with that. What more could a girl want?

One weekend, about four months into the pregnancy, Simon took us off for a romantic trip away. Think moonlit cobblestones, the Eiffel Tower sparkling in the distance and the aroma of authentic French cuisine gently wafting past us, inviting us in to eat and laugh and lock eyes as we fell deeper and deeper in love. Ha! How hilarious. Stop thinking about that, and now imagine a damp tent in the freezing early spring on a mediocre Lake District campsite and that's where we're at. Throw in a greasy fry-up in the site café, me looking like a dweeb in waterproofs borrowed from Mum and you've painted yourself a picture of reality. Not quite the lust-filled flair of a European city break. Pair the cold and damp with a constant feeling of nausea (why they call it 'morning sickness' when it lasts all day is beyond me) and you don't have the most incredible picture of love, do you? Still, on the second day, after a two-hour trek through the beautiful, if slightly grey, scenery, Simon got down on one knee and proposed.

I looked down at him in his wind-resistant anorak and sensible glasses and knew the right thing to do was say yes. The right thing, not the knee-trembling, holy-fuck-I-can't-believe-this-is-happening thing. I knew – or thought I knew – he'd look after me and the baby for all of our lives. We would do our weekly food shop on a Monday, have a take-away on a Friday and if we were feeling completely crazy, have a glass of wine on a Saturday night. He was never going to bolt, never going to upset the applecart. He was a safe bet and a decent man. I loved him. So I said yes.

Fast-forward two years, and my safe bet felt very dull, much more dull than I'd anticipated. Not only was I bored of Simon, Simon was bored of me. Lyla had come along after hours and hours of excruciating and sweaty labour during the hottest week of the summer, and we'd been thrown into a sleep-deprived world of stinky nappies, soiled breast pads, car seats so hard to figure out you practically need an Enigma machine, and pureed food. I'd never felt less sexy. I stopped taking on artistry jobs and lost myself in motherhood. I'd so wanted to be one of those yummy mummies who glides about in soft-stretch skinny jeans and floaty bohemian tops with chunky, wooden-bead necklaces and kind eyes. I'd wanted more than anything to have a gaggle of mummy friends to sit in cafés with on sunny mornings and chat about the funny things our doting husbands had said earlier that morning as we'd kissed them goodbye for work. As with a lot of things I'd discovered, expectation doesn't usually meet with reality and in fact life felt rather bleak. I found it hard to get out of the house with all the things you needed to pack, feeds to do and naps to time, let alone make a handful of glamorous mother friends for morning coffee dates. Early on into motherhood I gave up hoping for all that and resigned myself to our comfortable routine complete with daily scrambled-egg sandwiches and walks to the duck pond, just the two of us. It was lonely. So, so lonely. Despite the obvious, I really felt like I was the only person in the world looking after a baby, had nobody to talk to and felt as if one day just merged into another, with the only break being Simon coming home in the evening and watching his documentaries. Looking back, I think this was the start of The Emptiness. My mum 'didn't want to interfere', so Kath was a real saviour back then, stopping by for regular visits and filling the fridge with goodies.

Simon climbed the career ladder at the factory, and became deputy manager of the office there. We had nothing in common, nothing to talk about, nothing to love together, except Lyla. Our perfect Lyla Blue Wilde. Since we still hadn't tied the knot – it's hard to find any enthusiasm to plan a wedding when you're covered in spat-up milk and your fiancé barely speaks to you – she had my surname. We said that when we finally did make it down the aisle we'd change it to his.

Our relationship ended ages before he left. Had we not had Lyla, I think we would naturally have drifted apart as we grew up; I don't think he'd have proposed. We just weren't the same teenagers any more, banding together against our tyrannical mothers. Simon wanted to knuckle down at the office and have a perfect family with three more children, and I had just become a shell, forgetting my identity and turning into a bit of a mummy zombie; a 'mumbie'. I don't think I'd really worked out who I was before I had Lyla – I was so young – so it was hard to hold on to any of that when I spent all my days at home or at mind-numbing baby groups, doing my best for Lyla but not managing to reach out and make friends with any of the other mums. It's hard to admit it, but I think I was suffering with post-natal depression. I didn't dare talk to anybody about it, and didn't go to see my doctor in case she thought I was the worst mother on the planet, and so I did my best to muddle through and hide it all. Over time, and with a lot of chat in the mum forums (they were the most social thing about my day), I started to feel clearer and better again. I actually think those strangers on a forum were the ones who pulled me out of it, who made me feel like I wasn't alone and sinking into an empty void. I wish I could find them and thank them.

Seeing these baby pictures now, of the three of us all smiling at the camera and me hiding deep sadness, I wish I'd spoken out, got better sooner and allowed myself to enjoy Lyla's early months a bit more. I wish I was enjoying now a bit more too.

When Lyla was about sixteen months old, just before Christmas, Simon's dad was involved in a car crash which left him with two broken legs and a dislocated hip. It was terrible. His mother struggled to cope with his care after he left hospital – although being a proud woman she'd never admit it – and we spent a lot of time helping them both get back on their feet again. It affected Simon more deeply than we thought something could. His perfect, mundane, plod-along world had suddenly been violently shaken and he cracked. Something inside him snapped, and after applying for a three-month sabbatical from work he decided he needed to travel, see the world and experience life properly for the first time. And he wanted to do it alone.

He left us in May for a backpacking trip around Tibet. It was the most un-Simon thing he'd ever done, and I didn't think I minded. By this point I was so numb that I didn't have the fight in me to mind. I just let life wash over me while I cut up apples and gave baths and kept Lyla going. I remember Lacey being absolutely furious with him. 'Imagine if you wanted to fuck off to Tibet! You'd never be able to go! You'd never leave your baby! What a selfish prick.' As she ranted about Simon, I'd just hold Lyla and nod. I was so exhausted I didn't have much else to give. Having had these years to reflect, Lacey's point seems pretty clear. I never did get to just take my time and run with it. And I'd never have left Lyla. Ever.

I realise, looking back through these memories, just how much I need to ask Natalie for more regular work; I deserve to do what *I* want for the first time in I don't know how many years. I am going to talk to her today.

Back then I thought a break would do Simon and me good. Absence makes the heart grow fonder, and all that. Kath came over almost every day and I started to make regular trips out with Lacey, going shopping or to Dovington's or even for morning coffee dates. Then Lacey introduced me to her neighbour, Natalie, and after a trial run she put me on her books to assist her on shoots. I suddenly had a purpose that wasn't just making up bottles or feeding the ducks. I was going out alone and doing something I was good at – and Kath absolutely loved the opportunity to babysit more. We even built up a routine so I could have a night out with Lacey once a fortnight. I felt a little spark of myself come back – and I hadn't even needed to don a backpack.

Simon was finding himself too. Except he didn't just find himself – he also found Caroline, a nineteen-year-old masseuse from Peterborough who prefers to be called Storie ('with an I and an E, please'). She'd travelled to Tibet to find her earth mother, Nature. Simon said he felt a 'powerful, natural connection' to Storie during a hilltop retreat, and that Storie (*with an 'ie'*) had convinced him it would be going against Mother Nature's intent if they were to ignore it.

Surprisingly, I didn't care as much as I thought I would. Over the summer I'd come out of my shell. Not by much, but enough to feel alive again, and I realised it was better without him. I had learnt that I didn't actually need him to look after Lyla, or to have a social life. I was starting to earn a bit of money, starting to get out and about and being more than just 'Mummy'. We'd separated by the autumn, moved out of our rented terrace and arranged a fairly flexible custody schedule for Lyla.

Dad and Auntie Kath had moved my ailing granny into a lovely facility for the elderly, and so the logical thing for me to do was to rent her house. It was perfect for us: the rent was low, I was able to stay in the area and it had a familiar warmth to it, which is just what I needed in those early single days. That's how special Kath is. Even though I'm not her daughter, she treats me like one and didn't resent Lyla and me being given such a wonderful gift. Sadly the same could not be said for my own mother. Rather than offering to come and stay with me to help, she asked me what had I done, where had *I* gone wrong in the relationship, for Simon to have 'run off with some young floozy'. My mum, Mrs Wilde, the least supportive woman in my life. She still hasn't forgiven me.

Simon moved in with Storie to a home with solar panels, dreamcatchers and a biodiverse vegetable patch in lieu of a garden, and they are very happy there. Storie isn't a bad person, she's just very different to me, and in fact to Simon, which is probably why they work so well. Opposites supposedly attract, after all.

Flicking through the rest of the memories in my shell box and clicking the lid closed, I feel a sense of satisfaction. None of those memories hurt me like they used to. They're not personal attacks reducing me to tears and anxiety; they're just bits of my story, and today, I'm moving on with it.

TAKING A MINUTE TO look around at what I've achieved this morning, I feel a surge of real joy.

I've never let go of any of the stuff in the cupboard under the stairs because I would have felt like I was letting go of Lyla's babyhood, my life with Simon, the family I'd thought I was meant to have. All these *things* felt like mementos or trophies of an era, but now, strewn around the lounge on their side or upside down, they just look like bits of plastic I'm ready to say goodbye to.

And the cupboard looks absolutely massive!

I spend the next couple of hours with kitchen roll and Dettol, wiping everything down and stacking it more carefully in the hall. One by one I take each piece into the front room, snap it on my phone, list it on eBay and put it back in the hall. With each thing I list, I feel motivated to do more. I've been putting this job off for years, and doing it feels deeply cleansing, not just for the cupboard but for my mind.

By lunchtime I'm done.

The baby bits are cleaned, listed and stacked, the everyday use things are back in the cupboard and, hurrah hurrah, I've dragged my plastic drawer units under the stairs too, so – at last – I have a proper place to store my make-up artist kit. Now I have more room to organise and display it (this is an upgrade from the top shelf of my wardrobe!), and it takes no time at all to put it all away and take stock of what I actually have.

I put the memory box safely at the back of the cupboard, and pad into the kitchen to make a cup of tea. I feel great. I did something. I did it by myself, for myself. A little piece of The Emptiness falls away. Sipping my tea, I decide to take the plunge, harness this new-found energy and force myself into the gym.

Now I'll be the first to admit, I'm no gym bunny. I'm a healthy normal size but I have the fitness levels of a slug. A slug after it's slithered over the blue salt pellets. A slug after it's slithered over the blue salt pellets, has died and been pecked at a bit by birds.

I manage ten minutes on the treadmill, ten on the bike, ten on the cross-trainer machine of death and call it a day. I went into the room of torture and moved about. That counts. I 'worked out'.

My favourite bit of any gym experience (of which I have about four to choose from) is the changing room.

I luxuriate on the squishy stools at the mirrors and delve into my make-up bag, taking time with each process, doing my brows gently and carefully, fully buffing in my foundation and blending my eyeshadow until it looks like light and dark merging seamlessly into each other. Finally I apply the purple orchid-coloured lipstick I never wear. I want to play with it all the time but always tell myself it's not worth it; today's not special enough, or I'm not in a good enough place to deserve it. Well, I feel different somehow: the day feels different, I've turned a chapter in not letting my memories overcome me and I am worth it. I guide the coloured bullet of the make-up over my lips and instantly my face looks vibrant. I feel it too. I am vibrant.

I'm not the drudgery of my lonely days. I am the vivid colour of my lipstick. I'm worth good make-up and skinny jeans and time at the gym. I'm worth the extra space in my cupboards. For the first time in a long time, I don't feel the low fog of The Emptiness, and feel a spark of excitement. Like the first snowdrops in spring, can I feel myself coming back?

I collect Lyla from school, Val watched me with narrow

eyes as I said a confident 'good afternoon' to Mrs Barnstorm and looked away when I nodded hello to her. I took hold of Lyla's hand and walked out with my head held high, and we spend a lovely afternoon dancing round the lounge to that same 'Motivation' playlist, eating spaghetti and snuggling to CBeebies. I feel so much better today that I don't even mind the mind-numbing children's songs or surreal characters of *In the Night Garden.*

At bedtime Lyla says to me, 'Mummy, I love it when you're so bouncy.'

Me too, baby, me too.

ELEVEN

'SHOTGUN THE FRONT SEAT!' yells Piper as we leave Lacey's house.

'You know nobody cares about the front seat any more,' Lacey retorts to her sister.

'Then you won't mind if I have it then, will you?'

'Obviously not.'

'Hate to break it to you, but I actually *like* to sit in the back, so let's go in Lacey's car. Piper, you can sit in the front and I'll sit in the back and listen to you bicker all the way there.'

'We won't be bickering. Karl's car has inbuilt satnav,' Lacey replies smoothly.

'That doesn't guarantee anything with you at the wheel,' baits Piper.

'Oh my God, stop it! This is supposed to be a nice day! I

haven't been shopping in fuck knows how long, Lyla's with Kath for six solid hours and I want to treat myself. I've got no idea what to buy so I need you to not be like this!'

'Like what?' Piper and Lacey say in unison.

'Like this! Like sisters! Focus on your sad, unfashionable, frumpy-mum friend who finally has a little bit of money thanks to her eBay endeavours, and wants to be SEXY!'

'Sorry, Robsy.'

'Yeah. Sorry Robin. I'm just glad you've come out. You've been so down. This'll be a nice day, I promise.'

Sheepishly the girls get in the front of Karl's swanky black BMW X5 and I climb in the back, ready for the perfect girlie shopping day. After selling all the junk under the stairs, I'd got the bug, decluttered the attic and made quite a bit of extra money on eBay. Putting a little bit into savings so I felt like a responsible adult, I'd decided to blow the rest on myself. It was about time I updated my wardrobe and felt good again, and stopped hiding away in T-shirts and leggings with holes in them and food on them.

Plus, spring is most definitely in the air. Pink blossoms are blooming, we're not wearing our thick coats any more, and I need a bit of life and colour in my clothes!

Stepping into the shiny shopping centre, Piper snaps into leader mode. 'OK, we need to attack this head-on. The first thing you need are some good jeans. You'll need a casual pair and a dressy pair—'

'Dressy jeans?'

'You know, for dates, cocktails, going out . . .'

'Right, right.'

'Then you're going to need some tops. Something sexy and off-the-shoulder to highlight your collarbones, something loose and easy for gentle afternoon dates and something practical but cute for work. Then some decent heels. I bet you have plenty of practical flats,' she adds, looking at my very worn ballet pumps.

'Flats are comfy.'

'So? Heels are sexy.' Piper seems confused by my desire to feel at ease in my clothes.

'Once we've tackled those basics, we'll move on to dresses and accessories. What bag are you taking out with you these days?'

'I just shove everything in a tote usually.'

'A *tote*?' It's as if I've used a language she's never heard spoken.

'Right, yeah, a new bag, fine.'

We spend the morning being marched around various shops and counters by Piper, swooning over soft leather, warm cashmere and all manner of silky things that would look revolting on me. As we meander around, Lacey makes a photo log of things she wants so she can prompt Karl for her next birthday. She's so lucky to have someone who loves to treat her.

By 2 p.m. we're all officially shopped out. I'm on a new-shiny-treats high, Piper is exhilarated at her new-found role as Chief Stylist and Lacey, who I've noticed eyeing up the baby clothes with a sad look on her face, has nearly used up all her data texting Karl pictures of the things she wants.

We decide to call it a day and head into one of Piper's usual spots, Nola's, for some celebratory cocktails.

'To Robin and her Technicolor wardrobe!' exclaims Piper as she raises a glass.

'To Robin! Who is going to have to go on loads of fabulous dates now, to make the most of this!' joins in Lacey.

'Thanks, guys! You've been so good to me! I feel amazing! I know this sounds insane, but I feel like my whole life is going to change now. I have all the tools in my box to look and feel amazing. This really is going to be a big, big change for me.'

'Yeah . . . a change,' says Piper, looking out of the window at the shoppers mooching by, laden with bags or pushing buggies.

'Erm, earth to Piper, what's all that about, please?' asks Lacey.

'Nothing, nothing,' Piper says, fondling the stem of her cocktail glass and looking over to the other tables, filled with couples and girl groups, all with luxury shopping bags at their feet too.

'Don't "nothing" me. I can see it's not nothing.'

'Well, I wasn't going to say anything today because we're shopping, and I was going to wait until we were with Mum and Dad, but—'

'Oh my God, you're pregnant!' Lacey and I both interrupt

at once, and then give a satisfied glance to each other for doing that best friend thing where you're totally in tune with one another.

'No! Jesus! No! But I do have a big change coming up, and like I said, I was going to wait to tell you with Mum and Dad there, I just—'

'Spit it out. If you're not pregnant, then what is it?' There's a sharp tone to the word *pregnant* from Lacey that I don't think Piper has picked up on.

'I'm moving.'

'Well, that's not that big a deal!' Lacey says, clearly – if only to me – with a hint of relief that there isn't a pregnancy for her to be painfully jealous of.

'To New York,' Piper says, taking her fingers off her glass and looking up at us.

Lacey's stunned into silence.

Everyone's eyes dart back and forth to each other, wondering who should speak first.

I bite the bullet and say, 'Piper, that's amazing. New York is *amazing*.'

'Yes, thank you, yeah. I had a meet and greet in London in January, then a phone interview last month and I've been offered a work placement as an Assistant Contributing Curator for a gallery in the East Village. I figured it would be silly not to take it and see where it leads.' Piper looks at Lacey, waiting for her to say something. 'It's not forever, it's just a-try-it-and-see thing . . .' She trails off, noticing

Lacey's shocked face and is clearly desperate for her to respond.

'Robin's right, Piper, this IS amazing! I'm so proud of you. My little sister! New York City! Fuck, yeah!' Lacey gushes, her face snapping into action and lighting up with pride.

Piper and I both let out big laughs, relieved that Lacey is OK and shocked at her use of bad language.

Lacey raises her glass again and says, 'Well, here's to my little sister! Flying the nest all the way to the Big Apple!'

We spend the next two hours ordering more cocktails and discussing all the things she'll do, the celebrities she'll no doubt become best friends with and the visits we'll make to her out there. We're all on a bit of a high now, except somewhere very deeply at the back of my mind, a pang of jealousy is twinging. I hate it, but I can't help it.

I'm happy for Piper, of course. I want her to have the best time ever, honestly, but *I* want to have the best time too. I'm never going to be sitting in a bar with my sister and best friend telling them I'm moving to the other side of the world to live out an exciting adventure. For a long time now when The Emptiness has hit, even the smallest of outings can feel like an ordeal. I need to take a day off just to gee myself up for a night out, let alone a move halfway across the world. Plus, even if I was brave and trendy like Piper, I still couldn't go because of Lyla. I'm a mum and I can't put myself first, ever.

Still, I reason, I might just be Robin the Single Mum, but

now I'm Robin the Single Mum with dating apps on my phone, amazing jeans and red shoes that make me look and feel incredible.

So, no more dwelling on all the things that are simply out of my reach.

TWELVE

THINGS ARE HOTTING UP on the dating apps. Every time I have a free moment I check my phone and sure enough, there's a message. Sitting in the school car park in the mid-afternoon spring sunshine: have a little flirt. Waiting for Natalie to finalise on a job (she takes such care to make sure the client is completely happy with everything and seeks out any feedback so that she can always improve and grow the agency. It's impressive. Without her example, I'm sure I'd just pack up and go) so we can go home: flirty-flirt. Sipping a cup of tea in my nine-year-old dressing gown with a little barely-visible-but-I-know-it's-there period stain, oh yes I'm so sexy: let's flirt.

Craig is a personal trainer who loves the outdoors, good wine and travel. We've been chatting back and forth and the chemistry is fizzing. I've not lied but maybe glamorised the truth a little and said I'm a self-employed make-up artist and that I mostly work in London. Almost true; I do sometimes help Natalie in London and I do sometimes go to jobs alone, although they're always local ones like bridal make-up or home bookings for people who have a special occasion to go to. I haven't mentioned my penchant for very old pyjamas, my hatred of gyms or the fact that I've never been anywhere on holiday other than England and the South of France with Mum and Dad when I was little. Oh, and I haven't mentioned Lyla. It'll be fine.

Piper told me never to make the first move and to let him chase me, which sounds very archaic in this day and age, but she seems to do well for herself so I'll go with it. Eventually, after some cheery messaging, he asks me if I fancy a drink.

A date! An actual, real-life date! I am so excited about it that I screen-grab the entire asking-out conversation and message it to Piper, Lacey and, accidentally, the lady who bought some of my baby bits on eBay. After a few apologetic messages to her, I fully immerse myself in the excitement of discussing every potential date detail with the girls, and spend a merry evening planning my life with Craig. I'd like to say I didn't get carried away, but I think creating the wedding Pinterest board (sage and cream theming, lace details and the handmade flower girl parasol for Lyla) after that third glass of rosé was probably a step too far.

For the whole of the next day I feel wild with excitement, The Emptiness like a distant memory. I drop Lyla to school and have so much pep in my step I am almost skipping. Even Finola looks impressed, and she's been up since five to walk the dogs for three miles. I feel so good. Craig fancied me, he looked at me (well, my taken-from-good-angles pictures), and didn't see a frumpy mum with a messy life. He saw an attractive woman he wants to take for a drink. I feel validated. Only twenty-four hours to go.

Then, as I'm cheerily chopping carrots for Lyla's tea, he messages to say he actually doesn't want to meet up.

He thinks I'm a 'really great girl' but that maybe he wasn't looking for a relationship and stringing me along would be cruel.

Oh.

Another wonderful foray into the world of men. Validating bubble burst, pep completely dissolved and, though I'm angry with myself for it, I feel rubbish again.

Five days later and no endless, vapid scrolling through men on apps for me today. Lyla and I have – for the first time – been invited to Soft Play with Finola, Gillian and the kids. Soft play. The place where mothers go to let their children behave like savages while they drink cheap coffee and try not to think about the lives they had before. You know, when they went to restaurants without children's menus and didn't have half-used packs of wet wipes in their handbags.

The children run off like a pack of wolves to expend their never-ending supply of energy, and I'm determined to make

107

a good impression. Gillian starts us off with the mumsy pleasantries.

'I was so glad you suggested coming, Finola. Clara's been getting ever so restless at home on a Wednesday. She does swimming on Mondays and chess on Tuesdays, but by Wednesday she's bored and ready to blow off a bit of steam.'

Wow. Should I be putting Lyla in more clubs? I thought taking her to Dovington's was extracurricular, but apparently not. This is the first time Finola and Gillian have invited me along, and I'm already learning so much. Note one: put Lyla in a club or six.

True to form, Finola responds with all the tact of a smack in the face, but none of the malice. 'Absolute load of nonsense, all those prep clubs. What children need is a good run in a field or some solid exercise.'

'Like dogs?' I joke, although slightly relieved Lyla isn't missing out on chess and swimming, and goodness knows what happens on a Thursday.

'*Exactly* like dogs. If I leave one of the bitches in the truck while I see to the horses, she goes absolutely berserk. You need to get them out, get their hearts pumping, air in the lungs, and they'll rest well. Children are the same. Honor's not too bad, but if Roo doesn't have at least an hour or two of physical activity each day we're in for a ruddy awful time, I can tell you.'

She's so direct I almost feel like I've been sent to the headmaster's office.

'Well, he looks like he's having a great time,' I say as we look up to the ten-foot-high netted pavilion where all the children are running around, quite violently throwing balls at each other. Honor and Roo seem to be heading up the assault with Clara giving it all she has in return and Lyla hangs back a little bit, holding a ball nervously in her left hand and just watching. My heart goes out to her because I feel like I'm doing the same, but holding a coffee and listening. I decide the best thing is to leave her to it. Finola probably did, and look how hers turned out, I think, as I see Roo hang from a bar and simultaneously launch two balls at once at his older sister.

'Little angels,' offers Gillian without a hint of sarcasm, clearly not seeing what I'm seeing.

Disregarding further indulgent talk about the children, Finola steps in with no warm-up, 'Robin, I've been meaning to ask you what all the fuss was about the other week, with the hair and make-up and shiny, shimmy bangles and such?'

Assuming she means that morning I looked like a total babe, I say, 'Just for myself. Just making an effort.'

'A man on the scene, then, is there?' Finola probes.

'Ooohh,' Gillian chimes with an air of interest, while keeping an eye on Clara, who appears to be straddling Roo and hitting him over the head with a foam noodle. Little angels.

I don't want to be rude; these are potential friends, so nicely-nicely does it. 'Well, I'm not actively looking, but if one came along I wouldn't mind,' I say with the added extra of a nervous laugh to try to appear casual.

'I don't believe it. When one of our bitches is in season, you can tell; she has a way about her, and so do you.'

'Finola, ha ha, are you comparing me to a dog?' She'd better bloody not be. This blush I've been wearing is Charlotte Tilbury, not shades of dog period behaviour, thank you very much.

'Ha! We're all animals, dear, and you can tell a lot about a woman by the way she holds herself. I think you do a marvellous job with Lyla and all you have on. If you're looking for a chap to add into the equation then I'm all for it. Bloody good for you, I'd say.'

I think that's Finola being loving. I'll take the dog comparison, then.

'Oh. Well, thank you, Finola. Truth be told, I am looking, but it's not going very well. I don't think there's anyone out there for me,' I say, picking at the sugar packets on the table.

Gillian, lovely, soft, timid Gillian, reaches out and puts her hand on my hand, which is still holding the sugar that I now don't know what to do with. I just sort of leave it there, hoping she'll let go before the packet falls out of my hand or makes my palm all sticky.

'Robin, you work hard for Lyla and you're intelligent and smart. Any man would be lucky to have such a lovely woman as you,' she says in her soft voice. I can't imagine Gillian ever shouting. I can't really imagine her doing much at all except lovingly caring for Clara and Paul and crying at *Call the Midwife* every Sunday with a box of tissues and a chocolate orange by her side.

Gillian says this in such earnest that I think I might actually cry. I never knew she felt this way about me – to be honest, I didn't think anyone did. It seems so much for someone to say, especially someone from the PSM crew. I'd assumed they'd just invited me to make up the numbers.

Blinking back tears, I turn to the play zone, where Roo is now holding his own with a foam brick for protection and Lyla is trying to keep the peace with outstretched arms. Honor watches on, seemingly giving no shits at all.

'You know what you need to do, my dear?'

No, but I'm sure Finola is about to tell me.

'Get yourself back on the horse. No shilly-shallying around, just straight back out there, best foot forward. My brother Jeffery fell off a steed once when he was fifteen and broke both arms. Four months later he was back on, and we didn't hear a peep about it. That's what you need to do. Get all your lipsticks and eye wands applied, or whatever they're calling it these days, and try again. You can do it, girl!'

God bless Finola the Blunt and Gillian the Gentle. Like chalk and cheese, but both exactly what I needed. I still feel weird and out of place, and like maybe I ought to be wearing something navy-striped, but I think I might have started to love them a little bit.

THIRTEEN

I'M FINALLY DOING it. I'm grabbing the bull by the horns, I'm flicking through every inspirational quote I can find on Pinterest and I'm bloody well doing it.

I swiped him five long days ago in the car while I was waiting for Lyla to finish ballet. Charles, 32, data analyst, four miles away. He's local, a bit older than me and employed. The pictures were promising. One face on, one black and white and one of him skiing. Has every single man on every single dating app in all the universe been skiing? Or do they get some kind of single man's handbook which advises, *just so you know chaps, the ladies go gaga for a ski pic*. I flick through to the last photo of Charles in a fancy dress ensemble on a night out, probably included to show me what a cool and spunky kind of guy he is. Oh Christ, it's tragic when you think about it – but who am I to criticise! But his bio was fine: 'Laid-back, likes nights in or out, looking for a lady to spend time with and enjoys getting to know new people'. See, that's fine! He sounds totally normal and totally great. Lyla is tucked up safe and sound for the weekend with Simon and Storie; they're off to a soul festival, naturally.

I'm so used to life being the Robin and Lyla Show, and branching out feels terrifying, especially with spunky Charles. It feels like when you're twelve years old and you're going on your first school trip to the Lake District: it's all fun and games on the coach when you and Sarah McGarthy have eaten your body weight in M&Ms and read through the scandals on *Mizz*'s problem page. But then you get there, to the dark and dank boarding house you're staying in, the carpet is thin, the bed smells weird and you just want to go home.

Natalie says 'fortune favours the brave', and affirmations like this certainly seem to be working out for her. So here goes. Two weeks, fifteen matches, more swipes than I dare to count and the suggestion by me (oops, I've broken Piper's rule) to meet for a drink, and I'm going on this date. My first real date. It's time to leave, and I think I've done everything right. I spent a disgusting amount of time preparing, but I'm already slightly irritated by the idea that Spunky probably hasn't even bothered to brush his hair. OK Robin, stop. Try not to mentally attack and take down Charles before you get there.

I smell great; that's important. I hope I don't smell too

much, though – a perfume should whisper, not roar. I bathed in some Jo Malone minis that I nabbed from a shoot last week (it's not stealing – they'd been sent by a PR company and would have been thrown away if nobody had taken them at the end). I'd planned to save them for a special occasion, and this seemed good enough. I've shaved (not everywhere, just a respectable shave). I've exfoliated and tanned. Well, I've tanned the bits you can see: arms, legs, neck and face. Naked, I look like abstract art. But what if the thirty-two-year-old data analyst does see? No, of course he won't see, because I'd never do that on a first date.

Would I? God, I'm not even sure I'd remember what to do.

I decide to tan everything, but I feel very unnerved smearing Marmite-esque gloop on my bum cheeks. I'm wearing a navy cotton dress from ASOS which is cute, but modest, but fun, but . . . oh, I don't bloody know! It's fine, and I'm wearing it with my gold pumps. I feel OK. I mean, I feel like I might shit myself if I make any dramatic or sudden movements, but I think that's normal. We've agreed to meet at a trendy pub with tables by the River Cam at 8. The one where you can see the filaments in the light bulbs and most people drink Aperol Spritz. I've told everyone that cares (so Kath, Lacey and Piper) where we're going and set Find My Friends up on my phone in case of abduction. I considered bringing both the rape alarm and the pepper spray, but my clutch would only fit one so I've gone for the alarm. Auntie Kath told me never to leave the house without the alarm, reassuring me that she even takes hers to crochet class. I'm prepared.

I'm also early. Shit. Don't really want to go in and sit like a sad single watching the door, so I'm just going to have some Instagram time in the car. I hope he looks like his pictures. Instagram is so nice; why isn't my life like Instagram? Why don't I have the sun streaming in through muslin curtains onto a rose gold vase full of peonies that's perfectly placed on an antique coffee table? I should do that. I should lay out – shit, there he is!

A man vaguely looking like Charles's pictures walks past the car and towards the door of the pub. (And the use of the adjective 'vague' is being very kind.) He's definitely a crappier version of his pictures. Spunky Charles has decided to wear baggy jeans with one of those belts that looks a bit like a slimmer version of an airplane seat belt. He's matched this with battered brown loafers that he probably bought after he graduated from university and a short-sleeved grey shirt. Is there anything more repugnant on the face of this earth than a short-sleeved shirt? His face is pointy. Pointier than in his pictures, anyway, and his skin is sallow and makes me think he probably hasn't eaten a vegetable this millennium. Perhaps Charles never goes out. Or perhaps he's cobbled this outfit together and has really tried, and this is the most exciting night ever for him. I need to give Spunky a break. Best just to get out of the car, Robin, and see if his personality is a winner.

Forty-five minutes and a small glass of rosé later, and I am certain it's not. Charles isn't The One. Our conversation is drier than my brow after a half-arsed attempt at the gym and I'm running out of general topics of conversation.

'Soooo, you're a data analyst, then. What's that like?' I venture.

'Well, I'm not a data analyst in the traditional sense. I tend to focus more on making the database infrastructure that the analysts themselves use day to day,' is Charles's monotone reply. He seems to be having trouble keeping his eyes off my boobs. I am not impressed.

'Oh wow, that must be . . . fulfilling?'

'Yes, can be.' The chemistry is on fire. By the fifty-five-minute mark we've had a conversation about the pub decor, the relative merits of his car over my Micra, how Charles didn't realise make-up artists had assistants and we've also discussed how many other dates we've had off MatchMe. (Charles has been on the app for eight months and this is his second date.). I've also filled the time up by wondering aloud how strong the current in the river is. Because I want to jump in it and swim away.

Charles is talking about erosion levels, and I can't handle it. If I don't leave now I will actually have to bludgeon myself to death with the trendy wooden wine menu. I need to get out, but 'sorry, you're so dull I'm considering one of our deaths' seems a bit much. So I'm going to do the most mature thing I can think of – lie.

'Oh my God, Charles! I've just remembered, I need to be at home for a delivery! Oh, shit! I need to go! Shit, *shit!*' OK, so maybe not a good lie.

'A delivery at nine p.m.?' he says, looking genuinely surprised. Dammit, Charles, let me leave you with some dignity.

'Yeah, it's quite . . . specialist.' Where am I going with this?

'What is it?' Charles, please. He still seems very believing, which I'm not sure is a good thing.

'I'd rather not say. It's . . . medical.' Medical? Why have I said that?

Now I sound diseased, or like an addict. Probably more like an addict. I sound like a classy drug addict that has drugs delivered at nine on a Friday night, and I should have just said I had a headache. What's wrong with me? But it's too late; I have to carry this lie through to get out of here. I stand and grab my bag. Charles doesn't try to kiss me, but he's insisting on walking me to my car.

I scramble about in my bag to find my keys in order to distract him from any potential goodbye affections. I grab the fob and press the button before pulling the whole bunch out (he doesn't need to see the 'hilarious' key ring of a man's nether regions that I got at Lacey's hen do years ago) and WEEEWAAAHHWEEEEWAAAAHHHWEEEEWAAAHHH.

Jolly good, it isn't my key fob, it's the fucking rape alarm.

Every single person in the car park and smoking area is looking at me. Charles looks horrified and confused as I continue to scramble in my bag to silence it, but of course I can't. People are approaching now – probably thinking Charles is some kind of attacker – and it's still wailing. If I go any redder my face will literally melt off my skull.

Finally I manage to turn it off and mutter something about it being better to be safe than sorry. Charles looks aghast (I sort of did just accuse him of being a potential rapist, though). He wishes me well with my 'medical delivery', and I thank him for the lovely evening. Nobody kisses. We're all still in shock.

On the way home, I feel mortified and rubbish. What a massive fail. I'm never, ever going on MatchMe again. Never.

'So, HOW WAS HOT Jacob?' Lacey asks over a cup of coffee at my house.

'Mmmm, not the best, not the best at all, Lace.'

It's a rainy Saturday afternoon in late March, after the disaster date with spunky Charles, Lacey encouraged me back onto the dating app. and she's come over to hear the latest on my most recent date. Finola's rousing words still in my head I'd matched with Jacob Greener and he seemed cute so I was optimistic. Blond, swished-up hair, you know, the type that defies gravity thanks to clay or putty or general ego; gorgeous blue eyes with lashes I could only dream of having with extensions and a lot of arty black and white shots in his profile. A photographer by profession (that'd explain the high standard of profile pictures), and local. 'Into good gin, vegan food and good company. Love learning new things, photography and seeing the world', seemed like a great profile, and the messaging had been exciting.

Rather confidently, again it had been me who'd suggested a date – go Robin! – and so we met in the trendy new gin parlour on the high street for a drink. I'd had high hopes. Very slowly, though, they'd been dashed.

'What happened, then?' Lacey pushes, holding her cup to her mouth but not drinking any coffee, that desperate to find out the gossip.

'Well, he's a man-child,' I reply, matter-of-factly.

'A man-child?' Lacey seems confused by the concept.

'Yeah, you know, old enough to be an adult. He was twenty-six, so younger than me, but come on, that's old enough to have most of your shit together. But still living like a teenage boy. He walked in wearing jeans, all frayed at the bottom, with grubby black converse and a Star Wars T-shirt under a zippy-up hoody.

'Oh. Wow. OK,' Lacey says.

We're interupted by Lyla:

'Mummy, I'm bored,' she says, flopping her arms by her sides for extra emphasis.

'How can you be bored with a bedroom full of toys? Why don't you make something with your crafts or play with the dollies?'

'I don't want to,' she whines, leaning her upper body onto me. I knew letting her stay up an hour late last night to finish off *Pocahontas* was a bad idea. She's seen it fifty-five million times but still loves it. When she's tired, even the tiniest bit, there's a meltdown looming round the corner. I can't deal with it right now. I want to talk about the dates; I want to ask Lacey how things are going with the baby-making (I can tell she's a bit down about it all; they've been trying for a while now. I think IVF might be their next option), and I want to have twenty minutes of adult conversation. As Natalie says, you've got to pick your battles.

I know I'm on a losing streak so I pull out the big guns, my very last trump card.

'Do you want to play on my phone?'

Her eyes light up and I know she thinks she's struck gold. Usually such a treat is reserved for epic train journeys or at the hairdresser's, but today I'm desperate.

'YES!'

'OK,' I say, handing it over. 'Stay on your games, and if it rings or buzzes, bring it back to Mummy.'

'Thank you, Mummy,' she says, beaming. She hops off my lap with her prize and I turn back to Lacey.

'I decided to give him the benefit of the doubt and not judge a book by its cover. But he's not *technically* a photographer. He's "working on it". He works two days a week for his mum on her mobile dog-grooming van and takes pictures at the weekend for his Instagram.'

'Well, at least if you dated him your feed would look good!'

I give her a look. 'He spends the rest of his time playing *Call of Duty*, and he lives in his mum's loft conversion.'

'Oh, sleepovers would be fun for you, then! Maybe his mum could bring you up a cup of tea in the morning and pop your knickers in the laundry,' laughs Lacey.

'Don't joke!' I mockingly fight back. 'I'm never going to find a decent grown-up man to be in our lives!'

'So how did it end?' I can tell Lacey is loving living the dating life through me.

'Terribly! When it came to settle the bill – which we were supposed to split – he said he'd left his bank card at home and could I lend him some cash.'

Lacey just laughs.

'I paid and said I ought to call a cab. He asked to borrow my phone to call his mum for a lift because his was out of credit! I despair, Lacey. I can't have a long-term relationship with a man on a pay-as-you-go phone tariff and his mum on speed dial. That's not the woman I am!'

Lacey is laughing so much that I start laughing at the ridiculousness of it all. Another dire date to add to the slowly growing list, but at least I've cheered my friend up a bit.

'One step closer to Mr Right, though, Robsie,' she encourages, sipping her coffee and suppressing the giggles.

'Yep, he's out there somewh—'

'MUMMY!'

Lyla walks in with a panicked look on her face. 'Mummy, your phone won't stop buzzing!'

Surely I'm not getting that many messages and calls.

As I look at the phone, tens and tens of MatchMe notifications are popping up, one after the other. So much so that I can't even type in my passcode to get into the app and see what on earth is going on.

'What have you done, sweetheart?' I say, frantically swiping away the notifications and trying to get my passcode in.

'I was bored, Mummy! I went into your man game and moved them all off till more came on.'

'Oh my God, Robin, I think she's got into your apps!' says Lacey, half-shocked, half-amused.

'Fuck. Fuck, fuck,' I say, getting up so quickly I knock my chair back and let it crash to the floor, startling Lyla even more.

'Mummy, those are bad words!' she says, looking from me to the toppled-over chair.

'OK, I'm in! Yes, I know. Sorry.' Once in my app, I can see I have over two hundred matches and fifty-eight pending messages. 'Fuck! Shit. Fuck.'

'Mummy! The *bad words*!' Lyla says again, standing on the lino anxiously. Right now I'm too consumed by the crisis at hand to worry about my language.

'Lyla, is this the game you went on?' I say frantically, holding the phone up to her with my dating app open.

'Yes, and I swished my finger like this and a new man came into the game.' I can see she's looking worried based on my reaction, but right now I'm freaking out.

'Lacey, she's swiped yes to *hundreds* of men!' I say in horror, to which Lacey just cackles in response.

'It's not funny!' I snap a bit more aggressively than I mean to.

With all the intensity and my choice language, Lyla is clearly confused and begins to cry. Instant mummy-guilt washes over me and dissolves any anger.

'Nooo, it's OK, sweet pea, it's all right, you didn't know,' I soothe. Scooping her up onto my lap and picking up my chair at the same time, I look down at my phone as it continues to freak out on the table with *Hey babes* and *Nice profile pics, how's your day* messages.

'I was just playing the game, Mummy,' she manages between sobs.

'I know, I know, but this is a grown-up game, not a game for little girls. You know where all your games on the phone are kept, don't you?'

'I just wanted to play on your games, Mummy, and be like you,' she wails.

'Ooohh, sweet pea, I know. But I think we need to make sure we stay on Lyla-friendly games, so that you can have the most fun and we don't have problems like this, OK?'

As I say 'like this', I lift up my phone to demonstrate the incessant buzzing and a new message pings through, this time with a picture. The thumbnail is tiny and hard to see, but suddenly I realise what it is I'm looking at.

'Mummy, what is that?' Lyla asks, completely puzzled. 'What's in that man's hand? Is he holding a little snake?'

'No! Oh my God! I mean, yes. Yes. He's just holding a little pink snake! He's sending me a silly little picture of his pet! Let's put this away! We don't want to see snakes, do we? Ha ha ha,' I force out in a sing-song fashion, knowing that my sweet baby girl has just been exposed to her first (and hopefully last) dick pic.

Lacey grabs the phone and her eyes widen. 'Wow, that's a big pet snake he's got there!' Clearly all this is hilarious to her. She's not worried about the permanent mental damage we may have just done to my child.

'Mummy, can we get a little pink pet snake?'

'Umm, no. Maybe a dog or a cat. Or a hamster. Not a snake. Let's forget about the snake,' I gabble in panic, but starting to laugh. 'How about I give you some Smarties and I'll put the telly on and you can watch whatever you like for as long as you want?'

Right now I'd rather pump her full of e-numbers and let her eyes turn square in front of the TV than dwell on this stranger's erection situation for a moment longer.

Thrilled with this offer, she jumps off me, gladly takes the tube of emergency Smarties and settles herself down in front of the flat screen. I breathe a sigh of relief and head back to Lacey, who's entertaining herself reading through all the introductions from men I would *never* normally have swiped.

'Well, at least you're not going to have any trouble setting your next date up!' she says as I sit down.

'Now it feels like Jacob and Charles are the least of my worries!'

We both burst out laughing. Dating is turning out to be quite the adventure.

FOURTEEN

I HAVE TAKEN THE PLUNGE. I have asked Natalie for extra work to fill my days, boost my funds and, above all, give me something to do that I truly enjoy. I've told her I'm happy to do solo jobs or full-time hours while Lyla's with her dad. Natalie has emailed that she's thrilled to have me so on board, and straightaway gave me a community centre pamper party and an assisting job on an editorial set. I'm feeling really buzzed to have two good jobs on my hands.

After three days, Lyla stopped asking if we could have a little pink snake as a pet, and I promised her that we can borrow Mollie from Kath as many times as she likes and take her out for walks, groom her and let her sleep at our house. I'm hoping with all of that she'll have forgotten about the dick snake and we can put this whole fiasco behind us. I've got enough on my plate without worrying that Lyla is

126

going to be spending thousands of pounds in counselling as an adult, talking about her mother's strange aversion to snakes and how she can now never trust a man.

Lyla is spending the rest of the week with Simon and Storie, and I'm making the most of it. He's texted to ask me to pack her swimming costume, so with any luck she'll have some nice, normal family time at the leisure centre and won't be taken to an eco-swamp to dive for kelp or something equally absurd. At least he's actually thought ahead and planned something for her; I should just be grateful for that, kelp or no kelp.

The pamper party goes well. Every couple of months the council set up a bit of an afternoon for the elderly, hire a few MUAs, hairstylists and such and put on nibbles and cupcakes. All the local older ladies pop by and ask for a bit of blush or pink polish, and it's lovely. I've never taken on this kind of job before, and I'm surprised at how much I like it. I thought it might be a bit dull compared to photo shoots and editorial work, but it's one of the most heart-warming ways to spend an afternoon ever. They sit and tell you about their grandchildren, or their plans for their garden this summer and it's just a nice way to spend the afternoon. Arguably it's not the most artistic or creative job, but you work with great people and come away feeling really warm inside. What I also love is that Natalie waives 70 per cent of the fee. I'm not sure all the freelancers do that, but she does and I admire her for her altruism. Thinking about

Natalie's business and how she cares for other people, and how, in turn, this afternoon I've cared for other people, it touches me. It's hard to wallow in yourself when you're giving yourself to others. I should do this more often. Today wasn't just about make-up; it felt so much deeper than that.

The editorial set, though, is the polar opposite – the gazelle-like models are much more interested in their phones than in chatting to me. Natalie handles it and even an altercation with the photographer about late payment, with such grace. She's like a swan. Completely calm and elegant on top, but under the water, where you can't always see, she must be working her perfectly pert bottom off to keep things not just going, but thriving. Hats off to her. I love spending time with such a strong woman. Whenever I'm working with her I feel like she's teaching me how to be a better woman – without her knowing it. Working alongside her, being given these opportunities, watching her, learning from her, chatting to her, she makes me feel like I can achieve anything I want to.

But nothing prepares me for the thrill of the next job.

FIFTEEN

'OK, ROBIN, LET'S DO this!' Natalie smiles at me and I follow her through the huge glass doors into the studio's atrium. I've been looking forward to this high-profile job for ages, absolutely thrilled that Natalie's invited *me* to assist her, and I'm going to give it my best. I want to prove to Natalie that I'm serious about my work for her and appreciate everything she's letting me do.

Clive Fitz is a world-renowned fashion photographer, and he's been flown in from LA to work on *Glamour* magazine's spring fashion editorial. It's clear from the get-go that he really thinks he's something else.

There's a whole team of us on board to make ten of the UK's most coveted models look even more beautiful and intimidating than they already are. Looking around at the size of the team, this is my biggest job to date and I can feel butterflies in my tummy. It's been a long time since I've felt this excited and ready to get stuck in. The two stylists are having an argument about whether exposed hems are the next big trend or not.

'They're so *raw*, Elissa,' one of them shrieks.

'I just feel like they've been *done*, Cassy,' the other snipes back, threatening every stylist's worst nightmare.

Focus, Robin. This is your chance to show Natalie what you can do.

I look across the studio at the runners who are supplying the models and Clive with everything they could ever wish for. The PR girls are running around with their clipboards, headsets and barking voices, and the light guys, equipment guys, hair guys and other nondescript guys are all looking super-stressed and super-busy.

It's a big shoot in a big, shiny, London studio with impossibly high ceilings and a warren of side rooms for hair, make-up, food tables. Natalie and I are holed up in the make-up room with signature light-bulb-framed mirrors and swirly chairs. As I step into the room, I feel a buzz of excitement. I always feel surprisingly calm and in control in this environment, and Natalie and I move together in synchronised motion. Here I know what I'm doing and I am exactly where I need to be, part of an ace team of two. We have arrived early to unpack the kit and catch up on our lives. I love chatting with Natalie, but sometimes it feels like a masochistic act. Maxwell has just achieved eleven As in his

GCSE mock exams. Her life is perfect and together, and being around her makes me question if I'll ever get to that point. The point where I'll have the guy, multiple littles playing at my ankles, a golden Labrador and the perfect house in the village, on the corner, with the cherry blossom tree at the front. But she also shows what a determined woman can do when she sets her mind to it. I can't help but adore her.

The first beautiful model walks in and places herself in my make-up chair without speaking a word or looking up from her phone. I busy myself, moving my tools around, pretending like I'm not waiting for her to finish her message. There's something soothing about seeing all your brushes laid out in order, clean and untouched, ready to work their magic. Suddenly Clive swings his head round the door with camp vigour and in a forced American accent shouts, 'Naaatural glaaamour! I want them to look vivacious! Hollywood! Full-lipped, doe-eyed beauties! Minimal, though. Nothing false. Classic. You know, you know . . .'

Hollywood glamour isn't normally approached with minimalism in mind, but after a quick chat we set to work sneaking on natural-ish powdered eyeliner and tinted lip balm. Clive seems pleased (we presume; praise isn't really his style, but Natalie tells me the powdered eyeliner was a 'genius' idea and I felt like I was floating, I was so proud), and very few touch-ups are required. It helps that each model is the living embodiment of perfection. God, I wish I hadn't eaten that second cronut (though at least now I don't feel as hungry as a lot of these models look).

After ten hours of creating the perfect look for each girl, doing touch-ups on set and helping the hair department aim the wind machine while being subjected to Clive screeching, 'Hold it! DON'T MOVE!', Natalie and I are packed up and off for the night. It's a two-day job and we're staying at a nearby hotel, so when she suggests a few drinks I jump at the opportunity.

Lyla is with her dad, probably enjoying some angel cards and a documentary on Indigo Children, and I feel pumped after a day on set. Granted, the Grey Goose vodka going round after 3 p.m. has also helped. For once I've managed to push The Emptiness completely aside.

It doesn't control me.

I pop into the hotel room to slip on something glitzy, realise I have nothing at all glitzy so opt for my trusty emerald-green flowing skirt and a black wrap-around top with sheer sleeves that Piper picked out. Something about the sheer black fabric makes me feel special. It's a maxi skirt, so nobody cares about shoes and I just throw on a pair of ballet pumps from New Look. Bangles and earrings on, a final swish of lip gloss and I plod downstairs to find Natalie.

She's already there waiting for me, and she looks like an absolute bloody vision. How did she do that in ten minutes flat? She's transformed herself from her typical working uniform of black jeans, white cotton tee with her hair wrapped up in a Gucci silk scarf to effortlessly chic city girl in a soft beige shift and gold slingbacks. I look down at my flaccid sheer sleeves. If I didn't love her so much, I'd definitely hate her.

WE HEAD DOWN TO one of Natalie's familiar haunts in Covent Garden. She regales me with stories of how she and Martin used to go out for dreamy dates round here all the time before their boys came along (she's just always been cool), and as we descend the concrete stairs to the bar, I can feel the stresses of life slipping away, along with The Emptiness. Simon texts me some pictures of Lyla playing in the garden, I've just aced it at my job, I'm about to have drinks with an amazing woman *and* I'm not wearing leggings – things are good.

It's been *so* long since I've done this!

Loud music and the sound of cocktail glasses clinking give me a warm fuzziness in my stomach (again, though, it could just be the vodka). We nab a table, peruse the menus and order some drinks and nachos. As the prosecco flows, so does our conversation.

Natalie has formed a committee in Hopell Village to restore the local lake and bring it back to its former glory with grants, fundraisers and whatnot. Wow.

'Oh, Robin, it's going to be great fun. We're going to host outdoor cinema nights and community barbecues come summer,' she chimes. 'You and Lyla must come!'

How does she find the time to do all these things? Honestly, I call it a win if I've got all ten nails painted and have picked Lyla up – and not necessarily on time. I suddenly realise that I may *never* be the Head of the Lake Restoration Committee and disappointment sinks in – even though it's not a position I previously knew I wanted. To put a firm stop to this negative train of thought, I excuse myself and pootle to the bar to order more fizz. The bottles aren't being put in ice buckets today, instead they're being served in ice-filled wellington boots. Of course they are. The bar apparently likes to mix things up in a 'kooky' way, so sometimes they switch out the champagne buckets for other 'hilarious' containers. It's all very jovial and I try to blend in with the young professional crowd who seem unfazed by the shoe-shaped vessels.

I pay for our bubbly, pop my bag under one arm and clutch the slippery welly in my other hand. I prance off in the direction of our table, thinking that maybe, just *maybe*, I might make it as Assistant to the Head of the Lake Restoration Committee. Only the prance is more full-on than I plan and before I know it, the bottle has tipped up and Prosecco is pouring out onto the floor. Oh, hell! I quickly bend down to retrieve my welly, which has now lost all integrity and is flopping all over the shop like some kind of jellied eel. Robin Wilde, everyone: the biggest klutz in London.

I stand up flustered with sticky hands and – oh, my sweet Jesus, there he is.

The most beautiful man I've ever seen.

His thick, brown, wavy hair tickles his cheekbones enough for me to notice how glossy it is. Is it salon-fresh? Why does it smell so good? *Stop smelling him, Robin!* I look up and his eyes smile at me like they know just what I'm thinking. Oh, God, I hope not. He's perfection, dressed in a well-fitted suit like something straight out of a fashion house, and I notice I'm gawking at him. Gawking with my flaccid wellington boot, my soggy shoes and my soaking sheer sleeves.

Say something cool. Say a thing that showcases what a creative, coherent go-getter you are, Robin:

'My welly was wet and it slipped.'

Amazing. Ah-mazing.

'Ha! I bet you say that to all the men you launch drinks at,' Mr Perfection leans in to my ear to reply and I get an actual shiver down my spine. Fuck me, I'm in love. There's no two ways about it. I'm actually in love. Without missing a beat, he says, 'Let me replace that for you, perhaps with something that's not served in a shoe.' He orders who-knows-what from the bartender and I burst into apologies.

'I'm so sorry about your shoes, I didn't mean to get sticky fizz all over them. I mean, it was the welly that did it. Ha ha ha ha ha ha ha ha ha ha ha – drinks in a welly!' Chill out, Robin, you sound insane. Less manic, more, well . . . anything other than manic.

Before I can behave like even more of an imbecile, two sweet-looking ruby-red cocktails arrive and he's leaning over to cheers with me. I glance over to Natalie. She winks, blows me a kiss and turns back to her menu, more than confident to sit alone.

'Here's to our ruined shoes and your beautiful face.' We clink our glasses and I swoon, internally this time. At least, I think it's internal – I'm struggling to decipher the difference between what I'm saying in my head and what I'm saying to him out loud.

'Honestly, I'm so sorry. I was carrying too much, and—'

'If wet shoes are all it takes to be able to talk to a woman like you, I'll have them. I saw you walk in with your friend and hoped we'd have the chance to meet, so the shoes are a small sacrifice to pay.'

Wow. That was smooth.

'I'm Theo Salazan,' says Mr Perfection, offering his hand for a cordial handshake.

'Robin Wilde.' Please God, let the lighting be trendily dim enough to hide my red cheeks.

'So, other than being totally bloody gorgeous, what else do you do, Robin?'

'Well, I'm a make-up artist's assistant, and we're on a shoot this week so we're in London and thought we'd just have a couple of drinks to—'

'No, I'm not asking you what you do for a living. I meant what excites you, what do you get up to, what makes you tick?'

When he asks this question he looks only at me, eye to eye, and I feel like nobody else is in the room. The music is quieter, the lights are softer, it's just me and my cocktail and this rather enchanting man.

Feeling buoyed by the attention of the most charming man in the room, and boosted by the alcohol already in my bloodstream, I answer as coolly as possible.

'Creativity makes me tick. Making something myself. Seeing my ideas come to life,' I say, leaning in close to his ear to be heard above the music. Fuck me, that was impressive.

We talk for what feels like forever. I'd popped over to ask Natalie to join us but she simply smiled and said 'You go, girl' and left to give Martin a call. I find out that Theo is thirty-four, was born in the Cotswolds but now lives on the Thames and works in property. He's out with some of his senior team celebrating a big acquisition, but he's not feeling it. He'd rather be at home catching up with *Peaky Blinders* on Netflix, and it's at this point I suspect he's my soulmate.

As the conversation develops, so does the chemistry. Little arm touches from me, a brushing of my hair out of my face from him; he is gentle but in charge. He's taller than me, so I have to look up and I can't help but notice his lips, and I don't think I usually notice other people's lips. They're really good lips. Yes, I'm in love. I am head over wellies in love.

SIXTEEN

I T'S A FULL WEEK from the moment the angels came down from heaven to bring me the most perfect man on earth, and I'm not entirely sure yet if my feet have touched the ground.

We carried on talking into the night, and he kissed me on the cheek when I decided it was time to make a dignified exit.

Theo and I swapped numbers, and as we did, he joked that I'd better be waiting by the phone for him to call. I laughed, but instantly knew that's exactly what I'd be doing. I don't think I've spent more than eighty-five seconds away from my phone all week, and as sure as perfection is perfection, he did call.

An actual phone call. Who does that these days? Usually you're lucky to get a text message. Having spent the last few weeks logging in to various dating apps to check for inbox notifications, a phone call feels like a true luxury. A real-life, grown-up, lovely telephone call.

Not only did he ring me, he asked me out. Gentlemanly. 'I'd like to take you to dinner, Robin, what day suits you?' When I explained that I don't live in London and have a daughter, so couldn't really nip out for dinner, I thought it might be all over, but no: Theo the Perfect continued on the path to being the Greatest Man Ever and said, 'Well then, come and make a day of it! Let me show you the sights.'

Yes please, Theo Salazan.

I was almost hyperventilating and weeing at the same time (I wasn't even on a trampoline or sneezing), so I said it.

Yes.

And then I made up an excuse about having a 'business call' to take. I thought that sounded better than 'Gotta go, Lyla's Alphabites are burning'.

Every day there have been sweet texts, friendly texts, pictures and 'how are yous' and it's been bliss. I've even deleted most of the dating apps. I feel like I'm a better person for it.

EASTER WEEKEND IS COMING and among the other six million things I need to do today – including blocking all the men who keep sending me dick pics on the one app I have left; sorting through the laundry to find something half-decent to wear on the school run tomorrow; dealing with the angry, pink council tax letter; and drafting out a casual, breezy message to Theo – I absolutely have to call my mum.

She trilled to me months ago, at Christmas, in fact: 'We'll see you again at Easter, I'm sure.' The thought of going there for Easter, driving five hours just to be reminded over and over again how wonderful Mum thinks Simon is and what a mistake I'm (still) making – with Simon, with Lyla, with my life, with my choice of paint in the downstairs loo – is too much to bear. I'd rather spend the day cleaning my brushes and watching overstimulating kids' cartoons than sit at her dining table smiling politely and secretly wishing she'd choke on her pork. Well, that's probably a bit much. I don't mean choke to death. Obviously. Just enough so she coughs and splutters and feels silly.

Anyway, as Mrs Wate taught me in Year Seven after I broke the sewing machine and hid it in the resources cupboard, 'Honesty is *always* the best policy', the best thing to do is just call her and tell her. I'm a grown woman and I don't have to do anything I don't want to or that will make me feel bad. Self-care, Robin. That's what it's all about. You're worth it! No quibbles, no fuss: I'm not going.

She'll be upset, of course, but perhaps I can placate her with the offer of a visit in Lyla's summer holidays, and maybe I'll send her a little goody bag of make-up treats. She's been wearing the same frosted pink lipstick from Avon since 1989, and I bet she'd love a creamy nude. Oo-er.

I'm not worried about this. I'm just going to make the call, handle her disappointment and get on with my day.

Deep breath – it's ringing.

'Seven-four-eight-three-two-zero!' she answers in her high-pitched phone voice. Why does that generation do this? I know what number I've dialled. Why do I need a recital of it as my greeting?

'Hi Mum, it's me.'

'Robin?' I'm an only child. How many other people ring, calling her 'Mum'? Unless she and Dad are into some sick role play these days.

'Er, yes, Robin. Your only daughter.'

'Ohh, hello, sweetie. I was just on the phone to Barbara, telling her you never call, but here you are, calling me! How lovely of you.'

'You could call me, you know.'

'Oh, you never answer.'

I *always* answer!

'Anyway, you know how it is with the Rotary. I'm always there, slaving away for them.' She's not *slaving away*. She bloody loves the Rotary Club. Jillian is the head and Mum is her sidekick, so she's always dashing about doing something with more gusto than I manage for anything.

'Well, anyway, how are you, Mum?'

'Very well, actually, sweetie. The antibiotics have worked their magic and I'm back on my feet again.' I didn't actually know she was ever ill – another reason to feel guilty – but

I let her carry on. 'Dad's been working tirelessly on the village beds. We're putting in for Best Village Flora and Fauna this year, so it's quite a challenge to keep everything as it should be – though I'm really not sure about those gladioli; I mean, it's a really risky strategy, and Jillian has taken on more than ever at the Club. We're organising one of those musical festivals in the village this summer for the young people to come along to and raise money for the Reservoir Wildfowl Association, so as you'd imagine, we're up the wall with all that!'

'Oh. Wow. A music festival. That sounds . . . good.'

'Yes, sweetie. And how are you? Plodding on?'

I love how much faith she has in me.

'Yep, working hard with Natalie. Lyla's doing really well. She's started swimming lesso—'

'And Simon? How's he?'

'Um, yeah, good, I think.'

'Bless him.'

'Mmmmm. Anyway, before we get sidetracked,' i.e., before I have to hear any more about Mum's bottomless well of love for Simon, 'I need to talk to you about Easter.'

'Oh yes?' Oh no, she sounds almost hopeful.

'Yes. The thing is, Lacey is really feeling a bit low at the moment—'

'Poor girl. What's wrong? Isn't she pregnant yet?'

'Well, no, I think that's why she's a bit low, Mum.'

'She needs to hurry up! She's pushing thirty now, isn't

she?' So, so glad Lacey can't actually hear how insensitive my mother is being.

'Yes, she is, Mum. She's actually having quite the battle with it all, and it's weighing her down, so I think Lyla and I are going to spend some time with her over Easter, maybe cheer her up a bit.'

'So you won't be coming to us?' I can't gauge her tone, but I'm bracing myself for the inevitable distress. I take a breath and reply.

'No. Sorry. No.'

'All right, then! Not to worry! Dad and I have booked a table at the club and the Rotary ladies will be there, anyway.' Wait a minute. She sounds sort of *glad* I'm not coming. This is not what I expected. Why is she glad about this? Am I not good enough for the Rotary ladies?

'Oh good, well, I won't be missed then, obviously.'

'No need to be petulant, sweetie. You've got your life and we've got ours.' How warm and charming my mother is.

'Yep, absolutely. Oh, I think I can hear Lyla shouting for me, I'd best go!'

We say our goodbyes and I ring off, feeling a bit stung. I know I didn't want to go, but I at least wanted her to want me to go. It's bad enough that they never visit or phone, and Mum, at least, is *much* cooler towards me since Simon and I separated – Mum secretly believes I drove him away, I know it – but now I'm not even good enough for the Rotary ladies. How lovely.

SEVENTEEN

I T'S MONDAY AGAIN. Only five days until my date with Theo, and I'm feeling pretty excited about it. It's 3.15 p.m. and I'm walking cheerily through the school gates to pick up Lyla. I stand in my designated foyer spot and secretly hope Val isn't coming in today or that Corinthia is doing a club.

The bell rings, the children pour out of class clutching 'artwork' that parents will be obliged to keep and cherish, even though it's essentially just an old tissue box with sequins stuck poorly to it. Lyla is ticked off their list and we head to the car. Just as we reach it, like a lizard Val sidles up in designer gymwear.

'Oh, goodness, I'm so late, I must have worked out harder than I planned to,' she modestly brags.

'Totally know what you mean, I do that all the time,' I lie.

Val looks annoyed and straightens herself up ready for the next jibe. 'Ha! Of course you do!' she says, making a point of looking at my less-than-toned tummy. What a cow. 'I expect you're all ready for next week then, are you?'

'Yes, completely.' Literally no idea what she's talking about.

'Oh good. I've already bought all my supplies. We've had the silk specially imported.'

What the actual fuck is she talking about?

'Great. See you tomorrow,' I say with false ease and get into the car.

'Lyla,' I say as we drive out through the school gates. 'What's happening next week?'

'The Easter Bonnet Parade. You've got to make me one. Or Storie can – she's got organic hemp.'

Oh God. I've been too focused on Theo. I'd meant to go to Hobbycraft this weekend, and I've completely forgotten. How could I do that to Lyla? Gillian told me that every year parents have to make the hats for the children to parade around in. Apparently every year all the PSMs say it's not a big deal and that it's the smile on the children's faces that matters most. But that's clearly all crap. You just know Gillian is warming up her glue gun ready to whip up a masterpiece for Clara. Even Finola, who doesn't care for arts and crafts, will tear herself away from the horses for one night in a bid to snag the first place. This is not just a merry afternoon out; this competition is a serious business.

Well, I'll be damned if Lyla is going to have a rubbish hat.

Tonight I'm going to put all thoughts of Theo aside and do my daughter proud. I'll open a bottle of wine and spend the evening on Instagram and Pinterest searching for ideas, and Val will rue the day she was so smug and imported that wanky silk. She's clearly forgotten that I'm a new woman with a stunning spring wardrobe, an app full of men who want to date me (or at the very least show me their perky pink snake) and now an Adonis of a man courting my attention. Step back, Val Pickering: badass single mum coming through!

Part Three

I need a hero . . .

EIGHTEEN

APRIL

I DON'T THINK I'VE ever walked Lyla into her class with such pep in my step as I have today. I've been up since six hot-rolling my hair, doing my make-up properly (not skipping the base or finishing powder and just swiping on some moisturiser and lip gloss, like I normally would, even on a good Thursday). And for the first time in weeks I have actually worn something that isn't 95 per cent elastane. Mrs Barnstorm almost didn't recognise me when I walked in confidently with my hair bouncing and eyes shining. It's one thing to perfect your liquid liner and wear an expensive shirt, but this look is coming from inside. Theo Salazan, thank you very much!

'Mummy, you look like you're in a film!' Lyla said when I woke her up.

'Oh, thank you, sweet pea, that's a lovely thing to say.'

'Why aren't you wearing your normal clothes?' Bit concerning that she thinks tracksuit bottoms and a tee are 'normal clothes'. I do look half-decent *sometimes*.

'I'm having a special day in London and wanted to look extra pretty.'

'Are you going to work with Natalie?'

'Um, yes, with Natalie.' I feel a bit deceitful, but I don't think I can say, 'Well, no, I'm ignoring all the other things I should be doing and hopping off to London to meet up with a man I met in a bar a month ago. We're going to spend all day flirting and drinking and maybe, just maybe, we'll make sweet, sweet love all night long. Although it's been so long I've probably forgotten what to do with a man's penis, so I watched a bit of porn last night to remind myself and totally freaked out. Mainly because I don't look like a shiny Barbie doll but also because that's definitely not how I remember it . . .'

'Natalie and I are doing some work there, and I thought it would be fun to wear something nice and curl my hair,' I lie again. 'Do you like it like this, then?' I ask, trying to change the subject.

She reaches up, runs a little hand over my curls and says, 'Yes, you look like Princess Sophia.' Hmmm, Princess Sophia is a ten-year-old cartoon character, but I'll take it. Hopefully Theo sees a slightly more sophisticated edge.

'Come on, you pop your pinafore on and I'll make you some jam on toast. We're not going to be late today!' I sing-song.

'Really? Why?' Bless my small, bewildered child.

So off to school we go, me looking like a sexier version of a princess cartoon character and Lyla looking like the child of a woman with her shit together – Mrs Barnstorm looks like she's accidentally swallowed a calorie, she's so surprised.

'Oh, Ms Wilde, how very glamorous you look,' she says in a way that would suggest she thinks I usually look like a bag of crap. What's the matter with her? Yes, I do quite often look like shit, but not *every* day. I have made the effort before, for goodness' sake! I'm going to say something so cutting she won't know what to do with herself.

'Yes, thank you . . . you look lovely too.' What?! Is that the best I can do? Now she just looks confused and so do I.

'My mummy is a princess, Mrs Barnstorm. She can do magic on you and make you into a toad!'

'Aha ha ha, children say funny things, don't they? I'm sure I couldn't make you into a toad even if I tried!' Ha ha ha, we win. Good job, me and my girl. We saunter off and I mentally high-five us, giving Lyla's hand a little extra squeeze of love as we walk down to her cloakroom.

Once she's settled and I've driven home, I take five minutes to flit about making sure everything is sorted. After several assurances from Theo that he'd be a perfect gentleman and have the spare room cleaned for me, I agreed to stay overnight, so I've packed a bag and arranged for Simon to have Lyla (originally he was completely flummoxed at the idea of having her on a day out of our usual routine, but I blagged that it was all good for refreshing the flow of the earth's energy and he dithered a yes and agreed – success). I still don't feel nearly prepared enough, though. I asked what the plan of the day was and Theo rather charmingly said, 'Leave it all to me.' Well, yes, in theory that's wonderfully romantic but what if I'm not dressed accordingly? Will I need heels? Will we be on our feet all day and I'll want flats? Is he taking me somewhere that requires a dress? What if it's a spa? Do I need swimwear?

I throw a bikini in just in case, and thank the heavens that I've done a full body tan this weekend. Obviously just in case we go to a spa, not because I plan on him seeing me naked. I've packed silky pyjamas and lacy underwear but again, that's just to make myself feel good. Not because I'm trying to impress him. No way. Not a jot. Not one iota.

After one last mini-tidy round the house – well, putting the butter back in the fridge and taking the smelly bin out (oh, the glamour), I hop in a cab to the station, grab a large latte and I'm on the train.

I'm so excited. I feel like a teenager again, with that fizzy feeling in my chest and a constant grin on my face. Fizziness isn't something you can feel in The Emptiness, so this is a welcome change. I try listening to some soothing music to calm myself down, but I think the caffeine from the latte and his 'good morning, gorgeous' paying-me-such-lovely-attention texts have sent me over the edge. This man is an absolute dream. I've never done something so spontaneous.

Storie is going to pick Lyla up from school tonight – they'll crush some almonds or something equally thrilling – and Natalie said there's nothing in the roster until Friday so I figured there was no harm in taking the day for me. Obviously I'm not going to get ahead of myself, not after the disappointments of Charles, Craig and Jacob, but somehow, Theo seems different; I feel like he understands me, and I feel like I want to fall into this and let myself trust him. It's taken a long time to allow myself to feel that way about anybody – a big break-up does that to you. It leaves you with a scarred heart that only time can heal. Theo listens to the things I say, and messages such specific texts based on what we've talked about, not just the generic 'hey, how's your day been?' and has something about him. Everything he does has a sparkle to it. When I'm thinking about him, I feel like I sparkle too. I can't put my finger on why he seems different, but he just has this charismatic aura to him that wows me. He makes me feel funnier and prettier and glossier. I don't want to get too trashy-magazine-horoscope-pages, but I feel like we were destined to meet. Like we just click.

As I alight from the train, feeling like I might vomit with the anticipation, and see him waiting for me at the station, I don't run up to him and jump into his arms like I want to; I play it cool with an high-pitched, overextended, 'Heeeeeeeeyyy!'

That's right, Robin, nice and casual, you've got this.

'Ms Wilde, how ravishing you look first thing in the morning.' Oh wow, we're on level five flirting already. How exciting! I think I'm going to really enjoy the next twenty-four hours.

'Theo, I woke up like this, of course,' I joke with a little swagger to my walk as we head to the Uber he has waiting. Where has this confidence come from? I love it!

'I certainly hope I'll find out if this is the case,' he says smiling, eyes forward as we leave the station. Beyond glad I packed appropriately.

We get to his disgustingly impressive fourteenth-floor apartment. Wow! Floor-to-ceiling windows that overlook the Thames, and every stainless steel kitchen appliance you can imagine. The main living area is open-plan. It feels as though you could twirl around endlessly with your arms outstretched and never crash into anything. Unlike the chaos of our tiny house, this is what you'd call 'mini-malist chic'. The white marble worktops are clutter-free (unless a smoothie maker, a sleek coffee machine and toaster constitutes clutter), and the huge glass dining table isn't strewn with post, receipts and a few pens like my little one. Across the gleaming wood floor is a generously sized grey corner sofa facing windows that showcase the most incredible view I think I've ever had from a settee. From mine you can see the drive, the bins and a lamp post. There's no TV or stacks of DVDs, but fixed to the ceiling is a projector and rolled-up screen. Of course. Of *course* Theo has a projector. Every perfect dream man has these things. It's like when you're little and you wished you lived in the Polly Pocket Country Mansion with the ballroom that has the floor you can spin round so it looks like the people are dancing. Well, this is the dream-guy equivalent. Every man I know (which, alarmingly I realise, is really not very many, I do need to widen my social circles – maybe Theo will introduce me to all his friends), would love to have this flat.

He courteously shows me through to the spare room, again sparse but stylish, where I leave my carry case. I think we both know I'm not going to sleep there, but it's 11 a.m., so I'm going to enjoy playing out this merry charade for a while longer.

'I thought we'd try the National Portrait Gallery this afternoon. They have a new Picasso exhibition. A lot of his early work from private collections is being showcased, and some of it has never been seen publicly in England before.' I love how enthusiastic Theo is about something so refined.

'Oh goodness, that sounds brilliant!' I don't actually know quite as much as Theo seems to; I don't really know anything about fine art other than what we learnt in our GCSEs or what Piper has told me about her projects, but I'm on board for a trip to the gallery.

'I thought you'd say that. With you being an artist, I decided this would be the perfect place to take you.'

'I'm a make-up artist, and mostly just a make-up artist's assistant.'

'Don't sell yourself short, Robin. I admire what you do.' And with that, he ushers me to the front door with his hand on the small of my back (mmm, dreamy) and we hop into another waiting (when is he arranging all of these?) car to the gallery.

I'm sure that to Theo, whizzing through central London is nothing short of a chore, but for me, it's such a treat. Usually I take the tube or arrive on set somewhere so early it's still dark outside, so sightseeing is never really on offer. London is such a magical place. Every kind of building, business and person are all packed into this busy little hive, and are somehow all just moving forward in sync together. I wish my life was more like London: fast-paced and functioning perfectly.

We pull up on Charing Cross Road and step out of the car. The air is cold on my face but the sun is shining, so the chill is forgivable. Theo holds out his hand for me. It's been a long time since anyone over the age of six has held my hand. It feels really nice to be the smaller one for a change.

We have brunch, with champagne, in the rooftop restaurant overlooking Trafalgar Square. The gallery is gorgeous, and very quickly I can see why so many tourists make a beeline for it. I don't know whether it's the high, vaulted ceilings, the art or the hushed silence, but something about it makes me feel very still and very calm. My heart is beating slower and my mind isn't racing; such a contrast to how I felt a few hours ago. The Emptiness doesn't allow any space for calm but here, with Theo, in this place, that's all there is: calm. I'm still holding Theo's hand, and I feel like I'm melting into him, into . . . us.

Theo remarks on a lot of the paintings and I chip in with the odd thought or two. I love looking at all the faces of people and times gone by, all with a story behind their eyes. Were they happy or sad or scared or brave? Did any of them once feel alone, like me? I love looking at the way the artists have painted the faces – the blush, the creamy skin tones, the contours, the way they define the eyes or bring out the model's best bits. I love the ones who look like they're wearing make-up, and the styles of different eras. Mostly, though, I'm just happy to listen to his musings and be part of this lovely moment. This is the kind of thing I have wanted for so long, for so many years. All those days of standing in the kitchen cutting the crusts off jam sand-wiches, trawling round the supermarket looking for deals to make the budget stretch or staring gormlessly at children's TV, feeling low and working hard to hide it from Lyla. I would have loved to spend an afternoon in a London gallery, holding the hand of a charming man, and here I am, doing it. If I didn't think it would look like I was having a spasm, I'd shake myself.

*   *   *

157

For a good couple of hours Theo and I meander around the richly decorated rooms with jewel-coloured walls of green and navy and gold-gilded frames, taking moments to rest on leather-covered benches, holding hands. The weight of the world has lifted from my shoulders and I'm refreshed. I feel as if looking at all these people and sinking into their world has lifted me out of mine. I'm not thinking about the long, dreary drive back from the school run or the intimidating piles of unopened bills on the table – I'm not worrying about anything. I'm just here, in the moment, soaking in the thoughts on all the faces in the paintings and relishing it.

Theo is enthralled by each piece in the Picasso exhibition, reading each little sign below and telling me about it. Spending time with a man so enthusiastic is like a breath of fresh air. I don't care all that much for the Picassos – they're all a bit unfathomable for my taste – but to hear him speak about them with such passion makes me want to give a shit (at least a little bit) and want to hear anything at all that comes out of those perfect lips. OK, Robin, focus on the art, not the lips. Art, not lips.

We leave the gallery and take a walk by the river in the fresh spring sunlight. Winter has felt like it's dragged on *so* long. It's been so grey, inside and out, that I'm surprised I don't have rickets. It's so good to feel the sun on my face. After a short while of chit-chat and banter (I've no idea if

I'm doing 'all the bants', but when he says a thing, I try and say something mildly witty back and he laughs, so I think this is a success) and one too many 'accidental' brushes into each other ('Robin, your hands look very much like they don't know what to do with themselves. Do you need some help?' Smooth move, Theo, smooth move. 'Yes. They're very confused and alone. This is a very hard time for me,' I mock.) He takes my hand. It's glorious.

Everything about him is glorious.

As we walk along the Embankment holding hands, I wonder if all the other people think Theo is my boyfriend, my gorgeous, handsome boyfriend. I hope they do. For once I'd like to be that smug girlfriend with her hand being held.

Cold sets in, and as the afternoon sun fades Theo suggests a drink. Deftly hailing a taxi, we jump in and within minutes are at a private bar, specifically for the old boys of whatever incredibly poncy boarding school he attended. The kind Finola's Edgar probably went to and hated but would still send Roo to, to build character. I don't think I could send Lyla away. Even after a few hours today I'm starting to miss her, but I force myself to push her to the back of my mind. I know she's fine with Simon; I'm allowed to have my me time and I'd be silly to waste it fretting.

Theo orders for us both, choosing me a 'Hotsy Totsy', which is essentially just boozy fruity heaven and forty-five minutes and two more drinks later, I'm drunk. I'd love to say I'm just a bit merry, but no; these cocktails are lethal, I'm drinking them way too fast, we didn't have lunch and I'm a drunk lady with a crush. Shit.

Needless to say, late afternoon becomes evening, the cocktails keep on coming, at one point delicious food (honestly, it could have been one of those greasy meat kebabs and I'd have reviewed it as 'divine', I was so tipsy), arrives and we talk all night. Theo is the most charismatic man I've ever met. Everything he says is exciting or laden with possibilities. He tells me he loves to fly in helicopters, and when I say I never have, he exclaims, 'We'll do it! We'll absolutely do it!' with such conviction I actually believe him. Nothing is impossible to Theo. You want to go in a helicopter? No problem. You want to sit in his private member's bar with vaulted ceilings and smartly dressed barmen who never stop delivering cocktails? Let's do it. This is so far from the life I've led. Simon's idea of a magical night would be half a pint of shandy in the local pub with a portion of fish and chips on the way home. To me, Theo's way of life is the stuff of dreams, the kind of thing you watch in romcoms and sigh deeply about. But Theo's real. I can feel how warm his skin is and smell liquor on his breath, our faces are so close as we talk.

He seems to think I'm special too. He laughs at my stories of the PSMs and tells me he loves how sensitive I am. At every opportunity there's a touch. He holds my hand, rests his fingers on my knee when we're sat down, brushes my hair out of my face. Each and every time he does, I feel goosebumps prickling all over my body.

160

After six incredible hours of flowing conversation that's left me feeling like he's my soulmate, strong cocktails and the blurry memory of dinner, we head back to his apartment by the river. Shunning my good intentions, I don't sleep in the spare bedroom. In fact, I don't sleep much at all.

NINETEEN

I SAT ON THE train home from Theo's and scoured every possible place on the internet for inspiration (in between daydream memories of his hands on my thighs, in my hair, up my back, mmmm, must stop! I've got to get back to the project at hand). Pinterest, hashtags on Instagram, I even researched the royal milliners for any ideas on how to make Lyla's Easter bonnet stand out – and then it hit me! I was never going to beat the PSMs at their own game alone, so I ditched the idea of glue gun and fuzzy-felt bunnies, dumped my case, had a quick shower (I showered this morning but it wasn't alone, if you catch my drift) and headed over to Dovington's.

Lacey and I spent three hours creating a masterpiece, as I regaled her gleefully with *probably* more detail than she was comfortable with. More custard creams than I dare count the calories of were consumed, but by the time we were done, we were elated. Even Terri got choked up when she saw it.

It's amazing what a night off from real life will do for a woman's creativity. I haven't felt this alive in months.

'I can't remember the last time I heard you laugh like that,' Lacey says with a smile.

'I can't remember the last time I had something this good to laugh about,' I say, smiling back as the spring sunshine pours into Dovington's through the craft room window. I love this place, and I love what we've made.

Very slowly and very carefully, we had attached delicate, fresh spring flowers to the broad rim of a straw bonnet, and used violet taffeta silk and dusky pink velvet ribbon to tie in a bow under Lyla's chin.

We'd used periwinkle-blue forget-me-nots, pansies with lilac outer petals and buttercream innards, giant daisies, tiny soft pink rosebuds and white baby's breath to capture the essence of new life and fresh beginnings. The scent was gentle but beautiful, and every which way you turned the hat, it looked divine and unique – just like my baby girl.

To fill in the little gaps between flowers we'd adhered tiny speckled Easter eggs I'd bought in a craft shop and then, just to add the final cherry on the cake, Lacey had used a fine paintbrush to add a sprinkle of glitter to the tips of the petals. It was stunning. A visual masterpiece.

I was so excited to show it to Lyla. I took it home and sat it on the chair in our little lounge. After Simon had dropped

her home (accompanied by a paper bag full of wild mushrooms they'd picked that would probably have made us all
high as kites if I hadn't thrown them away immediately), I
took her into the room with my hands over her eyes. When
she saw it, she squealed.

'Mummy, it's so beautiful! My precious Easter bonnet!
The best bonnet anyone has ever seen! Mummy, I love it,
you're so clever,' she gushed as I held back tears.

Seeing her so pleased, and knowing she understood that
I had made this for her, as a currency of love, was all too
much for me. I could feel my heart expanding, and all I could
do was use an overly high-pitched voice to say, 'Yes, Lyla, it's
yours. You'll look so beautiful, I love you so much, to the
moon and all the way around the earth and back again.'

'Well, I love you to the moon and all the way around the
earth and then all the way to Saturn.'

We'd carried on with a few more rounds of how far we
loved each other (a game I never tire of playing), and I put
to bed a very happy girl with a very beautiful hat that I kept
in the fridge overnight with a few light spritzes of water
from a spray bottle to keep it going till morning.

Before bed I took a quick phone snap and sent it to Theo.
'Wow! Best Bonnet Ever!' he'd replied, which really was the
perfect way to end the day. Having Theo in my life, even if
just on the receiving end of a text, made The Emptiness feel
very far away. The Emptiness was a huge gaping hole in my
life, and Theo, it seems, thankfully, is now filling it.

TWENTY

I T's 10.35 a.m., and we've all taken our seats on the slightly chilly playground to watch the parade. I'm still fizzing with the memories of my day – and night – with Theo, and our steamy messages and phone calls since. He's away in Zurich, but we've got plans to see each other just as soon as he's back. A cool breeze brings me back to the here and now. We could have the event inside, but it's sunny and Mrs Barnstorm suggests it will be marvellous to feel the 'bracing air' as we sing. Sadist. The tension is palpable, with every PSM perspiring at the thought of their precious angel parading their masterpiece in mere minutes.

I snuck in earlier than the others this morning so I could charm the receptionist into putting Lyla's hat in the staffroom fridge to keep the flowers fresh, and although she now probably thinks I'm clinically insane, it'll be worth it just for the look on Val's face alone.

'Oh, we didn't bother with any of that craft shop tat in the end,' I can hear her boasting to one of the Year Three mums. 'No, Roger and I were on a coastal minibreak a few weekends ago and we specifically picked up some absolutely stunning shells from one of the harbour shops, and we've adhered those to a fantastic hat we bought in Harrods over the half-term and dressed it with very expensive Chinese Silk.'

'Oh. Are shells particularly seasonal for Easter?' I can hear the Year Three mum asking, bravely.

'Well, they're pink and pastel-coloured, aren't they? That's Easter-themed, I'd say!' defends Val, with a hint of irritation in her voice.

'Yes. Yes, I suppose so,' the Year Three mum says, backing down.

Poor Corinthia.

'Ohh, here they come!' coos Val.

'Stand tall, Honor! Stretch your shoulders back!' barks Finola lovingly at her obedient daughter.

Honor, Clara and Roo have beautiful little straw boater hats with fluffy chicks, fake grass, foam bunnies – the whole shebang.

Corinthia walks out pompously behind them in a lemon-coloured felt beret that's covered in shells. Poor kid looks like the beach has thrown up on her. I actually feel sorry for her. She'll be spending an absolute fortune in counselling one day.

I crane my neck to see Lyla and there, at the back of the line, she walks shyly but proudly wearing her fresh flower and silk taffeta bonnet. She looks beautiful. Her long lashes flutter as she turns to look at us all, and I feel my chest puff with pride. I might be imagining it but some of the other mums and dads (you know it's a big event when the dads come) audibly gasp.

'Oh Robin, it's beautiful,' breathes Gillian in awe. She has clearly taken this event very seriously. Her husband, Paul, gently reaches for her hand and nods in my direction very sincerely.

'Thank you.' They're a lovely couple.

'Are they fresh flowers, dear?' asks Finola.

'Yes. I thought they captured the essence of new life,' I say, exuding as much grace and dignity as I've ever mustered in my entire life. I'm practically floating.

'Well, blow me down with a feather, darling, I think you're going to win it. It's magnificent.'

Praise from Finola is rare, and to hear her be impressed with me might actually be one of the greatest moments of my life. Aside from Lyla being born, I mean. Or on a par with that, at least.

'Thanks, Finola. Honor and Roo look brilliant too. And Clara as well, Gillian; she looks so cute.'

The parade continues, and we're given the 'treat' of all the children singing a few songs. There's something about children singing songs that sets me off. I blink back tears as they all chorus: 'Dance, then, wherever you may be, I am the Lord of the dance said he' so beautifully. Lyla makes eye contact with me and I wave and smile. Looking at her singing with her bonnet on, smiling at me, she seems perfectly happy and settled. She doesn't seem like the kid of a broken home or deeply troubled (like me, perhaps); she just seems at ease with the world around her. Have I managed to ease her through the late start at this school and life as a joint custody child? Maybe she's going to be OK here. She's even looking at ease with little Corinthia, who has thrown several jealousy-induced shady looks her way, and one tongue poke. Lyla's risen above it, though; good girl.

Mr Ravelle, the headmaster, reads a passage from the Bible and then – the moment we've all been waiting for – Mrs Barnstorm announces the winner of the parade.

The bonnets were apparently displayed earlier this morning in the school hall – ours ceremonially removed from the fridge – for the 'esteemed panel' (a lady from the local church, a Year Five teacher and Mr Ravelle) to judge, and the votes have been submitted and counted.

The parents look tense, the children sit cross-legged on the playground tarmac staring with wide eyes, Mrs Barnstorm ceremoniously opens her envelope, pulls out a piece of white A4, unfolds it and and bellows, 'First place goes to Lyla Blue Wilde.'

All the children cheer, the parents clap, Val seethes and I lock eyes with Lyla. She's flushed with surprise and happiness, and so am I. I give my beautiful girl a thumbs up and a big smile and she does the same back, accompanied by a wriggly little dance. We finish with one final song from the children and she runs over, carefully holding the brim of her bonnet.

'Mummy, I won! My hat won!' she says, jumping up and down and tip-tapping her little blue patent-leather school shoes on the tarmac.

'I know, I know! You did so well, I loved your singing and your parading and you sat so nicely. Well, well, well done my little Lyla Bluebird. I'm so proud of you!'

'I was so careful with the bonnet, Mummy. I'm going to keep it forever!'

'Yes, we'll keep it very carefully and it can be our treasure.'

'Well, that's not true now, is it, Mummy?' Val sneers. In all the excitement of Lyla's win, I haven't seen her creep up next to us. 'Those are fresh flowers, so they'll be dead by tomorrow and you won't have your bonnet any more, Lyla.'

The joy from Lyla's face completely evaporates and turns to horror at the idea of her hat vanishing.

'Val, please. She's a little girl and she's happy. Lyla, my sweet pea, we can easily dry the flowers and keep the bonnet forever.'

I cast my eyes about hoping Finola or Gillian will come and rescue me, but they're talking to Mr Ravelle and have their backs turned.

Seeing she has the advantage, Val starts up again. 'Corinthia's hat is something she can treasure forever because we made sure to make it with things that last. Flowers rot.' She almost spits the words at me.

This is horrific. Why is this woman being so awful to my little girl? I would never say anything unkind to Corinthia, even if she does look like ocean puke.

Lyla's eyes are filling with tears at Val's cruel words, and she takes her beautiful bonnet off her head.

'My mummy made this for me. She loves me so much, to the moon and all the way around the earth, and my bonnet is beautiful,' she says, looking up at Val, voice quivering. 'Mummy, I want to go home,' she adds so meekly I think I might die.

Seeing her be so tiny yet so valiant makes my heart almost break.

'Well, she can't love you that much if she made you a hat out of mouldy old flowers. You might as well put it straight in the bin, sweetie.'

Nope. That's it. She's crossed a line.

'Valerie Pickering,' I say, my voice starting to rise, 'how dare you speak to my daughter like that? How dare you try to spread your poisonous insecurities onto an innocent little girl.' People are looking now. 'I know you can't bear to lose, I know you're so sad that you feel like you need to show off at every possible opportunity and flaunt any tiny thing you can, but for once, just once, have the good grace to allow someone else a little bit of the glory and back the hell away from my child.'

Silence has fallen across the playground.

'All I was saying—' she tries to weasel.

'I couldn't care less what you were trying to say. What you did say, directly, to a six-year-old girl, was that Lyla's hat would rot and that her mummy didn't love her enough.' Everybody watching looks equally appalled, but also thrilled at such school drama. 'Don't you ever, ever come near me or my daughter again. You are nothing but a pathetic woman with spite in her heart, and I'm sorry to say it, but a total BITCH!'

'*Mummy*! A bad word!' says Lyla, in shock.

'I'm sorry, Bluebird,' I say, completely flabbergasted by my own bravery. I think we all are. Val stands looking at me and then looks around at the other mums. Nobody comes to her aid. She grabs Corinthia's wrist, turns on her heel and storms off towards her shiny Range Rover.

Surprisingly, Gillian is the first to break the shocked silence.

She kneels down in her sensible navy-and-white-striped Joules skirt and says, looking directly at her, 'Lyla, I thought your hat was so beautiful. I wish I had a hat made out of real flowers. I would think that fairies would come to it and dance around and make little parties all over it, because did you know, fairies love fresh flowers.'

Lyla slowly nods and a faint smile reappears. Clara (whose bonnet is covered in fake grass and hidden eggs) steps forward next to her mother and says, 'If we put our hats next to each other, it will look like a whole fairy garden,' and this entices a full smile from both girls and they skip off to the bushes, where they carefully lay their hats down, crouch beside them and drift off into little girl chat about pixies and fairies and all kinds of magic.

Watching Lyla take control of her feelings, put Val's twattery to one side and allow herself joy and fun with Clara, her own little friend, refills my heart. So often Lyla copes with life better than I do. Amazing little thing.

When I look back up, the crowd is starting to dissipate and Val has vanished. Finola and Gillian are looking at me.

'Robin, my dear, that was tremendous.' Fuck me, two lots of praise from Finola in one day? I think we might very well be becoming friends!

'I can't believe I called her a bitch,' I say, starting to feel everything sinking in.

'Well, I think sometimes, just a bit, she is one . . .' Gillian says, looking around nervously as if someone is going to judge her for thinking a bad thought.

'Oh, God, you don't think I'm going to be in some kind of trouble with the school for causing a scene, do you?' I say, panicking now that I've realised quite what I've done.

And then, with impeccable timing, Mrs Barnstorm, the woman who thinks I'm the shittiest mother of the year, strides past and says, 'I didn't see or hear a thing, Ms Wilde. Congratulations on Lyla's win. We'll see you next term.'

I'm speechless.

'I think this calls for a celebration!' Finola says, and we

172

pile the children, and their bonnets, into our cars and drive to the ice-cream parlour to fill ourselves up on frozen sugar and victory. Huzzah!

A WEEK LATER, SAT in my lounge in my sagging PJ bottoms, a T-shirt I've had since uni and my dressing gown, I can't stop thinking about Theo. Ever since our magical twenty-four hours together, I've been on cloud nine. I've said it before and I'll say it again: the man is perfection. When he talks to me, it's like he knows me. He asks questions and he listens to the answers. It's like he's known everything I've ever been and everything I could be, and sees something in me that I so rarely see in myself. He told me he loves the way I see the details in things that other people don't. We watched a Netflix sitcom the morning after the amazing night, and I'd said it annoyed me that every single actress had the same style of false eyelashes on and how unrealistic that is. Rather than roll his eyes at me nitpicking, he said, 'I love your passion for the details. You're incredibly astute, Ms Wilde.' It amazes me that a man like him could be so attracted to a woman like me, and I love it. Every time he messages me I feel my heart fizz, and carefully crafting messages back to him is just about my favourite way to waste twenty minutes of my life.

When my phone pinged an hour ago I leapt across the room thinking it was him, but it wasn't. It was Kath, informing me that she'd 'pop by for a coffee and catch-up

173

around 10 a.m.' if I was in. It's a Saturday morning at 10 a.m. – of course I'm in.

All I really want to do is stay braless in my pyjamas, eat Nutella on toast, watch mindless children's TV with Lyla and read through every message Theo has ever sent me and analyse every detail of the punctuation he's used to see if anything has a double meaning or if there's anything about the promise of our magical future life together I've missed. Not that I'm obsessing. I'm just . . . being careful. Being watchful. Very acceptable behaviour for a together and winning person like me. I *am* winning, actually. The twenty-four hours of magic in London; our bonnet win; the Val victory; such a fun afternoon at the ice-cream parlour and then a great week have left me feeling more than a bit dreamy. I think I'm making good progress with the PSMs. Gillian has started a WhatsApp group between me, her and Finola 'so that we can coordinate play dates for the children'. I don't care what it's for; I'm just pleased as punch to be part of their gang at last!

Sure enough, at 9.59 Kath walks in (I can't remember the last time she bothered knocking) and 'woooo-ooooo's me from the hall. 'Wooooo-oooooo, it's only me! I'll put the kettle on. I'll make a cuppa.' If she really wanted to do it all herself, she would have just stayed at home and not dithered in at 10 on a Saturday morning (don't be mean, Robin), so being the good niece I am, I resentfully heave myself off the sofa, leaving Lyla zombied out in her PJs to some programme about animals that run a country (not too dissimilar to the current political climate, actually), and plod into the kitchen.

Not only has Kath put the kettle on, she's begun loudly scraping last night's dinner off the dirty plates and into the bin, run the tap to fill the washing-up bowl (except she's turned the tap on too hard and all the water is splashing up onto the windowsill and wetting my frames) and loaded the dishwasher. How did she do this in under three minutes? I stand there, embarrassed at the mess but marvelling at her. Here she is, at 10 a.m., dressed and functioning. Here I am, wondering if I could get away with an extra spray of deodorant until bedtime or if I really do need a shower this morning. Once she's done ninety things I didn't ask her to do, in ninety seconds, she moves on to opening my post. 'Oh, lovey, you really must open these bills – some are weeks old – you'll get behind! And your bank statements, where are you filing those away?'

'Just leave them, please. I just want to open them later when I'm a bit more up and awake, you know?' I say, flustered that she's dealing with something I've been deliberately burying my head in the sand over. I don't need this right now. I was happy thinking about Theo and watching Lyla's programmes. Bills and bank statements were not on my agenda.

'Rise and shine, lovely! It's a beautiful day! You don't want to spend all of it inside,' she trills, continuing to open my post and ignoring my protests.

'That's sort of exactly what I do want to do, really.'

'Nooooo, you want to get out and about, see the world. My Derek used to say, "Your days might be limited but your enthusiasm doesn't have to be". I've been feeling so under the weather, you know, with my headaches this week, but the best thing you can do is keep on going and shake it off.'

'Ahhh, bless him.' I never really know the best thing to say when she talks about Derek. Also I've left my phone on the sofa, and I think I can hear a faint buzzing sound.

'Of course, his days were limited, and now it's up to us to seize each one and make them count,' she continues, throwing things into the washing-up bowl a bit too vigorously and splashing soapy water onto the worktops. 'Oh, sorry love! I've not been sleeping very well; I'm not awake enough for this,' she chuckles.

'You do make them count. You do so much, Kath. Look at the clubs you run and the classes you go to. You do a lot, and he'd be proud,' I say lovingly. She's really annoying me with that water all over the counters, but now she's talking about Derek I can't really do much except be nice.

'Thanks, love,' she says, giving my hand a tap with a soapy rubber glove. 'Just hope I start feeling a bit less grotty next week, eh?'

I still think I can hear my phone buzzing, but it might just be desperation. With Kath chattering on I don't feel like I can just leave the room and get it.

Only one week until I see Theo. This time next week I'll

be on my way to a shoot and will have that butterflies-in-my-tummy feeling about meeting him afterwards. He's taking me out for a fancy dinner. Or maybe just to bed . . . I don't care which.

'Are you still all right to have Lyla for me next Saturday?' I double check.

'Yes, indeed, can't wait to have the little petal. Are you working on something nice?'

'Just a shoot. Natalie offered me the lead assistant spot. Since I decided to up my hours it seems like she's really keen to give me interesting work to do. I think she's quite pleased with my work, actually. I'm going to stay over.'

'Ohh, a two-day shoot. That'll be good for the bank balance. You can treat me to lunch, ha ha! Derek and I used to go to lunch every Friday, come rain or shine. It was our little treat to each other. Sometimes we'd have soup. Sometimes a ham sandwich. Oh, my Derek was so particular about his ham sandwiches. He'd—'

'Ahhh, that's lovely. Well, no, it's just a one-day shoot, but I'm staying with a . . . friend for the night and then coming back up on Sunday morning.'

Kath stops what she's doing and looks at me, eyes sparkling. 'A gentleman friend?' Fuck, she's astute when she wants to be.

'Ha, yes, no, well, yes.' Why do I feel like a teenager who's just been caught kissing her celebrity posters?

'Oh, sweetie, I remember those days,' she says, peeling

the soapy gloves off and leaning up against the sink. I can see her paisley floaty skirt getting wet with all the suds she's splashed everywhere, but she doesn't seem to care and keeps on talking. 'The initial spark of excitement, when everything seems to shine and the world suddenly sings to you. Derek took me for dinner at the Ritz when we first started courting. I wore a flowing mocha silk dress and tied hundreds of coloured ribbons into my hair. It was quite a look. You could get away with things like that in those days,' she moons. 'Derek loved it, he said I looked like a bird of paradise, and you know how he loved his birds.'

'He's called Theo. The man I'm sort of seeing. He works in property,' I offer from my spot at the kitchen table where I'm putting all the letters back into a pile that I can ignore for another week.

I don't think Kath is listening; she's rested her hands on the side of the sink and is just looking out of the window at this point.

I take the opportunity to give her a moment alone and fetch my phone. It hasn't buzzed; I really was just being desperate. I swipe it open to read the last message Theo sent me.

Goodnight darling. Sleep well x. He cares, and that means something. I can't believe I've landed such a catch.

I really want to ask him to a PSM thing that's coming up. Every now and then they organise a dinner out and other halves are invited. I've never been to one. It would be a lovely way to feel more part of things. It's not for a month or so, but already I'm trying to think of how to ask him to it. Or is it too soon? I don't know. This dating game is so much harder than the apps game was. I wish in real life it was as easy as swipe, swipe, tick.

After a couple of minutes Kath comes through looking a bit flushed and peaky and I feel guilty. I've barely listened to anything she's said because all I could think about was my phone and how irritated I was that she was looking through my unpaid bills.

Lyla looks over and jumps straight up to give her a big arms-flung-round-her-waist cuddle. 'Auntie Kath! I'm glad you've come to play!' she says, arms still holding on. Kath is almost knocked off her feet.

'Goodness me, that's a lot of love for such a little lady!' she sing-songs gratefully.

'You smell like gardens, Auntie Kath,' Lyla replies, inhaling deeply. She's right. Kath always smells like her patchouli bath oils; her whole house does.

'Lovey, I'm going to leave my tea actually and pop in on Moira. Alan said he'd be writing to the council today about people sellotaping unnecessary posters on the local lamp posts and I want to see the draft.'

'You what?' Once again I am completely at sea in Auntie Kath's mad world.

'People are taking the law into their own hands and adhering whatever they fancy to the street fixtures and

179

fittings. It's just not on. I'm all for a missing cat poster here and there, but now we see furniture for sale, jumble sale dates, all sorts. It's getting out of hand,' she says matter-of-factly, as though this is a heinous crime and I should fully understand.

'Oh, right. Wow. Terrible.' I'm not sure how we've gone from Derek at the Ritz to this. Should I have been more active in that conversation?

'Exactly. I do like popping in on Moira and Alan. It's lovely to see a happy couple at their age. I think Derek and I would have been the same.'

There we are, we're back to Derek. I knew it was too big a leap before.

'You and Derek wouldn't have been bothered about letters to the council. You'd still have been travelling the world, living every day like it's your biggest adventure, filling your house with all your amazing things. You'd have been a beautiful couple.'

I can see Kath's eyes are welling up, so I go over and give her a squeeze. She leaves, seeming a bit perkier but saying she can feel a headache coming on. I think she just wants to have a bit of alone time. I respect that and tell her I'm here if she needs me. Poor old Kath.

I go to the front window to wave her off. Something wasn't right this morning. I'm not sure if it's her headaches or if she's having a tough time missing Derek, but I definitely should have tried harder just then. I don't like seeing her so upset, and my heart feels heavy that I didn't help her the way she always helps me.

As the door closes behind her and I watch her disappear down the road, my phone pings. Yes!! It's Theo!

TWENTY-ONE

MAY

H E'S GOING TO BE here any minute. My God, I'm excited. It's not natural to be this excited at this age but honestly, this is more exciting than the time Dad gave me thirty quid to blow in Toys R Us (he won it on the dogs; Mum would've gone mad if she'd known he'd had a flutter, so we went into the toyshop, bought whatever we fancied and said I'd won it at the church raffle. To this day she doesn't know the sordid measures taken to get that game of Hungry Hippos).

The whole house is immaculate, I've dressed in what I consider to be yummy-mummy wear – a soft jersey maxi wrap skirt in mustard, a white long-sleeved tee, brown sandals and a denim jacket. I'm going to jazz it up a bit with a statement necklace, va-va-voom lipstick and sunglasses, but I don't want him to know I'm putting any effort in right now. I'm going to play this day so cool, I'm practically frozen. Lyla decided to dress herself, and rather than start the day with a battle of wills that would inevitably have ended in tears (mine, not hers), I'm letting it go. Very zen. Hopefully Theo will think it eccentric rather than completely batshit crazy. Much to my secret horror, Lyla has opted for knee-high Christmas socks, a tutu with a customised pom-pom trim (courtesy of Kath's pom-pom phase last summer), a top with a sparkly dinosaur roaring on it and more hair clips than you could shake a stick at. She feels great. What can I do?

Lyla and I have had a little chat about it being a special day, meeting Theo, being on our best behaviour and being a good girl, but I'm not holding my breath. Hopefully I can style out any minor outbursts, and Theo will be entirely won over by our sweet family, fall in love with us both, propose, buy a house in Primrose Hill and we'll live happily ever after. Not that I'm getting carried away. I'm keeping expectations realistic. Cool as that cucumber.

A few more spritzes of perfume (is Lyla coughing at the fumes, or just because her throat tickles?), one more whizz round the house to check I haven't left anything hideous out and oh my God I can hear his car pulling onto the drive. It's a big day. Deep breaths, deep breaths. I'm so thrilled he agreed to come up, I could burst.

Maybe slightly too keenly I've opened the front door before he's even out of the car, and I watch him come over to greet me. He looks completely divine, and says hello. As usual, he is ready to sit on the front row of London Fashion Week, wearing perfectly cut tan chinos, a very pale pink casual shirt with sleeves rolled up to the elbows (it takes a man with a strong game to pull off a pink shirt well, and, of course, he can) and brown suede lace-ups. His face is stubbly in a 'relaxed for the weekend' way, and his hair looks like it needs my fingers running through it imminently. If I smile any more widely I might lose my mouth off the sides of my face.

'Darling, you look gorgeous!' Theo steps into our little hall, pausing on the squeaky floorboards, kissing me on the cheek and validating everything I wanted validating.

He steps over to Lyla, who's hopping from foot to foot and has suddenly gone shy, and says, 'Robin, is this beautiful lady your sister?'

'Oh no!' I say, looking shocked and playing along. 'This is Lyla!'

'Surely not! I thought Lyla was a little girl, but this young lady is so grown up and beautiful she can't possibly be only six years old!' Theo says with a faux surprised look on his face that is totally fooling her.

Lyla giggles, and I know he's won her over. 'No, silly! I'm Lyla and that's *Mummy*, and she hasn't got a sister!'

'Good grief, you're right!' he mock-exclaims, bending down and offering his hand for her to shake. 'Hello, Lyla, it's a pleasure to meet you. I'm Theo and I think your mummy is very beautiful.'

Lyla takes his hand and they shake cordially as though this is a very important business exchange. Lyla is grinning from ear to ear at this extravagant grown-up treatment.

Excuse me while I just die at how perfect his introduction is.

'She is! Mummy is perfect! And she's so happy today because she hasn't shouted about her "fucking keys", or run around in her knickers saying "where are my bloody jeans! Where are my jeans!"' Lyla responds seriously.

I want to die again, but now because I'm so mortified.

'Lyla! Don't say those words! Those are grown-up words! Theo doesn't want to hear language like that from you.'

Thankfully, Theo just looks amused. 'I don't know, I'd quite like to help you in a game of "where are my bloody jeans" one day,' he says quietly to me.

'Sorry Mummy,' Lyla says sweetly, but with a wry smile on her face, knowing she got off lightly for saying 'bad' words.

'Ahh, she's such a polite little girl,' he says, defusing any potential upset and putting his hands on his hips. 'Now, Lyla, I heard you're taking Mummy and me out today, but I wondered if you wouldn't mind me driving us in my car?'

Lyla giggles, loving all the attention, and nods her approval. She's so easily charmed. I can't think where she gets that from.

In the car I feel dreamy. It's like the car is a bubble (a

BMW-flavoured bubble) and I'm enveloped safely in it. Beautiful, madly dressed child sat on her booster seat in the back, gorgeous man deftly weaving through the country roads, one hand on the wheel and one hand on my knee, and me feeling so blissful. This is what it was meant to be. Man, woman and child having a perfect day out. I notice in the wing mirror that I'm wearing the diamond stud earrings Lacey's lent me and feel pleased with myself. Theo's girlfriend would wear diamond studs. Glamorous yet under-stated. I'm so contented in this car. I almost don't want us to arrive.

We do arrive, though, and as I open the back passenger seat door I notice that Lyla has scuffed her shoes all the way up the back of Theo's cream leather front seat. Aghast, I just shut the door gently behind her and remind myself to clean that up later somehow when he's not looking. Perhaps tonight, while he sleeps. Shit.

'Just need to grab my sweater,' Theo says as he opens the other passenger seat door to pick up his navy cashmere jumper. Of course it's cashmere, and of course he's going to see the shoe scuffs.

Fuck, fuck, fuck.

'Oh,' he says, an octave higher than usual.

'Mmmm?' Going to just pretend I don't know what he means. That'll make this go away.

'I think perhaps Lyla has a bit of mud on her shoes.' He nods towards the scuffed-seat situation.

186

'I'm so sorry! I didn't realise, and I can absolutely get that off. It happens all the time in my car. I'm ever so sorry . . . You're not angry, are you?'

'Nooo. Absolutely not. Let's just crack on, shall we?' The vein on the side of his head twitches as he clenches his jaw and I can tell that, actually, he is quite angry, but I fall for him all the more for pretending it's no big deal.

'Auntie Kath says life is for living, Theo. We don't need to worry about a bit of mud,' Lyla pipes up. I love her free spirit; I would love it even more if she didn't share it at this precise second. That'll no doubt push Theo over the edge.

He's walking round the car to us, and I mentally brace myself for the fallout, but to my surprise, he scoops her up, swings her onto his shoulders and says, 'You are exactly right, Miss Lyla Blue. Let's enjoy the day and worry about that later.'

Wow, I'm impressed. He was very calm about that. Also, I'm amazed he's remembered her middle name. I think I only mentioned it once. I love him, I love him, I love him.

We meander through to the great courtyard of the magnificent stately home, Thropnon House (think huge pillars encasing the front steps, ivy crawling all the way up the stone walls and multiple chimneys attached to multiple fireplaces that the wealthy inhabitants enjoy sherry by at Christmas). We're visiting for their Spring Family Day, and I can't help but feel smug. At last, I, Robin Wilde, am sauntering around gorgeous grounds with my beautiful little girl, the light of my life, and a handsome man in tan chinos. I never thought I'd be this woman. I'm currently being the sort of woman I tend to look at and feel jealous of. I look like the kind of woman who has it together and has a happy and balanced life. We could be in a magazine, for fuck's sake.

'This is great, isn't it?' Theo muses. 'Reminds me of being a boy and going shooting with my father.' I'm secretly impressed that Theo spent his youth doing country pursuits on grand estates.

The courtyard is dotted with world food stalls selling every delicious thing you could want. Stone-baked pizza slices, tortilla wraps, hog roast rolls, fish and chips, steak-to-go and far too many treat foods to have near a small child. Cake pops, cupcakes, scones with cream and jam. It's too much to choose from.

Almost reading my mind, Theo says, 'Shall we go crazy and just get a bit of everything?'

'Are you my dream man?' I shoot back, laughing at the idea of all that deliciousness.

'Aha, quite possibly! Let's grab a selection and take it through to the lawns,' he says, striding off towards the first food stall.

And so we do, and it's glorious. I let him choose everything because I don't want to seem like a glutton, but I do insist on a box of cupcakes because Lyla loves them.

We leave the courtyard and find a spot on the great lawns

near the trees. This garden is so stunning. It makes me wish we had even a little patch of grass. Everything is carefully planted and precisely pruned. Tulips, peonies, perfect delphiniums, fat hyacinths and pink camellia flowers are all in full bloom and adding some much-needed colour to the day after months of grey nothingness.

'Lyla, look at all these cherry blossoms!' Theo calls excitedly to her. Unfortunately she gives zero shits, because I'm holding the box of cupcakes. She's more puppy than child sometimes. I give a little celebratory 'wow, so pretty!' to Theo, though, so as not to leave him hanging, and he looks satisfied with my acknowledgement at least. Look at us, being happy for cherry blossoms in the sunshine!

We set all the food down and, like the domestic goddess I'm pretending to be, I pull a little blanket out of my giant slouchy bag and lay it on the grass.

'Wowee, it looks like your mummy has it all, Lyla,' Theo remarks. I pretend to look bashful but don't manage it.

'Mummy has everything in her magic bag!' Aww, she's so sweet. 'Her phone and sweets and hair bobbles and money and toys and blankets and Tampax for her grown-up lady times.' Oh my God, of course she remembers that one throwaway answer I gave her when she asked if my yellow-wrapped tampon was a sweet!

'Oh!' he laughs back. 'Well then, she's prepared for absolutely everything, isn't she!'

I laugh too, but deep down I'm slightly miffed that our

perfect moment has now been tarnished by a flipping tampon. Next she'll be bringing up the wax salon visit.

We lay out all the boxes and containers of food and slip straws in drinks (which also distracts Lyla from any further chat about things I don't want her to remember). I'm glad we're sat by the trees, slightly hidden from the main crowd, because we actually look a bit deranged with this much food on a blanket. I love that Theo doesn't make me feel uncomfortable about enjoying my food. I wouldn't say I'm especially conscious of my figure; it's a good average size, but working with models all day does take its toll, and sometimes I find myself feeling really guilty for treating myself. Taking a hold of my thoughts and reminding myself that skinniness and happiness do not correlate, I'm more than happy to have a bit of everything and enjoy it. Lyla clearly has no issues either, sticky hands in every packet.

'I never get to do things like this in London – this is so great,' Theo says, looking into my eyes.

'Well, that's the joy of not living in London. Fresh air, open skies, I love it. I loved hanging out with you in London, but there's no way I could live there. I'd feel like I was suffocating. It feels so good to breathe deeply, you know?' I say, instinctively inhaling the sweet scent of the nearby flowers.

'And to breathe it in such good company too. I can be so relaxed with you,' he replies, lying down on the grass with his head resting in my lap, looking up at the sky (and, I hope, not my nostrils). Man, he's smooth.

'Well, I'll say cheers to that!' I say, raising a can of lemon fizz in the air.

We chink our cans (I reach over and chink his where it's sat next to his thighs), and turn our attention to the falconry display that's just about to start. This is supposed to be the highlight of the day, so I'm interested to see just how amazing it is.

'Oh, I love falcons!' Theo says, sitting up and looking over at them. I can't actually tell if he's being sarcastic or if he really does love these birds.

'Mmm, yeah . . . they're . . . really good.'

'They're such powerful birds, soaring through the air, spotting their prey and going for the kill. Efficient and ruthless,' he says, gesturing more animatedly than he has done all day.

'Like you?' I laugh.

'Ha! Maybe!' he laughs, leaning back onto his elbows now that his initial falconry excitement has passed.

Sadly, the falconry display leaves a lot to be desired. Out of the three birds performing, one saw something on the roof of the manor and has camped out there while the work experience boy stands below waggling a flaccid mouse about to try and tempt it down; the other flew to the nearest tree, perched on a branch and hasn't moved since, and the last one did three laps of the lawns (semi-impressive) and then

191

just went back to its enclosure, sort of giving up. I kind of get it; I'm not sure I'd make a good falcon, unlike Theo. Lyla thinks the flaccid mouse-wiggling is part of the show, though, and is utterly captivated by it, as though it's some sort of avian thriller. Theo seizes his chance to move his hand from its respectable spot on my knee much further up, sliding it under my skirt and across my inner thigh before I brush him off, laughing, 'Down, boy, you'll put the falcons off.'

'I'll turn them on, more like,' he whispers calmly. I blush, because he's so right.

'I used to hunt with my dad when I was younger,' he says, changing tack somewhat.

'Do you still hunt? I saw you as more of a charm-every-woman-in-London man rather than a shoot-animals-in-the-country kind of a guy,' I say, smiling and leaning in for a tiny kiss while Lyla's engrossed in the mouse debacle.

'Not any more; Dad's put his guns away now – at Mother's insistence – and none of my work friends shoot,' he says with the slightest hint of sadness, maybe about his dad.

'I'd love to meet your friends,' I say, putting my hand in his and tickling his palm nonchalantly.

'Yes, I'm sure; I'll introduce you,' he says, not looking at me but squinting into the distance at the guy putting the birds away.

We carry on with the picnic, and I pull Lyla onto my lap for a cuddle (Theo's hands are safely back where they should be), and gaze dreamily at the flowers and at other people. She smells gorgeous. Every mother thinks that about her own child, I know. They smell like love and sweetness, and it makes my heart squeeze for her. If I could bottle this comforting scent and keep it forever, I would.

Theo looks a bit disappointed. Maybe he really *was* into the falcons.

'You OK?' I ask, with a hand on his toned arm. 'You're not upset about Colin the falcon, are you?'

'No. No, no. I just don't like thinking I'm going to get something and then it not happening.' He frowns, a little sulkier than I'd have expected. 'I thought that was going to be really cool, that's all.'

'It was RUBBISH!' good old Lyla yells with her perfect timing. The work experience boy never did get the falcon down. Instead he just shrugged, threw the dead mouse back in a Tupperware box and climbed into the main guy's Land Rover and got on his phone. All a bit of a let-down, really.

'Shall we pack all this up, have a mooch round and head back, then?' I offer as a consolation. I just want to move on from the display drama, and we've eaten so much food I feel a bit sick now.

'Yes! I want something from the shop, Mummy! Can I pick something?' Lyla says, jumping off my lap and dancing about.

The craft marquee is the stuff of dreams. A huge tent filled with trinkets and gifts and handmade fudges that smell divine. The sun is streaming in through the vast open doors; men and women are holding hands looking happy and vendors are chatting merrily about their creations.

Theo has mellowed about the slightly shit birds, and has slipped his hand into mine. Lyla is dancing about in front of us and I want to stop time and stay here, in this perfect little moment. This is exactly how I wanted this day to be – it can't get any better.

Theo spends rather a lot of time looking at granite models of sniper planes, and I pretend to be really interested in how the propeller really does turn and Lyla is being good.

Lyla is in her element, having a play with everything, and finally settles on a painted black and yellow bumble bee wooden jigsaw to buy. She's been good so I decide to treat her.

The lady behind the stall looks up smiling and says, 'You must have been a good girl for Mummy and Daddy to buy you such a nice present!'

Lyla barely registers (she's just been handed a bag with a toy in it) but Theo and I do. We both stand stock-still, and I can feel my cheeks burning. I must look insane.

Calmly, Theo squeezes my hand and says to the woman, 'She has,' and we walk away.

Just like that, he's solved everything. He's amazing. Does he see himself as a father figure? I think this rather cements us.

After twenty more minutes of mooching (and rather a

lot of vanilla-fudge-purchasing), we walk slowly back to the car.

In bed, later, after *very* quiet but very satisfying sex, I lie there listening to Theo gently snoring. I can't believe how beautifully this day has gone. If it were possible for me to be floating, I would be.

TWENTY-TWO

JUNE

ONIGHT IS A SPECIAL night. Kath is picking Lyla up from school and keeping her overnight, and I'm giving myself a gorgeous treat. I'm blasting a romance-themed Spotify playlist and swooning about like the cat that got the cream. At this precise moment I am luxuriating in a hot, decadent, mid-afternoon bath. Everything's been going so well with Theo since our family day out – more dinners, a cinema trip (though he was clearly a bit bored), a couple of sleepovers – I decided to bite the bullet and ask him to the PSM Parents and Partners dinner. I went to a Parents and Partners drinks evening once in Lyla's first term, just before Christmas, when I was still very new to the school, and felt so alien that I wanted to scream, 'IS THIS HOW IT REALLY IS? ARE YOU REALLY HAPPY? IS IT THAT IMPORTANT HOW MANY TIMES LAUREN AND PHILIP WENT TO ROME THIS YEAR?' but

196

obviously, didn't. Instead I bit my tongue and nodded along with an inane smile on my face, hoping Roger (Val's balding, sleazy buffoon of a husband) couldn't tell that I didn't give a shit about his 'sometimes forty-five minutes, if traffic is heavy' commute to work. Some of them might be dull, but they're a gang, and I want in. All dinner parties have dull moments, and I think part of my suffering is that I've always been single at them. I don't have that teammate to bounce off, and so I end up sat at the end of the table with no anecdotes to share or tales to laugh over and nodding along to the likes of Roger and his enthralling chatter.

This time, though, it's different. Theo said yes! He's going to come to the Partners night, and we'll be that couple that makes everyone feel a bit sick. We'll be charming and funny and partake in scintillating conversation and offer witty anec-dotes. We'll be that couple that gently bicker, 'no, you tell it, darling, you tell it so much better', over our stories, and the other women will be sat secretly wishing they could have affairs so that they could have as much excitement as I'm having right now. Not that I want anyone to have an affair, of course; but you know, a little bit of other people's envy always goes a long way, I think.

I've told everyone I'm coming with Theo. I may have over-told them, actually, because even Gillian rolled her eyes and said, 'I know!' when I mentioned it briefly in the foyer this morning. I feel like that kid who got the best Tamagotchi for their birthday and feels like everyone needs to know, when in reality they don't give a shit. Well, maybe they give a little shit, but not a big one.

Theo was meant to take the day off today and drive up last night, but he's texted to say that because of the huge acquisition he's handling at the moment he needs to drive up this afternoon. It's 3 p.m. and I'm already preparing, I'm that excited.

It's not that the night itself is likely to be anything mind-blowing; it's only dinner and drinks in the new Italian that's opened up on the high street. But it's everything else. That feeling of walking into a venue holding your partner's hand, having your seat pulled out, perhaps; having someone to say, 'Shall I order chicken and you order beef, and we'll share a bit of each?' It's having your teammate there, and not just being on your own *all* the bloody time. It's been so long, years actually, since I felt like I fitted into an environment like that. I've longed for it. I've felt so far away when I've seen friends in couple bubbles, quietly laughing at a private joke, locking eyes with tilted heads. With such a long wait, having it now feels all the sweeter, and so I'm letting myself spend an entire afternoon luxuriating in the getting-ready process. I refuse to feel guilty or self-indulgent for it.

Hello gorgeous, how's it going there? I'm lying in the bath, thinking of you x, I send via text. I've definitely got the knack of a saucy text now, and feel a bit smug that I managed to basically say *where are you?* without sounding desperate. If I wasn't naked and immersed in bubbly bathwater I'd do a little victory dance for that one. Instead, though, I just screen-grab it and send it to Lacey with a sunglasses smiley face on. She replies with a thumbs-up emoji and the hand that's doing the 'OK' sign, which satisfies my need for validation nicely.

I do love a bath. Yes, all I'm doing is laying my body in a container of hot water and swilling about in it, which doesn't sound particularly appetising, but when you can smell your Lush bath bomb and your legs are smoother than Theo's one-liners, it feels like heaven. I lie in mine for a good forty-five minutes before jumping out, grabbing the nearest towel – oh, good, it's a Hello Kitty beach towel – and lavishly applying my good moisturiser that matches my perfume.

Trying to ignore the lack of message flashing up on my phone, I start blow-drying my hair. Instead of my usual tip-head-upside-down-and-blast technique, I'm taking my time. I'm channelling my inner hairstylist and clipping segments to blow over a barrel brush. Why don't I do this every day? It actually looks rather glorious when I spend that little bit of extra time on it. Soon those beauty bloggers will be asking *me* for tips.

Four o'clock, and still no message. I don't feel like I can send another *where are you* text, but being the new-found genius I am, I have an idea. A mirror selfie in my towel! I hunt down a normal woman's towel, though, so I don't have Hello Kitty's face stretched across my bosom, and I tousle my hair. Admittedly I did have to take my hair out of all the holding-segments-up clips, apply a discreet layer of tinted moisturiser and then heavily filter the snap (who doesn't love a high-contrast black-and-white with heavy vignette?) but on final review, I think it was worth the end result.

I send the snap along with *Thinking of you* and hope it nudges him to a) reply, and b) leave the bloody office.

At 4.45 p.m., my phone buzzes. Thank the Lord.

Theo says, *Hello my darling, you look sensational. Looking forward to dinner with you, leaving in ten. x*

Yessss! He's leaving in a moment, my hair looks amazing, we're in business!

To celebrate this, I message Finola: *Looking forward to seeing you later. Are you drinking?*

Yes, comes her reply.

I should have known Finola was the wrong person to try and spark a chat about Theo with, and try Gillian instead. *Ooohh, I'm so excited for tonight! What are you wearing?*

Slightly more fruitfully she replies, *I know, it should be lovely. I'm going for my navy trousers (bit tight though, oooer) and that nice floaty cream top with the gold buttons. See you shortly xxxx*

Since he messaged me, I think it's still casual and breezy to respond so just after five I text Theo to say, *I bet it's been so busy for you today! I'm just enjoying the peace and quiet and getting ready. Is the traffic heavy or are you making good time?*

He doesn't reply, but I think that's probably because he's driving and I open my make-up bag ready to transform my face from tired mummy to sexy mama.

I'm so happy with the way my make-up looks. I've blended in a heavy-cut crease, my eyebrows are well shaped, I've contoured seamlessly and set everything with transparent powder so we can fully enjoy the night and nothing's going anywhere.

To be there on time, we need to leave at 6.30 and it's 5.35 now. No message from Theo, but I'm not going to worry. He's an adult, a proper adult with a mahogany shoehorn and membership to swanky social clubs; he'll cut it fine but he'll be here.

In my eagerness I've got ready far too soon, so I pour myself a glass of chilled white wine, gently sit down (this dress is far too expensive to flop down in like I normally would: since even a bloody invite to the Partners night is a celebration, let alone Theo coming, I decided to treat myself to the most incredible floral embroidered mini-skater dress. Each jewel-toned petal is hand-sewn onto the sturdy navy fabric that clings and swings in all the right places. I feel amazing, but don't dare muss it up) and flick on Netflix. I've been slowly working through the Kimmy Schmidt box set so I sit back, click yes to a new episode and sip my wine. This is bliss. This must be what it's like to have a loving, doting husband. Gillian and Finola must feel like this all the time.

Six p.m. ticks by, and I'm starting to lift my neck up a bit every time I see a car come near the house, but it's not him. A message pings through. I'd have thought it would be easier just to ring if he's driving, so I pick up my phone.

My heart sinks.

Sweetheart, I've still not left the office. I'm going to have to give it a miss this time, but we'll definitely have dinner next week xx

He's not coming.

I've made all this effort, bought this stupid dress and droned on about his attendance not only to Finola and Gillian, but to the other mums, and he's not even coming.

Once again I'll have to walk in on my own. Sit at the awkward head of the table so that everyone else can sit opposite their partner, listen mutely to everyone else's couply stories about their recent weekend in the Lake Distrct, but this time it will be even worse because they'll pity me. Poor, single Robin, she'll never get the guy. They'll say things to 'help' like, 'Oh, Robin, I wish I were single! No shaving your legs, come home whenever you want'. But it's not like that. Not for me. So that's no consolation.

Suddenly I feel very low. I don't think I can handle going alone. I send a group message to Gillian and Finola.

Hi ladies, really sorry but going to have to cancel tonight. Theo's been held up at work and I'm a bit down, so don't want to spoil the night with poor company. Have a great time! See you on Monday! xxx I've tried to make that sound as cheery as possible, but my throat is already burning and I can feel tears threatening behind my eyes.

I put down my phone, carefully unzip my dress and drape it over the armchair (I might be let down, but I haven't forgotten what I'm wearing), flop down onto the sofa in my matching bra and knickers and hold a cushion to my chest while I take big gasps of air and let the tears come. They roll down my face, taking my perfectly applied black eyeliner with them.

How could he do this? He knew how excited I was. Surely he could have organised his work better? Or left it till Monday? Or had someone else take care of it? Or messaged me sooner? Before I poured myself into this dress, or glued on false lashes. He didn't even have the backbone to phone me and let me down. A last-minute text with zero compassion. I don't want to have dinner next week – it won't be the Parents and Partners dinner. I won't be able to say to them all, 'Hey gang, can you all find babysitters again because Theo might be able to make it this time?' This won't happen again for months. This was my chance finally to feel like I fit in, like I'm one of them, like I'm good enough, and to enjoy *not* being the one smiling and pretending being on your own is totally fine all the time. It's all been ripped up in front of me at the very last second. I feel like such an idiot. I don't know why I thought I deserved all this: this dress, the witty anecdotes, the tilted-head looks at each other.

A message pings through from Finola. *Nonsense. Have a stiff drink, put on your eye sparkles and call the taxi!* She's so forthright. I bet a man cancelling wouldn't faze her. I wish it didn't bloody faze *me*. I can't actually think of anything that would faze Finola. Six hours after giving birth to Roo, she says she was up and feeding the dogs. She's a machine to be marvelled at.

Gillian adds to the group chat: *Oh dear. I'm so sorry. I hope everything's OK for him at work. Why don't I pick you up and you can sit next to me at dinner? I don't want you sat in the house alone feeling so down. Let's go and have a lovely night and you'll feel better for it.*

I can imagine the tone she wrote that in. It's the exact same soothing tone she uses on Clara and right now I'm fine with it. Maybe she's right. Maybe sucking it up and going out would be best; after all, going solo isn't something I'm not used to and this dress needs an airing. Also, I note, this is the first time I've felt like Finola and Gillian really want my company. Theo might have stood me up, but these women certainly haven't and that warrants more than just moping at home.

Thanks, Gillian, that's really sweet of you. I'll come along. I'm not sure how much fun I'll be but it'll be nice to see you all. What time will you swing by? xxx

That's the spirit, lovey! Back on the horse! Finola adds in. Always the dogs or the horses. I dread to think what she considers dirty talk.

With more determination than I've had to muster in a long time, I pull myself up off the sofa, slip back into the dress – there's no way I'm wasting looking this good just because Theo's a bastard no-show – thud up the stairs to sort my face out (my tears have trailed through my foundation and left tracks like skiers on snow) and start to move from let-down and sad to angry.

By the time Gillian and sweet but quiet Paul pick me up in their pristine Range Rover and I slide into the back next to Clara's bumper seat, I'm hot with rage. I have to open the window a crack just to keep myself from sweating. Or as Mum would say, my gentle glow: 'Pigs sweat, men perspire and women gently glow.' Well, I'm gently glowing all right. I'm gently glowing at how little Theo seems to care about me when he makes out he cares so very much. He seems very able to put on a great show of charm and throw his cash and contacts around, but the first time I've asked him for anything, when I want him by my side, he's not here.

As we pull up to the restaurant, I can see Matthew and his partner Laurence from Year Three are just parking their car too, and I feel so embarrassed. I was meant to be stepping out of the front seat of Theo's BMW, not waiting for Gillian to click off the child locks before I climb out of the back seat of her car. I see them coming over to do the high-pitched 'hellos' and it starts. Matthew says, 'Oh nooo, where's your chap du jour?' and I want to curl up and cry all over again.

I make it through dinner. Of course I do. I'm an expert at pretending I'm managing perfectly well on my own.

TWENTY-THREE

I WAKE UP THE NEXT morning and the memories of it all wash over me again. Theo isn't lying half-naked next to me like he should be; he didn't come with me to the meal and, instead, I took my place as the sad single mum at the top of the table, with Gillian to my left giving me little knee squeezes every time someone said, 'And where's this handsome new chap of yours, Robin?' It was my own fault for making such a fuss about him. I cringe just thinking about it.

It's not so much that he didn't come to that specific night; it's the smack-in-the-face realisation that he means more to me than I do to him. To me, he's my potential future, but I'm wondering if to him I'm just a game. He's never free when I suggest a date. Every time he suggests one, of course I come running. I'm a walking, talking toy that he can pick up and shake about and play with whenever he fancies, but only ever on his terms. Bastard. I hope he enjoyed playing the fun weekend dad. I hope he enjoyed his ready-made family, putting Lyla on his shoulders, letting that woman in the craft tent think he was the doting father. How *dare* he use us like this? I'm starting to feel furious again, so I take a couple of minutes to stay in bed, and breathe deeply – I even download a mindfulness app – and I calm myself down.

Kath is dropping Lyla off at 9 a.m. and it's already 8.45, so I roll out of bed and wrap my old fleecy, stained dressing gown around me. At least I don't have to bother with trying to be sexy and alluring this morning. Thank God for small mercies.

Bypassing the mirror (I came back to an empty house, and it didn't feel good. One knock, and the sadness feels like it could overwhelm me. I cried more last night, before going to bed without removing my make-up, so I can't face my face just yet) I plod downstairs and switch the kettle on. I'd thought Theo would be here today and that we'd go out, all three of us, but now that's gone down the toilet I have no plans, except to try to keep The Emptiness I can feel seeping in at bay. I'm going to put decent mothering on the back burner and declare it a TV Day with beige freezer food for dinner and, for me, continuous cups of tea and custard creams. I had a creative briefing from Natalie that I was supposed to be researching this weekend, but the thought of working right now fills me with dread. I don't want to think about anything.

On the dot of nine I hear a key in the door and the familiar 'oooo-eeeee, only me' of Kath.

'Hello, love! How was your night? Was it as wonderful as you'd hoped? Is he upstairs still? Can I meet him?' she stage-whispers, looking round for signs of a man before clocking my grotty dressing gown and realising. Her face falls for me. Her face, by the way, is 'made up' with turquoise eyeshadow and purple lipstick. Bless her; this is for Theo's welcome, no doubt. She's mad and drives me nuts, but she's bloody lovely really.

I just stand there, next to the kettle, with red, puffy eyes, blinking back tears.

'Ohh love. What's happened? Have you had a falling-out?' Kath's tone has instinctively changed into something soft and warm and with that, I crumble all over again.

Big, blubbery tears fall this time, along with huge gasping gulps. The whole time Lyla stands by the door, still holding her Paw Patrol backpack, looking really worried. That makes me feel worse, of course. How many times is this poor kid going to have to see her mess of a mother like this? I'm sure this is damaging her. Instinctively I wipe away the tears and sing-song, 'Sorry, my Bluebird, I had a little moment but I'm all right. Silly Mummy crying about nothing, I'm all right, I'm all right!' to try to shield her. She comes over to me and reaches out for a cuddle. As soon as I feel her hot little body pressed up against my legs and tummy, I feel fresh tears pouring out again. It's all too much. I can't hold any of this in.

Kath quickly realises that I'm on a one-way track to melt-down and takes control of the situation. 'Lyla, petal, why don't you go and put your bag upstairs and see if you can find any colouring books to go through? I'm going to look after Mummy, don't worry. Robin, you sit yourself down and I'll finish this tea off and make one for me too. I can't stop long because Cupcakes and Crochet starts at ten and I'm giving out the patterns today, but I've always got time for a chat. A problem shared is a problem halved.'

Lyla senses the tone and doesn't argue. Once I can hear her footsteps going up the stairs and feel safe that she's out of earshot, I let it out, the whole sorry story.

'Oh pet, I know it feels like the end of the world now but I promise you it's not,' Kath says gently, taking over the tea-making I'd so far failed at. 'There'll be other nights and other dinners.'

The Emptiness feels like it's smothering me, like it's mocking me for ever thinking it was far away. I'm so angry at it and oppressed by it at the same time. 'You don't get it! I'm so sick of doing everything myself, sitting by myself every night, not having someone to say goodnight to, forever making just one cup of tea. I don't have anyone and I never will,' I say, taking a sip of tea and then putting it down so angrily it slops over the side and splashes onto the table.

Kath is silent for a minute. I look at her, and she's smiling tightly.

'Do you think I don't know what it's like to be on my

own?' Kath says quietly, indignant. She's standing stock-still by the kettle, two just-made cups of tea in hand but not bringing them over, her initial warm tone has cooled. She continues after a deep breath. 'I had to watch the love of my life slip away in front of me, Robin. I had to say goodbye forever to the man I thought I would say all my goodnights to for the rest of our days. I know what alone feels like. I know it and I feel it every single day.' She slams the cups down on the counter, sloshing tea everywhere, and brings her brightly manicured hands up to her face to rub her forehead and eyes, smearing the turquoise eyeshadow and pulling on her skin. She runs one hand through her over-accessorised-with-butterfly-clips hair and uses one hand to steady herself on the counter, not looking up at me, just staring down at the wood as if she can't bring herself to see me.

I don't think I've ever seen Kath so tense and so hurt. Fuck.

'Perhaps if you took a moment,' she says, lifting her head and looking right into my eyes with a hard look I haven't seen before, 'to look at all the wonderful things in your life that you *do* have, then you'd feel a lot better. You're not alone. You have Lyla. A beautiful spirit who loves you and wants you and needs you. I would LOVE to have had my own children to share those days with!' Tears are threatening, and her knuckles have turned white where she's gripping the counter so hard.

210

'You have us,' I offer meekly, realising my terrible faux pas and desperately wishing I'd never been so self-absorbed.

'I do. And I love you,' she says sighing, loosening her grip on the counter and reaching for a cloth to wipe up the tea. 'I'm so grateful for you, and grateful to have Lyla come and stay, but don't think for a moment that I don't feel the loneliness too, that I wouldn't like someone to hold my hand and take me to the pictures. I feel it too, Robin. I would give everything I have just to have one single day, even a moment, with Derek again.' Kath's voice thickens, and I can tell she's so upset. 'Now. I won't stop, I really do need to get to the club to hand out these patterns, but I love you and this won't last forever. It's just a hiccup. You WILL be all right. Focus on Lyla, and all the blessings you do have.' She starts walking towards the door, her chiffon skirt billowing behind her.

'Kath, I'm sorry, I didn't mean to—'

'I know, I know you didn't. Don't worry, love. We're not alone, we've got each other.' She walks back over to the table where I'm sat.

'I love you, Kath; I don't know what I'd do without you,' I say, relieved that she hasn't just stormed off.

'I love you too, petal,' she says, giving me a bending-down-breasts-in-face cuddle, and wafts out, leaving a trail of Giorgio Beverly Hills behind her. She really made an effort for Theo. As she leaves the room, I notice her wiping a tear from her face. She closes the front door behind her before I can get up and follow her.

211

I vow to spend more time with Kath and take better care of her. It dawns on me how self-indulgent I've been. I drink the rest of my tea in silence at the kitchen table. I don't look at my phone or flick through the TV or open my laptop; I just sit. I do have a lot that's good in my life already. I know I do. The problem is, when The Emptiness takes hold, it's hard to see that. It's hard to see anything.

'Mummy?' A very tiny voice comes from the kitchen doorway.

'Yes, Bluebird?' I answer.

'Are you still crying?'

'No. I've had a cup of tea and feel much better,' I try to reassure her.

'Are you sad?' she says, slowly walking towards me, still with the same worried expression on her tiny, elfin face.

Deciding to be honest, I say, 'Yes, I'm sad. Sometimes, though, it's all right to be sad, and I won't be sad forever.'

'Mummy,' she says with a weirdly authoritative voice. She's planted her feet wide on the lino and has her hands on her hips. 'We are a team. I'm on your side. Let it all out, we'll have a cuddle and then we'll get on with our day with happy faces, OK?'

I start to well up again. Good God, I'm more emotional than a chocolate-starved woman on her period. She's mimicking me. Those are the exact things I say to her when she's having a moment, and here she is, my baby, looking after me. She's so right: we *are* a team.

'Are you crying *again*, Mummy?'

'Yes, but with happy tears because I'm so proud of what a beautiful little girl you are, inside and out,' and I lift her onto my lap, wrap her into my dressing gown and give her the biggest, best cuddle I've had all week. Being with Theo makes me happy, but he can't touch this feeling; there is no greater cuddle than this one.

AFTER A DAY AT home full of cuddles, streamed films and an 'I deserve a treat' Chinese takeaway, I decide we need some air. The next morning the sun is shining, the birds are cheeping.

After a quick Google search we're in the car en route to a National Trust house and garden to enjoy the scenery and perhaps a scone or two (or four). I feel good about this. I'm actually channelling my inner yummy mummy vibe pretty well, Lyla's relaxed and happy and we're doing something I can tell the PSMs about at the school gates tomorrow. Who needs Theo Salazan? What a win!

Once we're there, I can see why every couple over thirty-five with Hunter wellies and privileged children do this, it's so, so lovely. There's something surprisingly soothing about well-manicured lawns and summer flowers, and as we meander through, holding hands and pointing out 'special flowers with magic powers, Mummy', I feel a deep sense of peace. Theo can't touch any of this, my perfect world with Lyla, just the two of us. He hasn't even bothered to ring me to apologise yet, so it's not that hard to be just a team of two right now anyway.

We admire each carefully kept bed of flowers and neat, winding hedges that lead you further and further through the gardens, down to a wild meadow and beyond that to a series of interconnecting ponds with mossy cherub statues all around them. Everywhere you walk the scent is light and fresh, and it's warm and bright. We pass couples and families and elderly people taking in the view too, and nod politely or have a knowing giggle with each other, both parties realising how nice it is here and how stupid every other person in the world is for staying at home or subjecting themselves to soft-play centres.

'Simon! Be careful! You almost stood on that mushroom!' A familiar voice shrilly permeates my serene thoughts. Whipping my whole body round with the speed of an Olympic gymnast, I see them. My ex-fiancé and his flibbertigibbet girlfriend, who is bending down surreptitiously bagging wild mushrooms.

Fantastic.

Of all the Gardens of Eden, and they have to walk into mine.

Lyla squeals 'DADDY!' as she hurtles over.

Simon looks horrified. He freezes to the spot in his brown corduroy trousers, sensible navy wellies and white crumpled linen shirt. His pale skin has flushed bright red and his eyes dart all over the place, probably looking for an escape route.

First, he probably didn't expect to see the estranged mother of his child here, and secondly, he nearly murdered a mushroom, and who knows what kind of effect that would have had on the delicate balance of Storie's world.

'Hello! Oh, ha, hello, Robin. Ha!' God, he's so lame, he can't even greet the mother of his child without making a div of himself.

'Hey, Simon, you OK?' I don't know why he gets so panicked when he sees me. I don't care any more. I haven't cared for a long, long time.

'Yes. I, we, ha, Storie and I are just out. You know, just, walking, having a walk here.'

'*Namaste*,' says Storie, nodding and putting her palms together as if in prayer. Oh Jesus. But then, thank goodness: 'Hi, Robin, how are you?' Storie manages to sound a bit more human than her less-than-eloquent boyfriend. I don't think we'd be friends in the real world (a world I don't think she inhabits anyway), but she's all right. She's not smug or spiteful, and you've got to give her credit for being so dedicated to her passions – including wild mushrooms.

'Good, thanks, Storie, we just fancied some air and to get out of town for a little bit. I've had a long week, and this is lovely,' I say, calmly and comfortably. I'm not the one who left and ran off with a hippy. I don't have anything to feel nervous about, unlike Simon, who's clearly feeling something, as tiny beads of sweat trickle down his forehead.

'Mother Nature, Robin. She really can heal anything,'

Storie says sagely. She clearly isn't worried about anything either.

'Yep. Of course. Good for her.'

Storie smiles.

Lyla seems beside herself with joy that we're all here together, and asks Daddy and Storie to walk round the ponds with us. Storie smiles again, serenely (water is made by Mother Nature too, after all), and Simon starts to melt down.

'Oh, er, I don't know, Lyla, maybe Mummy wants to, er, I, er, spend some time, errr . . .' His dithering is so painful I have to cut him off.

'Simon, it's fine, it's just a walk round a pond.'

As we set off, Lyla runs to her dad and slips her hand in his. He looks over at me awkwardly as if he doesn't know if this is allowed while I'm here or something. This is the first time in, well, ever, that we've all been in the same place at once. After we split up and arranged custody set-ups, we just kept things separate. I've never questioned it or had an issue with it because I was glad to distance myself from Simon. Before I can give any kind of meaningful look back, Storie walks over, takes Lyla's other hand and swings her high into the air with him. I take a moment to push down the lump in my throat. That should be me. I should be swinging Lyla like that, not her, not *them*. My heart doesn't ache for not having him, but it aches for not being in the Mummy, Daddy, Lyla trio. It almost takes my breath away to see what I almost had, and then I hear Lyla screaming

216

with pure delight. She loves it. She doesn't mind that it's Storie and not me; she just loves to be in the moment and feel the thrill of being off the ground and of having two adults who, in their own dithering, nature-obsessed ways, love her. The lump in my throat disappears. Storie isn't the enemy here. She loves Lyla. She clearly loves Simon too, to support him so well, and they provide something wonderful for my little girl.

Just as I'm coming over all zen about the situation, Lyla breaks free from Simon and Storie, runs back to me, jumps up and says, 'Come on, Mummy, you're my team, come and see the magic spell pond!' My heart almost bursts; she wants me as much as I want her. We squeeze hands, run down to the pond where Storie is now telling Simon about the nutritional values of algae and spend the rest of the morning as a happily dysfunctional family of four. Five, if, like Storie, you count the bag of mushrooms.

TWENTY-FOUR

I T IS A SUNNY summer's evening a fortnight later and, incredibly, everything is running smoothly. The chicken is in the oven, the veg is chopped and ready to steam and Prosecco is chilling in the fridge. Lyla has even eaten fish fingers, mash and vegetables, so I feel like she's well-nourished for once. She'd live off cheese on toast if she could. We're on schedule for a perfect evening.

Theo is coming round. He's driving over after work, and I want him to arrive to domestic bliss and see how lovely it would be to do this with me more permanently. He called me and we have thoroughly talked through the night he let me down on the phone, and he was so apologetic. Flowers have been delivered to the house, and lots of attentive and sweet messages and calls since. He says he'll keep making it up to me until I feel better, and everyone has to have their first row. He is trying. That means something.

So, the grown-ups' food is looking good (roast chicken with a lemon and herb jus) and Lyla is playing with her Female Scientists Lego – God bless the hours of entertainment Lego brings a child. I'm pottering around clearing up plastic, kiddie plates and shoving all her toys in the decluttered understairs cupboard – a slew of dollies, sets of Stickle Bricks and Peppa Pig don't exactly scream romance. Then I light every candle I own. The house looks glorious. I take a deep breath and look around: this is how life is meant to be. I'm actually nailing it.

'Come on then, Lyla Blue, let's get you to bed.'

'Why? Is your boyfriend coming round to kiss you?' she giggles.

'Ha ha ha, cheeky little thing!' Shit, how does she know? 'Yes, Theo's coming over for dinner.'

'Oohh, Mummy loves Theo! Theo loves Mummy!' she sings.

Secretly I'd love her song to be true. He's in love with me, I'm in love with him, then there's a proposal, a new house and more babies for me to Facebook the shit out of like everyone else I know and feel jealous of! I'll spend my life frequenting tiny cafés with scrubbed wooden tables, brunching on smashed avo on toast, which I'll Insta the hell out of. I'll laugh merrily with the other mums who, like me, have their shit together. It's on the cards. I should probably rein it in a little bit, but a girl can dream.

'Yep, OK, bedtime please.' And off we go upstairs for our regular routine: fairy lights on; PJs pulled on; teeth brushed; face washed; story read and cuddles administered.

Once that's done, I feel like I can relax. There's something very wonderful about 7.30 p.m., now that Theo is (back) in my life. It's no longer a lonely dinner for one with a cheap glass of wine and a night with no one to talk to, but some adult time to look forward to, some intimacy and warmth that's not in the form of a lovely but sometimes sticky six-year-old. Kath said to be grateful for what I have and I totally am, but right now I want to be grateful for Theo. I want him to stay in my life. It feels like the day moves from mummyhood to having my own brain back again, and I can turn my full, undivided attention to my night with Theo.

We can't go anywhere because I don't have a babysitter (and I don't want to go on bothering Kath, especially as I keep forgetting to ring her since my vow to check in a bit more and I feel like a bit of a crappy niece), but I'm going to show Theo how much fun we can have at home. I've preened, prepped and tweezed. I nip into the bathroom for a hot shower to freshen up. I'm just about to step into the steamy cubicle when my phone buzzes: *Be there in two!* from Theo.

Shit! No time for a shower, but I really do want to freshen up. I grab a flannel (really wish it didn't have Cinderella's face on it staring up at me), run it under the hot tap and give myself a little stand-up wash in my you-know-where. There's absolutely no dignity in this, but needs must.

I fling the flannel (sorry Cinders) in the laundry basket and pull on a lacy black thong and my dark skinny jeans – the good ones, not the ones where the inner thigh area is wearing away. I hate thongs, but it's imperative Theo continues to think I spend my life walking around in delicate matching underwear. I want him to be so enamoured by me he never stands me up again. He need never know that my pants of choice would be full cotton briefs with loose elastic.

Perfume spritzed, hair zhooshed, nether regions almost cut in two by undergarments: I'm ready for him.

I wait a few seconds after the doorbell's rung, just so he thinks I haven't been stood here watching him pull onto the drive and get out of his car, which I totally have. I open the door with a smile.

'Evening, gorgeous,' says Theo at the same time as bending over and kissing my cheek. He's clearly come straight from work, as he walks past me in his well-tailored navy suit, shirt already unbuttoned and tie in hand. Ugh, he's actually perfect. The last traces of my anger after the Parents and Partners night melt away.

He hands me a bottle of Malbec and bag of Minstrels (see? Perfect), and I stand there still smiling and wishing I could think of something equally perfect to say. We've done this for nearly three months now, but I'm still overwhelmed when he arrives. It's like that butterfly feeling but on steroids.

'Hi.' A good effort there. 'Wine and chocolates, you certainly know how to please a lady.'

'I know how to please the right lady,' he quips back with a wink, and walks off with a swagger to investigate the kitchen while I stand there in shock. Did he just call me Miss Right? Yes? No? Maybe? I don't know.

'Something smells amazing, Robin, you shouldn't have done all this.'

'Oh, it was nothing.' That's a lie. I've spent the best part of the afternoon on all of this. Breezy-breezy; he doesn't need to know that. 'I love cooking, and it's all the better when I have someone appreciative to cook for. Lyla doesn't really care for anything that isn't breadcrumbed and dipped in ketchup.'

'Bless her. How is she? Tucked up in bed?' I love how much he cares about her.

'Yep; she asked if you were coming, and I promised she'd see you tomorrow. I'm so pleased she's taken to you. I thought it might be a struggle, but I think you've really hit it off.'

'Oh, good. Now, where are the wine glasses? This red needs to breathe.' (I personally never bother, but this is the kind of man he is). As he opens and shuts cupboards until he finds them I start putting the veg in to blanch, check on the fingerling potatoes and I feel blissful. Just two happy grown-ups, making a meal, working as a team, enjoying the simplicities of life.

Before I can completely lose myself in the 'Robin and Theo' daydream, I feel Theo's arms wrap around my waist and turn me towards him.

'The green beans – I need to keep my eye on them,' I protest.

'Fuck the green beans,' comes the response very, very close to my face with his brown eyes glinting mischievously. 'I want to kiss you. It's been a long week, and you look like you very much need to be kissed.'

'Do I?' I ask in between tiny kisses from him on my jawline, neck and ear. Oh my God, I am losing my mind ever so slightly.

'Yes. On your neck,' kiss, kiss, 'on your cheek,' kiss, kiss, 'on your mouth.'

'Mmmm . . . OK.' And that's it. The beans are overdone. I don't care. I'd far rather be pushed up against the kitchen wall being kissed by the most perfect man in the world than have a good bite to my beans.

We stand there – well, I'm leaning because I can barely use my legs right now – kissing like teenagers until, just before it gets too hot to resist, I muster a shred of willpower, push Theo off and insist that the chicken needs taking out of the oven. I want this evening to be special and go the way I'd planned.

'This had better be the best chicken in the world for tearing me off you,' he protests.

'It'll be the most burnt chicken in the world if I don't dish it up right now.'

'Burn it, let me have you and we'll order pizza.' He sounds almost desperate. I quite like it, and although I'm toying with the idea, I'm going to make him wait. I love how much he wants me. Also I slaved hard over this chicken. Pizza, indeed!

Reluctantly he sits at my kitchen table (which, of course, I've cleared of unopened bills and debris) and I serve the food. We eat, and it's delicious. Theo tells me vaguely of his latest acquisition (I try to follow along, but he gives no real details and I don't really want to ask) and after a little while and a glass of red, we're done. All I can think about is how uncomfortable this lacy thong is and how much I'd like to be out of it.

'That was amazing,' Theo says, putting his knife and fork down and breathing out heavily. 'I forgot how much I miss home-cooked food during the week.'

'Yes; eating out in great restaurants every night must be so challenging for you, Theo. I don't know how you stomach it.'

'You tease, but seriously it's not as good as you think. There's something much more real about eating with you, at your kitchen table, with food served out of dishes you've used a hundred times and Lyla's paintings all over the fridge. It just feels like proper home food, like being a kid again. Mother was never very maternal, but before I went away to school we had this amazing nanny called Isla who used to cook every night and sit with me at the big oak table, and I loved it. I miss dinners at home like this.' Wow, I didn't know he felt so intensely about it. I'd have thought eating out every night was the dream.

'Do you miss being part of a family?' I ask, adjusting myself in my chair so I can listen to his answer without my thong cutting off the blood circulation to my groin.

'Yes and no. I've lived alone my entire adult life, but I do miss home life, or as much of a home life as I had with my parents both working a lot and me being mostly with Isla or away at school, I suppose. But then, I like my space and my tidy environment and the perks that come with that,' he muses, sitting back and taking a big sip of his Malbec. He looks so vulnerable when he's talking quietly about his family life like this. He isn't showing off or being the big shot in town, and I feel like I'm actually seeing a glimmer of his heart.

I'm not sure what to say to him, really. I'd like to go back to his apartment. Is it odd that he only ever comes to mine? I'm mostly just glad I hid all the toys and put all my junk away. I'm surprised he's lived alone his entire adult life, though. How has he not had a long-term girlfriend or something? When do I ask a question like this? Would he want to have a scatty woman and her energetic six-year-old running around his minimalistic glass and steel tower? He looks a bit forlorn, so this probably isn't the best time and I don't want to spoil a lovely evening. Plus I'm wearing a thong that I swear is slowly getting tighter and cutting off the circulation to my legs – so the sooner that comes off, the better.

'Shall we go through to the lounge? All the candles are lit and I can put a film on.'

'Why don't we go through to the lounge and skip the film?'

'That sounds like my kind of plan.' So very, very glad I violated Cinderella's face now.

Half an hour later and the Thong of Pain is a distant memory, as are all of Theo's clothes. We kissed again like we did in the kitchen, but this time more passionately, more boldly. The weight of Theo on top of me was so welcome. He makes me feel appreciated and protected when his arms are wrapped tight around me, and I like it. After a good while of kissing things get a bit heated, and with no struggle at all he deftly flips us over so I'm on him and he's lying down. His hands are in my hair and I think I'm about to have the best head massage of my life, judging by all the skills he's ever shown with his hands, but no; he's being quite clear with what he wants, pushing my head south.

I'm very generous. Twenty minutes and extreme jaw ache kind of generous. Theo, at this point, is a very happy man and I hope my generosity and its outcome aren't the finale, but despite my best efforts at hinting for more, it appears it is. I squash myself sideways between him and the back of the sofa and I nuzzle into his neck. He smells great. I don't know what his aftershave is but the crazy in me wants to buy it so I can smell it during the day and think of him.

I look over at him and he's closed his eyes. He looks so

content. I'd quite like to look content too, but it seems like that's off the cards. He's had a long week, though, poor thing.

You should be glad just to have a man here at all, Robin.

Realising we can't sleep naked on the sofa all night – imagine Lyla walking down to see that? It'd be far more mentally scarring than the dating app incident, and I'm still hung up on that – I heave myself out of my uncomfortable position and pick up all the strewn clothes.

'Theo,' I whisper. 'Theo, we need to go upstairs.'

'What?' he mumbles, clearly half-asleep.

'We need to go and sleep upstairs. Lyla can't wake up to find naked people in the lounge.'

'For fuck's sake,' he says under his breath, hauls himself up and walks past me to the stairs without so much as a half-arsed kiss on the forehead.

Not exactly how I'd hoped the night would end, but he probably has a lot on his mind. I'm sure he'll be cheerier in the morning.

I follow him up, nip to the loo and then get into bed with him. He's already asleep, facing away from me, so I scooch up to him and be Big Spoon until, finally, I fall asleep too.

When I wake up, he's already left.

TWENTY-FIVE

I 'M SAT ON MY hotel bed sandwiched between my laptop (essential for top work research and, mostly, Netflix) and a tube of sour cream Pringles from the corner shop which might be the saddest dinner I've ever 'made' myself. My excitement has faded to worry, which is now transitioning into humiliation. Hotel rooms are lonely places to feel sad.

Natalie and I have been working in Bath on the set of a new indie band's (apparently the next big thing) music video. We drove up on Monday, started on Tuesday and now, Friday, it's the wrap party. I say 'party', but really I mean pub crawl.

We were going to go for a few drinks, show our faces and be part of the team. I couldn't imagine Natalie on a pub crawl (the only pub I can imagine her in is a country bistro – one with a solid specials board), but in the end I didn't have to. Martin rang her several times throughout the job, and each time she'd finished a call she smiled even wider when she said, 'Fine, fine,' to 'Everything OK?' I don't think anyone else would have seen through her calm swanlike exterior, but I could see her feathers were ruffled, so I wasn't that surprised when she said she was going to drive back a night early and 'spend some time' with her husband. Natalie's so lucky to have someone so desperate to be in her company. I hope everything's OK.

Theo and I haven't seen each other in a couple of weeks. I messaged him a few casual, breezy texts, then a ha-ha-so-funny *have you fallen off the face of the earth?* text, and then followed that up with an *OK cool, I'll leave you be then* message. In fairness, that last one was hotel-bar-cheap-wine-induced, so I'm not sure we can count that one, but Theo did and replied this morning saying, *Gosh, so sorry, haven't seen any messages, just been so busy, let's FaceTime tonight at 9.*

Result! Admittedly there's no warmth, sweetness or kisses in there, but his text style is time-efficient, I guess. When he's with me he's so perfect, so attentive, and it's like he's reading me, working out what I like, what I don't, what I want, how he can make it happen. It feels exquisite to have someone pay you that much charming attention. So when he sends short, businessy messages, I don't sweat it, that's just how he rolls.

Once we'd packed up our kit, Natalie had driven home and I'd walked back to the hotel, past Bath's beautiful creamy stone buildings and wrought iron railings with the rest of the

229

guys from the shoot, I made my excuses in the lobby. Fearing they'd think I was a massive bellend if I said, 'Soz, guys, I can't come out, I'm waiting for the man I'm in love with but who sometimes ignores me a bit to call', I went with a different version of the truth and said, 'I'd love to come out but I'm waiting on an important call from a relative', and then pulled a pained face. Nobody questions a 'call from a relative' if you add a pained face. The British don't want to delve into that potential mess of awkward conversation, so they all just nodded, gave me hugs, ruffled my hair, said goodbye and thanks a lot and off I skipped, giddy that soon it would be just me and Theo alone in a hotel room. Sort of.

I FaceTimed Lyla at her dad's, washed my hair, packed my stuff for tomorrow and waited.

And waited.

And waited.

By 9.30 p.m. I caved and tried calling him, but there was no response. At 10 I texted casually, saying, *Hey, I'm free for a call now if you are? x*, but there was no response to that either. Bastard.

So here I am. It's 11.03, I'm alone in my Travelodge hotel room, not FaceTiming with my gorgeous man but eating an entire tube of Pringles and feeling hollow. It feels so shit to be picked up and played with and then completely discarded like this. I feel embarrassed at my own neediness. I wish I'd gone out and joined in the 'mad bants' after all.

* * *

A WEEK LATER AND Natalie and I are in the car home after a brilliant day on set for a short YouTube film.

The vibe was young and creative.

It was an action film, so touch-ups for the men, beauty for the women and dirt, gunpowder and general muck for everyone. It was easy to get into my rhythm and lose myself in the work. I chatted to the actors, deftly flitted between brushes and took great pride in seeing them leave my chair looking exactly like they'd been fighting heroically in a derelict building.

We're only an hour away from home, and I've been looking forward to a catch-up with Natalie.

'Were you OK the other night, after you had to drive home early?' I start as we set off in the car. I didn't want to say anything on set, but she'd seemed tense when she left.

'Yes, absolutely! Lovely to get home early.' Then, a lightning-quick change of tack: 'So, you did really well today, Robin, great work,' she says, keeping her eyes on the manic London traffic.

'Thank you! I really appreciate that, Natalie.'

'How've things been going outside of work, then?' she asks casually.

'Not too bad. I'm still sort of seeing that guy from the Foundation Bar I met a few months back, Lyla's great, I'm enjoying all the extra jobs you've had me on. Really happy, actually.' Natalie is a friend, but not like a Lacey or Piper friend. I never forget that she's my boss, and refrain from moaning about Kath's unsolicited 'makeover' of my bedroom last month ('I just thought you could do with a bit more lace in here, darling; lace is *very* sexy,' she'd assured me when I recoiled at the sheer amount of lacy fabric she'd glue-gunned to every nook and cranny that I've since had to peel off before Theo saw), or worrying about how snide Val Pickering can be. I give her the highlights reel and try to keep the focus on work.

'What about you? You look like you had a lovely time in Paris this weekend. From Facebook, I mean. I wasn't stalking you. Ha ha ha.' God, I hate my nervous laugh.

'It was lovely, thank you, Robin; glad you enjoyed our photos. Martin surprised me, actually. We've been so busy lately with Max and Daniel doing mocks and exams and Nathan moving to university and the agency doing so well, we haven't had a whole lot of time to just be. Now the boys are a bit more independent, Daniel and Nathan driving and Max so occupied with his sports and school, I think Martin's a bit restless, needs something more to do, you know? Something to focus him.'

'I know, it can get like that, can't it? When you just drift a bit?'

'No! No, no, we're not drifting,' she answers a bit too quickly. 'It's wonderful the agency has been so busy; it's afforded us so many fantastic opportunities and really given the boys a brilliant start, but I just mean it's an extra treat for Martin and I to jet off for a minibreak. It's not that we're drifting. We just need something special to focus on.'

Wow. That was only the second time I've ever detected a ruffle in Natalie's feathers. She's usually so unflappable. I don't want to pry, so I move the subject on to something much safer – business.

'Oh no, I didn't mean it like that at all! Martin's so lovely, I bet he's thrilled the agency's doing so well. I love it because it means I'm getting more jobs, Lyla and I get to have a few more treats and I get out of the house. It's great!'

'And you deserve them, you work so hard. I watched you today, and I think your technical work is coming on in leaps and bounds, and your confidence is shining through beautifully as well. I can see you love it.'

'I really do; it's such a buzz to be in that environment, talking to new people, doing something I'm so passionate about. Thank you, Natalie, for always being such a great mentor. It means such a lot, you know.'

'Well, I think you're about to thank me a whole lot more!' she says like a mother who's about to treat the kids to a McDonald's. Mmm, I'd be more than happy if she were about to do that, actually. I'm starving.

'Ooohh, OK . . .' I say, playing along with the excitement.

'Look. There's something I want to ask you. We've had something quite exciting in. A film franchise are set to make a series of horror movies, and they've heard great things about the agency.'

'Oh *wow*, how cool!'

'They'd like a senior artist and assistant to work on set for two to three weeks full-time, and I'd love it if you'd assist me. I know we've spoken before about you only working on local jobs, to be close to Lyla and home, but this one really is something unique. I think you're ready for a job like this. I think you're ready to push yourself to those creative limits and give it a go.'

'Wow! I'm so flattered to be asked. I think I could see if Kath would help me with school pickups here and there, and I'm sure Simon could have Lyla as well. How exciting! Thank you!'

'Before you agree to it, I should probably mention . . .' Natalie pauses excitedly, 'it's in New York! This is the first film, and it would be a trial contract. If things go well, we'd win the deal and work on all five of them over the next few years. The rest are going to be shot in the UK, but this first one needs to be filmed in part on location over there so they want to find the team they'll be using long-term in the UK. It'd be incredible for the agency's portfolio, but also amazing for your own personal portfolio. They already have a special effects team booked for the latex work, which I want to learn more about, and really challenge myself with some of that, but they need beauty work and touch-ups and creative support and advice. Seeing how hard you've worked all these years, and watching you when you're in the zone on a job, I just know this would be perfect for you. I think it's time you challenged yourself to do more. I know you have it in you to take on bigger jobs and step up to them. I want you to be my right-hand woman, Robin.'

I'm stunned.

For one, I can't believe Natalie has so much faith in me, Robin Wilde, the girl with mystery Sharpie all over her leggings, and two, New-freaking-York! For a second I feel excited. And then panic kicks in. I can't go to New York! I'm a mum! My mind starts going into overdrive as we turn onto the motorway and I don't know what to say. First, I can't leave Lyla. She needs me. She'd probably be all right with Kath and Simon for a short while, but maybe *I* need *her* – she's who I am. Without my daughter around, I wouldn't know who I am. Also, New York is so busy, so on the go. I like my pace of life. I like a quiet glass of wine at night. Well, I'm just used to it, I guess. I can't imagine myself in New York. I can't even imagine myself on the plane, let alone bossing a job on the other side of the world. What if there were an emergency at home. What if . . . What about Theo?

'Natalie, I'm . . . wow New York . . . that's so far. I don't know if I could leave Lyla. I'm not sure . . . Look. I'm sorry . . . I just can't. I'm sorry.'

'Take some time to think about it,' Natalie says calmly, eyes on the road.

Once she's dropped me off, I put my things in the house (months on, and I'm still loving my cleared-out cupboard and easy make-up kit storage, I feel so smug every time I use it) and go to collect Lyla from Kath's. I'm so looking forward to seeing her. I've felt a bit guilty for working so much these past few weeks, and even the prospect of going to New York for half a month, let alone disappointing Natalie because I simply can't go, has been whizzing around in my head and making me anxious.

I know having her home will soothe me, so I grab my car keys and head out the door.

LEAVING KATH'S HOUSE, I can feel my footsteps slamming against the concrete as I thunder down her drive to my car. I'm furious. Every inch of my body feels prickly with heat. How *dare* she? How dare she make this choice without me?

Opening the car door for Lyla, I seem to employ that super-strength you only have when you're super-mad and almost rip it clean off. Well, probably not, but it feels like I could, I'm that angry.

Lyla climbs in silently and I slam the door shut so hard I see her midnight-blue eyes widen in shocked fright. I feel instant guilt for scaring her. Brilliant. Another wretched emotion on top of the rage.

Thunder, thunder, thunder with my ballet flats on the tarmac, and I'm round to my side of the car and in the driver's seat. Good. The faster we get away from that selfish old cow the better. Driving away feels good. The sound of the car whirring washes over me and I can feel calm being restored. Thank goodness. Driving that angry was teetering on dangerous. The Mother of the Year Award committee won't be knocking on my door any time soon.

Very quietly from the back I hear Lyla's mouse-like voice tentatively ask, 'Mummy? Are you cross?'

'Yes baby. Very cross.'

'At me?' Her voice trembles as she queries, and the instant guilt at making her feel like it was her fault resurfaces.

'No. At Auntie Kath. She shouldn't have cut your hair without asking me first.'

When I say it out loud it sounds so trivial, like it's nothing at all; but it is something. A haircut is a thing. You see those poor children on the news with dirty clothes and scraggly hair and pity them. You assume they aren't well taken care of. You assume nobody is there to love them. You see a smart, well-groomed, clean kiddo and know they are cared for and loved. *Loved* is the key word here. I love Lyla, I'm her main love-giver, and so haircuts are on my shoulders. A haircut isn't a daily thing, it's an event. Arranging that would have shown that I have everything in hand, that I can balance home and work and that I can handle my life. I can manage it all. I can, I can, I can.

Then Kath muscled in and thought she was in charge. No call to ask, no consideration for me, just snip, snip, snip, done. I should have been in control of that. Not doing it has made me feel like crap. Like my life is the mess I secretly fear it is. I was going to book a salon appointment, but I didn't have time. Was her hair really so desperate? Did she look like the pitiful children off the news, and I'm such a shoddy mother that I just didn't notice?

I look in the mirror and I can see the cogs turning in her tiny head.

'Auntie Kath has all the best scissors, Mummy. We were playing salons and I told her I wanted my hair short at the front like yours.'

'In a fringe?'

'Yes! I wanted to have Mummy Hair, so Auntie Kath said we could surprise you and you wouldn't be cross because it's a "lovely surprise". Auntie Kath didn't cut my hair in a cross way, Mummy. She cut it in a loves-and-cuddles way.'

I can feel my heart softening. 'A loves and cuddles' way means Lyla felt cared for and special, and I can't begrudge her that, can I? That's how you want your child to feel always.

Cogs still seem to be turning. 'Do you think it looks rubbish, Mummy?'

'No, I love it, I just wanted to be there—'

'Then if you love it, why are you so cross?'

Can't argue with that kind of logic, I guess. Starting to feel like maybe I overreacted very slightly.

'Lyla, I'm your mummy and I love you so, so, so much. More than you can ever imagine. I love you so much that I want to be at everything you do. To help you do it right or not to feel scared or to protect you.'

'But I wasn't scared, and Auntie Kath did do it right

because she has all the special hair-cutting scissors from when she was a hair lady in the olden days.'

How am I being outdone by a six-year-old?

'Yes, I know. But I wanted to be there. That's all. I just wanted to be there.'

'Then how would you have been at work helping Natalie? Auntie Kath said you were doing a very important job and that you work *sooo* hard that we could do a lovely surprise for you.'

I love that she takes my job seriously. I'm sure everyone else thinks I do nothing all day, or that there is no skill in it, but the joy of children is that they have no judgement, and if you say you're working, to them, you're working. I hope she never loses that trust. I hope I never ruin it.

'I just wanted to be there, Lyla.'

Quick as a flash she replies, 'I wants don't get.'

Argh, why did I teach her that? I don't need my own quips thrown in my face when I'm so angry I've given myself a tension headache.

'Mummy, I don't want you to be cross with Auntie Kath or she won't want to play with us again. You've got to use your indoor voice and kind actions, or people will have hurt feelings.' She says this to me like I'm new to the world and haven't had any experience in basic communication before.

'I know, baby. I'm sorry. I shouldn't have been cross.' Hopefully that will placate her for now.

I pull into the drive and feel ten notches calmer already.

Nothing takes the edge off things like the innocent reasoning skills of a child.

Once we're in and settled (*Peter Pan* for Lyla, the secret Galaxy bar I hid behind the tinned beans for me), I look properly at my little girl. I'm constantly astounded at how perfect she actually is. Dainty rosebud lips; clear, pale skin with the faintest of freckles; deep-blue eyes and the kind of elfin nose that every 'it' girl in Hollywood would die for. And now she has a fringe, and eight inches has been lopped off her once bum-/waist-length locks. Does it look terrible? No, I suppose it doesn't. The fringe softens her slender face and gives it a sort of roundness I miss from her baby days. The length still swings down her back, but now it looks healthy and somehow thicker. I absent-mindedly stroke my hand down it and feel how silky it is under my fingers. God, I love her. Before I had Lyla I didn't have any comprehension of how much I could physically love a person. Sometimes when she's there, squeezed up next to me on the sofa, I run my fingers through her hair and feel like my heart could burst.

'Do you like it now, Mummy?' she says, jolting me back from my deep thoughts.

'Yes. It's lovely, just like you.'

'Will you be friends with Auntie Kath again?'

'Yes.'

'You were so cross and shouty. Do you think you'll have to say your biggest sorry?'

'I think so.'

I do think so. I was awful, and Kath knows it. Lyla is lucky to have her, and so am I. Time to get my grovel on, I think.

THAT NIGHT I CALL Theo to talk to him about everything. Communication has been really lacking lately, with a few sporadic messages since the night in Bath but nothing concrete, and I don't know where we are with things at all. After not really hearing from him, being nervous and confused about the New York offer and the whole Kath debacle, I'm feeling really anxious and I'm hoping that by speaking to him, we can sort things out and I can maybe get back on track a bit. I could do with the support, and Theo really is the person I want it from. I know he can make me feel better.

I've put Lyla to bed, settled on the sofa with crap TV and a gin and tonic and I pick up my phone to call. It rings out for a frustratingly long time but eventually, in true Theo form, he answers like nothing has ever been wrong.

'Hello darling, how's tricks?'

I don't know why, but I'm instantly angry. How dare he be so nonchalant about the fact we've barely spoken in a couple of weeks. Obviously, though, I must appear to be the very essence of breezy and let him think I've been having the best few days of my entire life.

'Hey! Yeaaahh, great, thanks! What about you?'

'You know, just up the bloody wall with things at the office, and missing my favourite make-up artist.'

If he was missing me that much, why didn't he just call? Maybe I don't want to offload everything on him. I feel like I could slap him for being so slimy.

'Oh really? How charming of you. Things have been quite busy here lately, with work and social life, crazy, crazy, as always!'

If by crazy you mean working three days this week, washing, shopping, cleaning, cooking, defrosting the freezer and playing a thousand games of Shopkins with a six-year-old.

'Absolutely. Yes. Very busy,' he says, clearly distracted by something. 'Why don't we have a weekend soon? Just me and you. Give Lyla to Kath, and let us have some fun, eh?'

I knew he'd pull through. A weekend of fun is exactly what I'd like right now.

'Amazing! I'd love that! Do you want to come up here, and I can rearrange dinner with some of my friends and their other halves? It'd be nice for you to meet them, and—'

'No; why don't you come down to me and let me treat you? We could do a spa, perhaps? Or a fun little day on the Thames if you fancy? Surely that's nicer than dinner with the mums from school?'

He's got a point, but I really did want them to meet him. I feel torn now. Boating on the river and a massage sounds better than a thousand custard creams alone or pasta with the parents, but I feel like he's saying spending time at our house isn't good enough. I want to let it go, but after my run-in with Kath, I'm not in a very agreeable mood.

'Theo, don't you like coming up here any more?'

'Of course I do, darling, but I think we both know it's more comfortable at my place, don't we?'

How rude! There's nothing wrong with my place! It might not be a city apartment with floor-to-ceiling windows overlooking the Thames, but it's got views, wonderful views, if you like the top of my neighbours' garage and an old Frisbee that's been there years. Anyway, yes, OK, maybe his place is nicer than mine – not that I really remember it very well, having only actually been invited once – but that's not the point. He should be making things up to me, after leaving me hanging so often, and if he really did like me, if I really was his 'favourite', then he'd be happy to drive up here and be part of my life. Wouldn't he?

I'm so sick of everything being hard work, and feeling so crummy all the time. I'm a shoddy mother, crap at dressing myself (I'm wearing a T-shirt with Sharpie on, for fuck's sake), Kath probably hates me and I'm going to be alone forever.

Picking up on the silence, Theo continues, 'How does the end of this month sound to you?'

Did I just hear that right? That's three weeks away!

He thinks he can just charm his way into having it however he wants. Well, he can't.

Summoning everything I have, I say, 'Look, a date every

six weeks isn't good enough for me. If we're going to be a thing, whatever this thing is, it should be easier than this. We should be in each other's lives properly, like normal couples are. This isn't working for me.' And then I go further than I'd ever expected I would. 'I need a break, Theo. From us. Anyway, I'm not free at the end of this month. Because I'm working on a movie set in New York.'

Drop the mic. That's decided, then.

Part Four

New York, New York

TWENTY-SIX

JULY

I DID IT! I, Robin Wilde, single mum and part-time make-up assistant, am here in the most amazing city in the world.

For a moment I was worried I was really going to hate it here. Stepping off the plane, I instantly felt overwhelmed. On the plane I felt fine. On the plane was safe and secure and cosy. I was squished up in my seat, shovelling sour cream pretzels into my mouth, and I watched all the films I haven't had the chance to see at the cinema because, frankly, I've got nobody to go with. Theo was more of a theatre person (and not fun plays like musicals in the West End, more confusing make-you-think plays with no real ending. We went to one back in the spring, and I had to use all my energy to muster a 'so abstract! Loved it!') but sometimes you just want to gorge on overpriced popcorn and watch superheroes smash up cities, right? My shoes were off, I had my blanket draped over me and I felt absolutely fine looking like crap. On a plane you're in a club where it's perfectly acceptable to spend a day out in public in clothes so comfortable they're practically pyjamas and hair so messy you look like you've just had sex. It's airplane chic. Everyone's in the same boat (or, well, plane) and everyone gets it. I'd love real life to be like that. Let's all just go around in grey jogging bottoms and call it quits. Saying that, I can't imagine Natalie in a pair of joggers; I doubt she even owns such a thing. Her version of relaxing is wearing her two-year-old skinny Armani jeans instead of the brand new ones.

But once we were off the plane, it felt very different. Gone were the days of a nice lady bringing drinks to my seat, and now it was time to leg it to customs. I didn't fully know why we all ran, but my God, run we did. It was like a herd of antelope running to the watering hole before the warthogs got there and spoilt it for everyone.

My feet felt quite swollen crammed into my flats (how in the name of absolute arse do celebrities disembark in heels and a bare-faced glow?). Airplane chic now felt less OK on land. I looked like I'd been living off the earth in a forest for the past eighteen months, not like I'd reclined gently on a six-hour flight. Obviously, Natalie looked incredible. Hair perfectly in position, skin glowing, feet not like slabs of swollen flesh. She's just winning at life again. You'd think she'd been in first class, but no; she just looks this way regardless. She's wearing some black pixie pants, a light-knit cream tunic and a huge, soft-caramel cashmere pashmina across her shoulders. If anything, celebrities get their inspiration from her. Oh, and she's wearing wedges, which I'd class as a heel. Jolly good.

We made it to customs – me breathless and sweaty, Natalie calm and collected – and spent fifteen minutes in the back-and-forth winding queue system. There's something really unwelcoming about customs. There are signs everywhere and tannoys barking rules and orders at us, aggressively telling us we can't bring seeds or tropical fruits into the country. Once I make it to the customs officer in his cubicle, he fires a lot of questions at me: What do I do? Where am I staying? What brought me to New York? I felt like I was on a very intense speed date but without the potential for a phone number and a snog at the end.

Eventually we were done. Customs was ticked, baggage was collected and now we're in a yellow cab hurtling (well, chugging slowly through thick traffic) towards the Big Apple! Suddenly a wave of fizzy excitement washes over me and I'm exhilarated at the thought of being here.

ONCE WE WERE OUT of the airport and the taxi driver had tried and failed making conversation with us so we could all settle into a comfortable, polite and thoroughly British silence, I stared out of the window at the rows and rows of wooden-slatted houses, all different colours, some with porches, some with American flags, some with broken children's toys in the front gardens, and imagine life here. Imagine if Lyla and I lived here, instead of on the outskirts of Cambridge, and for work I occasionally popped into Manhattan instead of London. She'd go to a New York school on a yellow bus and I could sit out on my porch steps in the evening, instead of the breakfast bar in the kitchen, scrolling through my dating apps. Suddenly that idea seems much more glamorous than my reality.

As we head closer to the city, we move away from the houses and apartment buildings, cross over a vast bridge (I wish I had noted which one, so I could make intelligent conversation or have some sense of direction – I feel very lost) and we're in the city. We are in Manhattan! I gaze hungrily out of the window just soaking up every ounce of what I can see. It's sensory overload. My first time in the Big Apple! YES!

The buildings are so tall and gleaming that I can't see where they end and the sky begins, and every space on the pavement is taken up by every kind of person you can imagine, walking briskly with purpose and importance. I can't imagine anyone I know walking like that. Maybe Natalie on the way to a meeting, but that's about it. Women in heels, men in dress shoes, teenagers in trainers, kids in pushchairs, old folk in sandals, dogs on leads, tired-looking individuals handing out leaflets and being ignored, suits yapping angrily into mobile phones and girls not looking where they're going while they text. Every ground floor bit of building is a shop or restaurant or business, with a stylish lobby of concrete furniture and one signature succulent on the trendy cardboard coffee table. We don't go more than ten seconds without seeing scaffolding or construction work, and we move no more than three centimetres without being in a total kaleidoscope of colour. Everywhere you look is a rainbow. Lyla would love the energy here, I think fondly. People are colourful, shops are enticing, lights are flashing in every direction. It's like New York took a look at itself and said 'more, we want more', and dialled everything up by 40 per cent. I have never, ever seen a place more alive, or felt somewhere with more energy. Manhattan makes the corner of Oxford Street by Topshop on a summer Saturday look sleepy. This place is incredible.

As I OPEN THE door to my hotel room, I feel a great sense of relief. As exciting as the hour-long drive from JFK was, I'm acutely aware that I'm not in sleepy suburbia any more and I'm starting to feel a little out of my depth.

The empty bedroom is a sweet refuge. I drag my case in (to say I've overpacked is an understatement), and leave it by the chest of drawers with a TV on it and take stock. The room is nice. Basic but clean; there's a decent en suite and a showstopping view of an alley with giant dumpsters. It's quiet, though, and for the first time in a while I'm completely alone. No Natalie, no Lyla asking questions, no Auntie Kath popping by unsolicited – just me, in New York, with a suit-case of clothes.

Good grief! I suddenly feel happy and homesick at the same time.

I message Kath and tell her I've landed safely and ask how Lyla's getting on at hers. I don't want to worry her with any feelings of homesickness; she'll only ring me excessively every day to check I'm all right and I'm sure, after a while, I will be. Ever since the haircut debacle and my heartfelt, grovelling apology to her, things have been a touch cooler. Not frosty, but not our usual easy-going warmth. It'll ease in time, but right now I don't feel she's the first person I should turn to.

Instinctively I reach for my phone and message Theo. We might not be a couple any more (if we ever were), but we can still be friends. We never said we wouldn't be friendly to each other. Theo travels all the time for work, so I'm sure he'll be interested in my trip and would offer some friendly advice and support. It's not a big deal; a friendly text here and there is actually a very mature way to handle everything I think.

I've arrived! New York is crazy! So busy! Feeling a bit weird and overwhelmed. Could do with a familiar face. Fancy a chat? As a friend. I think that's cool. Short and sweet, but clear that I want a bit of comforting and that I'm not looking for anything more than a bit of friendship. I hate myself as soon as I've done it, though. It's the first time I've caved in three weeks, but he did send me a friendly *good luck* message just before I got on the plane.

Quickly the dot-dot-dots appear and I'm instantly relieved. Like a knight in shining armour, Theo will know what to say to get me in the mood to face the city.

Hey! Great news! he types back.

Maybe he didn't read it properly.

Yep! So great! Do you want to FaceTime?

Dot-dot-dots bubble up.

Can't right now. Just heading out to the gym.

Oh cool. As long as Theo-the-selfish-prick is all right then, I'd best not make a fuss. I feel like throwing my phone across the room. Not so much because I'm angry at him (although I do want to scream at him for being such an insensitive dicksplash) – it's what I've come to expect – but because I'm annoyed at myself. Why did I make Theo the first person I went to for comfort or help? He's never really offered me any support unless it suits him. He's not a friend; he never was. Why did I let myself be fooled? I'm such an idiot.

I don't want to appear needy, so I resolve to be the bigger person and ignore him for a few days, as per – not that he'll notice. I'll be sure to post some really sexy black-and-white selfie shots to Instagram during that time. That will show him.

After a few minutes of venomous thoughts about Theo while checking out the minibar and sniffing the complimentary mini-toiletries in the en suite, I reach for my phone and pull up Kath's number in my contacts. It's late afternoon here, so they'll be awake over there. I'd spent a solid forty-five minutes explaining and practising FaceTime with her earlier in the week, so hopefully she'll answer.

Kath's face flashes up on the screen way, way too close. I can see up her nose.

'Robin!! Hello!' Kath booms. We clearly didn't practise volume control.

'Hello, Kath! I've arriv—'

'Oh, you've arrived safely, have you?' she booms back before I can even finish my sentence. She knows I've arrived safely. I texted her earlier. Deep breaths, deep breaths.

'Yep! Flight was quite g—'

'How was the flight?' she half-yells. She clearly hasn't yet mastered the art of FT.

'Kath, I can hear you really well. Just talk to me like you would normally.'

'Sorry, love, you know how I am! I'm just amazed I can see you all the way in New York! How is the phone managing with the time difference, eh?'

'Ha! I know! Amazing. How are you? Is Lyla being good?' Let's just get to the important bits.

'Yessss, here she is.' Kath swivels the phone around to reveal my sweet baby on the sofa covered almost head to toe in wool, string and ribbons. It's like a haberdashery has vomited all over her.

'Wow! Hello baby! What's happened?'

'We're finger-knitting, Mummy!' says Lyla as if all her Christmases have come at once.

'What's finger-knitting?'

'We ripped up your old jumper and now we're making something new with just our fingers!' Lyla replies very jubilantly. 'And Auntie Kath keeps forgetting my name! She calls me Robin or Mollie and Mummy, it's SO funny!' she chuckles. I can't think about Kath's ditzy brain right now; please God, not my good Zara jumper.

'You ripped up my old jum—'

'No, darling! No, no! I've got one of your woolly jumpers from when you were little. It's far too naff to be worn again, so we unravelled it and now we're doing some really marvellous finger-knitting. Suzanne at the WI does it all the time! She absolutely loves a good finger session!' chimes Kath.

'I bet she does.'

'She really does!' Kath smiles into the camera, blissfully unaware of the suggestiveness of her comment.

'Mummy, I'm going to finger-knit you the best dress ever, and you can wear it to a ball with a Prince Charming, and then I'll teach you to knit and we can do it all together. We can be the knitting family!'

Her enthusiasm is infectious, and before I know it I'm having a full-blown conversation about how many things I can't wait to finger-knit.

I feel wobbly when I blow them both kisses and their faces freeze then disappear. Even though I'm going to stick to store-bought clothes and give finger-knitted trousers a miss, I love that Kath is doing this. She's so like Dad, always tinkering away in the shed, making something and teaching me how to do it too. I miss those days, before they moved. Mum thought her health (she had mild asthma, but in her overdramatic mind she was at death's door twice a week) would improve if they lived by the coast and she could breathe the 'superior sea air'. Dad being Dad obliged her, of course. I'm *so* grateful for Kath, really, despite her passion for 7 a.m. 'let's get out and about' calls and her penchant for 'customising' my things. We managed to iron out the haircut incident before I left, and she has been so good about Lyla – she offered to take her as soon as I told her what Natalie had said. She's such a rock I realise I so rarely tell her that. I feel bad. Maybe I should message her again.

I ping over a text: *Kath, you're the best. Thank you for being such a star in our lives xxxx*, I'm already learning that you can be in the most incredible city on earth but that what you really need is your people, your team, and that's real happiness.

Well, that and a full minibar of tiny liquor bottles and no need for a babysitter. Hello, New York, I've arrived!

TWENTY-SEVEN

IRST DAY ON SET, and it's like nothing I've experienced before. Everywhere I look something is happening, and the atmosphere is electric.

Our make-up station is enormous, the largest I've ever seen, and rather than just our tiny team of two, there are three other MUAs focusing on more of the latex and special effects side of things, while we focus on the beauty aspect. Natalie is trained in special effects, but really wants to up her ante with it, so I'm sure she'll tackle some, but with my role as assistant I'll just be sticking to beauty, helping out where needed, applying touch-ups and observing. As I unpack all the kit, I feel that bubble of anticipation you get on your first day at a new school. Fresh new books and unfamiliar faces, but that fizzy sense of what's to come. I hope I'm good enough for this. This is big.

We introduce ourselves to the other artists, Marco Leonardis, Amy Stoke and Sarah Scott, and are called through for a team briefing. Normally Natalie would have dealt with all this information over the phone, but with this being such a big, complicated job, we sit around the set on anything we can find and listen to Anthony Langston, the set director, go over the shoot days, scene breakdowns, art requirements, styling requirements and safety details. I scribble notes furiously. It's incredible just how much goes into making something so creative, and I can't fathom how they're going to get through all of this in just a few weeks.

I've set up and had a meeting with the other MUAs and hairstylists, and now the actors and actresses start pouring in. With main characters and support actors, there's a lot of work for us to do and our chairs are never empty. It's a constant rhythm of having bums in seats, talking to people and checking my clipboard and schedule to make sure we stay on track with everything – this is far more than anything I've been used to back home. It hasn't escaped me what a step up this is, and I'm anxious to show Natalie I can handle it; that, like she said, I'm ready for this challenge. I want to prove it to myself, too, just so I know I can do it, I can do something well.

The whole day zooms past in a blur. It's exhilarating, thinking on my feet and handling such a huge range of work. As usual, I prep and base the faces, with Natalie finishing the eyes and details, but, in the spaces between actors, I observe and assist the special effects team, preparing the latex and cleaning brushes. By the time we leave that night, I realise I've been so busy I haven't thought of anything else except my brushes and applications and chatting and laughing with the actors. I look down at my phone and see a missed call from Theo.

I head up to my hotel room to return it, but by the time I've had a long, hot shower to wash away all the gunk and powders that I'm covered in, I'm too tired. My bones are aching like I've run a marathon, so I lie down and drift into a deep, jet-lagged sleep.

At 5 a.m. I wake up either with jet lag or excitement at being in New York, working on an actual freaking film, and we head to the set for 7. Make-up artists start early and finish late. I slept so peacefully last night that I'm totally ready to run at the day.

Like yesterday, time seems to be going at super-speed. No sooner have I applied powder and basic fake blood to one actor, I've another in my chair ready for a powder and set job. We work in a conveyor belt, with the special effects team working their magic on injuries, extreme gore and body blood, then I apply base work and brows and powder, and finally Natalie works on eyes, lips and lashes. Then we hand them over to the hairstylists to work their own magic. The whole sequence is a cacophony of chatter and movement, of people yelling, girls with clipboards, guys with headsets, nobody stopping to pause or rest because time is tight and we're all on our A-game. It's electric. I feel so happy to be here, so glad I was asked, and *so* glad I decided to come.

The momentum flows, and we all get on well. Sarah is my favourite. She lives in a box flat with two other friends and graduated from beauty school three years ago. She's sassy and upbeat and reminds me of myself before life happened and I felt The Emptiness. Talking of sassy and upbeat, I'm excited to see Piper and how she's getting on with her new job out here! We arrange to meet up in a few days when I've settled in a bit more, we're doing shorter hours (I hope) and the jet lag's subsided. She seems so busy living the American dream these days, and there's some new guy on the scene – it's hard for her to squeeze a night in to see me!

Like yesterday, time flies and we work quickly through the actors. Working with blood is something I'm not used to; there's not much requirement for it in bridal jobs or commercial shoots, but it's so fun. It's so exciting to be learning new skills and working with some of the best in the industry. Natalie has always been the person I've looked up to in my career, but now it's like I'm surrounded by Natalies. I'm going to observe everything they do and glean as much knowledge and skills from this trip as possible! I'm just going to ignore the fact that I've splashed fake blood up my fresh pale blue denim skirt, or that it's dribbled all over my hands and wrists and go with the flow. I can do this!

I've worked on films before – small homegrown indie

films with five or six actors and a 'make do' crew – but this is something else. There are more actors than I can remember the names of, but one stands out. Marnie is young and petite and sort of reminds me of Lyla. She has a lovely innocence about her that makes me want to talk to her with softer tones and mother her a little bit. While I'm priming her neck for fake blood, I notice some bruising on her upper arms and casually say, 'Ooh, little accident?' as I gesture to the blemishes with the end of my make-up brush.

'Oh God, yeah, ha, party, party! I dance like a crazy person, I've knocked into someone. No biggie.'

There are so many people on set and so many people to get through, I don't have any time to argue, but something about her overly sweet, happy-go-lucky attitude to bruising sticks with me. I cover them over and, like the good, well-brought-up Brit I am, I don't press further, and say, 'There we are, good as new,' and watch her hop off my stool and disappear back into the throng.

I WORK SO HARD. I lose myself in the creativity and the artist–actor relationship and feel like I'm on another planet, very far from the one Robin Wilde lives on. There's no angst; I'm just a woman who is good at a thing and I'm loving it.

Very quickly I work through my quota and move over to Natalie and Sarah to observe and assist. Watching them adhere and blend the latex wounds is amazing and after a little while, Natalie suggests I give one a go.

It turns out liquid latex is the most fun thing I've ever played with in my life. Remember Silly Putty when you were little? The same appeal as that! I practise a little bit on my own arm and then am offered the chance to try a very small bleeding scab on one of the extras. It works beautifully, and both Natalie and Sarah are impressed. I'm actually rather impressed with myself too. The joy of feeling proud of myself lingers and I'm eager to try more.

I spend the rest of my day learning new latex and blood techniques and practising on as many extras as I can lay my rather bloody hands on in between my own touch-up and powder work. By 7 my arms are aching but I'm elated at how much fun it's been and how much I've taken to the special effects work. I've always been good at art but, as per usual, lacked the self-confidence to really give it my all.

As we're cleaning our brushes ready for tomorrow's early start, Marnie quietly walks over and asks, 'Hey, do you have a minute?' Natalie lifts her head slightly, pausing to see if I'm going to handle this or if she needs to be involved (that's the manager in her) and I say, 'Yeah, sure, what's up?'

'I'm going out again tonight, premiere and a party.'

'Oh, lovely! How glamorous!' I say encouragingly.

'Yeah, real glamorous. I wanted to know what you used on my arms earlier? I hate turning up to jobs with . . . marks, but I know tonight might be a bit crazy too . . . lots of dancing.'

Something's not right here.

She's lying the way Lyla does – pausing, looking at the floor. It's painful to watch.

'Well, it's correcting cream, concealer and powder to cover everything up,' I say very gently.

'OK, thanks. Correcting cream. I'll get some of that,' Marnie says, getting up to leave.

'Listen, Marnie, I know dancing can get a bit crazy, but I also know that sometimes you want to stop and talk about that. I'm not on anyone's side, and I'm a good listener. This is my number. If ever you want to talk about that . . . dancing, let me know,' and I thrust a bit of blotting paper with my number written in eyeliner into her hand.

'Thank you,' she says stiffly, 'it's nothing. I need the work. He's OK, really . . . it's just too much partying.' She trails off and picks up her things. Before I can ask any more, she's left.

Langston, the formidable set director, approaches. Known for his no-nonsense demeanour, I feel myself stiffen in anticipation of something troublesome. 'Good job today, ladies,' he says in a booming voice and thick New York accent, as well as, amazingly, a smile, a very, very white smile, totally surprising me. 'Really happy with everything and *you*,' he says, looking directly at me, making my heart stop in panic, 'you were a little firecracker. What a credit you are to Miss Natalie!'

'Oh. Thank you. I'm really enjoying it all. Great to be working with—'

'Awesome. See you girls tomorrow!' and he walks off, not stopping long enough for me to finish my sentence.

'Look at you! That's high praise indeed!' cheers Natalie when she's sure he's left. 'He's right – you've worked so hard these last two days, I'm proud of you. You're really coming into your own, Robin.'

Langston and Natalie's affirmations have made a good day amazing. If I could bottle this feeling and keep it forever, I would. I love New York!

STEPPING OUT ONTO LEXINGTON Avenue, I notice the balls of my feet aren't burning and my head doesn't feel like it's full of sand like it does at the end of most working days. There's something about this city – I feel so energised even though sometimes you do need to take a deep breath and brace yourself. The streets are heavy with summer heat. People don't slow down for it, though; they march by, taking huge strides on the busy pavements, weaving between bins and signs and streetlights. Everyone here has an easy confidence. Nobody dithers or panics; they just step out from the precipice, adjust to the sirens and car horns, and, alarmingly, wiggle through the jammed traffic of yellow cabs and trucks – and everything in between – and crack on. I am surprised to find myself thinking I could get used to this!

On the way back to the hotel, I stop by a little kiosk selling fizzy drinks and papers, and buy a couple of postcards with the Empire State Building twinkling at sunset. The vendor sells them to me with stamps (and, amazingly, not even so much as an eyebrow raised at all the fake blood on my arms and top) and I take them to a little bench nearby. In just a few seconds I scribble, *Dear Bluebird, Hello, it's Mummy! I'm having a lovely time working in New York. It's so hot here and they have all sorts of yummy treats – the other day I had a deep-fried Oreo biscuit! When you're a big girl I'll bring you here and we can go to the top of the building on this card – it'll be like being a princess in her tower. Missing you lots, see you very soon, love you all the way round the earth and up to Saturn, Mummy xxx.* Then I take out the next one and write, *Dear Kath, Thank you for everything you do, you're helping me make my career into something, I appreciate you. Love always, Robin xxx.* I write Kath's address on the front and walk over to the blue postbox and drop them both in. Feels nice to be having a moment for Lyla. Things have been crazy out here, but I can feel myself starting to think more about things at home. I love learning new things and discovering I'm good at them – maybe I could carry on learning and really go places. Thank God for Kath and her support. I wish they could both be out here right now, sat on this bench, watching New York zoom by. Maybe minus the sweaty clothes and fake blood, though.

Three twelve-hour days in a row, and my body is clearly acclimatising to the work, which I'm so, so grateful for. I'm just over a week in and I've already found a new level of energy and respect for Natalie. This is the norm for her:

handling the entire cast; liaising with the art team and producers; overseeing touch-ups on set; leading the assistants – and that's before she's even laid her kit out and picked up a make-up brush. It looks exhausting, but there must also be a real thrill to it. The buzz of knowing you've done a good job and the satisfaction at the end of the day when you fold up your case and turn off the mirror lights, knowing you ran the ship. I feel like alongside Natalie I'm really learning and achieving something, and I love it.

And tonight I'm free. Time to explore this city and let my hair down!

TWENTY-EIGHT

I NEVER THOUGHT I'D BE one of those drinks-on-a-week-night people (I'm more of a go-home-and-get-pyjamas-straight-on kind of gal), but Piper has invited me out for a couple of cocktails at the Sugar Factory in the West Village. It seems wasteful to say no. I'm never not searching for a babysitter and never not on my hands and knees rummaging through a clothes heap at the bottom of my wardrobe, having to do the classic yet undignified crotch-sniff test to see if the jeans are wearable. I said I'd stay out for a couple and, for me, there's something quite liberating about that. I don't always have to just stick to my working/mumming/sleeping routine. I've still got it. I'm still young. If I want to say yes to cocktails, I can. It feels good to feel so in control and have this extra pep in my step. Even if my peppy step is slightly painful after twelve hours on my feet!

Nipping back to the hotel, there's just time for a 'bower' (at school Lacey and I made up 'bower' for when you have a shower without washing your hair, just a body shower. Yes, we were actually geniuses), a change of clothes (skinny black ripped jeans that say, 'oh hi, I'm so rock chic' and a black clippy-poppers-under-your-nether-regions top that gives an air of sex appeal but mostly just sucks in my mum-tum) and something to eat (a bag of vegetable crisps from Starbucks almost counts as dinner Stateside, right?). Yes, ready to go. Let's do this.

Pulling up to the bar and stepping out of my Uber, I think I look good – a bit like a dolled-up ninja, but still good. But this only lasts until Piper strides over from the entrance of the bar where she's been waiting. Legs like a gazelle, it only takes her about four steps to cross the street and she looks like she's just stepped off a runway. Her skin is glowy, her hair is gleaming and everything that should, twinkles: eyes, teeth, tiny diamond stud in her belly button. Who knew belly button piercings were still a thing? I don't think I've even properly looked at my belly button for about half a decade. My stomach is so untoned I think if I had a piece of jewellery in it, I'd lose it. Ew. Need to get off this train of thought and focus on Piper.

Jeans were clearly the right choice because Piper is sporting some herself, so that's a relief. Imagine two straws made of denim and stitched together. Those are Piper's jeans. I'm not even sure they would fit Lyla, they're so slim-fitting. Her legs look lean, her bottom pert and just above the waistband there is no bulge, just that twinkle. Not one to shy away from daring fashion, Piper has opted for a crop top made out of a metallic fabric, folded in half to make a triangle, attached by tiny strings and tied like a halter neck. Basically, she's wearing spray-on jeans and a golden handkerchief, and she looks sensational.

Suddenly I feel a bit meh. Meh ninja, not glamorous ninja.

'Hiiiiiiiiiii, I'm so glad you came!' Piper exclaims, four octaves higher than anyone else around us. 'Welcome to Manhattan!'

'Heeeeyyy!' I try to match.

Piper links arms with me and we walk in.

Without wasting any time, we order an Ocean Blue and after one sip from the giant sharer cocktail goblet, I can feel the blueberry vodka slipping down a treat. All the drinks at the Sugar Factory are insane. Served in giant fishbowl-style glasses, garnished with lollipops, jelly sweets, candyfloss or fruit, each drink is a sugar high waiting to happen. Located in the trendy Meatpacking District, it's become the place to try, and I'm not berating Piper for her choice. I don't think I could do this every night – I'd have no teeth left, and Diabetes, but for now, sipping a blue cocktail with tiny gummy sharks floating around in it is working for me. It's just bliss to be sitting on a bar stool and not flitting around the set with brushes in my hand and a million thoughts about liquid latex, blending creases or schedules in my head. I'm ready to zone out, let go and enjoy every moment.

We chat for a while about our days, and then about the weird man on the subway Piper sees each morning (he gets on at her stop and carries a tiny cocker spaniel dressed as a canine astronaut – only in New York!). Piper loves her job as an assistant curator at a small up-and-coming gallery nearby and to my mind, this is amazing. Ever since we were little she was into art; she'd tear the prettiest adverts out of Tina's magazines, stick them to the walls of her bedroom and make us come in to admire the 'art', while me and Lacey played the more classic 'Mums and Dads'. I admire her for following through on her dream. From small beginnings in the suburbs of Cambridgeshire to assisting in an actual gallery in the Big Apple! I don't think I could ever just fly out somewhere and start a whole new life with a brand new job. Although, if this week is anything to go by, maybe I'm wrong. Maybe I could.

'Piper, before the cocktails go to my head, I just want to say I'm really proud of you.'

'What? Don't be silly. You've not even had a drink yet and you're starting!' she laughs me off.

'No, I mean it! You've done incredibly, and been so brave. I don't know how you do it.'

'Yes you do! You're doing it too!'

'No, I'm not; this is temporary. I don't live here. I'm not making a whole new life here. Look at you, being amazing and totally embracing it all!' I say, gesturing at her and the bar around us.

'Robin, you're just seeing me now, now I'm settled. I was totally and utterly terrified when I first arrived! Was I making the right choice? Would I miss everyone at home? Could I handle the role?'

We carry on talking about how in time she settled, but I'm still mentally on Piper being terrified. I just never thought of her as someone who was scared of anything at all. She's so suave and vivacious. She's the girl at the party on the bar doing shots, not the girl by the wall wondering if her shoes are a bit boring. I suddenly feel a whole new wave of love for my little Piper, her secret vulnerabilities and her 'screw it, I'm doing it anyway' vibe.

Then we move onto Callum – her latest squeeze – and before I know it, we're playing virtual Shag, Marry, Avoid with the guys in the bar. I love this game. Zero consequences, zero chances of messing anything up. I wish real life could be like that. Just look at a man, pick 'marry' and then dream up the most wonderful life without any of the usual stress of a mediocre relationship. No second-guessing everything he says; no waiting desperately for him to message; no feeling shit when he runs his hand up your maybe-ready-for-a-shave leg and says 'oo, bit spiky, ha ha' as a 'hilarious' joke.

After a few minutes our eyes land on a group of men in suits by the back wall of the bar.

'Shag, Marry, Avoid the three closest to us?' asks Piper, with mischief in her already twinkling eyes and a wry smile on her glossed lips. .

I look over and see the three she means clearly. Stood about with beers (why would you buy a beer in a place where the cocktails come with lollipops in them?), they've all come from work, in their smart trousers, lace-up shoes, white shirts slightly crumpled from the day with the sleeves rolled up.

So: the task at hand. We've got an older, greying guy with a hook nose and a slight back-and-forth rock to his stance: Avoid. A fresh-out-of-college hottie with eager eyes who's clearly highly enthused to be out with the big boys: Shag, obviously. And lastly, the dish of the group – tall but not so tall people would say 'wow you're tall', as if the recipient didn't know, with dark brown hair, a decent medium build and a bit of stubble. Not 'oh my God I need new knickers' hot, but handsome enough. Someone your mother might like (although not my mother, because she still lives in hope that Simon and I will get back together so she can regale the ladies at the Rotary Club of our most happy ending). Anyway, Mr Handsome: Marry. He looks dependable.

Piper is impressed with my quick choices; this isn't my first rodeo. But obviously she'd marry the older guy because she reasons he'd have the most money and would be grateful to have her. Then she'd have a fling with the young hottie to keep life exciting. She tells me all of this in the tone of voice someone would use for describing a new washing machine they'd ordered.

We skim the menu for our next choices, and I opt for a

bubblegum-pink cocktail in a highball glass with a wand of candyfloss protruding from the top, and think about how Lyla would lose her mind over something like this (minus the alcohol, of course!). Still mid-thought about concocting some kind of candyfloss cocktail for my six-year-old, Piper has popped off her stool, is taking my free hand (the other one isn't letting go of this drink, that's for sure) and dragging me up to dance.

Thankfully I've been filled with enough sugar, booze and adrenalin from my day to have a 'fuck it' attitude, so I go all in, shake what my mother gave me (she'd be so very proud right now, *not*) and dance away with my beautiful gazelle friend. I can't remember the last time I felt so free and liberated on a dance floor. This isn't aunties swaying round the handbags at a wedding; this is arms-above-head, bending-my-knees-sometimes-more-than-ninety-degrees movement here. All too quickly I'm reminded of my somewhat lacking fitness levels (if only I'd taken a leaf out of Natalie's gym dedication book), so we head back to our stools, take a few sips and I let my heart rate get back into a safe zone.

'How often do you have fun like this on a weekday?' asks Piper, breathlessly.

'Mmm . . . never. I work, or I do the school run in the mornings, so dancing in a cocktail bar is far less important to me than having a bath or flopping on the sofa before an early night.'

'Oh, wow. Sounds fun,' replies Piper in a tone so dry you could set it on fire. 'Wanna spice things up a bit?'

Not really, I think; the dancing was spicy enough, surely. 'Er . . . yeah?'

'Why don't you actually go and say hi to Mr Marry? This is New York. It's what everyone does here!'

'Because he's having a night out with his friends. He doesn't want to be interrupted by me.'

'I bet you ten dollars he does.'

'Nooo, he'll brush me off.'

'I tell you what, go over and ask him any old question to start a conversation going, and if he doesn't brush you off, I'll buy you brunch at Sarabeth's.'

Well, she's got me there. If there's one sure-fire way to my heart, it's food. And according to Piper, Sarabeth's breakfasts are apparently the best.

After taking an unreasonably large gulp of my cocktail, I lurch off my bar stool in what I hoped would be an elegant hop but what probably looks more like a baby seal splashing into the sea for the first time, brush my already clammy palms down my jeans and stride over.

I can do this.

I'm Robin Wilde, who flew out to New York with barely any notice. I'm Robin Wilde, who deputised for Natalie and helped to manage the entire make-up department today. I'm going to stride over and say something charming, witty and hilarious.

'Hello.'

Hmm. Not as amazing as it could have been, but still confident.

'Oh . . . hi,' replies a slightly startled Mr Marry in an accent that's familiar.

'Oh! You're British. What a small world!' Stop, Robin!

'Yes! Hi! What a small world indeed. What brings you to this neck of the woods?' Mr Marry replies confidently and comfortably. Maybe America really is the land of opportunity.

'I'm just over here for a work thing, and my friend thought she recognised you but maybe she didn't – I . . . I'm not sure now.' Shit, I started strong but should have had more to say or at least some kind of plan. I look over to Piper, hoping she'll sense my panic and swoop in to rescue me, but she's occupied. No sooner was my stool next to her free, an indie-band kinda guy has hopped on and is trying to win her affections. Great.

'Lamest excuse ever, I'm afraid,' teases Mr Marry with a kind laugh. 'I'm Edward. Nice to meet you.'

'Robin. Hello. Again. My friend over there with the gold top, she, well, she dared me to come and say hello. Very grown-up of us, ha ha, er, yes, sorry. It's these insane cocktails!' I say, hoping that honesty really is the best policy.

'Not my good looks and potential charm, then?' Edward quips back. Oh my God, is he actually flirting with me? I should flirt back! This is my chance. All is not lost! I'm in a bar in New York City, flirting with a hot man. Shit me.

'Aha ha,' is what I actually manage. How poetic.

Edward's face is really very appealing. Dark green eyes with tiny flecks of tawny-owl brown in them, and such long lashes. The sort of lashes I usually glue to people on set. There's something about his eyes that just feels safe and gentle. He doesn't strike me as a murderer. These are the things a modern lady out in the world thinks of these days. It's what I look for on the dating apps. Is he wearing a decent shirt? Yes? Tick. Has he included any photos of him with sedated tigers? No? Tick. Does he have the eyes of a mass lady-murderer? No? Tick. So far with Edward we've got two ticks. I'm yet to find out how he feels about the tigers.

Piper's tap on my shoulder brings me back to the real world. Apparently Callum, the guy she sometimes sees, has buzzed her and she's going to go to his studio to 'check out his artwork'. This is what we're calling it these days, is it? I think we all know she will have her denim-clad legs over his 'easel' before you can say 'draw me like one of your French girls'. Cheeky minx. Good for her.

I consider leaving myself but, feeling brave, I decide to stay for ten more minutes and see what Edward's all about.

I tell her to be safe and that I'll text her when I'm home (I feel like that's the correct thing to say to your gal pal when she's decided to leave you for some male anatomy). I look back up at Edward once she's left. 'Oh great, I've been abandoned!' I tell him, with only moderate annoyance. I'm quite glad. I'm starting to think I might enjoy spending a bit more time with him, and goddess-like Piper is a distraction for any red-blooded man.

Without skipping a beat Edward says, 'Hang with us. I'm here with some of the chaps from work. Keith's leaving next week, so we're starting early on the goodbye drinks! The more the merrier. I'd be glad of a fellow Brit. We can talk about red phone boxes and Marmite!'

Normally I'd say no to such a hideous push into a group I don't know, but tonight feels different. I'm in New York City! I handled everything on set! I look incredible in these jeans! Why bloody not? I'm a woman of poise and substance, and if I want to stay for a couple of drinks with a decent guy, then so I shall! Look at me go, world, look at me go!

An hour later, and I haven't regretted my choice. 'The chaps' and Keith are an absolute hoot. Either that or they're not and the cocktails are a lot more potent than I initially thought. So far we've fiercely debated whether Hershey's or Cadbury is better (Edward and I passionately stick to our guns and agree that the Caramel Bunny is way too sexual to be selling chocolate), and gone through a lengthy list of things we name differently over in Blighty. Sounds like the most boring game ever played, but truly, after a few cocktails so sugary you're facing a coma, screaming 'BIN AND TRASH! CABS AND TAXIS!' becomes the absolute height of entertainment.

Before I know it it's 2 a.m., the Sugar Factory is winding down, Keith and the chaps are looking around for which chairs they slung their suit jackets on and Edward is talking in my ear about walking me home.

SOMETHING I'VE LEARNT QUICKLY in this city, despite its being a thick maze of buildings, roads and constant construction, is that walking is usually the easiest option. Well, the easiest option when you have your bearings, are escorted by your friend and it's daylight.

'I think I need a cab. Or I just need to check Google Maps. Or . . . I . . . erm.' I start to look wildly around, over and over, as if by doing this I'm suddenly going to see my hotel.

'Are you having some kind of fit?' asks Edward.

'No! I'm just not sure how close my hotel is to here. I've been using Ubers, or I've had Piper or Natalie with me. I'll work it out. My brain just feels foggy from all the drinks. And candyfloss. Ugh, I have so much regret for the sugar.'

'My place is two blocks away. Fancy coming back for a cup of tea, some Marmite toast and a chat about the merits of Wills and Kate?' Edwards gently laughs.

There's something really calming about him. I should be absolutely freaking out that Piper has left me, I'm half-lost and I'm about to go back to a strange man's flat. But I'm a big girl, and Edward has given me no reason not to feel safe, so I think 'you only live once!', nod casually (at least I hope it looked casual and breezy, and not like one of those little toy dogs people used to put in the back of their car) and we start walking.

278

About fifteen steps down the road, I notice our hands brushing against each other and less than five steps later, they're intertwined. All of a sudden I'm acutely aware that this isn't a chat with a new friend. I don't really know why I thought it would be. We had great chat all night, his attention was focused purely on me and the drinks flowed easily. Usually in those kinds of situations I'd feel self-conscious, but tonight feels so easy. I just let myself go, laugh heartily and actually manage to not worry about anything. I should do that more often.

Edward is handsome. Classically handsome, as in, he could be in a men's razor advert. He's taller than me but not crazy tall (six foot, maybe?), and pale with cheeks that would probably flush pink in the winter air. He has I've-worked-all-day stubble and sensible hair. He's no Theo, but right now I don't want Theo. I want calming, good-looking Edward, not stressful, unobtainable Theo. With his hand in mine, I don't feel lost. He strides confidently down the street and we dip in and out of the light from the street lamps. Conversation has stopped, but it doesn't feel awkward. It's amazing how a few drinks and a bit of chat in a bar can make you feel so all right with someone. It must be New York. I'd never do this at home.

His flat is tiny. I know people always say apartments in New York are small, but this is insanity. It's almost smaller than my single room at university. It's effectively a short, wide corridor.

As I go through the front door, I'm instantly in the cream-walled lounge and about thirty centimetres away from the two-man grey sofa (with no cushions or blankets – it's all very functional). If I swivel 180 degrees, there's a flat screen on the wall that's too close for comfort. Next to the sofa on the right is a light fold-up wooden table (I silently wonder if you could actually fully unfold it in here), and then the 'kitchen' next to it. The 'kitchen' is a clean stove, about nine inches of wooden worktop, a wall-mounted microwave next to a double cupboard and there's a fridge and some shelving for pots and pans and whatnot. The space in between is minuscule. If I breathed out I would get stuck. Melt an ice cube and we'd both drown. It's small.

'Oh, it's so homey,' I say in what I think is an encouraging tone, but in reality I sound like a children's TV presenter pretending to love the colour blue and the triangle shape.

'It's a box. It's smaller than my parents' shed,' nice Edward responds in a matter-of-fact tone.

Jolly good.

Realising a guided tour isn't necessary, Edward sidles past me, deftly grabs two glasses and a bottle of wine out of the fridge and pours. There's something sexy about his confidence in assuming that I like or even want a glass of wine.

I do want it, though. New-found confidence be damned; I'm sobering up, and the reality of the situation is starting to hit me. I was feeling so calm outside, but very slowly anxiety is creeping in. Hopefully a glug of wine will deal with that.

Edward starts talking, his voice deep and relaxed. He has the slow speech of someone who's secure in what he's saying.

'I like you, Robin. You made me laugh, you've got interesting stuff to say. You're hot. If you want me to walk you to your hotel, that's fine, but I want you to stay. Will you stay with me?'

I love how easy that was. No confusion, no innuendos, simple. I take a big sip of my (very nice, thank you kindly) white wine and nod, looking straight into his eyes.

He reaches out for my hand, leads me (by which I mean we take four steps to the left of the front door) to his bedroom and kisses me.

His kiss is authoritative. He takes the wine glass out of my hand and puts it and his own on the bedside table. One of his hands moves up my back, stroking my neck and into my hair, while the other lingers, gentlemanly, on the side of my waist.

I tumble down onto his bed with him, clothes are being pulled off (lacy thongs be damned – I'm in soft cotton briefs and feeling all the better for them), bodies are colliding. He gently caresses my thigh. He kisses my neck, moves down to kiss my belly. And . . . well, it seems Piper isn't the only one enjoying her evening.

IN THE COLD LIGHT of the next day, things feel very different. Gone is the giddy, liberated feeling of cocktails and sex with a man I don't know and, unwelcome, into its place rush utter panic and sickness.

I left Edward's place at 6 a.m. in an Uber he called for me (actually quite gentlemanly of him, I think) and came back to the hotel. I took my time in the shower, enjoying the free smellies and letting thoughts of last night wash over me at the same time as the hot water. That's when, on a bit of a freedom, first-time-one-night-stand and orgasm-induced high, I stepped out of the bathroom and saw my phone buzz.

Natalie's called. She's been up all night, too, but instead of having her head in a man's lap, like me, she's had her head in a toilet and is suffering with severe stomach cramps. She's not coming on set today for fear of infecting everyone, and because of the unpleasantness of not actually being able to leave the bathroom, so she's asked me to 'take the reins'. I'm utterly horrified by this, especially in light of this horrible hangover but obviously I've lied, said everything will be fine and 'you just get yourself better, I'll handle everything'.

My instant reaction – dammit – is to run to Theo. He'd know exactly what to say to calm me down and remind me that everything will be all right. He has a way with words, and his voice is so smooth and strong you can't not feel good after a call to him. I know he's not the answer, though. Too many unanswered texts have taught me this. Instead I remind myself of Lacey's words whenever I've felt anxious or like I couldn't cope. If I can get through childbirth, the first few months of motherhood plus nearly five years of single-mum-dom, then I can do anything. So, though I still feel wobbly, I take a smiley selfie, send it to Kath's phone (no need for filters) and write, *Hey Kath, hope everything's OK. Can you tell Lyla Mummy is missing her so much and can't wait for a big squishy cuddle on the sofa when I'm back? xxx.* That little bit of contact with my people feels good.

Suddenly last night doesn't feel so amazing; I just feel tired and overwhelmed by the day ahead, and like I want to be at home with daytime TV and a packet of fig rolls.

Realising there's nothing I can do about my frustration now – Natalie is depending on me – I get dressed. Black cotton skater dress, old white Converse, my brush belt and hair in a topknot. I'm not in the mood to make much more effort than that.

Our hotel is a short walk to the set, and outside in the blazing sun, I already feel too warm. I take the few minutes to myself to try and find some calm. Langston likes me, praised me, even; I'm good at my job, I've had plenty of practice, Natalie assured me on the phone that I can handle this, I can take direction and it's going to be OK.

On set, everything, thankfully, is OK. Sarah offers some lovely advice: 'Honey, everything is as it should be; the world longs for what you have to offer,' and, like a sponge, I absorb her wise (maybe from a fortune cookie or inspiration Insta account) words and give it my all. I set about priming, powdering, blending and contouring, and work up a good rhythm with the rest of the team. I channel my inner Natalie and, where needed, guide, advise and organise people in what they're doing. Occasionally Langston shouts me on set for touch-ups, and I scurry back and forth trying not to get in the way of his seemingly bad mood. Even his deputy seems tense about it.

By 11 a.m. I feel like I've been working all day instead of just a few hours and excuse myself to take a breather, dash across the street and buy myself a portion of deep-fried Oreos. These might be the naughtiest things I've ever eaten but my God, they are worth it. I sit myself down on a bench by a tiny patch of fenced grass posing as a city park and let the sun shine down on my face. I'm covered in make-up and smudges, my hair is a sweaty mess and my feet are sore, but I feel good. I take out my phone and, surprisingly, there is a message from Edward.

Hey Robin, it's Edward! Just checking your limo dropped you off safely this morning and you are enjoying luxuriating on set in your trailer, and then the old school camera emoji and a winky face. How sweetly charming of him. Buoyed by the sugar high from my deep-fried treats, I decide not to play the wait-thirty-minutes-to-reply game and respond.

Hi Edward, my chauffeur was excellent and dropped me right at my door as asked; please pass on five stars from me. Sadly they have misplaced my trailer and so I am being forced to actually work on the set today rather than lounge around and recuperate from my evening. It's a hard life but I've discovered deep-fried Oreos, so will survive. Hope you're feeling OK, not too hung-over. I really enjoyed last night x. I think this is a good mix of friendly, witty and sincere, so I close my phone and start walking back to work. I don't feel tight-chested about this man; it's very novel. Maybe this is how it's supposed to always be? Who bloody knows?

Things seem oddly tense when I walk back into work. Marnie is in my chair and I can't ignore the fresh bruises on her shoulders and collarbones.

'Marnie, what's happened?'

'Nothing. I went out and danced a lot and was just having a good time,' she says, looking at her lap.

'Marnie,' I say as softly as I possibly can, 'I don't think that's true. These are bruises from hands and fingers, aren't they?'

'Can you just cover them up, please? I'm on set in ten minutes and Langston is so mad at me, and—'

'Why is Langston upset with you? He shouldn't be getting you worked up this much, you poor thing,' I interrupt while she blinks back tears.

'It doesn't matter. I don't want to make a big deal.' She lowers her voice. 'We had a thing. It's not a thing now. Or maybe it is. I don't know. I just need you to do my make-up and I can suck it up and do my job. I've always wanted to be an actress, I can't blow it. I'm sorry I told you . . . If you say anything, I'll just deny it!'

I can see Marnie flushing red with panic at the thought of losing her chance, and probably for fear of Langston. He's a intimidating man, looming taller than most and having an air of authority you don't often see. I'm a bit scared of him myself, to be honest. Still, I know what's wrong and what's right, and that overrides any concerns I have for Langston.

'Did . . . did *Langston* do this to you?'

Marnie's silence confirms my suspicions, and as she looks up at me we meet eyes and she nods. Big, hot tears run down her face and I grab for tissues to blot her mascara.

'This is not OK . . . you don't have to put up with this. You could—'

'MARNIE! IT'S CALL TIME!' barks Langston, who's suddenly filling the entirety of my doorway. He's so abrasive I almost jump out of my skin. I can feel Marnie shaking.

'I'm sorry, Langston, we're not quite ready yet. We shall need five more minutes,' I deliver, channelling my inner Finola.

Taken aback either by my bravery or my absurdly posh accent, he glares at Marnie and leaves the room.

A moment or two later, Marnie has relaxed enough to start telling me her story. 'We were dating,' she says, twiddling her fingers as I fix her face and gently cover her bruises. 'He told me he worked in movies and would get me a part. Things were great for a while, he called me his little dollface and took me to premieres and parties and gave me roles in his films,' she continues, looking down at her hands and pausing as though unsure whether to go on. 'Then I noticed the way he would talk to the other girls in his films, how he'd take them into his trailer and call them dollface too. I knew I wasn't special to him, that I was just a plaything for him to amuse himself with, and so I tried to break it off.' Marnie looks up at me for reassurance and I nod encouragingly. 'I told him I didn't want this, and that he was welcome to the other girls. He was so angry. "You need me," he said. "You're nothing in this business without me." I said I didn't care and that I just wanted to go home, and he grabbed me.' She pauses and stops playing with her hands, looks straight into my eyes. I can see hers are full of tears, and she says quietly, 'He's so much stronger than I am. I'm going to leave for good when the shoot is over but for now, I just want this job – I need this job – and then I'm gone.' Fresh tears fall again and I grab more tissues and sponge pads to soak them up and save the newly applied concealer. I wonder what Natalie would do in this situation. She'd be so much better at this than I am.

'Oh Marnie, I'm so sorry. He's a bully. A bastard bully.'

'Yeah. Well, nothing I can do but leave and feel sorry for the next poor girl he calls dollface.'

Marnie's called on set, and I don't know what to do. I have barely any time to think because no sooner has she left my station than someone else is here, and I need to do mine and Natalie's load today. I wish she was here; she'd handle this so well. She's unflappable.

The next few hours pass in a blur of work and light chat, and all the while in the back of my mind I'm thinking about Marnie. I believed her when she said she's seen through him and she'll leave after this job and be OK, but what about Langston? He's going to carry on doing this.

My phone buzzes – it's from Kath. She's sent a picture of Lyla smiling and holding up a picture she's drawn of me and her and I could cry. I'm tired and emotional and trying so hard to hold it all together, but I can't. I take this Lyla-induced moment of bravery, unclip my brush belt and walk on set, where thankfully they are between takes and Langston is sat in his chair, scrolling through his phone.

As I walk over, thinking on my feet, my legs feel like they might lose all structure and buckle beneath me. But I take a deep breath and think about Marnie and how, if someone did that to Lyla, I'd kill them with my bare hands.

I have to be careful about this. I can't let him know my plan.

'Hi Anthony – Mr Langston – sorry about earlier. I'll try to be quicker next time.' I say as nicely as I can through slightly gritted teeth. How can he be so disgusting to such a sweet girl?

'Huh?' Clearly our interaction earlier has meant nothing and I'm just annoying him. I take a deep breath and carry on. I've got to get this right.

'With the actress, Marnie. She was talking and taking up my time. That's why we were running a bit late, because she distracted me.' I feel horrible for saying this about her, but hope my plan's going to work.

If he were a dog, his ears would have pricked up, such was his reaction to the name 'Marnie'.

'I was doing her make-up but she just kept talking and talking, very frustrating really. I just wanted to apologise to you.'

'She was?' he says, rolling his eyes. 'She's a fucking night-mare. Needs a bit of sense knocking into her. We're on a tight schedule!'

'Ha ha, I know, right? I could have slapped her!' I say with a fake laugh so convincing even I almost believe it.

And then it happens: the most horrible, wonderful thing.

Langston, obviously feeling at ease with me, his new comrade, leans in and says, 'You know what, Robbie,' I'll pretend he didn't get my name wrong, 'Sometimes I do.' With that, he laughs. And I don't.

I look him straight in the eye.

'You disgust me,' I say.

His eyes narrow.

'*What?*'

He speaks quietly. Gone is the charm. He is cold as ice and furious.

'You heard. You are a violent pig and I think you're revolting.'

'You want to watch your mouth, young lady, or you won't have a job to come back to tomorrow.'

'No, *Mr* Langston, you want to watch yours,' I say, starting to feel light-headed with adrenaline. Before he has a chance to say anything – or worse – to me, I walk briskly back to my station, throw my things in their case, stash it under the table and almost run back to the hotel.

Good grief. I think I am going to lose my job. And on this day, too, when Natalie was depending on me. But I know what I have to do.

Lifting open my laptop so forcefully I almost bend it backward, I plug my phone in to it and write the riskiest email of my life.

TWENTY-NINE

S SOON AS WE open the door to Sarabeth's on Park Avenue, I can feel my dopamine levels rising. This place is the best. The smell, the gentle colour schemes of creams and golds, the happiness of all the people inside. In the distance I can hear music playing, and instantly I realise it's mine and Simon's song. I haven't heard this in years, and wish I wasn't hearing it now. I'm already anxious enough worrying about what just happened with Langston and what Natalie will think if I get fired. This place was just calming me down, and now a song is set to push me back over the edge. It's funny how you can feel so completely over someone but then something hits one of your senses and you are utterly triggered. Hearing our song instantly takes me back to happy times when I felt secure and safe, and all of a sudden I remember I'm far from home and feel quite on edge. Determined not to let a song ruin my day, I focus on the food to come. The smell of French toast is in the air, and nothing can be that bad when brunch is on offer.

'You OK there, Twitchy?' Piper asks, noticing my obvious discomfort.

'Ha. Yeah, I was just thinking about Simon, actually,' I muse back.

'Ew! Why?' Piper asks in surprise.

'This music reminded me of him,' I say, in more of a sigh to myself than a response.

'Do you still miss him?' She places a hand on my arm. She's so sweet.

'No, I just have him in my memories. He was such a huge chapter of my life, I can't not think about him sometimes. I loved him. He was my everything, really,' I say, scuffing at the lobby floor with my foot, allowing myself a second of extra time to gather my thoughts. 'I thought we'd spend the rest of our lives together, grow old and die together and then *poof!* It's over. It's actually amazing how hard you can fall for someone and then, years later, how little they mean to you.' I look up at Piper, who is listening intently. I'm surprised at my own outpouring. I've been so used to just existing at home that coming here, to the busiest city in the world, is allowing my brain to be quiet and actually think for a second about what it's been through. It feels good, so I let it carry on. 'I mean, not *little*, he's Lyla's dad, but that magic is gone. That connection. I didn't think it would be possible to have something so special and then for it to be nothing. It's just a sad concept. I don't miss *him* so much as I miss what I thought I was going to have.'

Wow, that got deep quickly. I breathe out a sigh so big the woman in front of me turns round in shock. She quickly turns back when she sees me tearily blinking back at her. I didn't even realise I thought that. Sarabeth's is clearly a trigger point for more than just brunchy goodness.

'I know, yeah.' Except I don't think she does know. 'Let's just get some carbs and eat our feelings instead.'

'Good plan!' Eating my feelings isn't something I'm new to, so I gladly end the chat, hold back the waterworks and walk over to the maître d'. I've been longing for a Sarabeth's for days, and I'm not going to let my brain spoil it for me. Shut up brain, it's tummy's turn today!

We're led to a table and I almost physically swoon. God, that would be embarrassing: 'Oh, so how did you cut your head open, miss?' 'I physically swooned at the sight of a table filled with breakfast foods and fell and smacked my head on a hotplate.' 'Don't worry, miss, we see it all the time.'

Nested in the corner by the back wall and window at a table laden with well-polished silverware, we take our seats and open the heavy menus. Everything looks like heaven.

Leaning towards the berry bowl and then almond-crusted French toast, I close my menu with a satisfied thud and look up at Miss Dovington Junior. Of course, she looks relaxed and glowing. I can imagine her in the gallery, walking around looking effortlessly stylish and giving her opinions and instructions for how and where everything should go. She's so comfortable in her skin, you can't help but respect her.

Silver leather pointy-toe flats with a delicate buckled-up ankle strap, another pair-of-straws skinny jeans but this time in a very soft washed-out blue, slimline silver belt and a crisp white shirt tucked into her jeans with three buttons undone at the top, she looks simultaneously effortless and absolutely amazing. She's thrown her hair up in the type of topknot she'll claim only took three seconds but if I were to do it, it'd take forty minutes, and slicked on some popping-pink lipstick and a couple of layers of mascara. I think if Piper punched three holes into an empty cat litter bag and wore that she'd still look better than me. A bit like Natalie, really. I must attract amazing women. That's actually quite a nice thought . . .

I've gone for a more casual look, as always, but not for lack of trying. 'Boyfriend' jeans (such a cruel name for jeans – they're not my boyfriend, I don't *have* a sodding boyfriend, and even if Theo took the coveted title, I'm not sure my thighs would crush into a pair of his anyway), a slouchy black H&M cotton tee and once-white Converse that I bought because Lyla had a pair and I wanted us to match. My hair is also up, but in an it-really-needs-a-wash ponytail. Thankfully

I took the time to fully cleanse and moisturise last night, so my skin is glowy and my make-up looks chic. Gotta use the skills you have, eh?

Piper is finished with her menu and leaning across the table looking at me with mischief in her eyes.

'Go on then, it wasn't just admiring his art, was it?' I say with a faux sigh, because actually I love hearing about her exploits and adventures.

'Nooo,' she says, as if she's revealing the most tantalising piece of information you've ever heard. 'Ooohhh nooo . . . oooo he's incredible!'

'You say they're all incredible while you're with them, though.'

'I'm not with him *with* him, I'm just *seeing* him,' she retorts nonchalantly.

'What's the difference?' I ask.

'Well, I just go over and see him or hang out with him, but he's not my boyfriend. I'm not bothered about that bit.'

'Isn't that the best bit?' I'm amazed people feel this way. All I want in the world is the holding-hands-and-sharing-our-problems part. Sure, I want the fizz and thrill of the chase and the early days hot-sex-before-work, but mostly I just want that connection you don't find in a friends-with-benefits kind of set-up.

'What? Having to listen to their problems or hold hands at their boring work events or provide soup and tissues when they're full of snot? No, thank you! I just want to go over, have some company, hang out, go for drinks, maybe explore the city a bit and leave it at that. Simple, easy, exciting.'

'Wow. I wish I could see it like that.' It'd certainly make life with Theo feel a lot better. Maybe this is actually how Theo thinks?

'You can,' Piper says, sitting back, picking up her fork and putting her fingers on the prongs, gently musing her idea over. 'You just have to cut your heart off from your brain a bit. Maybe it'd do you good to put yourself out there a little more.'

I blush slightly, thinking about how much I put myself out there the other night, but I don't think she's noticed.

Best change the subject. 'So, Callum's just sex and fun, is he?'

'Yes. Oh my God, Robin, he's incredible. We went back to the studio, he took five seconds to show me a canvas and before I knew it we were all over each other. It was so raw and animalistic! I could barely even *think* it was so hot. He's ripped. And tall and strong and absolutely massive. I mean his dick is absolutely huge, and as he thrust into me he did this thing with his fingers that—'

'Yep! Yes! OK! Thank you, Piper! I've known you since you were five, remember. Weird, weird, weird!' When did my best friend's little sister become this sexual minx-like creature? I'm sure we were playing with Barbie and Ken about four nanoseconds ago. Now she looks like the Barbie and there are a lot of Kens playing with her. Ew, ew, *ew*.

'Shut up!' laughs Piper. 'We're all adults now! I'm sure you've had loads of hot sex in your life!'

Uh-oh, I can feel all the blood rushing to my cheeks again. I've not had lots of hot sex in my life but I've had pretty explosive sex this week. Every time I think of it my body tingles.

'Are you blushing?' Piper says, putting both hands flat on the table, clearly thrilled with her observation and what it might mean.

'Me? No, I don't think so. It's so warm in here, isn't it? Shall we order?' I say, reaching for the menu, trying to busy myself enough to distract her.

As if all the gods are smiling down on me, the waitress arrives to take our orders and I do go for the berry bowl, the almond-crusted French toast plus a hot chocolate. You're only in New York once, right? Piper orders fruit and granola and a green tea, and I realise she doesn't share my philosophy about eating everything in sight in this city.

Thinking we can move on, I start up the conversation again.

'So, Lacey called me the other day and said she feels like it might be a good month,' I offer, to fully swing the conversation round. 'The conception app thing says all the signs are good. And her nipples hurt, apparently. Maybe she's right! Maybe there'll be a new baby next year!'

'Lacey always thinks it's a good month, bless her. I try not to talk about all of that with her too much; I don't think I'm much help with ovulation chat, and I'm ever fearful that I'll upset her more. I just want to cheer her up and make her smile. Sex chat, that's where I am. So, tell me, Miss Wilde, what's going on?' Piper says, leaning forward, eager to work out what, indeed, is going on.

'I don't know what you mean,' I say, trying to look as innocent and confused as possible.

'Yes you do, you're bright red and being skittish. I've known you forever, remember. Something's up. You did something with Mr Marry, didn't you?'

She's literally a psychic now, is she?

'OK, yes, I did.'

'I knew it!' Piper is euphoric, for fuck's sake. 'Sooo, how was it? Where was it? Was he good? Are you in love? Are you going to marry him and have all his babies?' she says, overenthusiastically clapping her hands together and smiling wide.

'For someone who just had to explain the difference between seeing and going out with, you're awfully quick to jump the gun,' I laugh as the food arrives. I feel like a king looking at all this glorious breakfast food. Why isn't this more of a thing in England? Why have I spent 99 per cent of my life settling for non-brand cocoa pops? I'm clearly not living.

I go to pick up my fork, but Piper's huge eyes are piercing into me in a way that suggests she's not going to let me eat in peace until I spill.

'OK, Mr Marry is Edward. He works in creative design, is British and has lived out here a while but flits back and forth.'

'Oooh, a local boy!' Piper says, doing a little clap. She's so into this.

'I suppose so, yeah. So, we had a few drinks, quite a lot of drinks, actually, talked for a while and then the bar was closing. I didn't have my bearings and you'd abandoned me and so, well, we went to his,' I say, nodding and picking up my cutlery to eat. Even though I'm full of glee at having something exciting to talk about for once, I'm holding it in in an 'oh, I'm so casual, I always have hot sex with hot guys in New York City, don't mind me, la la la' kind of way. God, I love this place. I'm exciting in this place. I have actual exciting things to be coy about!

'So it's my fault then, is it?' Piper smiles as she eats a tiny spoonful of crunchy little brown flakes and yoghurt.

'Ha! Yes! Completely! His flat is tiny and there was nowhere really to sit and the drinks were really quite strong and Piper, I just thought, "Fuck it, I've been so good for so long, always trying to do the right thing, I'm just going to let it happen", and it did. He poured wine, we kissed, we did it.'

'"Did it",' Piper repeats. 'We're not in sixth form any more, Robin, you can say "sex", you know.'

'OK, we had sex,' I say, letting myself just say it with ease. 'Sex!' I add, once more with confident liberation.

'Was it *good* sex?' she asks, smiling, amused at my new-found brazenness.

'I think so.' I do think so. I don't have a lot to compare it to – there's only been Simon and Theo – but whenever I think about it, I feel good; sexy.

'You *think* so?' she says, looking at me over her cup.

'It was good, really good, actually. It was different, though. It's only ever been Simon or Theo, and then all of a sudden, with no warning at all, it's a new man and there are new things to deal with,' I say, hoping she'll pick up on my tone.

'By "new things", do you mean his dick?'

'Shhh, yes, Piper, yes, his . . . *dick*.' I'm blushing so hard at this point, I think people are looking. She's so far ahead of me in the confidence stakes, casually dropping the D-word over brunch.

'He was lovely; everything was lovely. He spent a lot of time on me, and I felt really good.' I hope this satisfies her. Thinking about it, Edward's the first man who really has spent that time on me. I smile at how much of a nice guy he is. There should be more Edwards in the world.

'But his dick, though.' Piper interrupts my thoughts matter-of-factly as she spoons more gluten-free nothingness into her mouth.

'You're not going to let it lie, are you?' I say, half-exasperated but half-amused at her boldness. I give in. 'He had a great dick! Very straight, very . . . thick.' I end up giggling. This time last week I was doing the school run, frazzled and tired, and now I'm in New York talking dicks over toast.

'You need to get a grip!' says Piper, alarmed at how inexperienced I am at this kind of chat.

'I already did!' I quip back, and we burst into full-on laughter.

We eat our way through our orders and chat a bit more about Callum. Piper clearly has no issues telling me every detail, every moan, every movement. I hear so much I almost feel as if I've had sex with the oh-so-marvellous Callum myself.

'So, how do you feel now you've had your first official one-night stand?'

I sit back, partly to take stock and partly because I've eaten so much it's hard to breathe, and think for a moment. I'd always thought that if I had a one-night stand I'd feel dirty and used. Mum used to refer to her friend's daughter Amy as a 'cheap tart' because she used to 'sleep around', and I think that sort of stuck with me. 'Nobody wants to marry a tart who gives it away on the first night,' Mum would say.

The thing is, last night I didn't care about that. I didn't want to marry Edward. I wasn't anticipating a relationship, or anything further than what was being offered in the moment. I felt free and liberated to just make choices on the spot without thinking about the future. Without thinking about the consequences. Without thinking about Lyla.

I instantly feel a pang of guilt for actually relishing the

thought of not having to think of her. Does that make me a bad mother? No, surely not. This won't touch her. She'll never know her mother went to a bar that served drinks full of sweets, drank too many and then went home with a man she didn't know. Talk about not remembering Stranger Danger! Jeez.

Despite all of that echoing of mum's dated sentiments, and my own motherly guilt whirring around in my head, I don't feel it. I don't feel cheap or bad or dirty. I went out and did something I wanted. I felt sexy. The way Edward touched me made me feel so wanted. It was urgent and fierce and passionate, compared to Theo's sometimes lack-lustre approach. Did the world shake for me when we finished? Maybe, yes, a little bit. Am I expecting him to contact me again? No, not really. Am I overly concerned about either of these things? No! Not really! The last thought makes me smile. How refreshing to feel so free. Not torturing myself with 'what ifs' and 'was I good enoughs', and just being happy about what happened. I went out, had fun in a bar, had decent (three positions and a bit of oral isn't to be sniffed at, is it?) sex with a decent man, and that's that. Move on. There's more of New York to see. And do, apparently.

'Piper, I feel great. I can do whatever the fuck I want,' I announce triumphantly.

'And what about Theo?'

'What about him? I'm not his girlfriend!'

With that, Piper enthusiastically throws both hands in the air and proclaims, 'Champagne! More champagne!'

'What? It's ten thirty in the morning!' But that doesn't stop us. We spend the rest of the day hopping from one 'this is my favourite little spot' to another – drinking and eating whatever we fancy off the menu on account of my new-found sexual liberation, and because Piper tells everyone who'll listen, 'It's about bloody time!'

ON MONDAY THERE'S A weird calm on set. The actors seem more relaxed, and Marnie in particular has such a light way about her, she almost seems like a different woman.

Natalie has recovered, and we set out our things in silence, quietly noting the difference in atmosphere but not yet asking why. Sarah bursts through the doorway, ecstatic.

'Have you heard?' she says, bounding over to us and clipping on her brush belt all in one movement.

'Heard what?' Natalie replies calmly, but I can tell she's intrigued too.

'He's gone! Got fired last night! Langston's off the movie and a new *female* director is being brought in today!'

'Good grief! What on earth happened?' Natalie says, slightly shocked.

'I dunno, but whatever it was, I'm glad. There were so many rumours flying around about the way he treats women. I'm glad he's finally had to face the music. He was a grade-A jerk.'

I'm about to change the subject and try to carry on with

the day as normal when one of the film executives we met on set the first day comes in. He gives me a knowing glance, and I instinctively look at my shoes as if I'm a five-year-old about to be told off.

Instead of scolding me, he asks for a word with Natalie, who puts down her palette and walks away with him, not even looking at me as she leaves. In the pit of my stomach I can feel a giant knot forming. What have I *done*?

'CHEERS!' NATALIE AND I both say, a bit too heartily since we're on our fourth drink of the night now.

'Robin, I've got to say it, you've astounded me. I always knew there was a spark in you, but this – well, this is something more. Recording that prick on your phone and sending it to the execs took such courage. I don't know what inspired it, but I'm proud of you,' she says with real sincerity.

'I didn't really think about it that much. I just knew there needed to be a result. I thought about Lyla, and how I'd protect her from anything, and it all just kicked into gear. After I sent the email I realised I needed Marnie's support – she's agreed now to back it up with a written statement but to be honest, I just went for it. I didn't have a chance to think about how it would affect my job or the agency or—'

'You're being utterly ridiculous! You've done wonders for the agency! We've been booked for the entire five-film movie franchise, thanks to our " outstanding code of ethics and moral integrity", Robin! *You* did that! I was trapped in a hotel room with my head over the loo feeling absolutely rotten, and there you were, sealing the biggest deal we've ever had! I'm amazed! Thrilled! More drinks, I think!' she says, downing the one we've only just toasted ourselves with. She's really going for it. I've been out for drinks with Natalie before, and she can definitely handle herself, but this added enthusiasm for drinking seems a little bit out of character, actually.

'Wow. I didn't think it would go that far. I just wanted to stop him hurting Marnie and the others,' I say, taking another sip of my still quite fresh cocktail.

'You did a good thing. I'm proud of you.'

With that praise from the woman I've admired for years, I say cheers again, down my drink and spend the night on a happy cloud of boosted ego and liquor.

THIRTY

A WEEK LATER, AND we're done. My feet are sore, my back aches, my suitcase is packed and bursting at the seams, thanks to a midnight spree in Sephora (a few extras for me, a couple of lipsticks for Kath and I'll pick Lyla up something at the airport), but I'm happy. I've taken myself off to Union Square, a big leafy block of space slap bang between massive shops like Forever 21 and Barnes and Noble, with a huge tree canopy for shade, walkways lined with benches, street vendors selling everything from acrylic prints to onions, and every sort of person you could ever imagine walking past and living their New York life, to sit with a Starbucks and watch the world go by.

New York has every kind of person, and they all seem to live and intermingle with each other in harmony. Surprisingly, there's a lot of wildlife in this concrete mecca, too. I take my phone out to snap a picture of a group of cute-looking squirrels and notice a message from Theo flashing up at me.

It's the first message I've had since that missed call I was too busy to reply too. Instantly my chest feels tight and I have that feeling when you're at the top of a roller coaster and you think, 'Why the fuck did I willingly get on this ride?'

I swipe it open.

Hi gorgeous, how's New York treating you? Shall we do drinks next week? I'm missing you xxx

I scroll up the chat feed and am reminded that the last message was me telling him I was homesick and him not really giving a shit.

The squirrels are starting to play quite animatedly and it's really distracting me from being angry about Theo. One of them is darting about with a bit of bread and the other two are dashing around after him. It's fun to watch, actually, like real live nature TV.

In the two weeks I've spent out here, I've thought about Theo so much less than I normally would. Little things have made my mind involuntarily go to him, and a couple of times I've wanted to text him but haven't. I've not been allowing him to take up that brain space, and it's felt great. I hadn't even noticed it's felt great because I've been so busy enjoying myself. I've proved to myself and everyone else that I'm good at my job, I've partied with Piper, made new friends, had hot sex and a non-chest-pain, anxiety-inducing text chat with hot sex partner and I feel good. The sun is shining down on my skin, the birds are cheeping, the squirrels are –

'ARGHHH, FUCKING HELL!' I scream at the top of my lungs in a crowded city park as I launch my Starbucks frap all over the floor.

The oh-so-cute squirrels have got a little more than animated and the head honcho has run up my bare leg and onto the back of my bench, enticing his sharp-clawed little friends to do the same, using me like a tiny critter transport ramp.

My leg is bleeding and I'm stood looking aghast at a) the squirrel attack, and b) my perhaps over-the-top yelling. This is New York, though, and clearly this happens every day because not a single person around me gives a shit. Not even the woman with a toddler attached to her breast seems to give a monkey's. I look over at her apologetically, and she just shrugs and smiles.

Man, I love this city. You can be whoever you want to be. You can save the day at work, ride hot men all night, ignore the man you foolishly thought you loved, be attacked by rabid rodents in the afternoon and everyone is just chill about it. Valerie Pickering would have an absolute meltdown. Ha!

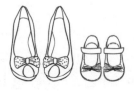

Part Five

Home is where the
heart is . . .

THIRTY-ONE

AUGUST

I CUT THE ENGINE of my car and look across at Lacey in the passenger seat as the late summer sun shines on us. 'Come on, lovely,' I say as cheerily as I can. Her eyes are still red from her tears, and I wish I could just make her feel better straightaway. We're on the way to a special place I know, because right now my bestie needs some love.

I've been back four weeks, and life has been crazy busy. After the success of New York, Natalie's booked me on more jobs than I'd normally take, and Lyla's summer holidays have whirled past so quickly I've barely had a moment to sit down. There have been some lovely days out as a twosome, and there was one day when Auntie Kath came with us on a day trip to the petting zoo; there were ice creams, a thrilling (feel the sarcasm) minibreak to see Mum and Dad for three (long) days in Cornwall. Lyla's seventh birthday party was a resounding success (Lacey, Kath and I perfected the wild animals theme – Wilde by name, wild by nature, ha) and Lyla really came out of her shell. She's now best friends for life with Finola's sturdy little son Roo, and for nearly all of this time Theo and I haven't been in contact. A few months ago that thought would be panic-attack-inducing but now . . . not so much.

It was initially hard not to message back to the couple he did send, a bit like that first week you go on a diet and have to resist eating the entire tube of Jaffa Cakes, but I did it. This is a big step for me. I'm always the girl on the diet that does eat the whole tube of Jaffas. Always. Theo texting made my heart race in a way I didn't like. Gone were the excited butterflies, and in their place was a tight, twisting sensation. But I remembered how different Edward in New York felt. No stress or fuss; I didn't panic or worry about anything. Edward's not on the scene, but that's how I need to feel about things. Theo induces a horrible, neurotic anxiety within me, and so instead of agonising over replies, I just ignored them, put my phone down and carried on with my day. Thanks to my willpower, my mind doesn't feel as foggy any more. I never thought I'd feel that way about Theo, or any man, actually, but I do. I feel clear-headed and able to see things for what they are; see myself for what I am.

At last, The Emptiness isn't here anymore. Although, with a new term looming and Lyla going back, if I'm honest I have to admit I'm worried it's hovering in the distance, just biding its time . . .

I've learnt that the key is keeping busy and booking positive stuff, for me as well as for Lyla, into my day.

This day, however, is about Lacey. As we walk in to the giant conservatory of Lawrence's, the smell of freshly baked cakes wafts around us and I can feel myself unconsciously grinning. I must look like an absolute lunatic as I walk over to our table smiling like the Cheshire cat, but how can anyone not feel joyous when they are minutes away from scones and pastries? I've worn my boyfriend-fit slightly oversized jeans and a loose tee on purpose, because I know I'm not going to hold back.

I've brought Lacey to Lawrence's because it's the happiest place I know (huge oval windows with striped canopies and swirling wrought iron frames adorning them outside; display cases full of baked delights to lure you in; tiny, pastel-clothed tables groaning under the weight of gilded china and the most incredible afternoon tea goodies), and right now she needs a boost. I popped into Dovington's earlier after dropping Lyla off at Simon and Storie's – apparently they're teaching her how to grow cress in eggshells this weekend; lucky little thing will be absolutely riveted, I'm sure – and found Lacey in the back room in bits.

Sat on the bottom rung of her storage unit ladder, Lacey's face was soaked with tears and her eyes puffy and swollen. Her lavender smock dress had dark purple splotches down the front where the tears had dripped off her face and all in

313

all, she was in a bad way. Apparently one of her suppliers had come in with the latest order and, with the sensitivity of perfume spilt accidentally on a cut finger, asked her if she was 'up the spout yet'. He, of course, had no idea how long she'd been trying or how increasingly hard she was finding the monthly disappointment. He probably just assumed someone married and her age was bound to want babies and had probably never given a moment's thought to the fact it's not easy for everyone, but really, he should have kept it to himself. If I'd have been there, I'd have told him, in no uncertain terms, that a) not all married women need to have babies unless they want to, and b) it's no one's bloody business but hers! Poor Lacey.

'I didn't know what to say to him,' Lacey stuttered between sobs, still perched on the ladder. 'I just stood there blinking and trying not to cry. My period came again this morning – just before he came in – and this month, after all the months of it not happening, I really thought it was it. I was four days late, Robin. Four.'

'Had you done a pregnancy test?' I asked as I squatted down beside her and stroked her knee.

'No,' she sobbed. 'The GP told us not to do a test until you're two weeks late, but honestly, all the signs were there. Tender breasts, cramps, fatigue – I really thought this was it, but it wasn't. It fucking wasn't. The cruel irony of fertility is that all the signs for pregnancy are almost identical to the signs of your period coming.'

'I'm so sorry, Lacey. I'm sorry it's not *the* month, and I'm sorry that guy was so insensitive. You'll get there. I know you will.' Poor Lacey. They've been trying for the best part of a year – she was full of glee when she told me they started on Christmas Eve. I don't think she ever imagined it might not happen. She and Karl have been trying all year to conceive, and it's clearly just not happening for them. I could see wasn't going to be on a good footing soon, so I suggested we throw in the towel for today, shut up shop (people can live without their bouquets for one day) and go to Lawrence's to fill our faces with deliciousness and put the world to rights. Without much hesitation Lacey nodded, flipped the little floral OPEN sign on the door to CLOSED and we headed off.

By the time we arrived, Lacey had stopped crying, but chat in the car was thin on the ground and she was distracted. I could tell she was thinking about it still. I found a good parking spot and we walked in. Located on the outskirts of Cambridge, Lawrence's is a hidden gem. You can always get a table but it's never empty, it being a favourite of the locals. I've been coming here with Auntie Kath, as a special treat, since I was tiny. Mum was always glad to let me go with her and I was always glad to feel indulged in such a sweet environment. I can't think of a better place to take Lacey right now. Lawrence's practically serves love on plates.

Once I've got over my joy at the very visible cake trolley, and we've rearranged the table so we can Instagram the living daylights out of it – even without the food on it, it's pretty – we look at the menus. Like everything else in here, even the menus are delightful. Light lilac card stock, printed with gold swirly ink and finished with a sheet of iridescent vellum over the top. If I ever do get married, my wedding stationery is for sure being based on these. I can see Lacey's eyes are looking a bit less red and swollen and she manages a smile. Unsurprisingly we settle on the full afternoon tea and sit back, happy with our choice and our unadulterated grown-up girl time.

Lacey looks out of the window for a second and says, 'I'd told Karl I was four days late. He told me not to get ahead of myself, but how can you not? We did everything right.'

'Of course you did, Lace, it just wasn't your time.'

'I'm starting to think it's never going to be my time, though. We're doing everything the apps say. We're waiting till the fertile days; I'm elevating my pelvis after every session; I'm checking to see if my discharge looks like school glue.'

'Wait, what? Why?'

'Because the bloody apps tell you to! Does it look like egg whites? Does it look like school glue? Is it thick? Is it clear? How hot are you? When did you last bleed? It's like the most intense personal interview of your life, but if it tells me the perfect time to conceive, I don't care. Once I tell it more about my vagina than I've told anyone in my life, it tracks my cycle and on ovulation day I get a notification. Like a text from my fanny, for fuck's sake.'

'OK, well, maybe next month is the month, then. It will happen, Lacey, it will.'

'I'm just so fed up. I'm so sick of hearing people say they didn't even have to try, or that it was a "happy surprise", when I'm trying so bloody hard all the bloody time, having sex on my optimum days even when neither of us are in the mood, taking every vitamin I should, already avoiding soft cheese and pâté! I'm starting to think there's something wrong with me or Karl, or that I'm letting him down in some way.'

I don't really know what to say or do, other than to just listen to her. I reach my hand out to lay it on her wrist. Lacey's usually the one pulling us both along, constantly propping me up. To see her so upset is unsettling, and I think all she wants right now is to vent; it's not like I have any solution to offer, after all. I was so lucky with Lyla, and as much as I won't say it now, I really didn't have to try. She just came along. I hate seeing Lacey struggle like this.

'Look, let's think of it like this, Lace: it's been what, eight, nine months since you really started trying?'

'Eight. Eight whole months,' she says in a thick voice that sounds like she might cry any moment.

'Well, that's only eight eggs. And like you said last month, it takes the average couple a year of trying, so you're only really three-quarters of the way through that, you're under average. I know it must be so completely shit when you both want it so much, but keep in mind that even the doctors say you don't need to worry yet. There's nothing wrong with you; it's just nature's timing. And when you do hold your beautiful little baby in your arms, it'll be all the sweeter. You'll be such a gorgeous mummy, I already know it.'

'Yes. You're right. It will happen. It's going to happen,' she replies a little too fiercely, more trying to convince herself than agree with me.

'Yes!' I say in the most encouraging tone I can muster.

The food arrives, and we're distracted by how amazing it looks. Everything looks almost too good to eat. On the bottom row, soft little sandwiches with straight edges where the crusts have been perfectly cut off. A selection of fresh fruit tarts; rose, mint and lemon macarons and miniature Victoria sponges on the middle row and then, oh wow, on the top row, two huge, warm scones with china pots of thick clotted cream and strawberry jam adjacent. I think I am in actual heaven.

I wish all my food was served on three-tiered cake stands. I might make that a thing. Buy a few colourful cake stands and just dish things up on them. If anything, it would be time-saving. No wasted trips back and forth to fetch the main course or dessert. I'd simply put starters, mains and desserts on each tier, and *voilà*! I could even do it with Lyla's food. Fish fingers on one layer, mashed potato on another and beans on the top. I take a moment to imagine her trying to eat baked beans off the top of a three-tiered cake stand, and realise how insane that would be. Not to mention how messy.

'Hello! Earth to Robin! Have you been hypnotised?' calls Lacey, waving a hand in front of my face. Wow, I was really getting into that.

'No; I was thinking about how I need to have more cake stands in my life. I'm going to treat myself in Lakeland next time I go.'

'I think I just need more cakes in my life!'

Lacey seems to have perked up. She's forgotten about being sad for a moment, and is stood up to hover her phone directly over the top of the stand to take the perfect picture. Nobody around us bats an eyelid, of course. They know when food is displayed this beautifully it would be a crime not to photograph it.

We dig into the sandwiches and swoon at how delicious they are. They're light and fresh and crisp, and I could eat a thousand more. Lacey has some colour back in her cheeks, and looks like she's feeling at least a bit uplifted. Good. We go quiet as we concentrate on the important job of savouring every bite.

'You know what, Robin?' says Lacey after her last bit of cucumber sandwich. 'If I'd fallen pregnant this month, I would have the baby in May.'

'Umm, yes, yep, that's nine months.' I'm not really sure where she's going with this.

'Well, May is the worst month to have a baby,' she replies drily. I see what's she's doing. She's trying to make herself feel better about it not being this month. I can't quite work

319

out why May is so bad, but I'm not going to stop her in the flow of talking herself into feeling better.

'It's the worst. May would be awful.' I think that's the right answer. She's nodding fervently, at least.

'It is, because it's the beginning of hay fever season; I could never take the baby out for a nice walk in the pram. Being pregnant in May would be horrible, giving birth in May would be horrible and having to look after a newborn in June would be horrible.'

'You're so right, Lacey. It's probably actually best that it didn't happen this month, really.'

'Yeah, definitely best.' And with that, we start on the second tier. I'm pretty sure we both know we're lying. Lacey doesn't get hayfever. May would be fine, any month would be fine, but it's not going to be May, so anything we can do to make that feel less painful for my best friend is OK with me.

The second tier is even better than the first. I usually think macarons are a bit emperor's new clothes. Everyone goes absolutely gaga over them, but I think they just taste like overpriced icing halves with jam between them. These, though. Oh, these are different. Each segment melts on your tongue and releases perfectly mixed, sweet, delicate flavours before you reach the filling, which compliments the meringue. I've never enjoyed a macaron more in my life, and suddenly I see what all the lifestyle bloggers get their knickers in a twist over.

Buoyed up by my magical macaron moment, I look up at

Lacey, who looks equally pleased, and says, 'I've got a crazy idea!'

'What?' Mischief glimmers in Lacey's eyes. She might be settled and married, but this girl loves a good time.

'Why don't we go out tonight?'

'What do you mean?'

'Out, out. You know, big hair, bright lips, high heels. Let's do it! It's Saturday, Lyla's with Simon and Storie learning how to live off the land or something, and what you need most, even more than these fucking delicious scones, is a cocktail. A big, strong cocktail.'

'One condition,' Lacey says, smiling.

'Anything.' I'm so eager to go, I actually do mean it.

'You do my make-up,' Lacey says, happily popping the last macaron in her mouth.

'HURRAH!' I say a bit too loudly, chinking my teacup against hers and sloshing tea onto the delicately embroidered tablecloth. 'I've spent five weeks rushing about in jeans or jersey skirts and flats. The last time I made any kind of big effort was New York. I might actually keep an eye out for a nice man this evening!'

'So Theo is *definitely* off the cards, then?' she says through a mouthful of pink icing.

'Nope, not really, I'm just not that bothered with him any more.' Wow, that felt weird to say and actually mean. I hadn't realised how little I cared until nudged.

'Oh wow, you've changed your tune.'

'Yep! About bloody time, as well! I'm starting to see what's important and honestly, it's not him,' I say, nodding on 'him' as if to really make my point.

'Hurrah again!' Lacey says cheerily, and we clink our cups once more.

THIRTY-TWO

ITH NEW YORK a blur of new experiences and, *cringe*, self-discovery, entertaining Lyla through the whirlwind of the summer holidays and work zapping all my energy, I'd forgotten how good it feels to let yourself relax and have fun with a girlfriend. God, it feels good. Like a really hot bath after a strenuous day, or a really cold cloudy lemonade on a summer afternoon.

After eating our body weight in miniature confections, we pop into Lacey's to select an outfit to take to mine. Her wardrobe is the stuff of any girl's dreams. Everything is neatly folded, carefully hung on matching hangers or stashed in its correct place and position. There's no 'crap pile' or plastic bags of junk at the bottom of the wardrobe, like mine. I need to take note. This is how to adult. Thanks to her immaculate system, it takes about thirty seconds to select a cornflower-blue embroidered shirt dress with a chunky tan belt and wedges. She folds them (of course) into a tote and we head back to mine, where the real magic begins.

It's late afternoon, so we're rich in time. It's been a hot, perfect late summer's day but the heat of the sun is fading and cooler air is wafting in on a welcome breeze. I open every window to allow it in and lay out my brushes on the bed as if I'm at work. The plan is to visit a couple of bars along the river, making the most of the late summer nights and not focus on anything except laughing and chatting.

Like old times, we spend forever on hair and make-up. False lashes (the subtle kind), backcombed hair, the good lipsticks that I don't use day to day – we let loose. We chit-chat about people we used to go to school with (we think Alison Berry from the year above us might be having an affair, judging by her weird Facebook statuses), Lacey and Karl's upcoming weekend break to Rome – poor Karl has been working all hours on a big new deal – how well Lyla seems to be getting on at school at the moment, and how that's such a relief. Standard chit-chat, lots of laughter and completely just what I need.

After twenty minutes of trying things on and taking them off again (nothing changes; it was like this fifteen years ago when we stood in Lacey's mum's house huffing and puffing while Tina told me I looked 'lovely in everything'), I settle on a denim playsuit with small wooden buttons up the side of each hip and gold sandals. It's fairly casual, but with my glimmering highlight and bouncing AF hair, I'm smashing it.

Once out and situated at a couple of sofas next to a low table near the bar, we don't hold back. It's as if we both inherently know that this is a treat, that it might not happen again for a while and that, maybe without realising it, we really, really needed it. We line up shots, we clink porn star martinis (even a bit tipsy, I shudder when it's my turn to order and yell 'porn star' across a busy bar, even if it is just a delicious cocktail and not actually an adult entertainer in a glass) and we shout into each other's ears about how much we love each other and how we'll never leave the other and how 'really, no really, you are the best friend I've ever fucking had'. We laugh and we dance a bit, and we have a ball. Why don't I do this more often?

At home in bed (I've managed to pull the sandals off and get the playsuit down to my waist, but those little wooden buttons are like tiny arrogant prison guards, and after a couple of failed attempts and a slight stagger and crash into the door frame, I give up and decide that wearing demin shorts to bed is fine), I text Lacey to make sure she got in OK after the taxi dropped me at mine.

'Yep, next to Karl, my second-best friend because you are my real, actual, forever best friend, Robin Wilde, I lob you.' She means love. I get it. I lob her too.

She's so lucky to be able to go home to her second-best friend. Her kind, handsome husband who loves her so dearly.

Suddenly the night isn't so fun any more, and my bed feels massive and lonely (even with my playsuit still on). I wish I had a nice man in mine like Lacey does in hers. I wasn't looking for a guy tonight, but then again, I wasn't not looking. A couple of decent-looking types caught my eye and one or two smiled but, unlike New York, I didn't feel brave enough to go over. Maybe I need Piper, or gummy sharks in drinks or just the buzz of the big city, but somehow I didn't have that confidence to waltz over and make small talk. Also, in fairness, nobody came over to me either. That's a bit sad, isn't it? I'm not awful to look at; I'm approachable, I think. But not tonight. And so here I am, sprawled out in a double bed with no one to share it.

I don't think it's unreasonable to text your friends when you're feeling a bit lonely. I'd text any of my friends right now, so it's no big deal at all. I would text Lacey, but she'll be asleep by now. Or not asleep with Karl, and I don't want to interrupt that.

I start to type. I know I shouldn't, deep down, but I carry on.

Theo, I miss you. I stare at the screen for a moment. Then: *What happened to us? I wish you were here to hold me.*

I hit send.

THIRTY-THREE

SEPTEMBER

S ITTING IN THE BACK of a black taxi, chugging slowly across Waterloo Bridge through the rush hour traffic (when is it not rush hour in central London?), I smooth down my gorgeous skirt and let my mind wander back over the last few days.

The drunken text, realistically, should have been a massive mistake. I sent it, passed out into the deepest sleep and woke up to not one, not two, but three messages from Theo.

I'm so glad you texted.

I miss you too.

Let's chat soon. Properly.

And so we did. I went downstairs (in aforementioned grotty dressing gown), poured the biggest glass of water, took a paracetamol, smiled as I dialled his number and forgot all about my hangover. It's like everything that went before was water under the bridge, and something inside me switched. That jolt of loneliness in bed triggered me into wanting him again. Life's too short. I want to be happy. After our long call and an intense exchange of messages I finally agreed to meet him. He asked me to dinner, and with a new wave of hope, I accepted.

The taxi slows and comes to a halt. We're on the South Bank, and I can see the bold red sign glowing on top of the OXO Tower.

Here goes . . .

WITHOUT SKIPPING A BEAT, Theo jumps up to pull out my chair. As always, he looks fantastic. He's styled himself perhaps on a magazine model, and I'm completely dazzled by it. Sharp navy trousers, expensive-looking leather belt, crisp white shirt with the top few buttons undone. On his chair hangs the navy suit jacket, and I can see a red pocket handkerchief just peeping out. I'm not sure if it's sexy or pretentious, but before I have a chance to mull it over, he speaks.

'You . . . you look incredible. You look so different. I can't get over it. Just beautiful,' Theo stutters in shock.

I think about how amazing it is that he can see how great I look. I mean, I thought I looked all right all the time we spent together, and I know I look a bit better now, but I wouldn't go as far as to say 'so different'. They say the sexiest thing you can be is confident, and lately, thanks to the success of the job in New York, the one-night stand, work life back in the UK going so well, I do feel more confident. I've shown myself how much I can achieve when I work for it, when I put my own mind to it. Maybe that's it. Or maybe I just contoured the shit out of my cheeks. Thanks, though, Theo. I guess.

In the glow of the golden fairy lights I realise Theo looks nervous. It's weird. The man who is usually cooler than Kanye is actually fidgeting a bit. It's like being on a first date, or perhaps this is what the start of a proposal feels like.

Oh my God, is he going to propose?

Is he going to actually get down on one knee and whip out a tiny box with the engagement ring of my dreams in it?

Hmmmm . . . I wonder if it's brand new, or an exquisite family heirloom from his mother's side? Oh, God, I'm so glad I painted my nai—

'Look, Robin. Darling. I'm sorry we've not spent much time together recently. Things at the office have been insane with the acquisition. I wish I had more time for just hanging about at home with you.'

Oh.

He's not going to propose. Of course not. Why did I go there?

'I don't just "hang about at home", Theo,' I say, slowly, because I'm silently kicking myself for going to Proposal Land in my head.

'No, I know that, I just mean, your life, it's more . . .

flexible, isn't it?' he says carefully, reaching out his perfect hand and placing it on my non-bejewelled fingers.

He's got me there. It is.

'Theo, this is all lovely, amazing actually, but haven't you noticed? The reason we haven't spent a lot of time together is because *I've* been really busy. I know you've been tied up with this new deal, but since I've been back from New York Natalie has been putting so much extra trust in me and loading more and more on, and I never thought I'd say this, but I'm really enjoying it. It feels good to have my own thing and to be managing everything else as well. I feel happy. I feel like I'm actually living life. Properly. For the first time in a long time.'

Theo sits toying with the stem of his wine glass, as if I'm boring him and he needs something to do.

'I'm sure you're doing a great job. Natalie's so lucky to have such a keen and efficient assistant,' he says with his head tilted in a sympathetic fashion.

I flinch a little in frustration. I don't want him to sense my irritation and know how much that bothered me, so I clench my thighs a bit and try not to let my eyes narrow.

'Yeah.' Time for a conversation change, I think. 'Well, it's nice we've both got a bit of time together now. This menu looks great. What are you going for?' I ask in a high-pitched, overeager voice that I silently pray he doesn't pick up on. I still have a glimmer of hope that we have something here. Why does he always make the assumption that we haven't seen each other because of *his* life? But then, a man doesn't rent out an entire freaking patio unless it's love. I'm sure it's fine. It's a new start.

Everything's going to be fine. Yes. Fine.

Pleasingly, there's a change in the air. He seems so much more . . . here. His phone is away, he's looking into my eyes, he's present. Now feels like a good time to explain to him that things need to be a bit different if we're going to try this again. To gently nudge him into treating me more like his equal and less like an afterthought. I think he'd do that for me. I think he wants to, actually.

This whole set-up is breathtaking. We are completely alone; even the staff are inside, patiently waiting for Theo's signal. The candles are gently flickering and the river looks beautiful, reflecting all the lights of the city.

I turn my head away from the view and look back at Theo's wonderfully chiselled face. 'Theo, why did you do all this for me?'

Theo shifts uncomfortably in his seat and starts. 'I've missed you, Robin, you know this. I texted you this. I've really fucking missed you. I did all this to show you how special you are to me and I wanted to impress you, to win you back, to have you as mine.' As he says it, I detect a very slight waver in his voice. I think he actually does mean it. I *think* he does want me in his life, as a permanent fixture. He seems so heartfelt that I can barely breathe; it's like all the wind has been knocked out of my sails by hearing him be so sincere. Must still try to remember what Brain said, instead of just letting Heart take over and completely melt any resolve. I need to stand firm here.

I allow myself to lean back in my chair and take a deep, long breath, as if the extra oxygen will help keep my head clear and stop me from spiralling into him, giving myself into everything he says.

'I've missed you too, Theo. The last few weeks without you have been so different. I've missed being able to call you or text you with little updates. Lyla's missed having you around to play with. I just . . . I just need things to be a bit different this time, to feel more like your actual girlfriend, maybe; to spend proper time with you – not just in the slots where you can squeeze me in.' I'm hoping my very gentle tone will help him see this in a positive light, and not feel backed into a corner. Natalie always says 'a threatened man is a useless man'.

He looks at me so intently, so sincerely, I feel butterflies in my tummy. I watch the cogs turn in Theo's brain.

'I get it; you want more time with me. Why don't you come to my annual work party? It's in Paris this year at Hotel Banke, and it will be fucking amazing, Robin. We have one every year to thank the staff and boost morale on the final leg till Christmas. They're always epic dos. I'd love to have you there.'

Whoa. Was not expecting that. An actual invite to an actual thing with actual other people at. What a turnaround!

'OK, so, we could spend the weekend together, maybe make a minibreak of it . . .'

Not missing a beat, Theo very quickly says, 'Yes! Amazing!'

Oh my God, a proper minibreak with Theo Salazan, my actual proper boyfriend. I'm stunned. Thrilled, but stunned.

I lift my head up to meet his gaze and open my mouth to say how incredibly happy I am, but before I can get the words out, Theo shifts around in his seat again and says, with a pained look on his face, 'Well, probably not this time, actually. It's on the Thursday, so we'd go in the morning. I need to see a couple of people about the contracts, and then I probably need to be back in the office on Friday afternoon. Obviously I'd love to spend it just with you, but these contracts, you know how they are. There's a spa, though; I'd book you in, give you some pamper time.'

I'm starting to feel like things haven't changed – this isn't a trip for us to spend time together. Why is he always trying to buy me?

Tensing my whole body again, but this time not trying to hide my narrowed eyes, I begin: 'So, we'd fly out, I'd spend the day alone, then be your plus one to a work function and then fly home the next morning? And that's meant to be a special treat for me?'

His eye twitches in the usual way that it does when he's getting annoyed.

'I'm offering to take you to Paris, Robin.' He takes a sip of his wine and puts the glass down a little too heavily, causing a tiny splash of red to hit the clean white tablecloth.

I watch the red stain spread out and suddenly I feel very angry. 'Er, no; you're offering to have me accompany you to a day I'd have to spend alone and then be introduced offhandedly to people you don't even care about before you pack me off home again!'

Twitch, twitch.

'Are you kidding me? This is such an amazing gift for someone like you!' he says, exasperatedly hitting the palm of his hand on the table, making the cutlery jump.

I'm not going to be intimidated. He's no match for Langston, and I stood up to him.

'"Someone like me?"' Wow. What a prick. He hasn't changed. I can't believe I thought he might have.

'Yes, Robin, someone like you. I hate to break it to you, but not a lot of guys like me would be interested in a single mother with a part-time job in applying lipstick! A lot of girls in your position would LOVE to come to this with me!'

Ooof, that hurt. That really fucking hurt. I feel like I've been punched in the middle of my chest and the wind has been completely knocked out of me. I can feel my skin burning and my eyes stinging at the indignation. He's revving up for more.

'Robin, you make no sense,' he says, leaning forward with both hands flat on the table as if he's having to steady himself. 'I'm offering you an amazing night in Paris, and you're turning it down because you think you've got something better to do, or what? Are you going to have your own party in Paris? You've spent the best part of this year hinting to come along to things like this with me, desperate to be by my side, desperate to be treated to things like this, and now you're saying no! One glamorous "work" trip to New York and you're a changed woman, are you?' He laughs at his final sentence, as if me being a 'changed woman' is such a hilarious concept to him.

'Wow, Theo. That was really nice,' I practically spit, struggling to let the words work their way over my tongue, I'm so furious. White-hot rage pours over me and I clench my hands in my lap, digging my fingers into my thighs just to keep myself from reeling. 'As it happens, I *do* feel different, and New York *was* glamorous. I worked my arse off, achieved more than anyone expected and, unlike you, the men there treated me like something they actually wanted!'

'You're not changed, Robin,' he says so quietly I can hardly hear him. His eyes are furious; I don't suppose he's ever been rejected before, especially not by someone 'like me'. Louder now, he continues: 'You might have flounced in here in your crazy-for-your-age dress and high heels, thinking you're something special, but you're not. You're a mess!' He gestures his hand to me as if I don't know who he thinks is a mess. Bastard. I get it; there's no one else fucking here. 'You rush around in a state of absolute frenzy not knowing your arse from your elbow, you message me every time you can't cope, you barely know how your car works, your idea of organisation is papers slung all over your kitchen table and I'm not sure I've ever seen you in something pressed! I'm amazed you can manage *anything* in your actual fucking life! Do you know how many men want to take on a woman like you and her poor offspring that gets thrown at every Tom, Dick and Harry you decide is flavour of the week? Not many, Robin, not many! You want to walk away from all this, do you?' Theo spits as he gestures at the twinkling surroundings.

I blink back tears. I always knew Theo had a ruthless streak, but this attack feels much more vicious than I thought him capable of, full of pure spite.

'Robin, I'm telling you this because I care.' His voice softens in alarmingly stark contrast to the one he used only a second ago, and he reaches out for my hand. Limply I let it stay there, shocked to feel how cold his hand is compared to my hot, sweaty self, flushed with horror at the way the evening is going. 'You're not as special as you think you are. Anybody with half a brain can do a bit of blusher on someone, and you don't even have Lyla all the time – Kath has to rescue you every time something pushes you over the edge. Oohhh poor, poor Robin, she's crying again. Lyla's spilt some milk and Robin can't handle it! Call Auntie Kath to save the fucking day, as usual!' He takes his hand off mine and sits back, clearly happy to have control of the conversation and relishing my distraught expression. 'And then, once you've dried your pathetic, snivelling face, you just come running to me for comfort and a good time, don't you? You don't want to come to Paris as my plus one, but I didn't hear you complaining about being my plus one when I paid for every dinner we've ever eaten together and treated you like a fucking princess.'

I pause to take a breath. A year ago – three months ago, even – I might have burst into uncontrollable tears or run for the hills. But now? Today? No. Not without saying my piece. 'You might view me as a big mess. And you might think I'm just pissing around with a bit of mascara and blusher, but that pissing around actually earns me decent money.'

I push my chair back to give myself some room. I feel like I'm suffocating, but can't let him know how close I am to vomiting/crying/fainting or all of the above. I'm going to bloody well stand my ground. My good, decent ground.

'Money that enables me to take care of myself and my daughter. And actually, Theo, I'm pretty fucking good at it. I'm not perfect, but I try every day to get my shit together. I'm doing my best and I'm managing – succeeding, actually! And at least I have the strength to be honest with myself about that. I haven't spent the last few years of my life trying to fix all my life moments – I've accepted the repercussions and I'm facing up to them. I'm just trying to move forward and better myself, for Lyla and for me.'

'Life moments?' he guffaws. 'So you meant to be a lonely single mother living in her granny's house, did you? You've got no real plan, Robin, and no aspirations. You're just happy

337

to trundle on, fucking your life up and showing no backbone to your child and hoping to God that someone like me will come with a new life on a silver fucking platter. More fool me – I'm offering you all this and you don't want it? Are you fucking *kidding* me?'

He's getting louder and louder, and as my eyes fill up with hot, heavy tears, I can't handle it any more. I didn't mean to be a lonely single mother, but I wouldn't change it. Lyla is everything. Every little insecurity I've ever felt is pouring out of his mouth and flooding over me. I've never felt more attacked, and not just me but my little girl too. He knew that using Lyla would break me, but I blink back the tears, not wanting him to have the satisfaction. The fairy lights and the river are dulled through my blurred vision. Everything feels disgusting and dirty; I can't quite breathe, and my hearing starts to blur along with my vision.

I'm drowning in his cruel words, and before I know it I've tipped my chair back onto the floor and I'm standing up, looming over the table with my hands resting flat on it, arms straight.

I'm wounded, and my head is spinning but, somewhere in me, there's a drop of strength – strength I didn't even know I had, strength I'd never found before now.

I look Theo dead in the eyes and say, 'You don't scare me, Theo Salazan. Your opinions don't define me. This is over.'

And with that last moment of valiance, I turn on my heel and walk out.

Not the graceful walk of a runway model, but an urgent stomp, knocking my hips past corners of tables and throwing my arms out in front of me to burst through the patio doors and escape all of this. I just want to get out, get away from this, run back through time to a place where I never knew Theo, where I never fell for him, thought I loved him and then felt completely and utterly destroyed by him.

As I leave I can hear him bellowing, 'Don't you do this, Robin, don't you *dare* do this!' I feel a burning sensation up the back of my right calf. Assuming it's the physical exertion, I despise myself briefly for not using that extortionately priced gym membership. I carry on to the lift, hit the down button so many times I almost induce RSI and hurtle into it before anyone has the chance to stop me. The doors close mercifully quickly, but it takes an eternity to go down. I take a deep breath. I'm shaking. In the brief calm, I have a moment to catch my reflection in the thankfully dimly lit mirrors. I'm crying. I thought I could hold it together, but obviously not. There's dried wax all up my tights. I must've kicked one of those floor candles up myself, for fuck's sake.

Fuck.

THREE HOURS LATER – one Uber, one painfully bright train, one black cab and a slow walk up the front path – and I'm home. The house is quiet and empty without Lyla. My heart is heavy, and I'm suddenly more grateful than I thought I'd ever be for the brushed cotton tie-dye nightie Kath kindly customised for me. I pull it off the drying rack and over my head; it feels like a cuddle from someone who loves me. I fall onto the sofa with smudged black mascara and a still perfectly painted pink lip. I let out a slow, quiet laugh.

Just a few hours ago I'd imagined an entirely different night. Gentle chatter about missing each other; exciting plans for the future; his hand on mine, eyes locked, delicious wine, then back to his for slow, perfect, loving sex and falling asleep wrapped up in his perfectly tanned arms. I wanted so much more from this evening, and now it's all gone, shattered, like I've been robbed. I replay his words over and over again in my head on a hideous, unstoppable loop. But the deepest cut is the hopelessness: for the first time since I met him, all the hope I had for 'Theo and Robin' is gone.

He's not in love with me.

And I feel empty, vacant.

'He's not in love with you.' I say the words out loud to make it feel real. To get my stupid head around the idea that no man like Theo could ever really love someone like me. I told him his opinions don't define me, but actually, very quietly, I wonder if they do.

I feel worthless.

'He's not in love with you, Robin.' I repeat it again to myself before getting up and standing in front of the speckled (wow, I should clean more) mirror above the fireplace. 'He does not love you.' I laugh, hysterical and overwhelmed with emotion. I let myself fall into this painful and oddly exhilarating moment.

I let myself laugh at silly old Robin and embrace the cruel hilarity of the evening, pushing aside the fleeting thought that the next emotion that'll seep in will be rage. An emotion far more exhausting.

THIRTY-FOUR

I SPEND THE NEXT three days in a daze. I can't focus on anything at all. I've let his words soak into me, permeating every part of my self-confidence. I don't even tell Kath I'm home for the first day, in fear of him being right about me running to her at every turn. She finds me the next day (I'll forever regret giving her that set of keys) after I ignored four of her calls and voicemails asking how my 'special night' went. Once in (and once she's had a bit of a go at me for not telling her I was home, which seems odd for Kath, who's usually so forgiving), she boils the kettle, wafts around fluffing pillows, opening windows (I haven't bothered to wash) and picking up empty food wrappers (I ate my feelings, apparently) and I tell her everything. I flit between laughing manically about how hilarious the whole thing is, crying my eyes out because I know it's truly over and wanting to go down to his office and flip the tables over because I hate him so much. He has validated everything The Emptiness was, and is. I've spent the best part of this year fighting my thoughts, proving to myself that I'm good, I'm worthy, but, right there, in that unreal, beautiful set-up, he laid out every hellish thing I think about myself. It's like he knew. He read me. He knew my secret list of painful fears and one by one he took them and stabbed me with them.

I have never, in all my life, felt as shit as I do now. The Emptiness feels vastly unforgiving.

Kath has faffed around me, making unwanted cups of tea, telling me about how she had to miss Cupcakes and Crochet for a headache (I'd love having a headache to be my only problem right now) and throwing out benign phrases like, 'there's plenty more fish in the sea' and 'it'll happen when you least expect it', which just make me cry even more because here we are, nine months past New Year and I'm in the same predicament. I ask Kath to leave me be. I can't handle her. I don't want to be force-fed cheery quips about fish. I want to sit alone and stare at the TV until I fall asleep and it fades into white noise. Lyla is at her dad's and I've texted Natalie that I have a stomach bug and can't take on jobs this week. I want to be as alone as I feel.

But on the third day, after I've sunk as low as I think I can, my tears dry up and I realise I'm not in the same predicament as I've been in the past.

I don't have to drown in The Emptiness.

I have a choice.

I can make this choice.

If New York taught me anything, it's that I can handle my life. I, Robin Wilde, am a confident and in-control woman, and whatever life throws at me can be managed. I *can* do this.

With my new-found determination and Lyla still with Simon, I decide it's time to stop living off cupboard scraps and go to the shops. I don't care what I look like – it's not important, I'm above all that now. I'm just going about my life, handling it.

If I want to handle my life in a matted, greasy ponytail and sagging-round-the-bum jogging bottoms, then I jolly well will. I'm sick to the back teeth of conforming to society's rules and being told what to do all the time. I'm rising far above all that. Find a man, be a good girl, bake a cake, take your child to soft play, don't be too loud, don't get too drunk, don't talk about porn, don't break out of your box. Fuck it all.

I park haphazardly across two spaces and slam the door shut as I march into the shop. I grab a basket and start walking through with the sole aim of filling it with whatever I want. I'm not going to do what I always do and try to be good. Why bother? I'm alone anyway, so I may as well enjoy my life. I walk over to the refrigerator aisle and dump in an eight-pack of white chocolate mousse, then I mooch over to the frozen foods section and throw in a couple of frozen pizzas, and finally I meander through the wine aisle, deciding which tipple tickles my fancy.

'Hello, stranger!' comes a familiar voice. It's Gillian. Lovely, kind, sensible-things-like-peas-and-bread-in-her-trolley, Gillian.

I stand there in my sagging joggers, BO-smelling baggy T-shirt and bedraggled hair and look at her. She's perfectly turned out. She's in a lovely Boden cotton jersey dress with pretty, comfortable flats and her hair, unlike mine, looks like it's been washed recently. A PSM is the last person I want to see. I feel like shit. A little part of me thinks maybe I *am* shit.

'Gillian, hi. I was just . . . looking at the wine. Things have been a bit crap, so . . . you know,' I say, trailing off.

I can see Gillian's politeness going into overdrive. She's clearly judging me and thinking I'm a disgusting mother for only buying chocolate desserts and frozen junk food. She's probably going to tell Finola, and they'll stop their children hanging around with Lyla because she's a scuzzy bad influence, and then, somehow, Val will overhear and say poisonous things to Lyla again. I can tell Gillian wants to say something, but my defiance gets the better of me and I'm not going to let her.

'Look, Gillian, like I said, things have been tough lately. The last thing I need is to hear your opinion on it. I know you're perfect, you all are, but I'm not and that's that. Let's just leave it, shall we, and I'll see you next week at school,' and I turn on my heel and walk as fast as I can, without looking like I'm going to wet myself, to the self-service checkouts.

I take myself and my eight chocolate mousses home and eat four in a row. Then, like the responsible adult I am, I feel sick, have a cry and go to bed. As Kath would, no doubt at the worst possible time, remind me, tomorrow is a new day. Thank fuck.

Except when i wake up, it's not a new day and a fresh tomorrow, it's the same day, just later and with some loud knocking at the door. Surely not Kath? She texted earlier saying she wouldn't be coming over because she's feeling a bit under the weather, and Simon isn't due to drop Lyla off till the morning.

As soon as I stand up, I regret eating the mousses and regret even more leaving the sticky pots all over the arm of the sofa as I knock past them and they all clatter to the floor. I check my phone and it's 8 p.m., and there are four missed calls from Gillian and two from Finola. Has there been some kind of school emergency?

Further banging on the door indicates that I need to actually go and open it and so I do, and to my surprise and horror, it's them. Gillian and Finola are standing on my step, holding a bottle of wine each, and I think I spy a large box of Ferrero Rocher too.

'We don't want to intrude or upset you further,' Gillian starts nervously, twiddling the sleeve of her navy cardigan and smoothing down her very lovely white dress. She always looks nice, I note. Not like me.

'But it sounds like you've got yourself into a state, darling, and we're not going to leave you like that. Nothing's as bad as all this,' Finola adds, gesturing at me and my haggard condition. 'Now, step back, let us in and let's see what we can do to help.'

It's pretty clear they're not going home, so, still slightly dumbfounded, I open the door wider and step back to let them in. I inwardly pray that there are some windows still open upstairs and that the house doesn't stink of mousse pots and sweat. I still haven't showered, and all pride in my home has disappeared. God, this is embarrassing.

Finola being Finola bulldozes straight through the lounge and into the kitchen. Gillian tiptoes after her, and a little part of me dies inside that they are seeing my home like this. There are wrappers, boxes, pots and food containers littered over every surface; old teabags sit in a cold pile by the kitchen sink; the recycling box is full of M&S individual G&T cans, and all over the floor by the washing machine is a pile of my dirty laundry. It was this morning's attempt at 'getting on with things', but I didn't quite manage to get as far as actually loading the machine. I felt that, given the circumstances, filthy clothes on the kitchen floor would be perfectly fine. Now that I'm having Posh School Mums over for the first time, I'm not sure it is. Walking through the house, I can definitely smell fustiness. I want to die a bit.

'Robin, where is Lyla?' says Gillian slowly and loudly to me, as if I'm not following her.

'She's at her dad's. Look. Obviously, all this will be cleared up by tomorrow.'

'Would you like us to help you? I'm always tidying up after Clara, so this is nothing,' she lies. Her wide eyes and furtive glances around at the chaos suggest that she's having some mild anxiety about the environment she's been thrust into.

'No, no, it's OK, just, er, sit down and I'll, um, make you—'

'Don't play silly buggers, my dear – let's pull our socks up and sort this mess out,' orders Finola, hands on hips, riding boots still firmly on over her cream jodhpurs, 'and then we can have a proper talk about what's going on and see if we can get you out of whatever pickle you're in. I've no doubt it's a man-shaped pickle!'

At that, Gillian and I exchange eyebrow-raised looks. We pause. I think for a moment I might cry. And then we both burst into laughter.

'Oh for goodness' sake! You know what I mean!' Finola says, ruffled at our immaturity but holding back a smirk herself.

We're still laughing. My belly hurts from laughing, and oh, wow, it feels good to use those muscles and have a huge smile on my face! As I laugh, I feel myself relax and give in to their help. By the state – and smell – of things, I need it.

For the next twenty minutes, these lovely ladies bustle around my house with bin bags and the hoover while I ferry things upstairs to find them homes and put away last week's laundry. It takes no time at all, and once it's done, we flop down on the sofa, still feeling a bit giddy about Finola's inadvertent penis joke.

'Thank you. This is so kind of you,' I say, still flopped into the sofa cushions, really very desperately needing a shower now.

'You looked awful in the shop, Robin, I was really worried,' Gillian says, turning her head to look at me but sinking into the freshly plumped sofa cushions too. I've never seen her look so relaxed. It's nice. *She's* nice.

'I'm sorry for being so rude. I don't know why I said those things. I was so tired and worn down. I'm really so sorry.' I get up to go and get the Ferrero Rocher. They bloody deserve one and I've never deserved one more.

'No, don't be, it's fine. I just want you to know, I wasn't judging you at all. I was concerned for you. I've never seen you like this,' Gillian says, waving her hand in my direction and raising her voice so I can hear her in the kitchen as I fetch the chocolates. 'You're normally the glamorous one of the bunch.'

'Erm, what?!' I say, standing in the kitchen doorway, completely flabbergasted.

Finola heaves herself off the sofa cushions and sits up straight to talk.

'You know, dear, the sparkly froofy-floofy one with your hair and your make-up all just perfect. Gillian was quite alarmed to see you looking so dishevelled, and to tell you the truth, so was I when you opened the door.'

Gillian sits up too, and blinks excessively like she does when she's about to say something big. 'Robin, I feel I should say, and I know Finola will agree, you are a wonderful woman. You are raising a charming little girl, you work very hard at your job, you always look so pretty and your home is . . . lovely.'

'Hear, hear!' cheers Finola with gusto.

While we all know the last bit of that statement is a stretch, everything else feels so welcome and much needed. Coming from two women I look up to and respect, this is such an antidote to Theo. I feel looked after and cared for and it's lovely.

THIRTY-FIVE

TWO WEEKS LATER

NOTHER MORNING, ANOTHER RACE to get in the car. I don't know if my house has some secret vortex I don't know about, but if I have to spend another minute searching for bits of school uniform it will finish me. I think I've spent 98 per cent of my income on replacing bits of uniform and yet we never have any.

Eventually, after Febrezeing yesterday's pinafore to get another wear out of it (don't judge me), we're in the car and heading to school. It's Harvest Festival day, so spirits are extra-high and Lyla treats me to a loud rendition of 'Autumn Days' while I try to apply lip gloss at the traffic lights. Nailing it.

Inside, the atmosphere is twice the intensity of that in the car. Children are dashing to and fro with their offerings for the table (we're required to bring in tins and packets for the local food bank) and mothers are dithering with complimentary cups of tea served by Mr Ravelle, who has a gaggle of women round him, hooked on his every very smooth word.

The children descend down the hall to their classrooms to 'prepare', and we let ourselves be herded into the hall past the offering table, which is decked out with vases of dried flowers and stems of wheat and barley. I've lost Finola and Gillian, but I can hear the shrill tones of Val behind me chatting with a Reception mum.

'Oh my GOD, Steph, look!' Val shrieks with excitement in her voice.

'Oh, what? What?' poor Steph asks.

'On the table. Some mother's brought in value beans! Ugh!' She points.

'Oh. That's all right, isn't it? It's going to the food bank. I suspect they'd be glad of any beans, really, they're in a bit of a muddle if they're using a food bank aren't they?' Steph replies kindly.

'But *value beans*? How revolting,' Val insists.

'We've had value beans quite a few times, and honestly, Val, you wouldn't taste the difference,' Steph says with a calm, kind tone.

'I would! Who on earth is so cheap as to bring value beans in? I'd be embarrassed!'

Feeling my blood boil over at this conversation, I whip round and without giving it a second thought, I snipe, 'Get a life, Val, it's a tin of beans. Most people would simply be grateful. Nobody cares except you.'

I turn back round and keep walking, leaving Steph looking smug and Val standing in her Valentinos with her mouth wide open. I don't care what she thinks of me at this point. Gone are the days of worrying about her opinion, and if I've learnt anything these last few months, it's to stand up to bullies.

We take our seats, I've found Gillian and Finola and Mrs Bell starts playing the piano. One by one tiny children file in, waving once they spot mums and dads and sitting down crossed-legged on the floor. Each child has a paper band round their head with foils and glitter in oranges, golds, browns and reds to give a seasonal theme to the production. Lyla waves and points enthusiastically at her headband and I excessively thumbs-up and wave back.

Gillian leans in and whispers, 'How's Lyla feeling about the dance routine? Clara's been practising for days.'

Errr, what?

I didn't know there was a routine. I've had no memo about this. I've heard the 'Autumn Days' song eighty times, but no dance routine. A little knot appears in my stomach. Have I dropped the ball? Was I supposed to parent this situation? Fuck.

Mrs Bell plays the piano, the children stand up and begin to sing. I don't know what it is about little children singing, but the hairs on my arms stand on end and I feel so over-come with emotion I have to bite my lip to stop myself from weeping.

Three gorgeous, slightly tuneless songs in, and Mr Ravelle comes forward. His shirt is awfully tight and he really is rather buff. I can barely look at his face.

'Welcome, ladies and gentlemen, and thank you, children, that was some fantastic singing, I think we'd all agree.' The audience give a murmur of appreciation. 'Now, as I'm sure you're all aware', he chortles on, 'some of the children have a rather special dance piece to perform for you. So, without further ado, I give you The Autumn Leaves!'

With a round of applause from Mr Ravelle as he walks backward off the stage with a flourish, all of Lyla's class stand up and 'Autumn Days' starts playing on the piano. I'm feeling very nervous. I know she knows the song, but choreography is another matter. Please let her be OK . . .

One by one the children find their spots and raise their arms. The music starts and they lower arms with wiggling fingers, like leaves falling from trees. So far, so good. Everything's going quite well until the second line. At 'smell of bacon as I fasten up my laces', the formation changes and they begin to do something else. Except Lyla doesn't. Lyla hurtles forward and flails around in what I assume is her idea of free-form dancing. My heart leaps into my mouth . . . But there's rhythm there. You've got to give her that. We're on the chorus now, and she's completely broken free. Some of the other children have stopped their dance to watch her – some are even starting to tentatively join in – and Mrs Barnstorm is kneeling at the side of the stage desperately pointing and hissing at them to get back to their places. Lyla hears nothing, though; she's fully feeling the spirit of the song and having the time of her life prancing back and forth, waving her arms and, oh my *God*, is she twerking?

They end ceremoniously on, 'I mustn't forget', and with it, Lyla takes her paper crown off her head and hurls it into the audience like she's at some kind of rock concert.

The crowd heartily applauds, the children walk off confused and Mrs Barnstorm looks close to a breakdown. I'm mortified. I should have taught her the routine, or at least practised it. Why didn't I know there *was* a routine? I sit through the rest of the festival with flushed cheeks, and by the time we're at post-show teas and coffees, I want to hide.

'What an enthusiastic performance from Lyla!' says Mr Ravelle, striding over to me with a cup of tea in hand. Wow, close up he really is quite handsome.

'Ha, yes, ha ha, she's very, er, energetic.' Of course it was *my* child who went AWOL. I bet everyone thinks it's because she comes from a broken home where her mother can't – but then I stop myself before the old negative thoughts take over.

'Do you know what I think, Ms Wilde?' Mr Ravelle says gently.

Oh God, I don't think I really want to know. He carries on anyway.

'I think it's marvellous to see a child with such a passion

for music. I could see all the other children were completely enthralled by Lyla's interpretation of the dance, and honestly, so was I. Wouldn't it be terribly boring if every child were the same?' He continues to look at me with kind, emerald-green eyes.

OK, was not expecting that. Could he tell I was mortified?

'Yes . . . it would. She's a special little thing. I didn't actually know there was a dance . . . I feel a bit silly, really, that I didn't help her learn it properly.'

'Ms Wilde,' he says, much more tenderly than I thought he was going to; it's actually a bit arousing to liaise with a man so tall and chiselled, yet so sweet and nurturing, 'Lyla is wonderful. She's quite a trendsetter here; all the other children think she's fantastic – I often see them following her lead. It's very rare to see a child as young as Lyla take such ownership of herself and display such confidence. She must have some excellent role models in her life. It's fantastic to see, and even more fantastic to see it rubbing off on some of the other, more guided children.'

Embarrassingly, once again I feel tears prickling behind my eyes. Here I was, always thinking we were being laughed at or that I was doing her a disservice, but all this time she's been the leader of the pack. I could learn a thing or two from her.

Before I have time either to weep over my well-adjusted trendsetting child or ask Mr Ravelle if he wants to father my next child, all the kids come running in from the hall, paper crowns in hand (even Lyla has hers back – clearly liberated from the floor of the hall), and find their parents.

'Mummy, did you see my dance? I practised it with Auntie Kath! Did you like it?' Lyla says so enthusiastically I almost can't understand her jumbled words.

'Like it? Lyla, I LOVED it!' I reply, wrapping her into a huge, squishy cuddle. 'Wait till I tell Auntie Kath!'

THIRTY-SIX

OCTOBER

I F I'M HONEST WITH myself, I knew something was wrong before I went away to New York, but I didn't want to admit it and she seemed pretty good when I got back. Kath had been having a lot of her 'off' days with headaches and tiredness and snapping at me for such small things, and now, after couple of months I fear the worst. I keep thinking about Derek and how quickly he went, and then feel like I'm going to throw up at the thought of the same thing happening to Kath, *my* Kath. Everything feels a bit much right now. Obviously everything with Theo has fallen away and I'm still smarting, Lyla's been so spirited ever since her Autumn Leaves dance triumph and I've barely heard a peep from Natalie – she's been sending me out on jobs mainly on my own. I really should check in with her, actually.

Anyway, right now my shoulders feel pretty heavy.

I'm so worried. I made Kath book in with her GP just to talk about her tiredness and headaches. She came over to my house the same day and said everything was fine but that she was being referred for further tests. I pushed her on it. 'You don't get referred to the hospital for more work if you're fine. What else is going on?' Well, apparently she'd collapsed a few days prior (prompting her to take me up on my advice about seeing her doctor), and was suffering from a fair bit of sudden blood loss after not having had a period in months. Naturally I'd googled this, and jumped straight to logical conclusions. Cancer.

Not letting any of this show, I turn the car radio down and say, 'I hope we can find parking – you know what they're like at the hospital, it's an absolute nightmare, isn't it?'

'I'm sure we will, lovey,' she says quietly, clearly lost in thought herself, hopefully not about cancer.

'I'm not having you walk miles though, Kath!' I'm starting to feel weirdly panicked now; I can feel all the things in my head swirling about, and the only thing I can seem to do is keep talking at a hurried pace about parking. 'I'm actually going to complain if we have to park miles away. You're a patient, you deserve a close spot!' I'm almost crying at this point, and I think we both know it's not about the parking.

'Robin, lovey, stop. Take a deep breath. I'm all right to walk, and I'm all right in myself,' she says, patting her ditsy-print gypsy skirt as if to illustrate how healthy she is and how far she can walk.

'All right, we'll see where we can find a spot. I just want to make today as easy as possible for you. I love you,' I say, looking at her briefly and trying to keep my eyes on the road at the same time.

Resting her hand on my knee, she says, 'My dear girl, I'm absolutely fine. We're only going to a hospital appointment – I'm not actually being admitted.'

I take a deep breath and remind myself that this is about Kath, that I need to pull it together and be supportive. 'You're right. We've faced far worse than this and we are strong. Let me get your coat out of the boot and we'll go inside.'

Walking round to the boot and brushing away my tears before she can see any upset, I take a big gulp of crisp autumn air and add, 'Better the devil you know, eh?'

'That's the ticket,' she says, and we head into the appointment.

*   *   *

WAITING THE COUPLE OF weeks for Kath's results is nerve-wracking. With the days drawing in and the clocks going back, play dates have migrated from National Trust grounds and adventure playgrounds to soft play centres and indoor trampoline 'parks' (absolutely hideous environments, where kids are worked into an energetic frenzy, dads insist on showing off, falling and pretending they haven't slipped a disc and mums cross their legs with every bounce). Last winter our only real outings were to the soft play centre, mums I didn't know to speak to all sat round the brightly coloured plastic tables sipping crap coffee and the children running feral through ball pools and rope mazes. Lyla never seemed to enjoy them that much, preferring to stick close to me and have me run the jumbo obstacle zone than play much with the others.

Lately, though, and to my delight, she's been asking more and more to visit friends or have them over, so I sent out a group text to the gang to see if they fancied a soft play date.

Sat round our table with drinks and packets of crisps we'll say are for our children, but it's not Lyla shovelling Wotsits into her mouth, I feel relaxed and happy to be with Gillian and Finola. How times have changed.

I'm wearing soft skinny jeans with an overgenerous give to them, a plain grey T-shirt, white trainers and no make-up. Once this would have sent me into a frenzy of self-deprecation, but not any more. I'm allowed to let my face be my face, to wear practical clothes, to just be myself and not worry. Theo, Val, anyone negative be damned – I'm a happy camper!

'What have you been doing with yourself then, deary? Spending the weekend with any dashing young men we should know about?' Finola asks with gusto.

Gillian titters excitedly on the other side of the neon orange table, bless her – she'd love a bit of gossip, I know.

'Sadly not, ladies; my life is a man-free zone at the moment, and it's going very well. I spent the weekend with my aunt,' I say, calmly taking a sip of my crappy coffee.

'The one with the crocheted socks?' Gillian enquires with earnest, trying to speak loudly enough to be heard over the din of screaming children in the nearby foam pit.

'Yep, that's the one. She's got a bit of a thing for handicrafts. I'm not sure there's anything she can't make. When Lyla was born, she made her a full set of clothes from this beautiful soft white wool with pearly buttons and lace around the cuffs and collar. She looked like a little angel.'

'How lucky! I'd love to have someone in my family who could sew. Paul's mother's idea of sewing is having something taken up in John Lewis, and my mum's too busy on her cruises these days to even see Clara, let alone knit for her.' Gillian actually seems a bit bitter about this, which is a surprise considering her usual meek and mild demeanour. I'd never really considered that other people don't have a Kath around to make mad things and teach mad dance routines. I had been so busy focusing on the fact that I'm a single mum, and that Mum and Dad had moved away, and I was so lonely, and then there was Theo, that I just hadn't stopped to appreciate just how big a space in my life Kath fills.

'I am lucky. We've had a bit of a scare with her health – we're waiting for the results now – so now we have regular "Kath and Robin" dates together. Kath lives and dies for charity shops. I go in and find total junk, and she'll go in and find couture – it's incredible! Kath used to look after me a lot when I was little, and she talks about how she spent many hours at parish hall Tumble Tots with me, and now

I'm an adult we do days like shopping in little villages, or crafts at her house. It won't be long before our lot outgrow the soft play and they're taking *us* out for lunch!'

'Now there's an idea! Perhaps Roo and Honor could send me off on a riding retreat as a thank you for all these early morning lessons I've been giving them all their lives!' laughs Finola.

'I thought you loved all those hours at the stables!' pipes up Gillian.

'Of course I do, my dear, but I wouldn't mind a morning fumble with Edgar every now and again!' admits Finola, still laughing and reaching quite a pitch with it.

The thought of Finola wanting or having any kind of sexual experience is enough to send Gillian and me into fits of giggles. All four children come running up and look confused to find their mothers have lost their minds, and beg us to come in and play with them.

Usually we'd say no, but since we've descended into hysterical chaos, we allow ourselves to be dragged into the mayhem and spend the next forty-five minutes laughing, running, sliding and falling all through the play zone.

Every time I make eye contact with Lyla I can see she's that kind of happy you normally only see when the birthday cake comes out, or when you switch on the Christmas tree lights for the first time. She's playing so well with Roo and the others, but I know that having me there, enjoying myself with carefree abandon, is thrilling her. It's thrilling me too. I don't care that my knickers are poking out above my jeans or that my hair is sticking to the back of my sweaty neck.

I don't even care when I get stuck in the curly slide and Gillian and Finola have to yank me out by my feet from the bottom. This is what proper joy feels like. In this moment, I'm not even fretting about Kath, but I'm living life, fully and happily. It feels great . . .

*   *   *

WE GET THE RESULTS. I haven't felt relief this overpowering since they placed a newborn Lyla on my chest and said, 'A healthy baby girl, Miss Wilde, congratulations!' I'm so relieved, I feel dizzy and sick and hysterical with laughter all at once.

'The menopause! You're starting the *menopause!*' I say over and over as Kath and I head out to the surgery car park.

'Yes, all right, dear, let's not shout it to all and sundry,' Kath says firmly, but she's also clearly relieved.

'Sorry Kath, but I'm just so happy! I was so worried it was something sinister,' I dance as we walk across the car park to our spot.

'Oh yes, so am I. I can't wait for the mood swings and night sweats,' she says sarcastically but with a smile creeping over her face. 'You just wait till it's you having to deal with dryness *down there*, hot flushes and forgetting your own name, my girl.'

'OK, sure, it's not ideal but it's not cancer! It's not a heart condition! It's not a disease! It's just the menopause!' I actually start skipping a little bit. But then I stop, 'In all seriousness, though, Auntie Kath, I get it. I do. We'll be there for you, I promise. I thought I was going to lose you. I thought Lyla and I would be orphans,' I laugh, realising how ridiculous I sound.

I look over at Kath, who has stopped still in her tracks and has tears welling in her eyes.

'I'm sorry! I shouldn't have said the C-word. Oh Kath, I didn't mean to upset you, I'm so sorry. I'm here for you. Lyla is here for you. Whatever you need, whenever you need us, our door is open to you. I won't even get cross when you try to open my bills or customise my clothes with pom-poms. I love you; I don't want to make you sad.'

'You haven't upset me, lovey. You said "orphans". All these years I've felt like you and Lyla are more daughters than nieces, and here you are saying it back to me. I should be sad about the bloody menopause, but this is a happy day! I've got my health, I've got my girls, I've got it all!'

'We've got it all, Kath, we've got it all!'

With that, we both skip to the car, probably looking like absolute maniacs, me in skinny jeans and Kath in a floaty maxi skirt, skipping out of a hospital to take on the world!

LACEY IS TRYING TO make the best of things, but I can see underneath it all she's broken. We're sat in Dovington's studio room with our standard cups of tea and custard cream biscuits and a stack of baby magazines.

'I really thought this was it, Robin. Honestly. Ten days late – *nearly* two weeks – and all the signs. I know I shouldn't have bought the tests yet, but they were right by the tills. I was buying them and I felt so confident. I had that glow, you know? The glow they talk about pregnant women having? I had it. So I just picked them up as I was paying and the test – ,' she says with a heaving sob, ' – the test was negative. Another fucking negative.'

'Oh Lacey, you'll get there, I know you will.' I put my tea down and stare into the cup. It's not just me that has problems and feels despairing, sometimes; everyone is fighting their own battle. I don't envy Lacey, my poor lovely Lacey.

'I know, I hope I know, but it's been so long. We're not far off the year mark now, and I'm so sick of it all. Sex isn't sex any more, and I resent seeing every one of my friends wheeling their beautiful babies around, or going to baby showers for girls who didn't even have to try. All I seem to do is try!'

We've been here before, many times, and I never know what I should say. I don't think she does either.

'I know there's nothing I can say to give you what you really want right now, but Lacey, I love you and I'm here for you. If you want to have a great big cry, go for it; if you want to smash things up in frustration, I'm here for you; if you want to go out and get absolutely shit-faced, I'm your girl.

You name it, I'm there. And then, when this fantastic little baby blooms into our lives, I'm going to be the best faux auntie it ever had! I'll babysit and take it out and teach it the ways of the world, and then when it's old enough, I'll pass it over to Auntie Piper to take out on the town and show it how it's really done.' Hmmm, turns out I did have something to say, I just hope it's what Lacey wanted to hear.

A thin smile crosses Lacey's face and she takes a sip of tea. Success!

'It's going to be perfect, isn't it, Robin?' she asks, looking for confirmation more than anything.

'Yes, it is – we just have to wait for it,' I say, giving her hand a little squeeze. 'In the meantime—'

I'm interrupted by the buzz of my phone vibrating on the huge wooden table.

'Oh jeez, it's Simon. I haven't left something out of her bag, have I?' I say to nobody really. 'Sorry, Lacey.' She gestures that it's fine.

'Hi Simon, everything OK?' I say, taking the call.

'Hi, yeah, er, now, Storie is away on an aromatherapy course,' he dithers.

'Right. OK,' I answer firmly, still confused as to why he's calling.

'Yep, er, Lyla is coughing quite a bit and, er, I wondered, shall I, er, shall I bring her home to you?'

'No, Simon, it's a cough. Can't you deal with it?' I'm glad he can't see me rolling my eyes.

'Deal with it how? Mother always gave me, er, a shot of warm whisky, ha, but Lyla's refusing to drink it,' he says, demonstrating how little he understands our child.

'Yep, well, she will, Simon, because that's gross and she's seven, so don't you dare give her alcohol. You need to go out and get her some children's cough medicine and then just wrap her up in front of the TV and make her some soup or something nice, OK?'

Fuck's sake.

'Right, right, yep, OK, so not to bring her home to you? It's just that, ha, Storie is away, so, er, it's just me here handling this,' he continues to dither.

'Simon,' I say, trying to talk slowly and clearly as he's obviously having a hard time understanding that this isn't a big deal. 'I handle everything on my own all the time, just fine. It's a cough. You can manage. I'm having some me time. If things get any worse then call the doctor, and then me, but for just a cough, you've got this.'

I put the phone down and roll my eyes again at Lacey.

'Bloody hell, that was painful,' I say.

'Poor thing,' she says supportively.

'Poor thing?! I deal with this all the fucking time by myself! It's about time he felt what my life is like for half a day!' I say fervently.

'No, no, Robin, I meant Lyla being poorly. Poor her,' she says, a bit taken aback by my outburst.

'Riiight, sorry! I know I seemed harsh there, but he's got

to manage. I think Storie does everything when they have her, and it's not right. Lyla needs her dad to step up, and for once I'm not going to enable his weakness. I'm strong enough to stand firm on this.'

Before I can change the conversation to something a little lighter, my phone buzzes again with an unknown number.

'You're popular today!' Lacey says, popping another custard cream in her mouth and munching it gladly.

'First time for everything,' I say with a smile.

'Hello, Miss Popular speaking!' I say in jovial, high-pitched tones.

'Robin, it's Natalie. Sorry to ring on a Saturday. Are you free for a chat? Do you think you could come over? Now?'

THIRTY-SEVEN

DECEMBER

A few minutes to midnight . . .

PLACING HER WINE GLASS carefully and importantly (it's quite the honour to be given a wine glass when you're only seven years old) on the marble worktops of our new kitchen, Lyla says, 'Mummy, this is our princess castle and you are the queen.'

'It certainly is, Bluebird, and how glad I am to be your queen! We've had quite a year, haven't we! What's been your best bit?' I ask, filling her glass up with more 'wine'.

It's 31 December. We're having our very own exclusive, only-two-invites-sent, New Year's Eve party in our new house, complete with actual breakfast bar (as opposed to my old stub of Formica posing as a one) in the very lovely marble-worktopped, under-cupboard-lit kitchen. We have Skips in bowls, cut-in-half Babybels, chocolate fingers and jelly babies as our buffet, and Appletiser on tap. It might not be the Sugar Factory with Piper, or even the stylish party Lacey and Karl threw last year but honestly, this might be the best New Year's Eve I've had. I'm so far from where I thought I'd be. I'm content.

After Natalie's big offer, we moved house. I loved Granny's house. It was everything I needed when Simon left and the familiarity of Granny's touches was like a warm hug. Now though, I realised it was time for something that was mine. Something I had worked for and that I can put my own stamp on. Also, something a little less draughty and rickety is quite the treat! I wasn't planning on moving so quickly but when this house popped up for sale in Figgsberry Village, a stone's throw from Lyla's school, chain-free, with a beautiful garden for her to play in and ticking every box I had ever wished for, I pounced. Martin helped me with all the paperwork and Karl and Lacey helped me move in the day after my 29th birthday at the beginning of December. We all regretted having one too many glasses of fizz the next day – my god, shifting boxes and hangovers do not mix! It's been a crazy couple of months and, thinking about it, I never imagined I'd have the strength to do any of this. That's the thing about change, sometimes you don't even realise it's happened until it has.

Lyla is twizzling around on her bar stool, surrounded by cardboard boxes of our possessions still waiting to be unpacked. She starts shouting out all her highlights: 'The Easter bonnet parade! When we took Auntie Kath on the dodgems at fireworks night! When Roo came to Dovington's and made flower crowns with me! When Auntie Kath cooked Christmas dinner and your paper crown fell in the gravy! When you made me the giant tent in the lounge with the sheets! This party right now!'

It's amazing how little something can be to be a child's highlight. I've always thought a yearly highlight needed to be a huge achievement: a holiday, a promotion or a big life step, but in Lyla's mind, each tiny life step is a highlight. She's not looking to jump her life forward or to keep up with an imaginary timeline of achievements she's imposed on herself; she just sets out to feel real joy, to sit in a tent made by her mummy or laugh with Auntie Kath at a funfair.

'Do you know what's been my best bit of the year?' I say, looking at my sweet girl, happy just to be with me in the kitchen and call it a party.

'What, Mummy?'

'You.'

'MEEEE?' she shouts, swirling round again on the stool, her feet almost knocking over a tower of boxes. We might see those jelly babies again in a minute.

'Yep. You. You've been my most perfect thing. You won't understand this yet, Lyla Blue, but sometimes, being a grown-up is quite hard. Mummy feels like she's made a lot of silly choices in her life. I worry about them a little bit because I want us to be happy and have the happiest life we can. I want to make sure you have everything you need and that I'm the best mummy to you. At the beginning of this year, I felt sad. It wasn't anything you'd done – never think that – and I worked very hard to fix it, but sometimes, I just felt a bit down. I thought if I had Theo – remember Theo? – that we'd all be so happy every day, but it turned out Theo was a worm.' Lyla laughs at the thought of me openly insulting someone.

'A slimy worm!' she says with glee, brandishing a jelly baby menacingly at the ceiling.

'A slimy worm!' I repeat, feeling a bit giddy, probably thanks to all the sugar. 'Do you know what, though? I went to New York and found out that I'm actually good at things, and then I came home and felt like I was good at being your mummy and good at doing all the things mummies have to do in their lives. I found all those things were possible without slimy worm Theo and without anyone else to help us. Our life was a success without a boyfriend or a husband on the scene. We can do it alone!' I raise my Pinot Grigio to my own speech and look at Lyla, expecting her to be ready to applaud me or something.

Lyla looks perplexed.

'Not alone, Mummy. Together. Always you and me together, the best Mummy and Lyla team in the world!'

With that, we both raise our glasses and have a celebratory spin on the new actually-really-fun bar stools, and spend the rest of the night dancing round the kitchen to the cheesiest Spotify playlists we can find.

As the clock strikes midnight, and it's time to put a very sleepy little girl to bed, I think about how much has happened since Natalie's call in October. I think about how far this year has taken me, and how much further I know the next one will go, with us always as a team, the best Mummy and Lyla team ever.

Two months ago . . .

AS I RANG NATALIE's doorbell a few hours after her phone call, I noticed my hand was shaking. Something about the tone of her voice really disturbed me. She's always collected and professional, so I wasn't expecting whoops and cheers, but this was different; something about her seemed so heavy, so finite.

'Robin! Nice to see you!' Martin said, as he answered the door. I don't know a single person alive who wouldn't like Martin. He's classically handsome with his dark brown eyes and smooth, dark skin, and his voice is deep and silky. Just being in his presence for thirty seconds calmed my nerves considerably. 'Come through, Natalie's in the drawing room.'

Of course they have a drawing room. It's actually just a casual second lounge at the back of their house without a TV in it, but if they want to call it a 'drawing room', I'm not going to argue.

Unsurprisingly, Natalie's taste in interiors is impressive.

The heavy, luxurious gold curtains compliment her bottle-green velvet sofas, placed opposite each other on a cream carpet with a gold and glass coffee table in between. She was sitting in cream jeans and a loose black sweater with her laptop and notepad resting on the table at her knees. She looked serious. I felt sick.

'Natalie?' I said, coming through the door.

'Come in, Robin, take a seat.'

Obediently I sat down and looked at her.

'Don't look so worried,' Natalie said, smiling.

'Sorry, I am worried, though. What's going on?' I garbled. 'Are you ill? Kath thought she was ill but it turned out it was just the menopause. Not that you're old enough to go through – ' Fuck, I didn't want to insinuate anything about age, especially if she was actually gravely ill.

'Stop, stop, it's all right, honestly. I'm not ill, nor am I going through the menopause' – I noticed an indignant raise of an eyebrow at my suggestion – 'but I am going through some changes, some life changes.'

Natalie took a deep breath and looked at the table. She seemed to be on the brink of saying something big, so I sat silently and waited, trying not to die from the tension.

'Robin, this is a lot to say so I'll say it all in one go and then you can comment.'

Efficient. Typical Natalie. 'OK,' I said.

'For a long time I've poured myself into the agency. I have

built it from the ground up, and I love it like it's one of my children. I know every detail of it and care about every choice made within it. I'm proud of my staff, I'm proud of our reputation and I'm proud of myself for cultivating this living, breathing, successful business. It's afforded me and my family a great deal. Private education for all three boys, a lovely house, fantastic trips and savings to fall back on.

'The problem is, I've spent every day there since Nathan was three. I've taken it on holiday; I've spent hours at kids' parties on my phone instead of chatting to the other mothers; I've missed school plays to work on jobs; I've been late for Martin's wonderfully prepared dinners more times than I dare to admit, and I don't think I've ever actually had a "girls' weekend".

'And while I might not be hitting the menopause yet' – I knew she'd taken offence to that suggestion – 'I'm getting older and I don't want to lose any more of my life to work. I want to see some of the world with Martin, I want to have dinner with my boys and I want to get to know my friends properly. I've been saying for a long time to Martin that I'm going to step back, but I've never had anyone to hand the baton on to. I want that person to be you, Robin.'

She paused. I could barely breathe.

'I needed someone with moral integrity and a strong work ethic, as well as natural talent. I'm not saying the business is yours. I'm still going to direct it, but I'm looking for a deputy to run things day to day and take the load off. We both know you're so much more than an assistant. You've showed me countless times that you have the skills to work on set and deal with people. I'm going to hire a manager for the office to handle the paperwork, but I'd like you to head up the big jobs, choose an assistant from our roster and schedule the right artists for the right jobs.

'Obviously this is going to require more hours, but there'll be a team to help you, and me, of course, so you don't miss out on the things I did and, naturally, a considerable pay rise.' She smiled and then continued, 'Winning the film franchise contract was in large part thanks to you – we all recognise that, and so, after some thought, I've decided I owe you a bonus. I'll have Sarah at the office include it in this month's salary.' She sat back in her chair. 'So. What do you think? Are you up for the challenge?'

I sat stock-still, as if I'd just had a full body epidural and all I could do was blink and move my mouth. That must be what a good shock feels like. 'Wow, Natalie, this is a lot. I'm honoured that you think this way of me. I can't believe I'm being given this opportunity. I've looked up to you for years. I don't think you've failed in anything; I think you are the perfect example of success.' I could feel my body slowly coming back to life. My breathing was embarrassingly heavy; I was overwhelmed that someone I look up to so much was inviting me to be an equal. It didn't need thinking about at all. I was so excited I wanted to run at it with both arms open. 'Natalie, I'd love to accept your offer. I think you're an incredible woman, and to work so closely with you would be a privilege. Maybe I'll even look as good as you in cream jeans!'

'Don't count on it!' Natalie said, smiling and giving a sassy wiggle on the sofa.

I PULLED INTO MY DRIVE and went inside. I was in shock. Everything Natalie had said was going to take a while to sink in. I'd always thought her life was so perfect. I didn't realise that she had her own struggles too. But I guess everybody does. It's how you deal with them that counts. She was the person I'd looked up to and had hoped to be like, and now, I felt like I was being given the chance to make it happen.

The house felt really quiet that day. Lyla was with Simon and I had had a good tidy round the day before, so there was something very still and tranquil about it. Against all the noise and buzz in my head, it was a welcome oasis of calm.

I flopped down on the sofa in my usual spot and switched on the TV, but I couldn't concentrate. I was on a crazy dazed high. What a day. I couldn't wait to get started.

Three weeks ago

WE'D MOVED IN IN mid-December but the house was still in disarray and there were boxes piled high in every room. Who knew I'd crammed so much stuff into Granny's old house, even with my big clear out earlier in the year!

Lyla was playing with her sticker books and just as I'd opened the four hundred and fiftieth box to unpack, my phone flashed.

Unknown numbers horrify me, ever since the Inland Revenue called me and screamed at me for not paying my taxes properly. OK, they didn't scream at me, but I did mess up my taxes, because being self-employed is complicated. In a fit of bravery – after all, if Natalie believes in me, plus I can move house without a partner and I can do the most perfect winged eyeliner you've ever seen, I must be doing something right – I answered.

'Hello?' I asked tentatively.

'Robin?' replied a man's voice.

'Yes, who's this?' I hate this game. Just start with who you are and what you want before you trigger my tax fears, dammit.

'Robin, it's Edward. From New York. Hi!'

Oh my God, why was sexy New York Edward ringing? I was both thrilled and confused by this. Obviously I wasn't going to show him that, though.

'Oh, hi Edward, how's things?' Yes, nailed it, so breezy.

'Yeah, really good, just working, playing, you know the drill.'

I wasn't sure I did, but hey, let's play the game.

'Yep, yep, ha ha, totally do! Me too. I just moved house actually, so I'm having a day of unpacking and organising.'

'Oh wow, well done you, that's awesome.' He might be English, but he definitely had that American enthusiasm to him. It was like when Marnie Facebooked me the month before to tell me about the *amaaaazing* pilot she'd started filming in L.A. I could feel her beaming. Edward continued:

'I'm actually ringing because I'm in your neck of the woods next month for a while and thought, maybe, if you fancy it, we could grab dinner?'

Shit me. Was I actually being asked out on a date by a one-night stand? This doesn't happen.

'Well, it would be rude not to celebrate my big move, so yes, sounds great to me!' I realised it would probably be a bit weird to celebrate moving to a new house by going out with a one-night stand months later but this phone call business was throwing me completely off balance. Whatever happened to a series of texts where you can't sense any tone but do spend plenty of time agonising over every full stop and emoji?

'Amazing!' he said, a bit more keenly than I think he meant to. 'I'd better dash, I've promised the chaps I'll meet them tonight, but that's great. I'll message you. Or call you. Or . . . yeah, message or call, ha ha.'

I loved that I was the cool, confident one here (on the phone, not in my head of course), and he was slightly floundering in a very cute way.

'OK, sounds good. I'll look forward to either a call or a message,' I laughed.

'Catch you later, Robin Wilde!'

We rang off and I sat back, sinking into the sofa. OK, then.

* * *

A COUPLE OF DAYS AFTER Christmas and Lacey popped round to drop off presents. She and Karl were on their way back from a trip to a rural lodge (complete with full maid service) in the Scottish Highlands to celebrate Christmas together as a couple. 'Just think Robin, this time next year I'll be here with my new baby', she said, a little too brightly, sipping her coffee and looking out of the lounge window at my new sprawling garden. Half the reason I snapped this house up was this garden. Granny's house had a little yard with an old crumbling shed but no grass or flowers – and no cherry blossom tree just waiting to bloom next spring.

'I know, it'll be perfect,' I said reassuringly. 'It's a good job you had this last Christmas as a romantic one because next year is for sure the year it happens, Lace, I can just feel it.'

'This month feels like a good month,' she said nodding – she thought I couldn't see the tears in her eyes – and continued to look out the window at a little robin hopping along the patio towards the seeds Lyla had scattered earlier. Lacey still thinks every month is a good month and I wasn't going to be the one who rained on her parade. I hated seeing my friend struggle like this. She reached in to her handbag for a tissue.

Maybe next year would be the year.

Maybe it wouldn't be long before Lyla had a little friend to play with on her new luscious lawn.

Breaking into my thoughts of frilly summer dresses and

tiny children running through sprinklers, Lacey burst out, 'Oh my God! I don't know how I didn't tell you this before! It's Theo! Look! Look!'. She brandished a battered copy of *OK!* magazine at me. 'I saw it on holiday and meant to call you but the signal up there was shocking so I've saved the article. I thought you ought to see this.'

Hearing Theo's name after all those weeks jarred and I reached for the magazine with shaking hands, trying to control my spiralling emotions. I opened the magazine to the page she'd bent down for me and there it was. A photograph of Theo at some swanky celebrity Christmas Gala, with a face like thunder. After the initial shock had subsided I realised it wasn't actually a photograph only of Theo. He was standing brooding at the edge of the photo with his back half turned, obviously not loving the camera, whilst a group of very well-to-do horsey-looking friends smiled beatifically down the lens. I read the accompanying article:

Lady Sophia Fennelsworth has announced her forthcoming marriage to Lord Freddie Goldman. Hot-shot property tycoon and only son of international financier Caroline Salazan, Theodore Salazan, 34, [also pictured, far left] has been linked with Lady Sophia on and off for more than 18 months, with bets being taken that he'd be the one to bag the heiress. But 'Always the bachelor, never the bridegroom' joked his school friend, Tommy Fitzherbert, adding that Salazan is currently on a two month-long ski break in Whistler nursing a broken heart. Sources close to Lady Sophia report she always knew there was only one man for her and marrying Goldman will make all her dreams come true. She and Goldman will tie the knot at Radboth Manor in early spring with Princess Florence of Denmark as the head bridesmaid . . .

I put the magazine down and expected to feel rage or anger or heartache. Lacey reached out to lay a supportive hand on my arm.

'I knew I never had his full attention. I knew I was always second best,' I said, still casting my eyes over the picture.

'You're not second best, you're . . . first best.' Lacey was smooth as always.

'You know what? This doesn't cut deep. This makes sense. Everything makes sense now.'

I put the magazine down and took a deep breath. I was exactly where I was meant to be, with exactly who I was meant to be with. If only Theo could have said the same thing.

1 January

My memory box lies open next to me on the sofa. I've had a good look through and it's time to close the lid and look forward. I open my brand new journal – a Boxing Day self-purchase from John Lewis – to a fresh page and start to write:

New Year's Day is back to being a favourite again. A lot of people moan when January starts because the magical cosiness of Christmas is fading away, decorations are being taken down and we're all back to real life, in the grey, and with substantially weaker bank accounts to carry us through.

I don't see it like that, though. For me, New Year's Day has nearly always been a chance to reflect on the year that's just gone and start afresh with the new one. I come up with goals (some more achievable than others – I never did become a minimalist or take up CrossFit) and I feel excited that, with a new year, there is a new chance to be the person I really want to be. To be content and able; to know deep down that I'm a good mother to Lyla without needing to be told it or have it validated in some way; to be able to walk confidently in skinny jeans, stilettos and a tucked-in shirt; to be proud of my home and make it welcoming (never having to shove chocolate wrappers behind the cushions when guests turn up unexpectedly); to have a secure group of friends and not be ashamed of being single.

Every year I dream up new ways to achieve those things. I've dated men, hoping they'll rescue me; I've tried faddy diets or going to the gym four times in a row thinking my jeans will look that much better for it; I've bought all the mum-erabilia like bento boxes and Trunkis and an iPad with the huge foam kidproof handles round it so I'd look like a Good Mother; I'd stick to

Lacey like glue, ignoring pangs of loneliness. I've been doing those things for years, in different ways and in different settings, and, let's face it, they've never worked.

Last year, though, was different. Last year I found that I didn't need to do all those things. Letting go of all my misconceptions freed me from being my own biggest critic. Theo wasn't the answer; no man is. I worked my (a bit untoned but who really cares?) arse off at work and it paid off; I didn't always send Lyla in to school with the right sodding socks and she didn't die; the PSMs aren't what I thought they were (except maybe Val, who's probably a lost cause); and the only person who was judging my mothering was me.

I've spent all these years looking for the answer, the thing or person to rescue me, but ultimately I just had to do it myself, for myself. It just had to be me.

This evening, as I gently removed each delicate glass bauble from the now sorry-looking Christmas tree and wrapped each one in newspaper ready for next year, I found big, hot tears rolling down my cheeks.

Lyla gently stroked my arm and asked me: 'Are you sad, Mummy?'

I smiled at my beautiful little girl, and answered: 'No. I'm so, so, happy.'

The End

ACKNOWLEDGEMENTS

Ahhh the Oscar moment of book writing, except here I'm minus a stage, a golden statue or a dress. I'm actually writing this at my kitchen table wearing a giant sweater and eating a packet of Wotsits – who says being An Author isn't glamorous?

I wouldn't have this oh-so-glamorous life if it weren't for some key people so, much like a lengthy but heartfelt speech at the Oscars, I'm going to share them with you now.

My first thanks are to Maddie Chester and Abigail Bergstrom from Gleam Futures. Maddie is my Manager and from the very first moment I said, 'I want to write a book about a single Mum and be totally realistic,' she was on my team, telling me I could do it and not to give up, even that time I rang her crying after eating an entire bag of chocolates and doubting myself – she's a good egg, the best egg actually.

Abigail joined Gleam as my Literary Agent and sat with me in the early days, listening to how I wanted the book to pan out and reading countless drafts of my first proposals and putting me in touch with the best publishing houses out there, most notably Bonnier Zaffre, of course. She has been a gracious soundboard, calmly replying to messages day and night (sorry for that 1 a.m. one Abi!) and without her, I don't think I'd have pushed through with my initial idea.

Thank you, thank you Maddie and Abi.

Through Maddie and Abi, I found the wonder that is my Bonnier Zaffre team. I knew instantly they were the team for me when Eleanor Dryden (my Editor Extraordinaire) took an idea I had for book two seriously and didn't try to 'fluff it up'. I have been continuously impressed by Bonnier's gusto for *Wilde Like Me* and the never dwindling energy of everyone involved. Particular thanks must go to Emily Burns, Stephen Dumughn, Georgia Mannering, Nico Poilblanc, Vincent Kelleher, Angie Willocks, Ruth Logan, Sarah Bauer and Alex Allden for being top notch all round.

On days when I've felt lack lustre and unenthused, I've remembered that there is a team of happy book bods working on the cover design and the promotion and the distribution (and forty-five thousand other things) and have been reminded that this is a team effort.

A couple of other people I feel important to mention for all their hard work are Tara, Jamie, Nick, James, Asmaa, Felice, Eleanor (a different one to Eli The Editor) Kate and Mark plus Jenny H, Jenny P, Katie G and Kati N. I'm so grateful to be working with such marvellous people and to be part of their world.

Eleanor Dryden, my Editor. Big, huge, wet sloppy thank yous. If I could stand on the spare pillar in Trafalgar Square and shout 'thank you', then I would. Since the day we rolled out a sheet of wallpaper over my lounge floor and scribbled all my ideas over it, to the day we sat in a swanky London hotel 'love suite' (long story) and said, 'that's it, it's finished', Eli has been incredible.

Eli has forced me to go deeper with *Wilde Like Me* than I thought I could and it's that pushing that, I think, has brought the very best out of Robin's first story. There have been a lot of highs (ever drank too much wine and had a disco in the vaults of a ye olde building? We have!), a lot of over-sharing (poor Eli, I'm sorry for the time I graphically described that thing to you) and, a tiny few, but worth mentioning, lows (a call in December when I thought I was writing rubbish and Eli told me to shut my laptop and go out for the day – thank you).

Through all of them, Eli has been steady, supportive, professional (we'll not speak of the wine and disco again) and positive. Eli is more than the editor of this book, she's also my friend and a joy to have in my life. Thank you Eli.

As well as my professional marvels, my friends deserve a firm and loud 'thank you'. Countless times I've declined invites for mooches around John Lewis (my favourite thing) or drinks at our tatty local pub (my second favourite thing) in favour of saying, 'Sorry, the book'. They've never rolled their eyes or been annoyed, but instead offered playdates with their children for Darcy so I could focus or told me they're looking forward to reading it.

Special thanks go to Clare, Esther, Vicki, Emma and Auntie Judith.

Thank you to Liam, the love of my life and man who has spent countless evenings sat next to me watching awful smashy action films whilst I typed and typed and typed. He's spent so much time with me as I've written this that he now says he finds the sound of my keyboard soothing! For every achievement (the first chapter written, the first twenty thousand words submitted, the first draft fully printed out etc.), Liam has celebrated with me. He's never complained that I can't come out to play and never begrudged the days when my laptop has seemed more important than him. I hope that one day Robin Wilde will find a man as good as him, just like me.

And finally, a funny thank you really because she can't even read the words I'm writing yet, to my daughter, Darcy. Having never sat down and expressly told her I was writing a book, I didn't think Darcy was paying my work life much attention. Why would you at that age? Occasionally she'd ask what I was doing and I'd say, 'just writing, my love' and she'd skip off to do something else. At her last parent's evening I was invited to look through her work and on one of the pages I saw something that almost blew me over. The children had been asked to describe their parents and Darcy had written, 'My Mummy is clever because she wrote a book'. I sat on the tiny made-for-kids-chair and cried. All these months when I've felt guilty for pouring so much into *Wilde Like Me*, she's known and instead of resenting me, she's been thinking I was clever.

Reading that gave me the boost I needed to continue giving *Wilde Like Me* so much and has given me such pride. Darcy, when you're older and you can fully read – thank you for thinking so highly of me. All of this is for you.

I'm all emotional now and I'm out of Wotsits, so this feels like a good place to wrap up my Oscar speech. Robin Wilde is everything I want her to be. I love her dearly and I'm so thankful to all the other people who love her too.

Dear Reader,

If you're reading this then you have a copy of my first novel in your hands and frankly, that thrills me!

Every word and page and chapter of this book has a piece of my heart in it. Aside from my actual human daughter, I don't think I've ever poured so much love and time into one single thing in my whole life!

There were times when I didn't think I would ever finish this book or ever manage to write anything worth your reading. There were times when I felt so elated from finishing an amazing section that I actually fist-pumped the air. Alone. Haha, how sad!

The thing that got me through those moments of self-doubt, though, was you. You holding this book in your hands (and, remember, thrilling me) and taking pleasure from reading it. I can't wait for Robin Wilde to be in more people's lives than just mine. I can't wait for more people to become her friend and love her for all her foibles. I can't wait for people to want to give Auntie Kath a big cuddle or give Lyla a tight squeeze. Most of all though, I can't wait for people to feel the warmth I hope this book exudes.

If ever you're feeling a bit low, if you feel like The Emptiness is knocking at your door, if you just fancy some company on a quiet evening or if reading is your happy place, remember you can always return to this book, visit your friend Robin and know that you, like her are surrounded by people who love and care for you.

I want you to finish this book knowing that you are your own hero and you can do anything you set your mind to, just like Robin Wilde.

Remember that you can, and should, always reach out to your friends when you need support. Or you can get in touch with me @LouisePentland (Twitter and Instagram), #WildeLikeMe

I always love to hear from wonderful people like you!

Big kisses and hugs,

Louise
xxx

JOIN MY READERS' CLUB

Thank you so much for reading my debut novel!

If you enjoyed *Wilde Like Me* why not join my Readers' Club* where I will tell you – before I tell anyone else – about my writing life and all the latest news about my novels.

Visit www.LouisePentlandNovel.com to sign up!

WILDE LIKE ME
AUDIO BOOK

AVAILABLE NOW TO BUY AND DOWNLOAD

Want to read
NEW BOOKS
before anyone else?

Like getting
FREE BOOKS?

Enjoy sharing your
OPINIONS?

Discover

READERS FIRST

Read. Love. Share.

Get your first free book just by signing up at
readersfirst.co.uk

For Terms and Conditions see readersfirst.co.uk/pages/terms-of-service